ALSO BY BRAD LEITHAUSER

Novels

The Friends of Freeland   1997
Seaward   1993
Hence   1989
Equal Distance   1985

Poems

The Odd Last Thing She Did   1998
The Mail from Anywhere   1990
Cats of the Temple   1986
Hundreds of Fireflies   1982

Essays

Penchants and Places   1995

*These are Borzoi Books published in
New York by Alfred A. Knopf*

A Few Corrections

A Few Corrections

[a novel]

BRAD LEITHAUSER

ALFRED A. KNOPF   *New York*   2001

THIS IS A BORZOI BOOK
PUBLISHED BY ALFRED A. KNOPF

www.aaknopf.com

Knopf, Borzoi Books, and the colophon are registered
trademarks of Random House, Inc.

Library of Congress Cataloging-in-Publication Data
Leithauser, Brad.
A few corrections: a novel / by Brad Leithauser
p.   cm.
ISBN 0-375-41149-6 — ISBN 0-375-72558-X (trade pbk.)
1. Businessmen—Fiction.   2. Middle West—fiction.   1. Title.
PS3562.E4623 F49 2001
813'.54—dc21
00-062010

Manufactured in the United States of America
First Edition

FOR THREE MIDWESTERNERS:

Neil and Debra Leithauser,
who provided a base
from which to reach Restoration and Stags Harbor,

and Mark O'Donnell,
that rare bird among humorists—
one who knows how to fly

Hic ego multas puellas futui.

Graffito preserved in a Pompeian brothel

So: one more infinitesimal shifting in the great human balance: a single unit subtracted from the unreckonably vast multidigit number of the living and added to the unreckonably vast multidigit number of the dead . . . Yes, there in black and white was the face of the deceased, and there as well were the life-statistics which said, finally, little about that life, and it occurred to me that a whole novel might be devoted to the rewriting of a single obituary.

The Friends of Freeland

A Few Corrections

CHAPTER ONE

RESTORATION—Wesley Cross Sultan, 63, of 2135 N. Westhampton, died suddenly in Lyon Hospital in Stags Harbor, of heart failure. He worked for Great Bay Shipping for 42 years, chiefly in sales. He began his career in the Stags Harbor office, and after stints in Kalamazoo and Cincinnati, Ohio, he finished his career back at Stags Harbor. He retired two years ago in order to pursue full-time his civic pursuits. He was an active member of the Rotarians, the Restoration Chamber of Commerce, the Stags Harbor Betterment Society, and the Thumb of Michigan Prosperity Council. He was also active in the Restoration Episcopal Church, where for many years he sang in the choir.

He was born in Restoration and was a graduate of the old High School on Cherrystone Avenue. He was the son of the late Chester Sultan, the well-known businessman, and the grandson of Hubert Sultan, who served as the mayor of Restoration from 1908 to 1912. Old-time Restorationists will recall Sultan Furniture on Union Street, founded by Hubert and presided over by Chester until he closed its doors in 1935.

He was married twice. His first wife was Sally Planter (Admiraal), now of Grosse Pointe, formerly of Restoration. They were divorced in 1964. He leaves his wife, Tiffany, and their two daughters, Jessica and Winnie; a son, Luke Planter, of New York; a brother, Conrad Sultan, of Miami, Florida; and a sister, Adelle De Vries, of Battle Creek.

There are at least a dozen errors here. Indeed, errors enough to leave a person wondering whether even what's known as incontestably true is true. The life commemorated in these three paragraphs—who actually lived it? What was Wesley Sultan truly like?

You might well ask, *Was the man's whole existence an illusion?*—and the answer you arrived at would naturally hinge on where you started. A philosopher might grandly inform us that all life's illusory. And maybe a speculative historian would announce that we have in Wesley Sultan a man who, prone to deceit, was himself surrounded by that comprehensive web of deceptions known as twentieth-century small-town American life, etc. And yet with all due respect to the pedants and the pundits among us, the deceased left behind a jumbled constellation of people—wives, girlfriends, siblings, children—prepared to testify that he was, if anything, all too real.

Our story begins on April Fools' Day. This would be a balmy spring morning in 1952, the robins and blue jays racketing in those big hospitable wineglass-shaped elms that reigned back then over the streets of Stags Harbor, Michigan, just as they did over small towns throughout the Midwest. Dutch elm disease wouldn't begin to take them down for another decade or two. On this April Fools' Day the streets are animate and graceful and Wesley is seventeen. He's a dapper young man whose lean face and compact squared shoulders make him look taller than he is. You might judge him to be six feet tall—the height which, throughout his adult life, he claimed to be. He is actually five ten and a half.

Although he might plausibly have wished to be taller, Wes could hardly have hoped to be handsomer. For here's a fact that is a fact: This boy is gorgeous. He's just now coming into his young manhood, when he will regularly be described as looking like a Hollywood matinee idol. Perhaps the chin could be a trifle firmer, the nose a millimeter straighter, but no film mogul, assessing young Wes in a screen test, would shift a hair on the boy's head: thick chestnut ringlets that throw off honey-gold sparks in the sun. And there are sparks as well in his electric-blue eyes . . .

Wes knows where he is headed. A preliminary scouting of the personnel building of Great Bay Shipping has already revealed that the first person he will be encountering is a woman and he takes this as an encouraging sign. He prefers to deal with the female sex. Palsied widows, grim girdled matrons, harried young nursing mothers who have neglected to tuck in their blouses as they run round the corner for a pack of cigarettes, acne-splotched teenagers who play the flute in the junior high school marching band—it hardly matters who they are, so long as they are members of the fair sex. He has come to consider women trustworthier than men, or more generous, or more forthright—whatever; he isn't somebody who analyzes his perceptions to a T. Wes simply knows how he feels . . .

Knows, that is, that men can be surprisingly hostile to him. Why this should be, he can't quite say (though he does have the feeling it isn't quite fair). Yet it seems other males, men and boys, frequently object to the way he talks (the wistful voice unexpectedly low, and its vowels, particularly *a*'s, softer than customary in his region of the Midwest). Or they don't like his looks (or like his looks too much). Or maybe his stylish clothes offend them—his bone-white trench coat, his paisley silk scarf.

Admittedly, these are not the clothes his friends or his classmates wear. As far as Wes is concerned, his classmates have *small town* written all over them, they have *Restoration High School* stamped on their foreheads. It's apparent in the way they dress, and talk, and even stand. It's as though they don't see what Wes sees: There is another—a larger and a brighter—world out there.

In truth, Wes has never been a reader, and most of his cosmopolitan dreams of a brighter life have their origin in the Mercury Movie Palace on Restoration's main street, Union Avenue. Wes is an avid moviegoer. But he also looks to magazines, to billboards, to the occasional tourist from the big city, caught pausing briefly in a Union Avenue service station or luncheonette. Wes keeps his eyes open.

If his clothes occasionally bring him a stranger's taunt—then so be it. He's used to being pestered and teased. For nearly the whole of his life he has been engaged in an intense civil war with his brother, Conrad, who is two years younger and who cares nothing for clothes or for movies or for the game of trying to charm the world's women. The brothers' battles are frequently public, and much appreciated as neighborhood entertainment. On ramshackle, struggling Scully Street in the modest community of Restoration (pop. 4,200), few neighborhood chronicles offer the long-term interest—few have done so much to liven up evening conversation in the street's cramped and poorly ventilated kitchens—that the Sultan brothers' ferocious, ever-evolving rivalry does. People regularly take sides, including their mother; everyone knows that Conrad is their mother's favorite.

On this brilliant April Fools' Day in 1952, Dora Sultan has been a widow for a decade. Her husband, Chester Everett Sultan, drowned in a swimming accident in Lake Huron on June 21, 1942. Chester was known to be a strong swimmer, and out along the edges of his small funeral service—like uninvited guests who keep a respectful distance but will not be chased altogether from the scene—a number of nasty rumors circulated. It was just possible that Chester Sultan had come to an unnatural end. Today, more than half a century later, when all the facts we have are catalogued and assessed (Chester's equable mood in the weeks before his death, his sedentary lifestyle and high blood pressure, his heavy consumption of beer on the day he died and the chilliness and choppiness of the water), suicide seems only a remote possibility. But we'll never know for sure.

Whatever was actually in the man's head as he stepped into the icy lake on that first day of summer, 1942, Chester had long been something of an aimless soul. He hadn't held a job since the dissolution of the family business, Sultan Furniture ("You can live like a Sultan too"), in 1935. The store's final days had been rancorous. In late 1934, with bankruptcy looming, Chester invited in a partner from outside the family. It seems there was little left to do but argue, and each was soon accusing the other of being a swindler. Their raging over the division of assets continued long after there remained assets to divide. The store, a Restoration town landmark, was boarded up.

The loss of Sultan Furniture altered Chester's life in various unexpected ways. It turned him away from churchgoing (he quit attending services at First Restoration Methodist). It led him to the Democratic party (he went to his grave insisting on Herbert Hoover's personal responsibility for the Depression which eventually sank the store). And it sharpened his thirst. He became a steady, a daylong, drinker.

Chester spent most of his days on Union Avenue, in the "library" of the Caprice Club, where over the last seven years of his life he played tens of thousands of hands of pinochle. When the weather was warm, he and his "gentlemen friends" (a term employed without self-conscious irony; by all reports, Chester was a constitutionally humorless man) whiled away their afternoons in Restoration's Toledo Heights Park. Chester showed something of a proprietary attitude toward the park, whose fountain had been inaugurated by his father, Hubert Sultan, mayor of Restoration from 1908 to 1912. (Hubert's failed 1912 reelection campaign was stained by accusations of financial irregularities—something of a motif in the Sultan family annals.) For all his fervent new Democratic ideals, Chester badgered the police to keep Toledo Heights Park free of bums and riffraff—those among the unemployed who, unlike Chester's "gentlemen friends," had failed to prosper even in pre-Depression days. In their search for a park, the lowlife settled literally lower: down in Restoration's Memorial Gardens, on the banks of the Michicabanabee (*Me-she-cah-bah-NAH-bee*) River— the very park that, as the family's fortunes spiraled downward, Chester's two sons, Wesley and Conrad, would eventually think of as their own backyard.

Chester's death soon confirmed widely whispered suspicions that neither the grandeur of the gabled gingerbread and fish-scale Victorian-era house on Crestview Boulevard, in the heart of Restoration's "Heights" section, nor the prestige of the Sultan family name would safeguard the widow and her fatherless children. (The family name remains something of a mystery. The Sultans originally came from Yorkshire, although their name improbably suggests a Sephardic Jewish or even an Islamic forebear, which perhaps accounts for the determinedly Christian Christian-names favored by the Sultans over the years—an abundance of Christophers, Luthers, and Marys, as well as Wesley.) The widow was all but bankrupt. Since the possibility of going to work was unimaginable, Dora took the only practicable line: She lost altitude, selling the mansion on the Heights and descending into a boxy duplex on Scully Street. Not surprisingly, she soon succumbed to a chronic illness which left her "not very well" in Sultan family parlance, and which justified her disappearance from those social pursuits that had previously consumed her. But if in hindsight Dora remains an authentically pitiable figure (someone who had every reason for feeling that the world had come crashing down round her ears), there's no evidence to suggest that she, who outlived her husband by four decades, suffered from any diagnosable physical malady. (Her mental health is another matter. In the final two decades of her life she seldom ventured outside her home, and even in her glory days on the Heights she earned a reputation for moody and erratic behavior. To be singled out as Dora Sultan's favorite child—Conrad's fate—may have been as much burden as blessing.)

Though there was little physical resemblance between the two brothers, Conrad was no less well favored than his brother: He too was surpassingly good-looking. His face was comparatively wide-set, with little of Wesley's angular fine-tooling in the nose and cheekbones, and little of Wesley's rich, contrasting coloring. Conrad's thick, wavy hair was sandy-colored, like his freckled skin, causing eyebrows and eyelashes nearly to disappear—a monochrome effect working only to enhance a pair of extraordinarily large, slightly hooded eyes (no less striking than Wesley's), whose irises were an arresting, exotic fusion of olive-greens and amber gold-browns.

Both boys were blessed with precise hand-eye coordination. Organized sports held little appeal for slight-boned Wes, whose athletic gifts were dissipated in contests that brought him little acclaim: He had a flair for Ping-Pong, for bumper pool, for the jangly contests of the penny arcade. Conrad was another matter. Equipped with strength as well as coordination, he was a rising school athletic star well before he reached his full adult height. In 1950–51, his freshman year at Restoration High School, wrestling at 120 pounds, he wound up with the team's best record, nine wins and two losses (a performance he would improve to 10-1 the following season). And the spring of his freshman year, he was promoted to the varsity track team after blazing through the hundred-yard dash in 10.6 seconds—a time trimmed to 10.4 by the end of the season. He was just one-tenth of a second away from the Restoration High School dash record.

That record was destined to fall, a prospect that offers one plausible reason why Wesley, on that April morning in 1952, scouted the personnel office of Great Bay Shipping. He may well have vowed not to be enrolled at Restoration High School on that imminent occasion when his baby brother broke the dash record and became the school's "fastest human."

Or maybe Wes's thinking ran this way: *What's the point in wasting three more months when nothing I'm "learning" will be of any future use?* He would take a shortcut, cut a corner—throughout his life, Wes was a great one for shortcuts, for corner-cutting. He sensed the existence of another sort of race out there, richer by far than any gasping sprint upon a graveled high school track, and he meant to get the jump on all rivals.

Meanwhile, in the Sultan household another life was unfolding. The boys had a little sister, Adelle, born in 1938, who was no athlete and no looker. In truth, many people in town viewed the extraordinary handsomeness of the Sultan boys as an undeserved bounty (neither Chester nor Dora was anything better than plain), and a certain reassured, neighborly comfort was taken in the appearance of this pinch-faced, myopic, large-nosed, allergy-afflicted little girl whose timid life seemed fated to bypass, for better or worse, most of the clamor and upheaval of the Sultan household.

A fresh, exploratory breeze is sliding over Lake Huron on this bright spring morning, a Tuesday, the first of April, 1952 . . . The bucktoothed woman who confronts our Wesley as he strides into the personnel office of Great Bay Shipping is a Miss Henrietta Scoobles. (The name survives to this day in the Sultan family oral archives—preserved, no doubt, by virtue of its humorous, antic oddity.) The confident young man with the breathy, throaty voice and the princely curls instantly charms her. Although Miss Scoobles discovers in the first minute or two that he's only seventeen (hence, at least a year too young for any position at Great Bay), she gives him the better part of twenty minutes. The two of them chat away. She has the largest set of front teeth Wes has ever seen.

She tells him about her memorable trip to Chicago (a thirtieth birthday present from her father), and she encourages him to return on his eighteenth birthday. And—smiling brightly—Miss Scoobles assures him that she will, personally, put in a good word in his behalf.

Thank you, ma'am, but Wesley Cross Sultan heads on home and turns eighteen that morning. In other words, he digs out his birth certificate and, showing more dexterity than you might suppose given his sprawling penmanship, amends a single digit. (Indeed, he shows sufficient dexterity to raise a question whether this is his first operation as a document-doctor.) Yes, he has cut another corner—slipped ahead of the others by a full year!

Wes doesn't hesitate—he returns immediately to Great Bay Shipping, waiting most of the morning in a diner across the street from the personnel office. When Miss Scoobles quits the building on her lunch break, Wesley scampers across the street. He speaks to another secretary and, charming her as well, is steered into an initial interview, and another, and—in short—Wes secures the job that very afternoon.

And Miss Henrietta Scoobles? Wasn't there a danger that she would expose him?

"Oh I squared things with *her*," Wesley used to explain, and the artful eyebrows would lift, fractionally, leaving his listener to surmise, although nothing so vulgar as a boast had emerged, that Miss Scoobles succumbed, in one fashion or another, to Wes's "way with women."

. . . Or at least that's how Wes might have recounted these events in the late fifties or early sixties, when he was still in his twenties. Back then, it was a beloved family story—"How Wesley Landed His Job"—one which, while dependably amusing its listeners, highlighted Wes's crafty charisma, and went a long way toward explaining the secret of his success at Great Bay.

Later, though, when Wes reached his thirties, many of his stories took a darker turn and the tale of Miss Scoobles lost its savor. Now divorced, Wes had gotten into the habit, particularly when addressing younger women, of trimming his age a bit. (Having once found it advantageous to be older than his years, he now found the reverse was oftentimes true. Only a few years late, the sixties reached even the town of Restoration, Michigan, by the early seventies, and Wes eventually discovered it didn't always pay to be on the wrong side of thirty.)

Meanwhile, those beautiful ringlets of his, while still abundant, lost most of their boyishness; he was graying fast. Wes took this hard, with a sense of personal betrayal—how could grayness befall one of Mother Nature's sunniest darlings? Even as he was subtracting a few years from his age, his hair was adding years to his face. Better, under the circumstances, to avoid specific dates . . . And so Wesley's past turned misty, as he learned to avoid, in the company of everyone but a few family intimates, the pleasures of specific, dated reminiscences. (With family, he would rake over the past eagerly, needfully.) And yet, even as his personal history receded, he deepened his allegiance to a sadly vanished era of honor and probity. Wes adopted a favorite grieving refrain called *These Days,* as in *You know, these days, you can't trust anybody.* Or: *These days, you can't leave a single door unbolted.* Or: *You've got to get it down on paper these days.* And this snowy-haired man—for the gray had turned white by the time he reached fifty—would shake his head with a dolor whose sincerity was unimpeachable. The modern world was operated by cheats, by scofflaws and check-kiters, by thieving fat-cats and do-nothing executives, and its debasement grieved nobody more than it did this wily and devious man.

Did he feel like a hypocrite, then?

No, it appears Wesley's pain was authentic, as was his piercing nostalgia for an age—lost back in the wood-frame contours and the primary colors of his childhood—when a man was as good as his word. Something had gone astray . . . Something in his *own* life indubitably had gone astray, and on those occasions when this fifty-year-old man turned to philosophy or social commentary, the solemn burden of his own message quite overwhelmed him. Into the gaze of this man who had outfoxed Miss Henrietta Scoobles, one April morning thirty-plus years before, tears would materialize (fierce little tears, gumming those plush black lashes which, even when he was a snowy-haired man, any woman might have envied). He took his country's moral decline quite hard, Wes did.

But there was another reason why the tale of Miss Scoobles and the forged birth certificate lost favor with Wes: Sometime in the sixties, his career at Great Bay Shipping hit a snag. Initially he'd been assigned to sales, and even in his teens, when no client with actual money might be expected to take him seriously, Wes demonstrated potent powers of persuasion. Back then, what his clients met as Wesley stepped forward with his hand extended and a big gorgeous grin in place was a young-blood in love with his job. Something in this fast-talking overdressed kid's zeal was infectious—he left them feeling cheered. While Wes still preferred dealing with women (and always would), before long he'd become fluent in a world of adult male exchanges: of cigarettes bummed and drinks downed, of companionable banter and good-natured griping (sports talk, spicy jokes, laments about taxes and Washington politicians and exacting bosses). He was at his best with an older crowd of men likely to look upon him with an amiable, avuncular eye. Often they could be cajoled, once the second beer had been drawn, into extending him a string of adage-laden career advice (Wes nodded thoughtfully, with genuine gratitude), or various admonitions about the wiles of loose women (here, Wes felt less need of instruction). At first, there were plenty of superiors eager to take him under their wing, and if that was a location where Wes never felt altogether comfortable (unlike Conrad the wrestling star, who, to Wes's unending puzzlement, had embraced a sport that necessitated spending long minutes of your life with your head wedged in another man's free-flowing armpit), it was a fine spot for getting business done. If something fastidious in Wes always recoiled from the stained collars and unbrushed teeth of bar-stool confidences, he was reconciled to the notion that his job required sacrifices. Hey, he was growing up fast.

What significance lay in the seventeen-year-old's choice of Great Bay Shipping as future employer? It's hard to say . . . Blind chance may well have been steering Wes on that April morning. Or there may have been other, previous visits to potential employers, later excised from his narratives because he'd met with no success. Or the choice may tell us something about what it was to have grown up in Restoration in the forties.

On that mitten which is Michigan's Lower Peninsula, the town of Restoration lies not far from the base of the thumb-knuckle (close to the outside—the eastern—edge of the state), on the banks of the Michicabanabee River. The surrounding countryside, low and flat, is misleadingly nondescript. Four commercial worlds once intersected here. In the forties and fifties, Restoration lay along the ragged southern verge of what was being sold to city-dwellers from Detroit and Cleveland as the "real North woods": Above the town stretched pine forests and cedar swamps, the lair of bear and deer, and farther north, wolves and caribou: the land of Hiawatha. Closer to home, westward across the state, stretched cornfields and cherry orchards, acres and acres of white navy beans, and—most important—sugar beets. The town's leading employer was Restoration Sugar, through whose factory gates, every autumn, makeshift mountains of muddy, skull-sized sugar beets went in and eventually came out in neat paper sacks of pure white-grained sweetness. Meanwhile, some thirty miles to the south lay Flint, and some sixty miles south of Flint, Detroit: home to the greatest industrial complex the world had ever seen. Finally, less than ten miles away, along the shores of Lake Huron, at the mouth of the Michicabanabee, lay the port of Stags Harbor: Restoration's link to a maritime world.

Arriving at the personnel office of Great Bay, then, Wes may have been symbolically heading off to sea. Perhaps he recalled that legendary Yorkshire farmer's son, founding father of the Michigan Sultan clan, who in 1836 tramped all the way to Liverpool to sign on as a cabin boy.

Yet commerce at Great Bay Shipping had come a long way from the Golden Age of Sail. The company was in constant flux. Founded in 1868, in Cleveland, GBS had made fortunes for its founding partners through the transport of iron and copper ore from Lake Superior to foundries to the south. Later, in the final decades of the nineteenth century, it was active in the razing of northern Michigan's white-pine forests—a harvest whose ultimate value surpassed that of the California gold rush. Along Stags Harbor's Majestic Avenue, mansions went up to rival anything in Detroit, Chicago, Cleveland. Nonetheless, it soon seemed that the company, while sited on the planet's greatest freshwater system, had run out of things to ship. Its directors looked elsewhere and the business drifted ever further from its name and charter. If Wesley Sultan joined Great Bay Shipping in the expectation that he would be (metaphorically at least) heading out to sea, he soon discovered that what he was peddling to the world was mostly paper products and auto supplies—envelopes, calendars, spark plugs, windshield wipers.

Envelopes, calendars, spark plugs, windshield wipers . . . Wes sold them with brio and a likable grace. He was burning up the road, first in a maroon-and-gray DeSoto and later, as he continued to prosper, in a '67 tomato-red Bel Air convertible with Ramjet fuel injection. He met people from all over the place: from Saginaw, Pontiac, Lansing, Mount Pleasant, Detroit. The jaded weariness that slumped the shoulders and coarsened the language of most of the other GBS salesmen was something that, frankly, he couldn't understand, at least during his first few years on the job.

No, it took a long time to see that in the particular game he was playing, the one called Making a Career at Great Bay Shipping, the real winners were not the salesmen but the executives. To them went the respect, the social standing, the bulk of the money. Moving up meant moving over; Wes needed to change departments.

What he needed to do was apparent and yet—and yet none of the various attempts to transplant him to a stationary desk job was a success, quite. The failure dogged Wes through the years. Was it true he lacked certain organizational and planning skills? Or was it merely a matter of his heart lying elsewhere—of his being, as he liked to assert, "a people person, not a paper person"?

Or was it a case (a doubt that increasingly haunted him) of some quiet personal resistance among the bosses, the bigwigs, the hotshots? As a grandson of the mayor of Restoration, Wesley Cross Sultan theoretically held an impressive, career-advancing pedigree. Yet he was a womanizer, and an occasionally reckless boozer, and while neither practice was alien to the (all-male, naturally) management of GBS, Wes pursued his passions with a flagrance that chafed a few sensibilities. After all, a Great Bay executive was accountable to the community. A salesman was different. He could be something of a hell-raiser.

Mostly, Wes kept his worries and complaints to himself. Day after day, he climbed into his car and roared off to his next appointment. Yet toward the end of his career, sometimes he would compare his job to one of those soured marriages whose partners, despite a hundred incompatibilities, cannot quite bring themselves to cut the marital bond. Wes held on at Great Bay through the decades, and the company, relocating him here and there (Stags Point, Kalamazoo, Cincinnati), held on to Wes.

Hence, the tale of how, at the age of seventeen, he outwitted the personnel department of Great Bay Shipping eventually lost most of its luster. In time, Wes—an indefatigable storyteller—all but dropped it from his repertoire. And yet the little ruse fashioned on April Fools' Day, 1952, stubbornly persisted. In March of 1994, company records revealed that, having reached the age of sixty some months before, Wesley Sultan was eligible for early retirement, and Wes (though with bitterness and resentment, feeling backed into a corner) accepted the offer. After forty-two years, he was an independent man at last. He was out on his own at sixty— even though he was only fifty-nine.

CHAPTER TWO

RESTORATION—Wesley Cross Sultan, 63, of 2135 62
N. Westhampton, died suddenly in Lyon Hospital in
Stags Harbor, of heart failure. He worked for Great
Bay Shipping for 42 years, chiefly in sales. He began
his career in the Stags Harbor office, and after stints
in Kalamazoo and Cincinnati, Ohio, he finished his
career back at Stags Harbor. He retired two years
ago in order to pursue full-time his civic pursuits.
He was an active member of the Rotarians, the
Restoration Chamber of Commerce, the Stags Harbor Betterment Society, and the Thumb of Michigan
Prosperity Council. He was also active in the Restoration Episcopal Church, where for many years he sang
in the choir.

He was born in Restoration and was a graduate
of the old High School on Cherrystone Avenue. He
was the son of the late Chester Sultan, the well-
known businessman, and the grandson of Hubert
Sultan, who served as the mayor of Restoration from
1908 to 1912. Old-time Restorationists will recall
Sultan Furniture on Union Street, founded by Hubert
and presided over by Chester until he closed its
doors in 1935.

He was married twice. His first wife was Sally
Planter (Admiraal), now of Grosse Pointe, formerly
of Restoration. They were divorced in 1964. He
leaves his wife, Tiffany, and their two daughters, Jessica and Winnie; a son, Luke Planter, of New York; a
brother, Conrad Sultan, of Miami, Florida; and a sister, Adelle De Vries, of Battle Creek.

On Wednesday the seventeenth of May, 1958, Wesley Sultan met
Sally Admiraal. Twenty-four years old on the books of Great Bay
Shipping, Wes was actually twenty-three. Sally was nineteen.

As she describes it: "You must understand: He was unlike anything or anybody I'd ever known. It wasn't just his looks, although of course you can't underestimate the effect of those ice-blue mesmerist's eyes of his. Honestly, he was too much for me."

And she for him, probably. Wesley the salesman prided himself on being able to charm the shoes off a duck, but his tools of persuasion were comparatively crude: persistence, amiability, repetition, sincerity of expression, repetition. Sally had it in her power to do something he could never quite manage—she could turn a phrase. She too loved to tell stories, but hers had the authoritative, graceful, allusive cadences of a lifelong bookworm. Words would always have a way of tripping up Wes. In social gatherings particularly, he slipped into malapropisms that mortified him—pointing up, as they did, his lack of formal education. But Sally (who later in life would spend twenty-one years, contented years, editing text for a small Detroit newspaper) loved words for their own sake.

Eventually, Wes learned to take pride in Sally's gifts. He especially relished her "superlative vocabulary" (a phrase he employed so invariably as to wind up not praising her breadth but unwittingly highlighting his own limitations). Academically, Wes had always fattened the middle of any classroom's bell curve, whereas Sally was always found out there where the elite end of the curve grazed the axis. Most years she was first in her class, and in 1956, four years after he'd dropped out, she was senior class valedictorian at Restoration High.

As such, she'd been the logical recipient of the newly established Albert Kakenmaster Fellowship, awarded to the graduating senior "of greatest scholastic achievement and promise." The fellowship would have permitted her to attend the University of Michigan, in Ann Arbor, with all tuition fees and incidentals paid. However, since it was only appropriate that the scholarship be given not to a girl but to a boy, on whose shoulders must fall the responsibility of supporting a family, Sally was bypassed. As was

Beryl Vestrand, the salutatorian. The Kakenmaster Fellowship went to Tom Hendrix, who stood third in the class.

The rationale for the decision had been explained to her by kindly Mr. Hennepin, the sweaty-templed principal of Restoration High, and, given the prevailing mores of the time, his logic made perfect sense to Sally, who enrolled instead at little Bayview College in Stags Harbor. Though far less prestigious than the University of Michigan, Bayview had the advantage of convenience; she could commute from home, from nearby Restoration, thereby deflecting the objections of her parents, neither of whom saw much point in her attending college at all. She took up the study of English, reasoning that it would prepare her to become a schoolteacher. She'd always liked school.

And she liked home. An only child (a few months before she was born, an older brother with a congenital heart defect passed away, one day before his third birthday), Sally had felt little sense of solitude or loneliness while growing up: The sparkling little bungalow on the weedy outskirts of Restoration had felt densely populated. In addition to her watchful father, Henry (who owned a little grocery store in downtown Restoration), and her watchful mother, Kathy (who kept a house so clean, a visitor could have dined confidently off any floor), there were near-daily visits from relatives: uncles and aunts, cousins and second cousins. These were big, overspilling Dutch immigrant families, who operated truck farms and dairy farms, automobile repair shops and hardware stores. And in addition to her parents, and her relatives, there was the Lord Himself—Who tenanted every one of the Admiraals' dustless rooms.

The Lord of that household? As Sally would later describe it, He was not so much a jealous as a zealous God: It turned out He had very strong views about everything under the sun. Sally was in junior high school before she came to the confounding realization that the God Who oversaw the homes of her classmates was often unclear in His dictates, leaving the Presbyterians, even the Catholics, with a great deal of maneuvering room for discussion and interpretation. This was decidedly *not* the case with the Lord of the Restoration Christian Reformed Church, Who, through his agent the Reverend Karl Koekkoek, forbade dancing, cursing, and gambling, as well as scores of less speakable vices. If He did not expressly forbid, He certainly frowned upon, moviegoing and smoking and music-making, as well as all reading pursued for pleasure rather than instruction or gain. (He was oddly lenient toward coffee—though preferably served weak—but He had no use for soda.) Any woman caught with her nose in a book before sundown was patently guilty of neglecting her duties to home and family. The underlying point seemed to be that the human soul was the very fuel for the fires of Hell—and hellfire, like fire anywhere, was always hungry . . .

Later, Sally would joke a little, good-naturedly, about a God Who was the "finest chaperone a girl could have." But no degree of subsequent joking, no classes in the worldly philosophers or readings in comparative religion, could dislodge from her mind her Dutch ancestral inheritance: the unshakable solidity of His omnipresence. It had come as another shock, when she reached her teens, to discover that for some of her friends God was not actually *in* the school desk standing before them, *in* the clock on the classroom wall, *in* the whirrings of the projectors in the audio-visual room.

It was a simple, an unquestionable, and a life-defining proposition: God was everywhere. He was like the sun in the blade of grass, and if no biology lab scalpel or microscope could ever hope to unweave and isolate the golden thread spun throughout the green fabric, the grass stalk was nonetheless inconceivable without the preexistence of the solar flame. No sun, no grass; and no God, no world . . .

And yet He was an altogether more accommodating Presence (as Sally learned early on, long before reaching high school) when encountered within the confines of her own bedroom. She'd been a sickly schoolgirl, and as she would lie in bed, awaiting the delayed arrival of a healthy adolescence, it became apparent that He was willing to overlook her delinquency if she chose to while away the long daylight hours with a book. She read voraciously. It was a practice tacitly agreed to by her parents—who, for all the exigencies of their faith, occasionally turned an indulgent eye upon their frail, sole-surviving child . . .

When in 1958 she met Wesley, in a Stags Harbor luncheonette, Sally—nineteen, about to turn twenty—was all but engaged. An "understanding" had been arrived at. Her all-but-fiancé, Jacob Slopsema, was likewise planning to become a schoolteacher, in pursuit of which he'd journeyed all the way to the holy city of Mecca—or what stood for such in the minds of the congregation of the Restoration Christian Reformed Church. For Jacob had enrolled at Calvin College ("My heart I offer to you, Lord, Promptly and Sincerely"), in Grand Rapids, on the western, the even more Dutch, end of the state. Jacob's father was a deacon of the Restoration Christian Reformed Church.

Sally naturally assumed that the announcement that she was "spoken for" would put an end to the attentions (rather flirtatious attentions, to be sure, but honorably so) focused upon her by this odd gentleman with the odd name, Wesley Sultan, who trained upon her the bluest, most potent gaze she'd ever encountered. And yet her announcement seemed only to enhance, to quicken, his interest.

"Of course it must be duly noted that he was extremely good-looking," she would later explain, in her roundabout and quaintly literary way, "but that was only the half of it. The smaller half, you might say. First and foremost, there was the urgency of his pursuit. In my nineteen years on the planet, I'd never seen anything like it, except perhaps on one of my rare trips to the movies. *Could we meet at ten tomorrow morning?* Ten tomorrow?—I'd reply—That's out of the question. I have a class then. *All right, how about eleven?* Eleven? Well goodness gracious, I wouldn't even have time to set down my books. *All right then, what about eleven-fifteen?*

"Pressing—that's what he did to you. Wes was always pressing, pressing, pressing."

In time, Wesley Sultan called on Sally at home, pulled right up with a squeal of brakes in front of the Admiraal house in his tomato-red Bel Air convertible. So charmed was he to meet Sally's parents, and to view the Admiraal homestead, that he apparently failed to perceive just how chilly a reception he'd been accorded. Five minutes after his departure, Henry Admiraal made it clear to his daughter, in no ambiguous terms, that this wasn't the sort of single gentleman she ought to be entertaining: a convertible-driving salesman who, to make things worse, didn't even belong to the CRC—the Christian Reformed Church. There was, in addition, the issue of whether it was proper for her to be receiving *any* gentlemen callers, now that she was virtually spoken for.

Sally's mother, while professing to like Wesley (and indeed Kathy *did* like Wesley—what woman didn't?), reminded her daughter of the deep ties of friendship and faith uniting the Admiraal and Slopsema families . . .

And Sally saw their point. Far better to sever all such relations at the outset. Only, it wasn't quite so near the outset as she'd led her good, trusting parents to believe: On the Bayview campus, Wesley had already contrived to meet her a few more times than she'd let on to Henry and Kathy. She'd spent enough time with Wes to owe him, anyway, some brief explanation about why future meetings were impossible. Which is how it happened that the two of them wound up side by side, one warm June afternoon, on a bench in Restoration's Toledo Heights Park (the very park in which Wes's late father, Chester, had once taken a proprietary interest). It was an afternoon Sally would recall vividly for the rest of her life. She was wearing a pink-and-white seersucker shirtwaist, white pumps, and—an extravagance—nylons purchased in Saginaw. Wesley was wearing a white shirt and a narrow red-and-blue tie. The blue of his necktie was in fact azure—precisely the color of his eyes.

The sun was fading behind them. Far away, to the north, Lake Huron could be glimpsed, a patch of crystalline blue, moment by moment turning the pink of a Dutch tulip. Wesley listened somberly as she laid out her careful reasoning. When she concluded, nothing could be clearer: They must stop seeing each other. Although no date had been fixed, she was going to marry Jacob Slopsema.

And then in Wes's hands the conversation veered off. (It was just the way he drove his Bel Air convertible: one abrupt, unexpected turning after another.) Their talk shot off in an unbelievable direction. Sally probably would have jumped up and walked away in indignation, had she not been so astounded. Wes wanted to know: Was she a virgin?

Truly, that was the juncture the two of them had arrived at. Sally was sitting in a public park with a blue-eyed businessman who wanted to know whether—whether she was a virgin!

And Sally (blushing less than you might suppose, for she had righteousness on her side, the impregnable knowledge that—in this matter anyway—she'd always been a spotless girl) explained that, yes, of course she was a virgin. Good heavens . . . Jacob was an utterly honorable man, you see. Otherwise, she would never have *considered* marrying him.

And once more Wesley's talk angled off unexpectedly. Some of the icy-fiery intensity drained from his gaze, replaced by an ample ease and sweetness. His voice, too, altered. It lifted, until he sounded just like a boy as he told her, as he chanted at her, "It's all right, then, everything's all right, then, everything's all right." He took her hands in his—which, too, felt less odd than you might suppose: to be holding hands on a public bench, in Toledo Heights Park, with an older man who wasn't your fiancé . . . And he made her a solemn avowal: "I promise you, dearest Sally, one thing: Everything between us is going to be all right, forever and ever."

And Sally, recalling his pledge thirty-nine-plus years later (recalling it while slicing into a plate of *poulet de Bresse à la crème,* in a sunny restaurant in Domat, a little ruddy-walled town in Burgundy), cries out, "What fools, fools, *fools* we were!" And yet her protest rings with more amusement than despair. She's on the verge of uttering that phrase which crystallizes so much of her life: *Back then, we didn't know any better.* For these days—a widow one year short of sixty, her fair, undyed Dutch girl's blond hair beginning to turn the wan straw color of a cobwebby broom—she carries everywhere a sense that what little clarity she has achieved on her existence has arrived late in her life, just as this gentle, generous French sun came late in life. It sounds like such a trivial accomplishment, but in truth it is the most thrilling state imaginable: At fifty-nine, Sally has begun to make sense of things. From some unimaginably distant corner of the cosmos a light has come down to illuminate her personally.

But if Wes's vow, recalled thirty-nine years later, brings tears of vexed amusement to her eyes, it brought tears of a different sort to the nineteen-year-old girl sitting on a bench in Toledo Heights Park. She'd never met anybody so romantic, so devoted, so good-looking, *so greedy for her time.* (Not even when, some three years later, she became a mother, would she feel so unreasonably needed.

Her child—a boy—would prove to be a "good baby" who slept well and ate well and solemnly enjoyed watching the world go by. The baby seemingly recognized that she needed a little space—a life of her own. Wesley, however, clutching her hand in Toledo Heights Park, recognizes no such need: He wants to swallow her up, to absorb her, or to be absorbed in her. He wants to merge with her and, his hips only inches away from hers on the bench, she wonders, with a little shiver, whether this is what love must be, whether this is what—her virginity having somehow become fodder for public discussion—sexual intercourse will be like: that union so complete, a man and a woman fuse into a single creature.)

It was never quite clear to Sally when, exactly, marriage to Jacob Slopsema became an impossibility. During this period in her life, somebody else must have stepped in and taken over her body, for surely she herself (meek little Sally Admiraal, who had nodded understandingly, *sympathetically* when Mr. Hennepin explained that the Kakenmaster Fellowship would go to Tom Hendrix) wasn't about to face down Jacob, to say nothing of her mother and her father. Yet face them down, face them all down, Sally did. ("And I'm afraid"—Sally explains, over another sip of wine—"we mustn't discount the persuasive power of what might also be called the glamour factor. After all, when you got right down to it, the question confronting me was: Did I want to spend the rest of my life as Mrs. Slopsema—or as the wife of a Sultan?")

Wesley helped her, of course—he stood staunchly beside her. He vowed to convert to the CRC, and, during the period of their courtship anyway, never missed a single service. And if he was that suspect thing in her parents' eyes—a salesman—there was no disputing his professional success. Parked out front, Wesley's tomato-red Bel Air convertible cast a robust glow that warmed the very walls of the Admiraals' modest living room. And he was the grandson of the mayor himself, Hubert Sultan.

In the end, Wesley won them over—he won them all over—so that no more than a momentary flutter resulted when Sally's father happened to discover a slight irregularity in the sketchy oral résumé Wes had provided. Though Wes had once claimed, or at least strongly suggested, that after leaving high school he'd subsequently gone back and got his diploma, it seemed he'd somehow neglected to do so. Wesley was a dropout.

For her part, Sally hardly needed from Wes the reassurance of his Bel Air convertible, or the dynastic splendor of his grandfather the mayor, nor was she fazed by his lack of educational credentials. (Sally the valedictorian had enough of those for both of them.) Oh, she had the reassurance of love everlasting, expressed in a vow of unsurpassable beauty.

"Now can you imagine," she says, washing down the last of her *poulet de Bresse* with a sip of Mâcon, "how utterly unprepared I was to learn, after I'd been married for three years, and now had a child in my tummy, that the very man who'd made such grand vows to me in Toledo Heights Park, *that my own blue-eyed Wesley,* had already, already, three years before, walked down the aisle with another woman?"

CHAPTER THREE

RESTORATION—Wesley Cross Sultan, 63, of 2135 *62*
N. Westhampton, died suddenly in Lyon Hospital in
Stags Harbor, of heart failure. He worked for Great
Bay Shipping for 42 years, chiefly in sales. He began
his career in the Stags Harbor office, and after stints
in Kalamazoo and Cincinnati, Ohio, he finished his
career back at Stags Harbor. He retired two years
ago in order to pursue full-time his civic pursuits.
He was an active member of the Rotarians, the
Restoration Chamber of Commerce, the Stags Harbor Betterment Society, and the Thumb of Michigan
Prosperity Council. He was also active in the Restoration Episcopal Church, where for many years he sang
in the choir.

He was born in Restoration and ~~was a graduate~~ *attended but*
~~of~~ the old High School on Cherrystone Avenue. He *did not quite*
was the son of the late Chester Sultan, the well- *graduate from*
known businessman, and the grandson of Hubert
Sultan, who served as the mayor of Restoration from
1908 to 1912. Old-time Restorationists will recall
Sultan Furniture on Union Street, founded by Hubert
and presided over by Chester until he closed its
doors in 1935.

He was married twice. His first wife was Sally
Planter (Admiraal), now of Grosse Pointe, formerly
of Restoration. They were divorced in 1964. He
leaves his wife, Tiffany, and their two daughters, Jessica and Winnie; a son, Luke Planter, of New York; a
brother, Conrad Sultan, of Miami, Florida; and a sister, Adelle De Vries, of Battle Creek.

Here's Photo #1, a bleached-out color snapshot of the two brothers. It's 1954, it's Conrad's high school graduation. Arms are
planted fraternally upon each other's shoulders, yet neither brother
looks altogether at ease.

Conrad is seventeen and Wesley is nineteen. At this point in their lives, each is thriving. In two years at Great Bay Shipping, Wesley has emerged as a natural salesman. He's wearing an expensive-looking silver suit and a pink-and-silver tie. The ungainly crook to his arm suggests a proud desire to throw into the camera's eye affluent glints from the face of his wristwatch. Conrad, too, has trophies to display. He has received the school's Mulholland Prize, also known as the "leading man of letters" award. These are varsity letters. It's an old but dependable joke: The man of letters award customarily goes to a semiliterate. But not this time. Conrad not only has received eleven letters (three in football, four in wrestling, four in track) but has also posted a more-than-respectable 3.5 GPA. He has been accepted at every college he applied to: Kalamazoo, Michigan State, the University of Michigan, and faraway Vanderbilt, in Nashville, Tennessee. Tennessee? Vanderbilt's the alma mater of Coach Cairoli, Conrad's wrestling coach, who steered him this past winter to the state Class B semifinals in the 148-pound weight class. Conrad will be heading south.

In the photograph Wesley looks like the taller of the two Sultan boys, though this must be a matter of positioning, or posture, or perhaps simply the unobtrusively elevated heel of a shoe. In this particular brotherly battle, height off the ground, we have a clear winner: Conrad, by half an inch. He has reached his full adult height of five eleven.

If the snapshot memorializes a day of triumph, it hints as well at some of the pitfalls in store for the Sultan brothers. In Wes's too-wide and rather brittle smile, there are traces of the small-town smoothy—he doesn't look too many steps removed from one of those slick, Brylcreemed men in pointed two-tone shoes who calls his women prospects *Sugar* and refers to their daughters as *purty ballereenas*. And Conrad? There's a suggestion of something thick or occluded in his fierce gaze. You sense a tunneling approach to life—a forward-looking drive that dismisses as irrelevant the peripheries, the qualifications and the nuances, of the world around him.

And yet with hindsight, what's most interesting about the photograph are the various ways it could mislead a viewer. In the breadth of Conrad's face, the smoothness and regularity of his features, you might detect a touch of blandness—envision him eventually becoming, say, a slow-rolling bore among a crowd of Restoration Rotarians, a big-shouldered man in a powder-blue Ban-Lon shirt who tends, over a third whiskey sour, to amble back through the fields of his ancient athletic triumphs. But in fact with each passing year Conrad will cultivate a wilder appearance, wilder observations. No, if either brother ultimately becomes something of a bore, it will be Wesley, with his stalled career and gnawing self-doubts. Like a dog chained to a post, he will be forever winding round a central pivot—his fear of having "lost his stuff," particularly with a female audience. For a couple of years in the early seventies, while living in Kalamazoo, Wes will take to dyeing his hair, a practice that will not relieve but merely relocate his anxieties: Are my roots showing?

Eventually, Wesley's search for some explanation to his life's various disappointments will take a broader sweep. His conversations will grow increasingly political. In this, ironically, handsome Wes will come to resemble homely Chester, his likewise-stalled father, who after the loss of his store in 1935 regularly launched into tirades against Hoover and the Republicans. Wesley's condemnations will be wider still. It will be typical of him, as he downs the last of a beer and swabs delicately at his lips with a monogrammed handkerchief, to conclude that "Each political party's worse than the other," and "The whole rotten thing's a racket." If the sixties are destined to be America's Golden Age of

Conspiracy Theories, they will find in Wes an easy recruit and fervent disciple. He will discern in each of the decade's political assassinations a collusion of actors and analysts—obviously the newspapers are in on it too. And in the seventies, he'll begin sounding like something of a crackpot on the subject of Japan's conquest of the American automobile industry. Isn't it all clear? The bigwigs, the politicians and the CEOs, they've sold the average Joe down the river, haven't they? Payoffs, bribes, cowardice, and greed. They've peddled away our *industrial base,* and in the modern world, hell, you lose your *industrial base,* man, you've lost everything . . .

The photograph might also be misleading about how the two brothers will weather the years. From the hints of something dandyish yet heedless in Wesley's looks (note the cigarette dangling from the hand slung over his brother's shoulder), you might think he will eventually let himself go, subsiding into a potbellied and short-winded middle age. Wes looks a little soft beside his younger brother, whose graduation gown cloaks but does not conceal a sprinter's supple springiness, a wrestler's compacted reserves of power.

In truth, it's Conrad and not Wesley who will let his body go—spectacularly. This is all some decades off. For many years to come, Conrad will maintain a spartan discipline; in his thirties, in his forties, he'll beat and whip and starve his body into a state of perpetual honed fitness. But in his fifties, the sprinter will drop by the wayside, the wrestler take a tumble, and Conrad's body inflate into a sort of overstuffed lounge chair—a transformation so complete that you can only wonder whether the woman who appears in Photo #2, the boys' mother, Dora Sultan, would have recognized the figure he's destined to become: the mammoth silver-ponytailed man in the lime-green T-shirt who sits before me.

He's my guest. We're in a Miami restaurant of his choosing called Bar Barcelona. Prices are steeper than either the food or atmosphere might warrant, but Conrad seems pleased with his choice. At my urging, we've brought along the graduation photos.

The images work on his imagination, they stir him up. After telling me he doesn't recall a "single damn thing" about the day on which they were taken, Conrad gradually embarks on an unbroken thirty-minute reverie. He talks constantly. He eats constantly too, one little dish of tapas after another—scallops ceviche, shrimp in garlic, spicy olives, a little bowl of chorizo stew, slices of ham cut translucently thin, meatballs, a sturdy wedge of salt cod. As though to minimize the risk of being interrupted, Conrad seems always to be taking his bites in midsentence; in this performance of his, nothing ever comes to a complete halt. Food goes in and words spill out in a hectic, dynamic equipoise.

We've brought along three photographs of that high school graduation. Photo #1, the two brothers. Photo #2, the two boys flanking their mother. And Photo #3, the three siblings.

This third tableau, too, seems pointed and symbolic. On Adelle's left stands the graduate, the man of the hour, his sunlit face a smooth clenched fist of determination. To her right stands the dapper businessman, and his face too is sunlit. He's clowning around, having donned his brother's tasseled graduation cap. Perhaps some tree-shadows have fallen on the girl's features. Adelle is not sunlit. She is eclipsed and her gray face can hardly be made out. What *can* be discerned, even so, is how her upturned energies are trained not on the brother to whom this day belongs—not on the school's "leading man of letters"—but on the other, whom she idolizes: the deathlessly beautiful one to whom not only this summer day but every summer day belongs, and the one destined to be the first among the three Sultan children to die.

"Of course you do understand that absolutely nothing Wes

said or did was to be trusted. The picture where he's fooling around, wearing my graduation cap? That's not *fooling.*" Into Conrad's mouth goes a baby octopus. A pair of tentacles, trailing from his lips, writhe frenziedly for a couple of seconds, as if the creature even yet were struggling to escape. "He wanted to know what it felt like. To be a"—slurp: no escape—"high school graduate. He envied me *desperately.* Told some people he'd gone back and finished up those last few credits. Told others he'd done his equivalency elsewhere. Lies. Big fat lies. You do see, don't you, that Wes was an instinctual"—Conrad swigs his piña colada—"liar?"

Me? Is this an actual, a nonrhetorical question? Is the monologue about to become a dialogue?

I say: "He's a real puzzle, isn't he?"

Conrad's indignant talk of *lies* unnerves me, since I myself am here under false pretenses. I've led Conrad to believe I've come to Miami on business. In fact, I have no *business,* here or elsewhere. My time is my own. As of four weeks ago, I've quit my job on Wall Street, as a partner specializing in debt restructuring at the investment firm of Gribben Brothers. Conrad has already made a couple of references to my "expense account"—seeking, no doubt, to excuse the extravagance of his monumental gourmandizing. But he needn't apologize. Oh, it would be a shame to correct him—to diminish even by one baby shrimp his delight in this meal. He is draining his fourth piña colada.

"Wes a *puzzle?*" Conrad manages to sound incredulous. "Sure, and maybe I'm a genuine two-hundred-fifty-pound eggplant. Wes a puzzle? You got to be kidding, it's the simplest thing in the world, actually. Take it from Conrad, the trustworthy accountant. There was nothing puzzling about Wes. You just have to know the system. The system? Conrad's system for dealing with Brother Wes. Now all you ever had to do with Wes was this: first, listen to what he said; second, note it down carefully in your brain; third, put a negative sign in front of it. And then you had the truth, simple as that."

"Well, maybe the whole story's more complicated than that. Tell me about Wes's first wife."

"Klara?" He gives me a challenging look.

"Yes," I say. "Klara."

"Miss Klara Kuzmak."

"Yes. I gather it's all pretty complicated. Quite a jumbled story."

"Complicated? Jumbled?"

To anyone who didn't know Conrad well (and I don't, yet), this particular mannerism might be unsettling. You utter a word or phrase and instantly hear it come booming bombastically back at you, loaded with exasperation, mockery, pity, dismay. It pains him—that's what he wants to convey. Your stupidity *pains* him. He says, "Why, it's the simplest thing *in the world*. Wes was young, he was twenty-one, he was packed with juice."

"I think he was nineteen, actually, when they met. Twenty when they married."

"All the more whatever. The *point* is, he had no more brains, especially back then, than an Irish setter. Maybe later he got smarter. Smart as a poodle, say. As far as Klara was concerned, he had one thought in his brain. It was, *I'm going to get into that girl's knickers*—a goal that was all the more exciting because she's fresh from Warsaw."

"I think it was Cracow."

"Wes wasn't particular. Didn't know Poland from Pittsburgh. And when she announces she's pregnant, he has a second thought: *Avoid a public scandal.*"

"Was she very beautiful? Sally says so."

"No doubt Sally called her 'a beautiful creature.' Or 'a ravishing being.' Or some other Sallyism that no one else on earth, unless they were trying to make a joke, would try to get away with. But was Klara beautiful? Not later *on* she wasn't. The girl was ballooning before she was out of her twenties, and in her thirties the *real* weight problems started. You see I had occasion to see her, a couple of times, later on . . . But let's say, yes, the girl had her moment, her glory day in the sun. The point is, Wes hardly knew her, hardly knew his wife. Wes didn't *want* to know his wife."

"But now that he's gone, you must miss him terribly."

"*Miss him? Terribly?* How much do you think Wes would miss *me,* if I'd gone first? How much do you think he could have missed anyone? Wes was looking out for number one—and how did he do that? By convincing everyone around him he *was* number one."

Conrad pries with a fork at a dab of cheese, congealed against the slope of one of his many plates, stabs it, and pops it into his mouth. The way the old wrestler hunches over his plates, you'd swear he expected me to go after one of them. Still, he looks terrifically pleased with himself.

But then into his once hauntingly beautiful eyes—those eyes whose whites have yellowed, whose voluminous green-gold irises have receded beneath the chubby puffiness of his cheeks—a flash of pain glints. Or maybe it's a look of fear. Conrad is—so Sally has advised me—a man in *very* shaky health.

Conrad sips from his piña colada and then, with a fastidiousness belonging more to Wes than to himself, applies his napkin daintily to his full lips. He says, "But of course I do feel his absence." And adds, with just a hint of affection in his stylistic snappishness: "Damn it, he was my brother, after all."

CHAPTER FOUR

RESTORATION—Wesley Cross Sultan, 63, of 2135 *62*
N. Westhampton, died suddenly in Lyon Hospital in
Stags Harbor, of heart failure. He worked for Great
Bay Shipping for 42 years, chiefly in sales. He began
his career in the Stags Harbor office, and after stints
in Kalamazoo and Cincinnati, Ohio, he finished his
career back at Stags Harbor. He retired two years
ago in order to pursue full-time his civic pursuits.
He was an active member of the Rotarians, the
Restoration Chamber of Commerce, the Stags Harbor Betterment Society, and the Thumb of Michigan
Prosperity Council. He was also active in the Restoration Episcopal Church, where for many years he sang
in the choir.

He was born in Restoration and was a graduate *attended but*
of the old High School on Cherrystone Avenue. He *did not quite*
was the son of the late Chester Sultan, the well- *graduate from*
known businessman, and the grandson of Hubert
Sultan, who served as the mayor of Restoration from
1908 to 1912. Old-time Restorationists will recall
Sultan Furniture on Union Street, founded by Hubert
and presided over by Chester until he closed its
doors in 1935.

He was married twice. His first wife was Sally *three times. His*
Planter (Admiraal), now of Grosse Pointe, formerly *first wife was*
of Restoration. They were divorced in 1964. He *Klara Kuzmak.*
leaves his wife, Tiffany, and their two daughters, Jes- *He then married*
sica and Winnie; a son, Luke Planter, of New York; a
brother, Conrad Sultan, of Miami, Florida; and a sister, Adelle De Vries, of Battle Creek.

"Isn't it all too gorgeous for words? I think I'll have a cigarette."

"Probably a good idea."

"It's my first one of the day," she explains to me.

The stone wall the two of us are leaning against commands the surrounding countryside and if the scene isn't "too gorgeous for words," it's probably too gorgeous for *my* words anyway. What could be more beautiful than the Burgundian countryside, and who could do it justice? Certainly not a jet-lagged foreigner who flew into France yesterday and is on only his second visit to Burgundy.

This is wine country, where everything your eye settles upon conveys a feeling of meticulous cultivation. It's as though it's all being minutely monitored—the soil, the rainfall, the flow of the air itself—as though the entire landscape is steadily amassing toward that concentrated moment when, some years from now, a cork will be tugged free with a little *pop* of anticipation and a fine purple rivulet spill into the sun.

And everywhere you look, history looks back at you. The stone wall we're leaning against—does it date back a hundred years? Two? Seven? Eight? In the distance stands a tumbledown Cistercian abbey whose oldest ruins—so Sally informs me—do in fact date back eight hundred years. The Cistercians began here in Burgundy. Sally has taken for a month a little house in a little town called Domat, and has rented a car. The house belongs to friends back in Michigan, and a last-minute cancellation has recently opened the place up for another month. Sally has decided to take it. She will have two months in France.

We've stopped on our drive to peer at the abbey in the distance. The combination of the weather and the scenery and my jet lag and my recent and still-not-quite-real but nonetheless heady and liberating joblessness all conspire to render my imagination particularly lively and susceptible, and the distant abbey yields a dizzying chain of images: generations of monks rising to the sound of bells . . . bells ringing across the decades . . . decades interchangeable as acorns ripening and dropping away.

Good Lord, what a day this is! The colors are subtle and *perfect*.

The hills drift away in a marriage of dusty greens and tawny browns, and overhead two long chains of white cumulus clouds extend like mountain ranges. Between them lies an unsounded blue valley, down which a silver aircraft, traveling south, trails a silken line. It's but one strand of a projected web—a strand destined to dissolve, probably, before being linked to another.

Generally, Sally allows herself one pack of cigarettes a week, which she purchases on Monday mornings. This rations her to three cigarettes a day, with the complication (which she welcomes—a little variation that keeps the game interesting) that there falls one day per week when she must restrict herself to two. It's a good game, which she has played successfully for decades now, and there are times when you'd swear it's a defining gesture, that there's no other region of her life where Sally's quite so idiosyncratically and appealingly herself as in this business of her smoker's arithmetic.

The game engages, first, her resolute self-discipline—she will keep this potentially deadly vice in check! And, second, her fondness for ceremony, exhibited not only in the strictness of her schedule but in her habit of publicly declaring her intentions before lighting up. (You can imagine her, alone back in her house in Grosse Pointe, Michigan, announcing to her house cat—or even to a potted cactus—"I believe I'll have a cigarette." And adding: "This will be my first one of the day.") And, third, it engages her submerged but spirited pleasure in rebellion. She may be just a year shy of sixty, yet there's a trace of schoolgirlish mischief in her gaze when she lifts the little cylinder to her lips, as though she expects to have some stern taskmaster—her father? Mr. Hennepin, the high school principal?—snatch it from her fingers at the last.

But there's more, even yet, to be read into her smoker's motions, for there's a touch of fumble to them, even after all these years—from which a stranger might extrapolate, accurately, to Sally's struggles with locks and keys, with corkscrews and blenders

and VCRs and safety pins and manual transmissions and can open-
ers. Although she strikes a tennis ball with a certain amount of
hard-won grace, Sally's approach to the world of mechanical
devices is adversarial; in her hands, objects are all too eager to snap
when meant to bend, to bend when meant to hold fast.

Finally, a stranger could hardly fail to note her infectious relish
in the whole process of lighting up. This isn't a desperate smoker,
longing for a fix. Even if she flounders a bit, this is someone whose
every gesture—the scratch of the match, the dancing link of flame
and cigarette end, the first sweeping inhalation of smoke—says,
Isn't this a treat!

Seeing her keen pleasure as the smoke fills her lungs and her
eyes drift over the French landscape, I'm reminded of pleasure of
another sort—a far more earthbound pleasure. I'm reminded of
Conrad, hunching protectively over his many dishes of tapas. "I
haven't really told you about my trip to Miami," I say.

"How is Conrad looking?"

"Terrible, frankly."

"Do you mean fat-terrible? Or do you mean sick-terrible?"

"I don't know. I guess I mean so-fat-terrible-it's-hard-to-say-
if-he's-also-sick-terrible."

"I worry about him. I hate to be the bird of ill omen—literally
ill omen. But I can't help feeling he's *very* sick."

"I can't imagine he'd conceal it if he was. He seems to conceal
very little these days."

"Oh but that's just it: He *would*. I had to prod and prod before
prying out of him the information that his doctor's urgently calling
for bypass surgery. Advice which I fear he plans to ignore."

"I suppose he's frightened."

"Maybe *bitter* is more like it? Feels they've mistreated him? And
by 'they,' I mean the entire American medical establishment. It
seems he doesn't feel he's really been himself since he had the last

surgery—the prostate surgery a couple of years ago. Of course the weight gain started some years before that."

"And he isn't so ill it took away his appetite. He consumed enough at dinner to feed your average slim-hipped French family of four."

"Well isn't that the point? After you're told you have ninety percent blockage in one of your main coronary arteries, what do you do? Do you consent to bypass surgery? No, you go out and eat enough for a family of four."

"*And* drink six piña coladas."

"I honestly think I'd feel better if you told me six martinis. Truly, that man's sugar consumption is horrifying to contemplate."

"*And* ate two pieces of mango cheesecake."

Sally flicks the ash on her cigarette and inhales pensively. "And I remember when Conrad didn't like sugar. For twenty, thirty years, he didn't like sugar. He had me convinced, maybe he had himself convinced—I suppose it was the old wrestler's attempt to keep the weight off by eliminating the very *thought* of temptation."

"And eventually the sweet tooth came out of the closet."

"Out of the closet and straight into the pantry. I was with him not so long ago when he ate seven brownies. *Sizable* brownies. It's as if Conrad just said to himself one day, I *like* sugar and I *like* cream and I won't be deprived of them any longer. He'll give himself diabetes . . ."

"We talked about all sorts of things. Including Klara Kuzmak."

I watch Sally's face closely. A fine net appears: delicate vertical fissures around her lips as she draws tightly on her cigarette.

"Poor Klara," she sighs, releasing the name on a cushion of smoke. "She died before any of us and who would have predicted that?"

"Conrad tells me that in later life she got fat."

"So I've heard. I only saw her the one time. Still, she made an indelible impression. And you know what? You want to know something that surprised me, that may not be altogether believable? When I heard she'd died, I truly felt bereft. Oh I did, I felt so sad. A light had gone out. She'd been *such* a beauty."

"Lou Gehrig's disease."

"Yes. God help her, such a gruesome way to go."

"But something troubled me later, something I didn't think to ask Conrad at that time. He spoke, rather mysteriously, of keeping in touch with her. Why would he do that—in what connection? And what about Wes? Did he stay in touch with her too?"

One second, two seconds, three, four, five—Sally, staring out over the French hills, ponders my question. Then she says, "Did Wes stay in touch with Klara? Possibly. If so, he obviously wasn't about to tell *me*. Yet I don't think so. I don't think he wanted to, frankly. I think he wished she would just sort of go away. But Conrad? Maybe. Maybe he was acting as what I guess you'd call Wes's liaison? The dealings between the two brothers were always so unbelievably complicated, really. And if Conrad was always sniping at Wes—indeed, still is—nonetheless he could often be prevailed upon to serve as Wes's deputy."

"Surely Wes could have found somebody more reliable?"

"Than Conrad? In his way, Conrad can be quite reliable."

"You ever notice when he tells a story, he's always got some crucial detail wrong—some name wrong, some fact wrong? I can't imagine what sort of accountant he was . . ."

"Well perhaps I don't mean reliable so much as discreet," Sally says.

"Discreet? Even *less* true, I'd've thought."

"You're thinking he's a gossip? Because he likes to be in the know? But Conrad can keep a secret when he wants to. He'll amaze me sometimes with some little nugget he's been hoarding away for twenty years."

"Even so, in the end he gives the game away."

"In the end, maybe we all do. Maybe *you* do?"

But what does Sally mean by this?

She goes on: "Anyway, I can understand how Conrad would have wanted to follow up on Klara Kuzmak. The journalist in me recognizes it as 'a great story.'"

For twenty-one years, from 1971 until 1992, when her second husband was diagnosed with colon cancer, Sally worked at a suburban Detroit newspaper, the *Eastsider,* briefly as a reporter but mostly as an editor. It was a job that suited her—working for what she called "our little paper." Its small circulation scarcely mattered in the end: She enjoyed, for its own sake, correcting typos, solecisms, dangling modifiers. The *Eastsider* was a surprisingly literate and, in an old-fashioned way, literary paper. It says a lot about Sally, surely—raised on the Reverend Karl Koekkoek's rhetorical flourishes, on Victorian novels, on spelling bees and recitation days— that one of her favorite anecdotes recalls the occasion when she managed to slip *rodomontade* into an article about sewage recycling. "I don't know. It's as though Conrad always wanted to see the outcome of Wes's adventures—or misadventures. As if he was more curious about Wes than *Wes* was. Or less willing to put the past behind him anyway. For many years it was Conrad, not Wes, who kept me posted on Sultan affairs. He would tell me how Wes was *really* doing, and I suppose he'd share with Wes any news of mine. He made himself an indispensable presence somehow."

"A sort of diplomat."

"Yes, the world's most undiplomatic diplomat. *That's* Conrad."

"Tell me about the one time you met her. Klara."

"That's a very familiar story by now."

"Even so, I'd like to hear it."

"And it's a long story."

"I'm not going anywhere. I don't know when, if ever, I've liked a stone wall as much as this one . . ."

It was a raw January afternoon in Stags Harbor [so Sally begins, opening a tale of midwestern sleet and darkness while looking out over French hills basking in a high-summer sun], and this would have been, I don't know, 1960 I guess. No, '61, '61 of course, because I was pregnant. That's a key element to my story.

This was in the smallest house on Majestic Avenue—in what I liked to think of as *downtown* Stags Harbor. I was terribly proud of the place. I remember the walls boasted some "original art"—a pair of watercolors painted by the chairman of the art department at Bayview.

Wes had gone off early to work and I'd spent all morning reading. That was one of the great unforeseen advantages of those first years of marriage to Wes; I don't think I ever read so many books in my whole life. He didn't want me to work, of course, which would have impugned him as a provider. Actually, back then my thinking wasn't much different from his, and it would *certainly* never have occurred to me that I, as a pregnant woman, belonged in the workplace.

When I was growing up, there'd always been such a wrangle over my reading—burying my nose in a book, as Poppa used to say. (Poppa never caught me reading—he always caught me "burying my nose in a book.") And of course he looked down especially on novels, which were a frivolous form, and I know this makes me sound like I'm a hundred and fifty years old, as if I grew up in another country *and* another century, but I can only assure you that that's really how things were, in the Admiraal home, growing up in Restoration in the 1940s. Right in the middle of America, right in the middle of the century. *That's how it was,* and I can only apologize so many times for not having been reared in a great Parisian literary *salon.* You reach a point where you do have to say, *But that's how it was. That's what the Church told us. That's what we all believed.* I wasn't really free to read all I wanted except when I was sick.

["And so"—I interject—"the little girl bookworm arranged, psychosomatically, to have a sickly childhood."

This observation amuses her—and yet I can see that she weighs it seriously, too. I can see her filing it away, for examination later. For the moment, she has a story to tell, and Sally loves to tell stories . . .]

Wes, on the other hand, *liked* my reading. He was forever embarrassing me by boasting about my having been class valedictorian. I compensated for his shortcomings as a student, I suppose. Or that's the pejorative way of looking at it. I choose to think he was proud of me.

Anyway, I'd spent this particular January day reading—reading *Jane Eyre,* I'd like to say. Given the afternoon's later events, *Jane Eyre* would have been the most appropriate choice; I was about to be paid a visit by the first Mrs. Rochester.

But I honestly don't recall what the book was. I know it held my attention, all day, while a freezing January rain came down, until finally even *I* had to feel guilty about neglecting the housework. So in penance I went down and cleaned the basement. It was dirty work, dust and cobwebs everywhere, and when I finished I needed a shower. And I was just getting undressed when the doorbell rang.

Well, you get the picture. I couldn't have looked more slatternly. I was dusty, and my hair was full of cobwebs, and I hastily wrapped myself in a ratty old bathrobe. I was a perfect Cinderella, really, and I opened my front door to let in a fairy-tale princess.

[Sally pauses, for emphasis. Or perhaps it's to marvel once more, in her mind's eye, at the beauty of her visitor—to pay due homage to someone whose life ended so prematurely and so tragically.]

Actually, I let three creatures in out of the freezing rain. For our princess was accompanied by what I thought of as an older woman—I suppose she could have been as ancient as thirty-five, or even forty—who was leading by the hand a little boy.

Neither the older woman nor the child looked any too healthy. Both had circles under their eyes, and hacking coughs. Absolutely resplendent, on the other hand, was the princess. I'll never forget the moment when she pulled off her hat and out came this marvelous thing, this marvelous cascading flow: I swear that Klara's red-gold hair lit up the entire room. And her skin really was as rich as cream, with a faint lovely nutmeg-dusting of freckles across the bridge of her nose and on the backs of her hands. Really, the whole business was surreal. Out of the storm had come this fabulous glowing creature, with this exotic accent, who seemed to know who I was: She'd asked me, when I opened the door to her, whether Wesley Sultan lived there. I'd hardly understood her, if you want to know the truth; she called him *Vesley Sooltan*. But I let her in quite eagerly, for this was clearly the most wonderful and exciting thing that had happened to me in months: one part fairy tale and one part espionage thriller.

Once they were inside, it was the friend who did most of the talking. Klara's English was quite rudimentary back then—and I don't suppose she ever came close to complete fluency.

[I interrupt again: "According to Conrad, she wasn't the smartest soul he ever met."

Sally replies: "I'm afraid that, according to Conrad, *no* one's the smartest soul he ever met. Besides, if your criterion for stupidity is being bamboozled by Wes at one time or another, there aren't many of us who wouldn't qualify."

And she goes on . . .]

Anyway, the friend did most of the talking. She was all rather clipped and businesslike. She would *not* accept any of my hospitality. I offered them tea or coffee (I felt they needed something warming—I was worried about that cough of hers). No, they wouldn't even accept a chair. It was the oddest thing. So there we all stood, the four of us, in my living room. I was dressed in that ratty old robe, and I was just pregnant enough to look fat rather than pregnant, and all the while I was being fixedly scrutinized by this gorgeous creature who looked gotten up for a party, with all sorts of bracelets, and big pearl earrings.

[Sally's hands rattle with imaginary bracelets, her fingers reach up gingerly toward her own ears to touch imaginary earrings. She is enjoying this process immensely: recounting what was perhaps the most horrifying day of her life.]

But I used the word *surreal* a moment ago, and truly that's a word that fails to do justice to this particular occasion. Honestly, truly, *there are no words!* The older woman, Klara's friend, I don't think I ever caught her name, she asked me whether Wesley was living there.

Well of course yes he was; I'd already told them that.

And was I living there too?

Living there? Of course I was living there—just where I belonged. With Wesley, my husband. In our home. We were expecting a baby.

And did I know that on January twenty-seventh, 1955, Wesley and (and I'm afraid I couldn't quite catch the name, for when Klara Kuzmak is pronounced in a thick Polish accent, it sounds a lot like *cataclysmic*) had been married?

I beg your pardon.

And this was the signal, the dramatic cue. The friend nodded at Klara, who with a powerful flourish produced from her purse a wedding certificate that might well have been my own. After all, Wesley's name was on it. But where my own name was supposed to be, there was another name. A stranger's name. Klara Kuzmak.

Well, do you know what I felt like then? I felt like a heroine in one of those cheap old-fashioned movies where there's simply no budget for special effects, and so in order to indicate to the viewer that everything's topsy-turvy, the cameraman tilts the camera at an angle, or twists the lens in and out of focus. You know that old cliché, The mind reeled? Well, that may have been the only occasion in my life when I can literally say my mind *reeled*. The walls moved, the floor tilted, the furniture danced around . . . I thought I was used to Wes's keeping me off balance. He was always saying and doing outrageous things. (For instance, when he'd take me out to dinner, before we got married, he'd sometimes say to the waitress, What do you recommend for a couple of newlyweds? He thought you got better service that way. But of course it *mortified* me. It meant the waitress naturally assumed we were intimates, and of course we weren't yet intimates.)

Anyway, anyway I thought I'd grown used to surprises from Wes, but *this* one—this Klara Kuzmak and the wedding certificate—was something well beyond my furthest imaginings.

Is it any wonder if it took me quite a while before I understood why they'd come? They'd come, I'm afraid, for financial reasons. Klara felt that Wesley owed her money.

The friend explained it all to me. There'd been a "settlement"—a divorce settlement—and Wesley had promised to provide Klara with twenty-five dollars a week, which, back then, actually struck me as quite a substantial sum, I have to say. And I remember feeling, as I came back down to earth, a slight but growing resentment. Okay, even if one accepted the authenticity of this document, even if one were to assume the whole business wasn't some terrible mistake or misunderstanding, why was Klara coming to *me*? Hadn't all of this ended long before I'd come on the scene?

Do you see how confused I was? I suppose I was in a state of shock. I'd naturally assumed that the child belonged to the friend—*she* was the one holding the little boy's hand, after all. The two of them even had the same *cough,* for heaven's sake. I suppose I was busy throwing up strong internal resistance to any recognition that those payments were meant as child support. You see? I didn't understand just how deeply Wesley's involvement ran.

Well, perhaps Klara mispronounced Wesley's name, but she had a better claim to it than I would ever have—for she had the prior claim. Now can you imagine? I had a baby in my belly, and here I was already looking into the eyes of Vesley Sooltan, Jr.?

Another jet passes overhead, moving from left to right, from east to west. It may well be flying off to America. It slides across the cumulus mountain range and bursts soundlessly into the blue valley, the heavens' cheerful void. The earlier jet stream, which might have met it at a right angle, has bled away. The web fabricated by multiple aircraft exists only in the mind.

"It's such a beautiful day," Sally says, "I think I'll have a second cigarette."

Her hand trembles and flounders with the pack.

CHAPTER FIVE

RESTORATION—Wesley Cross Sultan, ~~63,~~ [62] of 2135
N. Westhampton, died suddenly in Lyon Hospital in
Stags Harbor, of heart failure. He worked for Great
Bay Shipping for 42 years, chiefly in sales. He began
his career in the Stags Harbor office, and after stints
in Kalamazoo and Cincinnati, Ohio, he finished his
career back at Stags Harbor. He retired two years
ago in order to pursue full-time his civic pursuits.
He was an active member of the Rotarians, the
Restoration Chamber of Commerce, the Stags Harbor Betterment Society, and the Thumb of Michigan
Prosperity Council. He was also active in the Restoration Episcopal Church, where for many years he sang
in the choir.

He was born in Restoration and ~~was a graduate~~ *attended but*
~~of~~ the old High School on Cherrystone Avenue. He *did not quite*
graduate from was the son of the late Chester Sultan, the well-
known businessman, and the grandson of Hubert
Sultan, who served as the mayor of Restoration from
1908 to 1912. Old-time Restorationists will recall
Sultan Furniture on Union Street, founded by Hubert
and presided over by Chester until he closed its
doors in 1935.

He was married ~~twice. His first wife was~~ *three times. His* Sally
Planter (Admiraal), now of Grosse Pointe, formerly *first wife was*
of Restoration. They were divorced in 1964. He *Klara Kuzmak,*
leaves his wife, Tiffany, and their two daughters, Jes- *He then married*
sica and Winnie; a son, Luke Planter, of New York; a
brother, Conrad Sultan, of Miami, Florida; and a sister, Adelle De Vries, of Battle Creek. *with whom*
he had a son,
Wesley Jr.

I'm wandering the streets of Restoration and something is missing—where are the people? It's as if I've stepped onto a movie set
when everyone's on lunch break. Where are the people?—where's
the life? Long blocks of dilapidated houses, boarded-up storefronts,

weedy parking lots, and the few straggling souls I do encounter might have been put here expressly to illustrate just how moribund the town's become. A drunk fishing with a stick through a trash can. An aged orange-haired woman with a cotton ball in her ear, marching out of the post office and shaking her head combatively at a fire hydrant. A couple of ashen men lounging in mostly deserted Toledo Heights Park, where Chester Sultan used to while away warm afternoons, their collapsed faces so weathered it takes you a moment to recognize they're identical twins. A shirtless, towheaded, obese young man wheeling a pair of shirtless, tow-headed, obese babies in a stroller that isn't a stroller but a super-market cart. And not a single child on the elementary school playground—only a child-sized elderly woman dressed all in black who sits motionless on a swing, staring up into what is in fact a lovely blue sky on this sunshiny day in August. Where are the people?

"Where is everybody?" I ask at a gas station, and wind up following the cashier's directions a few miles out of town, on Route 272, where the new Fairplay Mall has gone up, serving the twin populations of Restoration and Stags Harbor. It seems I've been here before: the plastic palms, the International Food Court, the vast wooden mill wheel beside the Food Court—a mill that turns but grinds nothing, and is nightly shut off with the flick of a switch . . . I don't linger long at the mall. It's Anywhere USA, but I'm looking for Someplace in Particular, for the town of Restoration, Michigan, in the forties and fifties. I'm looking for what Sally calls "a vanished world," and I get in the car and circle back to Restoration.

I have a few addresses. I check out first the grand manse on Crestview Boulevard, where the Sultans resided until Chester's death and the crash of the family fortune. And the sullen modest duplex on Scully Street, down by the Michicabanabee River, where Wes and Conrad and Adelle grew up and where old Dora, turned agoraphobe, cached herself in her final decades. I drive to Stags Harbor and find the little house on Majestic Avenue (quite sprightly, actually, in a coat of canary-yellow paint) where one rainy January afternoon, after a day of reading and basement cleaning, Sally opened the door to Klara Kuzmak. And I make my way to the later, grimmer lodgings on Downward Lane, the basement apartment that Sally took after leaving Wes. Each of these places interests me, but none evokes quite as much as I'd hoped. I'm waiting to feel that a key has been turned—a squeaky unused door been shouldered open.

I do better in the afternoon, after a diner lunch, when it occurs to me to explore the Restoration Christian Reformed Church, over on Grand Elm Street. I steal in through a back door and find my way to a punitively uncomfortable pew. The bareness of the whitewashed walls ought to speak of grandeur but seems merely dour. The carved oak pulpit, though, is prepossessing, with its zigzagging vines to suggest how, week after week, Reverend Koekkoek hurled premonitory lightning bolts—foretastes of the sizzling fireballs of Hell—at a cowering congregation. (To Sally's young but literary imagination, the Reverend's outsized magnificence was embodied and enhanced by the crisp cacophony of his name—the only name she'd ever encountered that held four *k*'s.) Even more evocative is a room in the basement, called the Consistory, with its friezelike line of black-and-white photographic portraits. These are the souls who have presided over the church since its construction, in 1909. Names like Vanden Akker, Dykema, Jacobusse, Ingelhousz, Opdyke. All men, of course. And all brothers in their sibling look of sustained rigor—in their resistance to any suggestion of latitude or hesitancy.

Of course I would love to have a look at the old high school on Cherrystone Avenue, but a Farmer Jack's supermarket stands on its former site. The new Restoration High School, built in the seventies, holds little interest for me. Meanwhile, as I drive around in my rented car, I keep hearing an inner voice remark, *You're missing something important,* and I have to remind myself, *You'll be back.* Where I have the best luck is, unexpectedly, in the new and ugly town library, built in 1984, well after Wes and Conrad and Sally and even Adelle had left town. In a bright little nook in the back, aswim with blazing dust motes, I chance upon a collection of old Restoration High School yearbooks, including the '52 edition. Will Wes be in it? Or, as a dropout, will he have been omitted?

I thumb slowly through the alphabetical gallery of the senior class. A businesslike list of honors and extracurricular activities anchors each photo. They're a solemn lot, who often manage— boys with their flattops and sports coats and ties, girls with their starched fussy hairdos and starched plain white blouses—to look precociously middle-aged. I come near the very end of the S's, reaching bespectacled, square-faced Thelia Stoneleigh, who looks less like a high school student than a professor emeritus of Latin. If Wes is present, he ought to appear on the following page.

I turn the page and—and my heart sinks. No Wes. Missing once more . . . And then I realize my mistake. A statistical aberration: an influx of *Su* names. Wes may still be present, pushed back a page by Sonia Sudbury (Future Homemakers Club) and Pierre Suffren (President, Microscope Club) and Wilhelmina Sugman (Vice President, Diary Club) and a host of Sullivans (Gerald, Nina, Stephen), who don't go in for clubs at all.

I turn the page and—and there's our Wes. A late arrival at the party, perhaps, but as buoyant, confident, and *winning* as he can be. Not a single hair, in the edifice of his pompadour, out of place. The gaze forthright and soulful. Wesley Cross Sultan. Social Committee. Future Businessmen of America Club. Although the picture is of course in black-and-white, you'd know those eyes of his must be a freezing and fiery blue and you can understand how a bright and pretty but inexperienced nineteen-year-old girl, sitting on a bench with him in Toledo Heights Park, might trust him utterly as he pledged, "Everything between us is going to be all right, forever and ever."

A white-haired woman approaches the information desk and asks, in that querulous, slightly aggrieved tone common to the partially deaf, "Where do you keep the large-print books?" She might well be Sonia Sudbury. Or Wilhelmina Sugman, ex–vice president of the Diary Club. Or Nina Sullivan. Meanwhile, outside the library, the town of Restoration goes about its business—its slow business of dying. On a front lawn, someone hammers in the stakes of a FOR SALE sign; in a back parlor, someone else packs up a footlocker. But here in the library, Wes gazes up at me, invincibly youthful, and time itself is arrested. How long do I contemplate Wes's photo? Five minutes? Ten? As he and I regard each other, the bravado leaches from his expression, leaving him less winning but even more appealing. A note of entreaty filters through his eyes—a look that says less *I'm lovable* than *Love me.*

I'd like to take this yearbook home with me for a while. Perhaps Sally has a copy I might borrow? Or Conrad? And then it occurs to me that, charming as the photograph is, this yearbook isn't a volume that anyone associated with Wes would be likely to treasure: the graduation keepsake of someone who failed to graduate.

I spend the rest of the afternoon inside the yearbook's pages. It's the closest I'm ever going to come to entering the classrooms and corridors of the old Restoration High on Cherrystone Avenue. For here, truly, is "another world." The Future Nurses Club. The Radio Club ("aims to interest boys and girls about radio"). The Square Dance Club ("helps promote social adjustment among the students"). The Ushers Club ("composed of uniformed girls who are on call for working the checkroom at school parties"). And my own favorite, the Lost and Found Club ("formed to aid the school and students in locating their lost articles"). Page after page, all stringently devoid of levity, prankishness, humor. Most of it's intended to be as funny as your average utility company's shareholders' report. No, these were young people launched on a grand and grave mission. The class of '52, Restoration High School, Restoration, Michigan, clearly was intent on declaring, to a nation they never seemed to doubt was listening to them, *Having now reached the brink of adulthood, we stand prepared, as responsible and square-thinking young men and women, to take our places in American society.*

Even the advertisements are wonderful, everything from the watch repairman, whose little meditation on punctuality soon embraces larger themes ("Young people, you need to know the time *and* the times, especially now when the communist threat is at our Gates"), to the men's store ("the smart look for the young man with smarts"), to the daring plug for ladies' swimwear ("A classy lassie has a streamlined chassis").

A soft bell pings and an almost comically mellow woman's voice announces that the library will close in ten minutes. It's only then that I discover, tucked away in the back of the yearbook, behind the advertisements, a sort of parting gift. There are four pages of "casual shots," complete with what I suppose are "arch" captions. On the penultimate page, I find it. I'm drawn to a caption that reads "The Master of the Mats,—or, The Fall Guy."

It's a skinny little kid in an old-fashioned, loose, singlet-style wrestling tunic, knees bent and hands outstretched warily before him. In 1952, though only a sophomore, he was already the mainspring of the wrestling team. And though he can't weigh more than 130 pounds, the penetrating scowl he levels at his opponent—at the camera, at the world at large—does not seem ludicrous. No,

Conrad's fierceness survives the translation into a little black-and-white snapshot. He looks formidable.

Another penetrating scowl: "So: back in Miami, are we? Business seems to be booming for us in the Sunshine State."

"Travel comes in spurts. I'll make three trips in a week, then nothing for months on end."

But is he on to me? Beginning to suspect that this time, as was true last time, I flew down here expressly to see him?

"And you've been to France, so my spies tell me."

"That was purely a vacation."

"And how's the rich widow? I thought she was heading over there for only a month."

"Seems fine, actually. She's extended her stay. I should have guessed she would from the number of books she shipped over there. Incidentally, it's a lovely place she's taken. You should reconsider your ban on European travel. You'd like Domat. Lovely hills. Wonderful food. Good cheap wine."

"And no sun, to judge from the look of you. You're even paler than last time I saw you."

"It's the light in here."

Again I've left up to Conrad the choice of restaurant, again under the pretense that it's a dinner I'll be charging to my firm. In truth, nearly two months have elapsed since I cleaned out my desk at Gribben Brothers. For the first time since my earliest childhood, I'm neither a student nor a wage-earner. But this isn't something I'm about to let Conrad know. I don't want to deflect him; don't want to have to explain myself.

The name of the restaurant is Pastures. Though it specializes in pasta, its atmosphere is far removed from what I think of as Italian dining. Where are the candles? The browns and reds? The watery operatic voices swimming over the loudspeakers? The music is the sort of jazz seemingly sprung direct from a computer's innards, unfiltered through any human lungs or fingers. The light's a cool, anemic blue, and the wood is blond, as are most of the servers, both men and women.

I've ordered prosciutto-and-figs for an appetizer, and a glass of Pinot Grigio. Conrad has ordered fried three-cheese ravioli, and a Brandy Alexander, and a second Brandy Alexander. He has already consumed four warm sesame breadsticks, with butter. This has all the makings of quite a night.

"Moved away permanently, has she? The rich widow?"

"One more month definitely, a few more months possibly. She's finally getting some time to herself. Every woman friend of hers from Grosse Pointe has gone out to visit."

"How gruesome: rich widows descending on a rich widow."

"I think it's great. She's talking about heading farther south. To the Mediterranean. She wants to take some French classes."

"Oh Lord save us."

"And she says she isn't coming back to the States until she's read all of Proust."

"All of what?"

"A modern French writer." It reassures me somewhat (never having read, if the truth be told, a word of Proust myself) to play the literary guide. "He wrote a four-thousand-page novel."

For somebody who probably hasn't cracked a work of fiction in thirty years, Conrad manages a sharp, if slightly confused, response: "And what will she do when she takes up *Kim*? Move to Baghdad? And has she thought about *Around the World in Eighty Days*? That's some life she's got."

"I asked her about Klara Kuzmak."

"Tactful of you."

"She didn't seem to mind."

"And?"

"And I got a different sense of Klara than I got from you last time."

Instantly Conrad's voice turns a little testy: "How so?"

"What Sally kept stressing was Klara's beauty. At least on that day when Klara first came knocking on her door."

Conrad hangs back a moment. Clearly he doesn't like the thought of Sally's contradicting him. But how is he going to challenge her?

Of course when he plunges in, he plunges in boisterously: "Oh now *that's* a scene I'd give my eyeteeth to have witnessed! The Day the Scales Fell from Sally Admiraal's Eyes. She was quite remarkably slow to catch on to our Wesley."

"She doesn't deny it. She calls herself Sally the Much Misled."

"But the odd thing is—have you noticed?—this particular misled woman always winds up better off than before . . . Richer, richer, richer. And socially grander. She trips *upwards*—that's our dear clumsy Sally. Give her enough time, she'll slip and stumble her way into being crowned Queen of England. Or even of France. Do the French still have queens?"

"I think they have film goddesses."

"Maybe Sally has a future in Hollywood . . ."

It's something of an obsession for Conrad—this railing about the "rich widow" and her endless good fortune. I work to deflect him: "But Klara *was* a beauty, yes?"

"Oh I suppose she was." Conrad scowls at me. "And perhaps that explains, to a degree, Wesley's otherwise inexplicable attraction to her."

"Inexplicable? What do you mean?"

"Look, don't be a dumb cluck. Obviously. *Obviously* inexplicable."

I'm growing somewhat used to Conrad, but he can still make

me flinch, especially when he meets with what strikes him as a stu-pid question—and half the questions I ask seem to fall into this category. To say he's in a cantankerous mood tonight would be charitable. Still, he'll probably soften as the evening wears on. Each bite on a breadstick, each slurp on a Brandy Alexander, mellows him a little.

"What's wrong with you?" he goes on. "Don't you see any-thing? Klara's English was negligible, so what possible use could she be to Wesley? She couldn't understand his *rap*, and what was any woman in Wes's eyes but a chance to weave his little spell of words around her? She was a sweet piece, okay, and maybe even some sort of 'beautiful creature,' as Sally might say, but in the end she wasn't challenge enough for our handsome blue-eyed sales-man."

I seek to soften his tone: "Actually, you were completely right about that. Sally really did refer to her as a 'fabulous glowing creature.'"

"Those Sallyisms," Conrad says, with a stiff, disapproving shake of the head that doesn't fully conceal how much they amuse him, even appeal to him. "Who else do you know, who else could pos-sibly have said, 'The automotive term *to total* entered my vocabu-lary under most unfortunate circumstances.' Or how about, 'That McNally boy would perhaps be better employed employed'? In terms of verbal dexterity, it's quite a long way from there to Klara Kuzmak, I can tell you."

"Still, Klara can't have been *all* that dumb. She caught on to him in the end."

"Cluck, you're being a dumb *cluck,* don't you see that? The day she materialized so dramatically on Sally's doorstep, Miss Klara Sul-tan, née Kuzmak, was every bit as confused as Sally herself. In fair-ness to Klara, she probably didn't give a good goddamn about the truth one way or the other. Give her the benefit of the doubt and assume by then it wasn't Wes but Wes's money she hankered after. Hell, she'da stayed nice and quiet if he'd kept up the payments. She'd stayed quiet all along. Wes had her totally snowballed about his dying father and the inheritance and all the rest."

"The—I'm sorry. The what?"

"You don't know . . ." And it seems every cell in Conrad's broad, bloated face—millions upon millions of cells—radiates a bathing joy. My ignorance elates him. "Well well. So so so. Haven't yet broken through the big conspiracy of silence, have we, kid? I guess Sally wasn't quite so forthcoming as she might have been and you could have saved yourself a trip to France. Miami's got to be a helluva lot cheaper and as informants go I don't think I've got quite so many *scruples* as our Sally does."

Conrad signals to a waitress (not *our* waitress, but this is typical: Conrad can never keep straight who has been serving him) and calls, "More breadsticks! More breadsticks!" It seems his rudeness customarily goes unchallenged—and I think I know how the waiters and waitresses feel. For there's something awesome and overmastering about Conrad's bulk, his forward-thrust shoulders, his booming voice, his thinning silver hair gathered into its tight ponytail. Then he turns back to me and says, "Apparently you don't know yet that Wes had to keep his marriage to Klara under wraps. Because? Because our father would have opposed his marrying a Catholic."

A crowd of objections immediately raise a clamor in my head—until I identify the one objection that renders all the others irrelevant: "But Chester was *dead* by then. And had been for many years."

"Precisely. So wouldn't you have thought Wes might prefer to say it was *Mother* who disapproved of marrying Catholics? But then why, assuming you're Wesley Sultan, would you ever stick to the possible when the impossible is so much more glamorous, and colorful, and *fun*?"

Conrad bites the head off another breadstick. The look he gives me is bellicose. He appears to be awaiting some challenge or objection. But I say nothing. And Conrad, seemingly satisfied with my silence, goes on:

"Okay, he confided in Klara that his father was very sick. In fact, poor old Dad wasn't expected to live more than a year or two. And also happened to be quite rich. So you see where this is going? If Wes didn't do something rash or stupid, well, he stood to come into a tidy packet. Hence, the two of them kept their marriage a secret."

This time I do speak up. I remember Sally's saying that Conrad occasionally served as Wes's "deputy," and I can't resist asking, "And you? How long were you in on the little secret?"

For a couple of moments Conrad steadily ponders my face, which I'm afraid falls short of his hopes or expectations. He gives me a dismissive shrug and says, "Jesus, dig, dig, dig, that's all you do, and the dirtier the dirt, the better you like it, isn't that right? Next thing, you'll be asking me the *really* sordid stuff—like what Wes was up to with the Zidlers in Kalamazoo."

"The Zidlers? Who were they?"

"See, didn't I tell you? I said it's the next thing you'd be asking me, and now it's the next thing you're asking me."

"So who were the Zidlers?"

"Another time, buddy boy. Another time."

And again he eyes me—the old wrestler sizing up his opponent. Our arena may be an elegant table rather than a sweaty mat on the floor, but the battle is no less genuine for that. Lunges, feints, takedowns and escapes.

And yet this remark of Conrad's simultaneously may extend an invitation. Isn't he saying, albeit as ungraciously as possible, *Come visit me again . . . ?*

I agree to his implied conditions. I say to him, "Okay, okay. We'll save it for next time." Then I impose a new demand: "But at least tell me when you were in on the secret. About the secret marriage."

And Conrad, after a heavy pause, decides to meet me halfway: "It was after the baby was born. When Wes realized he'd taken on more than he could handle. Occasionally the point would be driven home for him: He knew how to dive, but he didn't know how to swim."

"That's very neatly expressed."

"For an old dumb jock—that what you mean?"

"For an anybody. That's what I mean."

"High praise from a Princeton boy."

"Praise from a Princeton boy to a Vanderbilt boy—a pair of Yankee boys at southern schools."

And again I've pleased him. I've found the right mixture of solidarity and contentiousness. I stir him up for all sorts of reasons, I suppose—and not least because of my career at Gribben Brothers. Conrad spent his working life in solo practice. He had plenty of years, based in an office on the outskirts of a Miami mall, to build up resentment toward the "hotshots," the "megabuck boys," the "fat cats." Although he has retired, he remains vehemently hostile toward "Manhattan finance"—that exclusive zone where multinational, multimillion-dollar deals are transacted on a scale far beyond anything ever overseen by Conrad Sultan, CPA.

He orders up another round of drinks.

I ask, "But why did he marry her in the first place?"

"Because he was an idiot? Because he was infatuated? Because the girl was pregnant?"

"Maybe he was in love."

"Maybe I'm a monarch butterfly."

"According to Sally, it was a question of honor."

"Honor? Honor?" Such is his shocked tone, Conrad might well be crying out, *Horror, horror.* No doubt about it, mine is the flat-out *dumbest* explanation he's heard in quite a while. "No. *Hell* no no no. It was an opportunity. It was a chance to have a *secret family.* Don't you see anything? To be husband and father in your every-day, open, acknowledged family—well, that would be nothing special, right? Wes had spent his whole life around such families. But a *secret family*—that was different, that was right up Wes's alley."

"But where did he get it? I mean, where do you think it came from, this appetite for . . ." And while I'm searching for a tactful term, Conrad again comes crashing down, like a wrestler throwing a body to the mat.

"His appetite for dishonesty? For crookedness? You asking me why Wes was a pathological liar? How in hell should I know? Christ, I'm only his brother. Maybe it was genetic, and if so it's got to make you a little uneasy, hm? After all, *I've* taken part in my share of deceptions, and of course Mother was, in her way, more devious than either of us."

"I beg your pardon?"

The light in this restaurant is, as I've said, an icy inhuman blue, but on the table stands a little garnet-red glass lamp. Into the left corner of each of Conrad's eyes it deposits a hard jewel-like glint. His gaze is burning. Febrile? Demented? Satanic? What extraordinary utterance will next emerge from his lips?

"Okay," he says. "All right, kiddo. I suppose it's time you were told what you should have guessed on your own, if you were only half as psychologically acute as maybe I was at your age. Look around the family tree. Ask yourself the old accountant's question: Does it compute?"

"I'm not sure I—"

"Ponder poor Adelle."

"Adelle?"

"My sister, Adelle? My kid sister? Blood of the Sultan blood, flesh of the Sultan flesh? Adelle Marie Sultan. Well, she's not my sister. She's my half-sister. Her father was Mel Bellamy. Does that name mean anything to you?"

"Bellamy? Wait a minute . . . I don't think so."

"And why should it? It's all before your time. But a name to reckon with on Crestview Boulevard, I can assure you. When I was a little kid, the Bellamys were my parents' very best friends. Constant companions. Mr. Bellamy owned the Commodore Hotel, in Stags Harbor, back when it was a place of some elegance, before it became a haven for pimps and druggies. Mrs. Bellamy was a sweet woman with a strong sense of justice—I remember she once went to Mackinac Island and brought me back a bag of taffy and nothing back for Wes, because so many of the neighborhood women babied and spoiled him. And I still remember her doing that; you don't forget thoughtful little kindnesses like that. But Mrs. B. had lupus, the sun was deadly for her. She stayed out of it—she was as pale as you—but she died before her time just the same. Are you with me so far?"

"I think so."

"All right. So then add this to the picture. In my entire life, I saw my mother cry only once. Wanna guess when? Are you guessing June of 1942, at her husband's funeral? If so, your guess is wrong. It was much later. No, the only time Mother cried, she was sitting in our living room, our embarrassingly *little* living room on Scully Street, with a neighbor who happened to mention that that eligible bachelor and widower and wealthy man-about-town Mel Bellamy was going to remarry. At first Mother flared up in anger— she actually called her guest a liar—and then? Then she burst into tears."

"But that hardly means there was anything going on. You said yourself, they'd been good friends."

"And when her guest went home, she retreated into her room and cried some more."

"Okay sure, maybe there was some attraction and disappointment, but it's hardly the case that that necessarily means Adelle—"

"Ah, but you never saw Bella."

"Mm?" I say.

"Bella Bellamy. Sorry about the name. Forgive me, and forgive my parents' friends. Mea mucho culpa. Your crowd, the Princeton/Wall Street, making-megabucks crowd, they don't have names like that, do they? I suppose most women you meet are named Priscilla Pettingfarm."

"A fair number. But not *most.*"

"But stop and think—hey, you can understand the logic. Mel Bellamy says to himself, I've got an atrocious name, but if I give my kid a worse one, hell, no one'll notice mine. He was a pushy son of a bitch. Anyway, Bella was their daughter—the only Bellamy child. And yet a dead ringer for—for who? For Adelle Sultan. As like as twins, the two of them. Even named like twins, Bella and Adelle—makes you almost feel sorry for that poor pinochle-playing knucklehead Chester Sultan, doesn't it? Bella and Adelle—twins right down to the same exact unmistakable honker of a nose. The Bellamy beak. Unmistakable."

"But it's—well, it's hard to picture, isn't it?"

"Is it? Doesn't it above all and everything make perfect sense? Mother was a proud woman, proud to be a Sultan, God help her, and when Mel decided to remarry? The poor girl felt *dumped.* It was humiliating—she'd cried in front of her son and an old snoop of a neighbor. Surely she was dreaming every day that old Mel would swoop down and rescue her—restore her to Crestview

Boulevard and the Heights, where she belonged. And what better explanation to explain the rest of her life? How else do you account for that cold, determined, shuttered-up widowhood of hers? Hell, she'd borne the ugly-nosed child of a man who, later on, when they both were single and free, still wouldn't make an honest woman of her . . ."

"I can think of all sorts of reasons why she might never have remarried."

"Can you? And I can think of all sorts of reasons why she bedded Mel Bellamy. Let me tell you another: The man she was married to had all the raw animal drive of . . . of . . ."

Conrad's eyes fly round the room, seeking out some apt object of comparison, before at last alighting, with seeming inevitability, upon his own dinner plate. The entrées have arrived. "Of a bowl of cold pasta."

Actually, the meal before him is steaming mightily. Conrad has ordered a Toscana wrap (thin slices of veal wound round spicy sausage and melted cheese, served on a bed of angel-hair pasta), with a side order of ziti Alfredo.

"But how in the world would you know anything like that about your own father? Come on, who would possibly tell you such a thing?"

"Maybe in the past I did a little of what you're doing now— maybe I did a little digging? This was years ago, incidentally. A little party at Adelle's. You can imagine what a lively affair *that* was, what with Bernie as host."

Bernie De Vries is Adelle's husband. He's a retired plumber, originally from the Upper Peninsula.

Conrad goes on: "By the way, do you know what Bernie's short for? It's short for *Hibernation*. I greet him, I say, 'Hi, Bern'— and what's he do? He takes it as a cue, wanders downstairs for a nap. At the gates of heaven, Saint Peter'll ask how he enjoyed married life, Bernie'll be able honestly to say, *Don't know, slept through.* Anyway, who do I run into that afternoon at Adelle's party? None other than Mrs. Hornman. That name, too, means nothing to you and I wish it meant nothing to me; we called her 'Mrs. Horrorman.' She was an old neighbor. A really terrifying woman."

Actually, I am finding all the names a little confusing. But I'm getting the gist, and I'm eager for more . . .

Conrad says, "But where was I? Well, the years hadn't been any too kind to Mrs. Horrorman, who'd apparently gotten in the habit of washing down her wine with a couple martinis. She and I weren't five minutes on Adelle's living room sofa before she's talking about how she used to throw herself bodily at old Chester. But never with any success."

And there's something about Conrad's free-flowing, hell-bent taste for the scandalous that, after a while, seems to spur in me some earnestly sophomoric need to protest. I was—I'm afraid—captain of the debating team at my high school, and even now Conrad rouses in me old schoolboyish calls for *fairness.* I find myself saying, "But that hardly means he didn't have any . . . any sex drive. Has it occurred to you, maybe he was simply being faithful to his wife?"

"Well. I *like* your theory. It's very tender. Got one hole in it though. How you going to account for what Mrs. Hornman tells me next? This look comes over her face, this hideous, gloating, almost flirtatious look—it was a frightening moment—and then she offers up 'a little secret.' It seems that Mother, in an uncharacteristic moment of openness, one afternoon went to Mrs. Hornman with a problem. What was she going to do about Chester? Mother wanted another child, but how was she going to have one if . . . if there was no longer any . . . how would Mother have put it? Relations? Activity 'of that sort'?"

"Did you ever communicate your suspicions to Wesley?"

"*Communicate? My suspicions?* What the hell's this, a goddamn court of law? Incidentally, you made a big mistake not ordering the veal, this was one little calf whose blood wasn't spilled in vain."

"I'm quite happy with my—"

"Actually, actually I *did* communicate my suspicions, and it turned into one of the most laughable encounters I ever had with Wes. You know what? He becomes indignant. *He* becomes indignant. Wes the legendary skirt-chaser absolutely won't *countenance* the notion that Dora Sultan might once have taken a tumble in the hay with Mel Bellamy."

"Well isn't that only natural? Aren't children always doing that? Holding their parents to a standard of behavior, of uprightness, they themselves don't begin to uphold?"

It's Conrad's gloating look that makes me go on this way, I suppose. Or the fact that—unwisely trying to keep up with him in another sort of arena—I'm now on my third glass of Pinot Grigio.

"Not bad. Okay, that's not bad. Far as it goes. But the waters are deep here. Can you swim? My father couldn't swim—or couldn't on the day when it counted, June twenty-first, 1942. And you know what I think happened on that day? I think the lake was very cold—it's never *warm,* not even in the real heat of the summer— and his heart stopped. He was too much of a coward for suicide, if you want the truth, and there are faulty tickers up and down the Sultan line, my own included. Hell, let's roll out of here. Go for a drink at my local."

"Your local?"

The next thing I know, I'm a passenger in Conrad's car and nighttime Miami is racing by—a city I don't know and tonight enjoy not knowing as it breezes past my lowered window in all its colorful, jangly, palm-tree-crested unexpectedness. Loud shirts, loud neon signs, loud music from the overlapping, competing rhythms of car radios and boom-boxes. The wine has made me sleepy.

Conrad's local? It's a dingy little Mexican place called La Rosa Rosa. The air conditioner is ailing and the posters taped to the walls (Mazatlán; a jaguar peering out of a jungle; a pop singer in an old-fashioned pink party dress) have begun to buckle. All of the clientele (four older men at a back table; three kids at a table by the door; two off-duty security guards in one of the two booths) are male, and Spanish-speaking.

Still, Conrad appears to feel at home. He settles into the remaining booth with a grunt. "Where was I?" he asks me.

"You were talking about Wes's resistance to your theory that—"

And Conrad launches right in: "When I questioned Adelle's paternity and Wes got so indignant? At first I thought he was just being a stuffed shirt. You have to understand about Wes: In his ideal world, everybody else would behave impeccably. Hm? He was very keen on virtue—for everybody else. Because everybody else's virtue was what made it so much fun. Other people's virtue was the most piquant spice imaginable. For his own vices. You see? What's the fun of being bad in a truly evil world?"

"I do see your point."

"And then I thought, No, it's just egotism. It's Wes in some cockeyed way defending himself by defending his father. After all, how could Wesley Sultan's old man fail to be anything other than some bangety-bangety stud? You get the idea . . ."

The elderly waitress is slow to approach our booth, and yet Conrad—another surprise—addresses her mildly. "Evening, Graciela," he says. "How *are* you?"

She shrugs and lays a hand on her flank. "My hip," she says. She walks with a limp.

"I'm sorry," Conrad says.

She sets a bowl of taco chips before us.

"We'll have two rum-and-Cokes," he says, ordering for me, and adds, "Please."

We sit in silence for a minute or two. Not until the drinks arrive does Conrad begin again, as fervently as ever: "But finally I find out, years later, that one of the women Wes so gallantly seduced in his youth (and what I want to know is, Did the seduction take place in the cramped backseat of his red Bel Air? And did our gallant lover-boy spring for a couple of chili dogs first?), that one of his many conquests was—can you guess? Bella Bellamy. So that when I'd pointed out, when I'd *innocently* pointed out, the sisterly resemblance between Bella and Adelle, what had I inadvertently done? Hm? Well, I'd effectively accused Wes of incest. Going to bed with Bella was tantamount to going to bed with his kid sister—a kid sister who, let's face it, was nobody's idea of a looker. It would have been a different kettle of fish, I guess, if Adelle'd been a looker. But as it was, Wes could get quite indignant on behalf of Mother's honor. Oh, Wes could get quite huffy—and Wes was always at his *godawfulest* when he was being huffy. You'll have to excuse me. Piss time."

Given Conrad's bulk, this is something of a production: the unpacking himself from the booth and the rising to his feet. As a speaker, when indefatigably holding the floor, Conrad could be something of an ageless presence. But he is something else again when glimpsed from the rear as he shuffles off toward the men's room at La Rosa Rosa: an elephantine soon-to-be-elderly man, at once pitiful and poignant and silly as he retreats in search of relief for his overloaded bladder. The Master of the Mats. Or so he'd once been called. Now he's a sixty-one-year-old man with high blood pressure and a heart condition who ten years ago decided he'd lived long enough without cream and sugar. The Fall Guy.

Even so, all his vital energies seem replenished when he

squeezes into the booth once more. He tosses down a handful of taco chips, drains the last of his rum-and-Coke, and says, "I feel you resisting me, but you have to embrace it. Embrace the ironies. As for me, I *like* the ironies. Given all the problems and upheaval and torment that arose over the years as a result of Wes's sexual impulses, to say nothing of my *own* impulses, it tickles me pink to suppose the two of us sprang from the loins of a man with sleepy balls. I'm telling you the straight dope: Between his legs, Chester carried a toy boat. And *that's* what launched me and brother Wes on the great seas of life. Ironies? You see before you, in all my rolling mountains of flesh, dramatic proof that life is, above everything else, a succession of ironies. I used to be a sprinter and now I weigh more than an eighth of a ton. Wrap your head around that one and then tell me you think it's implausible that Adelle is Mel Bellamy's daughter."

CHAPTER SIX

RESTORATION—Wesley Cross Sultan, 63, of 2135 ~ 62
N. Westhampton, died suddenly in Lyon Hospital in
Stags Harbor, of heart failure. He worked for Great
Bay Shipping for 42 years, chiefly in sales. He began
his career in the Stags Harbor office, and after stints
in Kalamazoo and Cincinnati, Ohio, he finished his
career back at Stags Harbor. He retired two years
ago in order to pursue full-time his civic pursuits.
He was an active member of the Rotarians, the
Restoration Chamber of Commerce, the Stags Harbor Betterment Society, and the Thumb of Michigan
Prosperity Council. He was also active in the Restoration Episcopal Church, where for many years he sang
in the choir.

He was born in Restoration and ~~was a graduate~~ *attended but*
~~of~~ the old High School on Cherrystone Avenue. He *did not quite*
was the son of the late Chester Sultan, the well- *graduate from*
known businessman, and the grandson of Hubert
Sultan, who served as the mayor of Restoration from
1908 to 1912. Old-time Restorationists will recall
Sultan Furniture on Union Street, founded by Hubert
and presided over by Chester until he closed its
doors in 1935.

He was married ~~twice. His first wife was~~ Sally *three times. His*
Planter (Admiraal), now of Grosse Pointe, formerly *first wife was*
of Restoration. They were divorced in 1964. He *Klara Kuzmak,*
leaves his wife, Tiffany, and their two daughters, Jes- *He then married*
sica and Winnie; a son, Luke Planter, of New York; a
brother, Conrad Sultan, of Miami, Florida; and a *half-*sis- *with whom*
ter, Adelle De Vries, of Battle Creek. *he had a son,*
Wesley Jr.

"Sure now? You don't want me to wake him?"

"Absolutely. Absolutely sure."

"I hesitate to only because he didn't sleep last night. Not a
wink."

"Then you mustn't," I say. "Absolutely mustn't."

"He'll be getting up soon anyway. On his own steam," Adelle reassures me.

It's four in the afternoon. Her husband, Bernie, is napping in the basement of their bric-a-brac-packed ranch house in Pheasant Ridge, a suburb of Battle Creek. She and I are sitting catercorner at her little kitchen table, under a framed needlework sampler that reads HOME IS WHERE THE HEARTBURN IS.

"I was so pleased to get your card. I didn't expect to see your business bring you to of all places Battle Creek."

Had I said as much in my note? Surely I hadn't stretched the truth so far as that . . . "Well to Detroit, actually. But it's an easy drive."

"You haven't been here before."

"Not to this house. But your old house in Restoration. I remember you had a swing in the tree."

"The city cut it down. The tree. On account of the Dutch elm disease. Then, after we moved away, the house itself burned down. To the ground. They were terrible people, the Mendozas. They came from Cuba."

"That's where my wife's family, her parents, came from."

Mine's a precautionary reminder, and probably unnecessary, but I'd just as soon the conversation didn't take a creepy, bigoted turn. Actually, the hard glint in Adelle's eye doesn't seem to reflect any sort of prejudice, only simple inquisitiveness: She's as curious about my story as I am about hers. I add, "My ex-wife."

"Let me offer you a cup of coffee."

It turns out to be instant coffee. I'm grateful for it anyway. Winds are whistling and a chilly rain slaps against the windows. This early September weather's unseasonably cold—autumnal. And here in the "breakfast capital of the world" (where, a hundred years ago, the city's favorite sons, Dr. John Harvey Kellogg and younger brother Will Keith, were visited by a vision of a flake), Adelle pushes toward me a plate of cookies made of various breakfast cereals glued together by marshmallows, chocolate chips, butterscotch chips. I select the smallest cookie on the plate and take a hesitant bite. But as the child within me eagerly responds to its overload of sugar, I'm grateful for the cookie, too.

In the foreground of the needlepoint sampler, a man reclines in a living room lounger. Spokelike lines of pain radiate from his chest and his throbbing heart is stitched in flaming red yarn. In the background, a woman stands in the kitchen, industriously stirring a pan on the stove—no doubt concocting another dinner disaster. HOME IS WHERE THE HEARTBURN IS. Adelle's actual kitchen partakes of the sampler's cartoon atmosphere. A chartreuse-haired ceramic troll stands guard over the sink. A bespectacled raccoon peers down from the top of the refrigerator.

Adelle offers me a plate of charred gingerbread men. There must be a dozen of them, all dry as dust. I break one in half and chew on a cindery leg.

Over refilled cups of coffee we talk for half an hour without touching on anything of much use or interest to me. That's all right. I'm glad to be here, grateful to be experiencing so heightened a sense of shelter. The cold rain against the glass lends to the afternoon an air of amplitude: Adelle and I, we have all the time in the world.

In back of or underneath the drumming rain, there's another sound, which I'm slow to notice and slower still to identify: It's the tranquil din, muffled behind a couple of closed doors, of Bernie's snoring. It makes a shuffling and leisurely fall, like soil sliding down a chute. Conrad's arch little gibe comes back to me: Bernie is short for *Hibernation*.

Adelle talks, I nod; Adelle talks, I nod. Her monologue is a wandering creek of so gentle a propulsion, you have to take on faith the notion that you'll eventually get out of the woods and into open waterways. I eat another cookie. I finish another cup of coffee. We're pared to elementals: falling earth, winding water—and outside a raw wind ripping at the first leaves of the season to call it quits. Adelle's talk slides along, taking in her neighbors, the local school board, Bernie's hateful ex-boss (now retired, in disgraceful affluence, with his ex-secretary in Tucson), Bernie's sensitive digestive tract, America's trade imbalance, the problem with dental floss, falling standards at the Big Hatch supermarket.

Meanwhile, I'm busy with a clandestine task: I'm studying Adelle's fifty-nine-year-old face, seeking to piece out some resemblance to either Wesley or Conrad. But in truth, I can find little of either brother in her eyes, eyebrows, forehead, lips, ears. She's a long way from either, certainly, in her bulldog jaw, and further still in what Conrad, with typical gallantry, calls her "honker"—a big cartilaginous slab of a nose, outfitted with various surplus curves and knobs. This nose of hers bears no resemblance to either Conrad's flat, vaguely Asian wedge or Wesley's arty, aristocratic prow.

Certainly there's nothing bland about Adelle. She looks like *somebody's* daughter, bears *someone's* distinctive stamp and irrepressible genes. And why shouldn't that somebody be Mel Bellamy? It doesn't appear to be Chester Sultan.

The possibility opens up for me dim inklings of another world, that murky and musky and ever-alluring zone called Sex Before One's Own Birth . . . It's a notion that's hard to believe when you're quite young: Somehow, our ancestors managed to figure it all out without us—got the mechanics down, anyway. Really? You mean even the *very* elderly, those gray figures hunched over their walkers, even *they* may once have been driven into acrobatics of clawing desperation? It's not a notion that fits very well into a twenty-year-old head. You have to get partway down the road, I guess, to make sense of it.

Could Adelle truly be the offspring of a scandalous union between Dora Sultan and Mel Bellamy? If so, where did the lovers do it? How often did they do it? Were there other lovers in Dora's life—was her affair with Mel notable chiefly because of the birth of the woman sitting before me? Or was Mel Bellamy (as Conrad seemed to believe) the one great explosive irregularity in Dora's existence, bringing in his wake a pain so deep she retreated for the rest of her life behind a barricaded, spinsterly widowhood?

If I can't quite imagine it all, for just a couple of moments I can *almost* imagine it all. Another erotic world beckons to me: desperate assignations with their own outmoded undergarments (girdles, garter belts, middies) and their own scents (cut-glass bottles of eau de toilette, men's hair tonics, medicinal aftershaves), rushed gropings with their own unspoken inhibitions and prerogatives and obstacles and liberated, the-hell-with-it pantings. And then, with a half-awakened, reality-restoring snuffle rising up out of the basement—an arrested rattle and a bold, pathbreaking snort from the depths of Bernie's nasal passages—the moment closes.

Is the bear in his lair about to crawl up into the light? A long silence ensues, followed by the sound of soil again subsiding down a metal chute. No, Bernie has taken up his burden of excavation once more.

Adelle and Bernie have no children. (And why not? Doubtless there's a story there, too.) But various kids' photographs and drawings adorn the refrigerator. Neighbors' children? Probably. It's easy to imagine how the kids on the block would find a refuge here: the warm kitchen stocked with bowls of candy and little toy knick-knacks, the plates of cookies, the kindly gray-haired woman who talks incessantly but doesn't seem to expect anyone to pay her any mind . . .

Adelle asks me about Sally and I tell her a little about the house in Domat, the French lessons, the open-air market where pheasants hang upside down, the eight-hundred-year-old Cistercian monastery. And it's apparent from the rapt but dazed expression on Adelle's face that I could just as well be telling her that Sally had settled in Alexandria or Zanzibar, Constantinople or Kathmandu, Troy or Tenochtitlán: Anything is possible for the former Sally Admiraal. (Anything is possible for the woman who once got Wesley Sultan to marry her, and then divorced him, and somehow managed nonetheless to inspire his lifelong loyalty and devotion.)

"But tell *me* about someone," I say. "I'd like to hear about Tiffany." Wesley's last wife. "You know I've never met her?"

"I have no problem with Tiffany."

And Adelle's mouth snaps shut upon this declaration, her sizable jaw swells. In her voice, defiance contends with pride, as if she fully expected me to challenge her on this very point.

"What's she like?" I ask instead, and this woman who has been talking so volubly hesitates, falters, halts. She's momentarily at a loss for words.

"Well, she's quite pretty," Adelle eventually pronounces, and adds: "Though nothing like as pretty as some of the women Wes used to go around with. Nothing like.

"She's quite young," Adelle continues, and again immediately qualifies: "Though maybe not quite as young as she acts."

"But what's she like? Did they have much in common?"

Adelle ponders. "Well-l-l, I don't think they had anything in common, f'you want to know the truth. The woman has two interests: talking on the telephone and watching television. Preferably at the same time. But neither activity ever had much appeal for Wes. Her interests *bored* him, you want my honest opinion, just as his interests bored her."

"And what *were* his interests?"

Coming from me, the question admittedly might seem a little odd; in any event, Adelle again fumbles for words. "Well, he . . . Wes was somebody who . . . There were all sorts of things—"

I try to help her out: "Those last couple years, after his retirement, how did he prefer to spend most of his time?"

"Well. The thing with Wes was simple, really: Wes was a people-person. He really loved *people.* He liked to talk, to socialize, although not on the telephone—I don't think I ever had more than a twenty-minute phone conversation with him in my life—but in person, where he could look you in the eye, and maybe lay a hand on your shoulder."

"Actually, twenty minutes doesn't seem *all* that—"

"There was this *warmth* about Wes. Lots of people who deal with people, people like politicians and newscasters and ministers, they spend years trying to develop that kind of warmth, but Wes had it right from the go. Everybody felt it, and many people envied it. I don't know if I've ever known any man who had to struggle more often with envy on a daily basis. And yet it didn't get him down. Wes stayed Wes. Envy's what kept him back at Great Bay Shipping. I'm not telling tales—everybody knew that. The other salesmen were jealous of his special gift, his talent for people. Mr. Haight, his boss, he was especially jealous, and a lesser man than Wes would have packed up and gone elsewhere. But Wes was loyal. He liked to start what he finished. Great Bay gave him his first real job, when he was only seventeen, and he stayed loyal to them."

And again Adelle's lips clamp shut; she offers another big-jawed nod of conviction.

"Do you have any photographs of her?"

"Of who?"

"Of Tiffany."

"Photographs of Tiffany?" It seems I might just as well have asked Adelle if she kept a pet rattlesnake. "No, not really. Nothing of that sort. No."

"But they were in love, Wes and Tiffany? Despite their lack of interests? I understand they were deeply in love."

"Oh *Wes* was in love. *Wes* was always in love with her. Till the day he died. It's what I was saying: Wes was loyal. You mustn't listen to anybody tell you otherwise. I tell you honestly: Wes was the most misunderstood man I've ever known.

"Let me tell you something. Tiffany? She broke his heart. I can still see him like he's alive right here today. He was sitting exactly where you're sitting. 'She has broken my heart,' Wes announced, and you could see the man struggling ever so hard to keep back the tears. 'That woman has broken my heart in two,' he said, and you could see how those tears were struggling to get out."

Adelle herself puts up no such resistance: With startling rapidity, the lower rims of her lids redden and spill over—tears that somehow reproach me . . . Why am I here? Am I meddling among powerful loyalties and heartaches where, for all sorts of reasons, I have no business? Why am I conducting this (or so I term it in my own mind) interview?

Adelle wipes away the tears with an appealing matter-of-factness, and continues: "And that's how his life ended—in a heart-broke state. That's what that woman did to that man."

"You're saying she never loved him?"

"I honestly don't think she did. F'you want my opinion. And that's not a criticism. I'm not criticizing Tiffany if I say I don't think she's really capable of loving a man. Any more than she can love her children."

"But I've heard them described as very much in love, at least at first. You know, I was in Miami not long ago, on business, and I had dinner with Conrad, and the subject of Wes and Tiffany came up—"

"Conrad?" On either side of her colossal nose, Adelle's eyes narrow into slits. "Now listen: You should *never* listen to Conrad on the subject of Wes. Conrad is my brother, and I love him dearly, and I'm as sorry as sorry can be that ever since he's been ill he doesn't want to accept the family pity we're all ready to extend him, and prefers feeling self-pity rather than having us doing it. But you must understand one thing: Conrad has never forgiven Wes Wes's *way* with people. And Conrad's always, always been so competitive, if he couldn't beat Wes at something he simply wouldn't try it even one bit. And that's why he's often the rudest person who ever lived. If you can't be most charming, well then you have to be most rudest." Yes—and isn't Adelle in fact on to something? "That's Conrad."

"When I've gone out to eat with him, he terrorizes every waiter and waitress."

"Sometimes he terrorizes *me*. I suppose he never has forgiven me for not siding with him when he and Wes had the fight about the painting. You heard about that?"

"The painting? Conrad and Wes once fought about a painting?" But what could *be* more improbable?

"Uh-huh. A painting belonging to Mama. When she passed away, and nobody wanted it, I took it home. But then later Conrad decided he wanted it, so I said all right. But then after Wes heard Conrad took it, he decided *he* wanted it, so I told Conrad he had to let Wes have it for a while. Only, Conrad thought I'd given it to him. Not lent it to him. So he thought I was siding with Wes all over again. When really I was just being fair."

"I never envisioned the two of them fighting over a *painting*. What was it of? Was it valuable?"

"I don't think maybe *too* valuable. Maybe it wasn't a very great painting? It's called *Michigan Avenue in the Rain*. That's in Chicago. Someone who visited there brought it home to Mama as a souvenir. Wes and Conrad, they were always finding something new to fight over. I don't think they talked to each other for a year over that one."

"And all because of an ugly painting?"

"I didn't say ugly. I just said not very great."

"Who gave your mother the painting?"

"I . . . I don't recall."

"But you were talking about Wes and Tiffany. Conrad described the two of them as very lovey-dovey. He called them 'the necking newlyweds.'"

"Oh it's true Tiffany was all *over* Wes, and if your idea of love is somebody munching away like a caterpillar on somebody else's earlobe I suppose you could say she loved him. But Tiffany wasn't prepared to sacrifice *any*thing. It was his age as much as anything. Rock concerts is I suppose what she expected him to be taking her to. Handsome as Wes was, and he remained so right up till the very day he died, eventually it dawned on Tiffany she'd married a man nearing sixty. And she. Was. Not. Happy. About. That. A sixty-year-old man with health problems to boot. Because Wes knew he was sick, and you couldn't have lived with him day in day out and not known it yourself, even if he never complained much. He wasn't that sort."

"So how did the heartbreak come about? When did he come to feel she'd broken his heart?"

"When she threw him out, course that's what brought it home, but you can be sure he'd been ailing at heart for a long time before that."

"Threw him out?"

Adelle's face studies my face; my face studies her face. Un-expectedly, we have crossed a threshold together.

She speaks warily, but I know a revelation is at hand. "Well, I assumed you knew. They weren't living together. When he passed away."

"No, I didn't. Know. Where was he living?"

"Two months before, she threw him out. And I'm not making any accusations, I'm simply stating a medical fact when I say that the shock of it, the blow of having to live alone, especially when you're a warm people-person like Wes, with health problems to boot, it contributed to his death. I do think we have to face the truth square on and admit that that woman contributed greatly to his death. Why did he have a heart attack, except he was first heart-broke? Not that Tiffany wasn't fully in her legal rights to do so, legally speaking. Bernie disagrees with me, but I do think we have to face the truth square on and admit she brought it about just as surely as dumping arsenic in his coffee. It's exactly the same thing. Just the details different."

"I didn't know he'd moved out. Where was he living?"

"See, I'm not accusing her of being malicious. I have no bone to pick with Tiffany. I accept her for what she is. Tiffany is Tiffany, and you don't start there with her, you miss the whole point com-pletely. But *self-sacrificing* isn't the first word you'd use to describe her."

"Where was he living?" I ask a third time.

"Well at the Commodore Hotel, you know, downtown Stags Harbor, but that was only a way station. Wes was finding his bear-ings. He didn't have to stay in a place like that, with all those ratty old winos and fallen women and druggies and God knows what all." And when was the last time I'd heard the phrase "fallen women" used without irony? And yet what could be more ironic (which is perhaps to say, more plausible) than the discovery that the very woman now employing the phrase might herself be the off-spring of an adulterous union? And what could be more ironic than Wes's winding up at the end of his life in the very hotel once owned, in its elegant heyday, by Mel Bellamy? "He could have stayed right here. In our guest room. It has its own separate john and everything. We both, Bernie and I, we both practically begged him . . .

"But you know what? It was almost as if Wes *wanted* a scummy place like the Commodore. Because, you see, that's what that woman had reduced him to. She'd heartbroke him. Not that he didn't retain his pride, it wasn't like he went around advertising about living at the Commodore. Quite to the contrary. Most people didn't know. And of course he continued to get his mail at Tiffany's.

"I understood Wes, you see. He was preparing to make another leap. It was like he needed to focus in on his pain. That's why he moved there. And didn't come here. And why we didn't see more of him when she threw him out. Why nobody saw much of him. He needed to focus in on his pain. He was preparing for another leap, you see. And if he'd lived, that's exactly what he would have done. Would have taken off. And surprised a lot of people, I can tell you."

CHAPTER SEVEN

and the Commodore Hotel in Stags Harbor,

RESTORATION—Wesley Cross Sultan, ~~63,~~ *62* of 2135 N. Westhampton, died suddenly in Lyon Hospital in Stags Harbor, of heart failure. He worked for Great Bay Shipping for 42 years, chiefly in sales. He began his career in the Stags Harbor office, and after stints in Kalamazoo and Cincinnati, Ohio, he finished his career back at Stags Harbor. He retired two years ago in order to pursue full-time his civic pursuits. He was an active member of the Rotarians, the Restoration Chamber of Commerce, the Stags Harbor Betterment Society, and the Thumb of Michigan Prosperity Council. He was also active in the Restoration Episcopal Church, where for many years he sang in the choir.

He was born in Restoration and ~~was a graduate of~~ *attended but did not quite graduate from* the old High School on Cherrystone Avenue. He was the son of the late Chester Sultan, the well-known businessman, and the grandson of Hubert Sultan, who served as the mayor of Restoration from 1908 to 1912. Old-time Restorationists will recall Sultan Furniture on Union Street, founded by Hubert and presided over by Chester until he closed its doors in 1935.

He was married ~~twice. His first wife was~~ *three times. His first wife was Klara Kuzmak,* Sally Planter (Admiraal), now of Grosse Pointe, formerly of Restoration. They were divorced in 1964. He *He then married* leaves his wife, Tiffany, and their two daughters, Jessica and Winnie; a son, Luke Planter, of New York; a brother, Conrad Sultan, of Miami, Florida; and a *half-*sister, Adelle De Vries, of Battle Creek. *with whom he had a son, Wesley Jr.,*

"I can't believe my good fortune," Sally says.

"To be here? In Domat? It really is an amazing spot."

"I mean to see *you* again. Here. I never thought you'd be jetting over the Atlantic like this. I worry you must be spending a fortune."

"I told you before. I've banked enough frequent-flyer miles to keep me airborne for months yet. At Gribben I wouldn't think twice about flying to L.A. for a one-hour meeting. First-class. With triple the mileage credits."

"And I can remember a time when I thought a trip to Detroit was quite an undertaking. I'll have you know, I felt quite daring and worldly. I'm referring to the morning I set out from Stags Harbor for the Detroit Institute of Art—the day I happened to meet Gordon. And if I hadn't set out that morning, if I hadn't met Gordon, what's the chance I'd be walking today through an abbey in Burgundy? Really, life is too peculiar for words. If you wrote it down as a simple factual account, wouldn't it lack all plausibility?"

"You're saying it would call for quite a skilled interpreter?"

"I suppose that's the question, isn't it? The one each of us ultimately faces? Whether we're skilled enough interpreters to make even minimal sense of our lives."

"You're sounding like quite the philosopher."

"Am I? And is that a worrisome thing? Actually, I think I'd rather be known as a contemplative. You know something? I can remember the first time I ever encountered that word—I mean as a noun."

"You can really? You're amazing."

"I was reading a novel," Sally tells me. "I don't remember which one, but I remember I was a child reading in my bedroom when I came on this amazing notion. A *contemplative*. And it seemed such a weird, wonderful, thoroughly *unnecessary* word . . . After all, isn't contemplation something everybody does? I remember snow falling, and looking out my window at the snow, and reciting the word over and over like a talisman."

"And this somehow explains what you're doing here in France?"

"I suppose it partially does. I feel as though—well, as though my whole life has gone by and I somehow never had an opportunity to think. What was I *thinking* when I wasn't thinking? I don't know. As I say, it's all a bit odd and unsettling."

"But you're enjoying yourself?"

"You know I *am*."

"From the look of you, life here agrees with you."

Sally has lost weight—a fair amount, maybe ten or fifteen pounds. For years now, she's been a self-described "round-faced little Dutch girl," and yet here in France, week by week, the bone structure in her face has been reemerging. She says, "I can't believe I've stayed this long. I'm working on two months. Just reading, and food shopping, and becoming a contemplative—or at least going over my past."

"And it's a good feeling? Not too many regrets?"

"Let's say I'm amazed, anyway, when I look back at things, at how often good fortune stepped in to rescue me from my own ignorance."

We're strolling through the grounds of the abbey glimpsed at a distance on my last visit, three weeks ago. It's an old Cistercian monastery, Coppée, built in 1196. Most of it lies in picturesque ruins. The little guidebook, purchased for ten francs from a surreal figure, a—truly—giant hunchback, is written only in French, a language I haven't studied since high school. But I can decipher enough to see that it records the usual chronicle of construction and destruction: new buildings erected in 1302, and 1492, and 1601, and fires bringing them down in 1386 and again in 1547. There's a beautiful pond, on which a pair of swans are floating with otherworldly grace. The refectory, where long-vanished monks once dined twice a day, has lost its roof. Sprawling, angling swatches of sun spill across a floor that must once have been, every day of the year, a place of flickering candlelit shadows.

We climb stone stairs that lead us to the roof of what seems to have been a granary, now overgrown with grass and flowers. We walk across, in a field of sunlight. French bees are busily pawing at French flowers and I'm acutely, elatedly aware of how foreign is the scenery, how far I am from home.

The chapel itself has been spared from fire, from lightning, from the whole fearsome armory of the Lord's instruments of destruction. We step inside—the only visitors on this weekday morning—and take a seat in one of the narrow wooden pews. We inhale a smell as old as any odor on God's green earth, indeed older than the green earth, older by far than chlorophyll: the smell of chill damp gray stone.

Sally and I sit side by side, looking not at each other but at the altar, where our drooping Savior, carved in dark wood, hangs— His three hours on the cross ramifying out across the soul's dark eternity. Sally says, "I mentioned earlier that I've been replaying various scenes of my life. And one of the things I've come to realize is that there really were two gods in my childhood household."

"Tell me."

"There was God Himself, naturally, to Whom we paid our respects before we broke bread in the evenings, or even had a glass of milk in the mornings. And to Whom we dedicated our Sundays, of course. It was to please Him that Grandma Admiraal was never glimpsed seated in anything but a straight wooden chair before evening; anything resembling an easy chair was reserved for after supper.

"And then there was the other god, the God of Money or Mammon, or whatever you want to call it. I know that sounds a little harsh, and the last thing I want to do is to be harsh toward either Mama or Daddy, but the fact is that Daddy's little store, though he slaved away day after day inside it, never really prospered. All the other Dutch immigrant families in Michigan seemed to flourish so naturally, and so many of the relatives had these big handsome homes and motorboats and suites of fancy Grand Rapids furniture, and I don't think either Daddy or Mama could every fully shake the suspicion that their relative poverty was some sort of divine judgment. Oh we weren't poor—only relatively less well-off than the others. But if you habitually see everything as a sign from Above, what do you make of the fact that your bankbook's empty? Maybe the two of them weren't among the Elect? They'd both gone through the Depression, and in the back of their minds was always the fear of losing everything—of being cast into outer darkness.

"Why did they agree to my marrying Wes, despite all the strikes against him? Why did they allow me to marry someone who was *niet een van ons,* who was *not one of us* at the CRC? Surely one of the powerful reasons was that tomato-red Bel Air convertible of his. This all sounds so crass and cynical, and that's not at all how I mean to sound. I'm talking about two kindhearted, God-fearing people who brought to every large decision in their lives the question, *Is it right?* These were lives utterly permeated by a sense of moral imperatives. But who can blame them if Wes seemed *blessed* in their eyes? Does this make any sense to you?"

"A lot of sense. I've been thinking along the same lines."

"Well now we come to the really odd and funny part, the little twist in the story . . . Obviously those two gods in our household were very harsh gods—or at least exacting gods. There was the Lord Himself, who watched over your every move with an unblinking and reproachful eye, and who might very well have selected you personally for eternal damnation. Calvin was our patron saint, after all. And then there was this other god, the God of Money or the Marketplace, who was always conspiring to take your little grocery store away from you, to see that you wound up begging for bread in the street . . ."

And while she rattles on, I begin better to understand her

A FEW CORRECTIONS

underlying seriousness of a moment ago, when she gaily, face-
tiously described herself as a contemplative. Sally has, these past
few weeks, entered one of the oddest eras of her life. She who has
never had an extended overseas sojourn has left her home and her
friends and come to reside in an old French village—has come, as
much as anything, to ponder her existence. She has shipped over
dozens of books that bear in some way on her upbringing: books
on Calvinism, and the Dutch emigration to America, and Michigan, and social histories of America during World War II, America
in the fifties. She is taking stock. Her month here has already
stretched into two, and as we sit in the chapel her words flow with
the fluidity of practiced reflection:

"And you know what the odd thing is? In many ways the oddest thing in my life? It's the way in which, as I myself moved
toward old age, both gods metamorphosed into kind old warmhearted gentlemen: Santa Claus figures. (Which is ironic, since the
CRC always disapproved of Santa.) The God of Money? From the
moment I met Gordon, I never had another realistic money worry
in my life, though sometimes I maybe thought I did.

"And the other god? The one to whom this chapel was erected
all those hundreds of years ago?" The light in here, indeed, is kind
and warmhearted, one of its shafts falling through a high little window on our left, to curl up like a kitten at our feet. "Well let me tell
you a little anecdote. Last spring, when I was back in Restoration
visiting some friends, I found my way over to the Christian
Reformed Church, where so many loads of fire and brimstone
were dumped on my cowering head when I was a little girl.
Though I left those fierce Calvinists definitively back when it
became clear I was irredeemable in their eyes—back when I
decided to divorce Wes—that particular stone edifice on Grand
Elm Street will forever be the most resonant place in the world for
me. Of course I'd been back now and then for funerals, including

services for both of my parents, but it had been thirty years, more than thirty, since I'd last sat through a Sunday service there. And you know what? It was one of the great shocks of my life. The whole business was changed utterly. The minister was this folksy kid with a mop-top haircut—he looked like a fifth Beatle—and he had the oddest manner. He had all these *facial* expressions, these I suppose you could call them *moues*. One minute he's looking quizzical, and the next minute studious, and the next minute outraged, and the next minute analytical—and gradually it dawns on me that in finding a preacherly style he hadn't apprenticed himself to the men he'd seen in the pulpit when he was growing up. No, you know what he was exactly like? Like one of those talk-show hosts, a sort of young Phil Donahue or heaven help us Jerry Springer. It was people like *that* he'd emulated. Everything he did was for the benefit of the TV cameras, and for the TV audience— only, only there *were* no cameras and no television audience. Church services are supposed to be aimed at an invisible presence, I know, but this was something else again, this was something novel and *weird* . . .

"And you know what happened next? As God is my witness (I'm speaking now of the old God, the fierce overwhelming God of my childhood), as God is my witness, they brought in a rock band. The POOF Band. The Praise Our Original Father Band. To play us some inspiring music. Do you believe it? I mean, do you believe it? And I realized then that He was dead and gone—the Calvinist God under whose immense shadow I'd grown up. He still went by the same old name, but He'd been replaced. God— really—was dead. He'd endured for hundreds and hundreds of years, He'd survived transplantation from Holland all the way to the American Midwest. He'd persevered intact through the Civil War and the Great Flu Epidemic, the Great Depression and a pair of world wars. He'd survived endless schisms and purges, because those dour Dutchmen were in fact terrific infighters. But in the end, what did Him in? Things like rock music and TV talk shows. He, too, had been replaced by a sweet old gentlemanly Santa Claus of a god, maybe it's time to get out of here?"

We step out of the pew and walk back out into the sun—out into a world where all the deities are kindly. Somehow the prospect doesn't cheer Sally as much as it might. We head in silence toward the pond, on whose smooth surface the swans have been replaced by a duck. Sally says, "You've seen some people since I saw you last."

"Well Conrad. And Adelle. They both send greetings."

"Tell me about them."

"Well, Conrad really outdid himself. After this absolutely *gargantuan* dinner, which included veal stuffed with sausage and ziti in Alfredo sauce, he orders two desserts. And then finishes mine."

"And Adelle? I hope you're not going to tell me she's still holding that poor girl Tiffany responsible for Wes's death."

"Afraid so. She also told me something you hadn't told me, by the way."

"Oh?" Even while keeping my eyes on the pond, I feel a stiffening at my side.

"She told me Tiffany threw Wes out at the end. Is that true?"

"So I never did tell you that? No I guess I never did, and I suppose, even at this late date, I've been wanting to shelter Wes. The fact is, he didn't even want *me* to know—I think he was deeply embarrassed that another relationship had soured. I didn't really know until after he died."

"She said he was living at the Commodore Hotel."

"Yes—that's right. It was only temporary."

"Temporary? Meaning what? Was he going to move back with Tiffany? Or find his own place?"

"I don't honestly know. You're asking what Tiffany was planning? I don't think *she* knew. Whatever a *contemplative* is, Tiffany isn't. But I do know that after Wes moved in at the Commodore, Tiffany started dating somebody else."

"A serious relationship?"

"Not so serious that it lasted. But I suppose serious enough in Wes's eyes. He'd been supplanted. By someone young enough to be his son . . ."

"Adelle says she broke his heart."

"Maybe. Yes, I suppose she did."

I say, "You know I think I'd like to meet her. Tiffany. What do you think? I'm not sure she'd be willing to meet with me."

"Why not? Under the circumstances."

"I don't suppose I absolutely need to meet her. But it might be useful."

"Useful?"

What am I on the verge of revealing? Has Sally begun to see that I'm out for more than talk? That I'm pursuing this subject systematically? That after each of these conversations I'm transcribing every last detail?

I retreat a bit: "Useful for understanding the situation. As you know, I'm trying to sort of sort out Wes's life."

"'Sort of sort out'? I suppose I'm meanwhile trying to sort of sort out Proust."

She discusses, as we round the lake, how her reading is going. She's in the second volume of *In Search of Lost Time*. There are seven interlocked novels in all. She's very excited. For years and years now, she's been meaning to read through the whole of it, savoring every word, and already she's feeling, only two volumes in, that the experience will be even more rewarding than she always envisioned, although she *is* having trouble keeping track of all the characters. In truth, I'm having trouble keeping track of what she's telling me. (It seems the novel takes place in the French countryside, or maybe a portion of it does—for suddenly the characters she speaks of seem to have all gone off to the seashore. And the protagonist is never named—though she has been advised that if she merely waits a few thousand pages, his name will appear . . . But who's got time for such devious games? My mind is on other things.)

—Therefore, she now finds herself wondering whether she should perhaps start the whole project over again, go right back to page one, this time compiling some companion notebook of notes and names and impressions . . . Could it be, she appears to be wondering now, that her great literary undertaking, deferred until the approach of her sixtieth year, has somehow been fatally impaired at the outset?

We find a bench and sit down. The pond stretches before us, with the abbey in picturesque ruins on the other side. I've heard enough about books and I return to the subject that weighs on me: "I'm thinking I need to see Tiffany if I'm ever going to make sense of Wes's last years."

"You keep calling him *Wes*. In a certain tone of voice. Almost as if he were no relation to you."

"No relation?"

"As if he weren't your father, Luke."

"Not my father?" The last bird on the pond, a duck, breaks and lifts into the air. One more vanishing act . . . "Well yes, in a lot of ways I don't feel he *was* my father. Now that's not a complaint, as Adelle would say. But maybe I should point out that that's what makes this all the more interesting. All the more challenging. In many ways he's a complete stranger."

My mother says: "I think it's time for the day's first cigarette."

She looks harried, even a little desperate as she fishes in her purse for her pack of Salems. For all the artful games she plays with her "filthy habit," she might be just another sixty-year-old woman who's never quite had the gumption to kick her addiction.

Behind a voluminous cloud of cigarette smoke, she delivers a mild reply: "Of course you might want to meet Tiffany. She's your stepmother, after all."

"And *you* can't use the word and keep a straight face any better than I can. Stepmother? She's younger than I am."

"Wes *did* leave a bit of a tangle, didn't he?"

I say, "You have to understand, I have virtually no memory of Wes as my father. The two of you were separated by the time my memory was up and running. I think of Gordon as my dad. I'm not blaming Wes, but the simple fact is, I hadn't seen him in many, many years when he died. By his choice more than mine, you'd have to say."

"But he was always proud of you."

"How would I know that? I never heard from him."

"Wes always had so many balls in the air . . . Maybe you were the one thing he knew was doing fine."

"You mean I was off at an Ivy League school? Or I was making money?"

"And I'm afraid he felt ousted. With no real role to play. Certainly Gordon didn't make Wes any too welcome round our house. Gordon was a true saint in many ways, but he could be a jealous man."

"Okay, it was everyone's choice. *I* certainly didn't do anything to keep in touch with Wes. I was busy, I was making a career, I was visiting Gordon after he got sick. And then there was no funeral for Wes, just an odd little family service."

And Sally's tone is suddenly defensive: "Just tell me how, under the rather bizarre circumstances I found myself in, we were going to arrange any sort of regular funeral. *I* was in no position to organize it—I'd thrown him out more than thirty years before. And can you imagine anything more grotesque and unfair, more disfiguring to Wes's memory, than to let Tiffany loose on the ceremony? The grieving widow who'd already found herself a new boyfriend? Let me tell you something else, something Tiffany conveniently seems to have forgotten: She'd filed for divorce just before Wes died."

"I didn't know that . . ."

"I'm telling you, Tiffany doesn't either. It seems to have skipped right out of the head of the grieving widow."

"Listen, don't think I'm criticizing you. About the lack of a funeral. I'd honestly like to think I'm not criticizing anyone. And the simple fact is, his death happened to coincide with a phase in my own life when everything had gone smash—as you know all too well. So back then I was simply in no position to do what I'm doing now: to look at Wes dispassionately. You say I talk about him as if he were no relation. Well, I'd like to think this sort of pilgrimage, or whatever it is I'm pursuing—this attempt to clarify things, to make a few corrections—will ultimately be taken as an expression of filial piety."

If I'm feeling a need for self-justification, so is Sally, no less urgently than I, and in our momentary, jostling neediness neither one has time for the other. She reproves me: "After Gordon arrived, everyone thought it was better for you if we just started over. That was the point in Gordon's formally adopting you. A fresh start. We were thinking of *you*, Luke."

And I counter with: "And Wes wasn't thinking of his own convenience? Maybe—just maybe—he had too many items on his plate to be worrying about a kid who was safely provided for? When I was growing up, *years* went by and I didn't lay eyes on him. He became some sort of remote, vaguely disreputable uncle."

"I think he felt he had nothing to provide. In some ways he'd made such a botch of things, and there was Gordon, offering so much security . . . Maybe Wes felt bested? Unneeded? I don't know—I'm sure we should have done things differently. But Gordon thought—*we* thought you at last had a father, a real father, in Gordon."

"But what about after I'd grown up and moved out? D'you know how many times Wes wrote when I went off to Princeton? Zero."

"Wes was always a hopeless correspondent."

"You know how many times he telephoned in those four years? Two? Three?"

"I'm afraid he wasn't much of a telephone-user either." She adds: "Were you telephoning him?"

I ignore her question. "You wouldn't call that being disowned?"

"What I would say is that Wes always had trouble with Gordon. Gordon was jealous and Wes was—what? Bewildered? Truly, in his heart of hearts, I don't think Wes fully believed Gordon was *real*—that I'd honestly gone off and found another man."

"And what does Gordon have to do with it? At least Wes could have kept in touch *after* I'd left home. When I was in college, or later in New York. And what about after Gordon died?"

"You're right, of course you're right, Luke, maybe we should have tried to get things on a new footing after Gordon's death. But I thought—oh maybe this is all my fault. But you see, Wes was starting a new life, a new family, Tiffany and the twins, and I *so* much wanted this one to work for him. I wanted Wes to feel that he'd done it *right* this time, that he'd become a real family man. I wanted him to invest everything he had, emotionally, into that marriage—was I wrong to want that? Maybe I was wrong to want that . . . The truth is, I do believe Wes would have had an easier time of it if you'd been born a girl."

"Meaning what?"

"Oh I don't mean the very obvious thing—that you were a source of competition. Or I suppose I do, but that's the smallest portion of what I mean. But Wes never knew quite what to *do* with a boy. He had no interest in sports. Oh he had wonderful coordination—"

"Unlike his son."

"Whereas, if you'd been born a girl, he would have had a natural role to play. His role would have been to charm you, honey. He would have sung you songs—you remember he really did have a lovely delicate voice, a fine clear tenor, and if he wasn't very keen on teaching you tennis or bowling, he was absolutely *adroit* when picking his way through a tune. To hear him singing 'Danny Boy' or 'The Streets of Laredo' or 'Waltzing Matilda' was enough, I can assure you, to bring tears to any girl's eyes."

To judge from the rapt look on her face, Sally can hear him singing even yet. Meanwhile, what *I* hear is a bird in a branch overhead, issuing a message that may well be territorial or amorous, but which appears to express, on this sublime summer day, nothing but unalloyed joy.

"But I'm losing the thread," Sally says. "What I meant to say is that being the father of a girl would have fit him—father to some little bright-eyed, curly-haired Tammy or Bonny or Shirley."

"He got his daughters in the end."

"Yes, in the end. But before they came along he was given this somber, and very cute, but deeply *contemplative* little baby-man. . You scared people off with your grown-up look! You made it so obvious, in your scowling owly way, that you were thinking harder than anybody else in the room."

"You're saying I made Wes nervous?"

"Everybody, you made everybody nervous. You were this mini-magistrate."

"Conrad says Wes would never have married Klara if she hadn't gotten pregnant."

"Perhaps not. But perhaps he would have. Wes loved her, I'm sure of it. She was an extraordinary beauty. At one time, he must have loved her very much."

"And he told me Wes concocted a very elaborate story about why they needed to keep the marriage a secret. About Chester Sultan's being opposed to his son's marrying a Catholic, combined with an upcoming inheritance—all this at a time when Chester Sultan was already dead and buried."

"Oh my." All at once Sally looks very tired; that thinner, French version of her face has become drawn. She turns away from me in order to address her words across the pond, as though speaking to the souls of the ruined abbey. "You have to understand: Wes was very young. And very ambitious. And very confused. And also: stories grow. This isn't to say Wes was fully honest with the girl. But especially with someone like . . . like your father, Luke, people are always wanting to exaggerate his exaggerations. It's an interesting process, actually: the way that even very honest people will feel not the slightest compunction about embellishing a story when it concerns somebody with a reputation for stretching the truth."

And whom is Sally—that born protectress—protecting now? Wes again? Or this time is it Klara Kuzmak whom my mother feels an impulse to shelter?

"And Conrad also said the main reason Wes married her was because it allowed him to fabricate things—to live a double life."

She turns toward me once more: "Now that's just not so. The *main reason?* The main reason was that the girl was pregnant, and, according to the moral code of the time (ridiculous as it now may look to you), a young gentleman had to marry a girl he'd 'got in the family way.' All the more so when the girl was a Catholic.

"Honey, you've got to take everything Conrad says with a

grain of salt. On the one hand, he probably knew Wes better than anyone else could. Good heavens, there was such an intensity between them—I've seen few relationships, even between man and wife, as intense as theirs. On the other hand, in my entire life I've never met anybody like Conrad for saying things purely for effect."

"So where did it come from—that degree of competition? Given how different they were . . ."

The two of us seem to have located once more, after a troubled interval of resentments and self-exculpations, a happy armistice. Sally is again my interpreter of a mysterious past—one that I never saw but one that circumscribes me yet. And I am (through my curiosity, through my hunger for amplification) the validator of that past of hers.

"Oh you'd have to say from Dora chiefly. I don't mean to malign the dead, but she was capable of astoundingly poor judgment. On the one hand, she made it clear Conrad was her favorite. On the other, she made it clear even *he* couldn't depend on her. She'd go from rages to funks to sulks. She was unbalanced, you'd honestly have to say."

"But exactly how did she display her preference for Conrad? How did she show it to Wes?"

Indignation fires Sally's gaze, and to my mind there's something deeply stirring in this urge of hers to stand up for a man whom she herself, for more than ample cause, threw out of her house a third of a century ago. Injustice remains injustice to her. She says: "How did she do it? She did it in ways so blatant it would make your head spin! Ways so heartrending and comical you want to put them into a textbook called *How Not to Be a Mother*! I could give you hundreds of examples. Start with this: One Christmas, the two boys receive identical bow ties from an aunt, and this worries Dora. How are the boys going to tell them apart? Now you may ask,

Why in the world was it necessary *to* tell them apart? But Dora was firm on the need to do so, and so she goes and sews a name tag into Conrad's. *Only* into Conrad's. Do you get what I'm saying? Conrad is, effectively, the son with the name. And Wes? He's the nameless boy . . . And how are you going to tell apart their two identical model airplanes, their two identical toothbrushes? Draw a gold star on Conrad's, or tie a blue ribbon to it . . .

"I honestly think a lot of Wes's womanizing was attributable to Dora. He could win the heart of every woman in the world except his mother. He certainly won over poor Adelle, who will never in her life meet another man who glows the way Wes did. You know you sometimes meet a grown woman who's still a 'daddy's girl'? Well, Adelle is still a 'little sister.'"

"You don't find her devotion touching?"

"You don't find it sad?"

Sad? A garrulous, good-hearted woman in a Battle Creek suburb turning out batch after batch of burnt gingerbread men on a rainy September afternoon while her husband snores in the basement—yes, sad. But sad, too, the former wrestling champion turned fat-man-with-a-heart-condition biting down with spiteful recalcitrance into his sixth buttered sesame breadstick of the night. And sadder still the thought of the other Sultan child, the white-haired golden boy in his room at the Commodore Hotel, thumbing through an address book of prospects as his heart was slowly giving out. And their mother, a shattered agoraphobe, and their father, a possible suicide—something sad, and more than sad, to the whole Sultan clan . . .

Sally continues: "Now Wes would have charmed the world's women no matter how he was brought up, it was simply his destiny, but I can't help feeling he wouldn't have gone about it so desperately, compelled to win over every female he met from the ages of two to ninety-two, if he'd had a different mother.

"And I don't think it did Conrad any good to be quite so blatantly the favorite son. It would be one thing if he'd ever been happy in his as I guess they call it now orientation. But so far as I know, he's never formed a real, a lasting love-attachment to anybody. When I first met him, it wouldn't have occurred to any of us to doubt Conrad's interest in women. And the funny thing is, I think he *was,* I think he still *is,* partly, interested in women. But he had no notions of how to deal with the opposite sex. On the one side, he had this unbalanced mother, and on the other, an older brother who, by the time Conrad discovered girls, had seemingly cornered the market on feminine affections."

"I'd have thought Conrad would have no trouble with girls. Assuming it was girls he wanted. A bright guy, a champion athlete, and good-looking besides, or so the old photographs suggest."

"Heavens yes he *was* good-looking, and yet there was something off-putting about him, Luke: He had no banter, no small talk. I can see how a girl would have been attracted to Conrad, to this burning assemblage of muscle and drive and ambition—but I can also see how she'd find him unapproachable. I suppose you have to take this on faith, now when he's seventy pounds overweight and throwing one chocolate eclair after another down his gullet, and as full of banter and small talk as any man alive. Really, the man's metamorphosis *is* extraordinary."

Sally draws morosely on her cigarette. "Let's go," she says, but does not rise.

Across the pond, a couple of teenagers appear, a big athletic-looking boy with a crew cut, wearing a rugby shirt, and a thin leggy blond girl in black jeans. They're holding hands. Suddenly he scoops her up into his arms and marches—unswervingly, robotically—toward the lake's edge, as if about to toss her in. The girl's legs kick and her arms thrash, and her cries of protest flutter across the water. At the very brink, the boy halts, raises her wriggling body as if to hurl her far and high—and sets her down upon the ground. They walk on, hand in hand. And thirty yards farther down the path, they repeat the whole process: He scoops her up and marches menacingly toward the water's edge, she screams and wriggles in panic and alarm, he deposits her on the ground once more, they walk off holding hands . . .

"But I seem to have lost my train of thought," Sally says.

"Conrad. His metamorphosis. His competition with Wes. His lack of banter. Dora. Her favoritism, as expressed in name tags, gold stars, blue ribbons."

"You really are something. It's as though you've been taking notes."

I continue my catalog: "Wes being able to charm every woman but his mother. Adelle as the smitten 'little sister.' Wes's decision to marry Klara Kuzmak. The moral code by which—"

"*That's* what it was. I knew something was chafing inside me. You see, you mustn't let Conrad convince you that Wes got married purely out of some twisted love of intrigue. For Wes it was also a matter of honor. In his way, your father was a very honorable man. As one of his primary victims, I can attest that his code wasn't the usual code—but the truth is, Wes really did want to do the right thing by everyone. He wanted them to be happy, especially if he could be the source of their happiness. There was nothing *cruel* in Wes, though I suppose there was enough selfishness, and immaturity, to ensure that he sometimes hurt people more than an overtly cruel person might.

"D'you see what I'm saying? There *is* cruelty in Conrad— maybe no more than in your average person, but it seems like a good deal more, since for obscure reasons of his own he's chosen to put his cruelty on display, to enlarge and expand it, just the way he's enlarged and expanded his body. And I think this explains a lot of Conrad's hostility toward Wes. Conrad couldn't quite forgive Wes, in the end, for being a really nice man."

It's a declaration that ought to be cheering, but Sally's despondency is palpable. It's in the hope of lifting her spirits that I say, "You were talking about Gordon before. About meeting him the first time, at the Art Institute."

"You've already heard that story any number of times."

"Tell it to me again. Every time you tell it, there's something new in it."

"I suppose you want the long version."

"The longer-than-the-long version, if you please."

And as we sit on the bench beside the pond across from the old Cistercian abbey of Coppée, the story Sally unfolds (with a few of my own attempts to correct for her reticences or modesties) goes like this:

In 1968 Sally was living with her asthmatic seven-year-old son in pretty much the worst lodgings in Stags Harbor: a dark, damp basement apartment on laughably named Downward Lane, not far from the (closed) Hyperion Fittings factory. The apartment was undeniably a drain on the boy's health, and not much better for the mother's health either.

Even so, things were looking up—somewhat. Sally's divorce was now a few years behind her, and she had reconciled—somewhat—with her parents. When she had first declared her intention of filing for divorce, Henry and Kathy Admiraal had cut her off. Their Church hardly countenanced divorce, particularly when instigated by the woman, and what had ensued were the grimmest days of Sally's existence. She'd needed her parents' help, financial and emotional, but they had cast her aside, and the worst of it—the guilt that had nearly overwhelmed her—was the realization that the two of them were suffering over her as acutely as she was suffering for herself. They were decent, good-hearted, loving people who were weeping, and praying—praying with all their hearts—that their sole child might be restored to them. And by their lights, by the One True Light, they were doing everything they could to aid her. They sent round to her apartment (her sunless, damp, tomblike basement apartment, where her son, Luke, wheezed in the back room) various emissaries from the Christian Reformed Church, who patiently pointed out to her that she had, through sheer headstrong pride and willfulness, fallen upon evil ways. Pointed out that were she to divorce Wes, the Church would not recognize the divorce; were she to remarry, the new marriage would be invalid. Oh, she might be married in the eyes of the law, but in the eyes of the Church she would be living in a state of "continual adultery." Henceforth, the world of romance—of men and love and passion—would be off-limits to her. That was the only future she had to look forward to . . .

In the end, it was Wesley who set things right. Once he finally, finally accepted the notion that the marriage was truly over, and under no circumstances would Sally ever take him back, he chose to do the honorable thing. He went to Henry and Kathy Admiraal and told them it was he, and not Sally, who was insisting on the divorce. He informed them (which was mostly true) that he had fallen out of whatever belief he'd ever had in the Christian Reformed Church. And he informed them (which was hardly true) that he'd fallen in love with another woman and wouldn't consider returning to Sally. And at this declaration of their son-in-law's apostasy, in combination with the prospect of his public infidelities, Henry and Kathy conceded that their daughter could do nothing but end the marriage. Reverend Koekkoek concurred. Sally had chosen unwisely in welcoming Wes as a suitor; now she must face the consequences of that choice.

During the worst of the worst, when she was broke at the bank and all but broken in her spirits, Sally found a job as a cashier in a Kroger's supermarket, while taking classes to get her teaching certificate; she still dreamed of becoming a schoolteacher. It was an almost impossible schedule, made possible only by a neighbor on Downward Lane, Mrs. Breskin.

Judith Breskin, now many years dead, God rest her soul, was then a widow in her fifties, and a Jew—one of very few Jews in Stags Harbor. She was a little gray wisp of a woman, notoriously short-tempered, who didn't seem altogether to like or even approve of Sally. Still, she'd taken an interest in Luke. She was drawn to him partly because (so Sally learned only subsequently) she'd lost, thirty years before, her sole child, a son, to infantile leukemia, and partly because of Luke's already-evident flair for mathematics (he liked to do sums in his head), and perhaps partly because her convictions of elementary justice led her to sympathize with Christianity's outcasts. In any case, Judith Breskin was, in Sally's words, "a lifesaver." She would baby-sit Luke while Sally was off at work or at her classes. And wouldn't accept a dime for it. (Of course this was one more dubious step in the Church's eyes— Sally's leaving her only son to be reared by a Jew.)

That grim apartment on Downward Lane had a single artwork adorning its living room walls, a reproduction of a Winslow Homer watercolor of a pair of trout leaping from a brown mountain lake. (Sally's "original artwork"—a pair of watercolors by the head of the Art Department at Bayview—had fallen victim to a burst pipe.) The actual Homer painting was to be found only a few blocks away, in the Stags Harbor Historical and Art Museum, a whimsical miscellany assembled by the wife of one of the founders of Great Bay Shipping. The Homer watercolor was the jewel of the establishment, and throughout Sally's childhood, when the museum, Stags Harbor's sole museum, had served as a popular school field trip, the painting had represented for her the very apex of mankind's artistic achievements.

And now, in that spring of 1968, something unprecedented occurred. Sally read in her local newspaper about an exhibition in distant Detroit—only one hundred miles south, and yet, for all the traveling Sally had done in her twenty-nine years, a city at the edge of the known world. The Detroit Institute of Art was hosting a Homer show composed of sixty (sixty!) watercolors.

It had been years, literally, since Sally had taken a day out from the constricted routine of her days—her job, her classes, Luke's asthma, Henry Admiraal's objections and doom-laden prognostications. To an extent that she couldn't bear to confess even to herself, the daily atmosphere she breathed was poisonous: air reeking of failure, and suspicion, and stigma, and hopelessness. (It was no easy thing, back then, to be living in Stags Harbor as a lost daughter of the Christian Reformed Church and a divorced single mother.) And Sally decided she would make the pilgrimage, drive all by herself to Detroit. Mrs. Breskin agreed to watch Luke for the day.

This had to be a covert operation, naturally. It would never do to confess to her parents she was leaving their grandson for the entire day in order to drive all the way to Detroit for the purpose of inspecting an exhibition of paintings. Sally prudently stopped once for gas, two dollars' worth, although her tank was far from empty. Otherwise, the trip was happily uneventful. She even found a free parking space.

Yet the exhibition, the unimaginably vast expanse of sixty Homer watercolors, unnerved Sally more than it pleased her. Oh, it was all too much—too many scenes, moods, colors! She was feeling jumpy and guilty and flustered. The polychromatic worlds that Homer conjured up (sullen silvery Florida coastlines massed against a coming storm; Cuban highlands basking in a tropical sun; deep Adirondack ravines where ferns wrestled with boulders) were evidently situated too far from the apartment on Downward Lane for her to bridge the gap. It occurred to her—an intimation that burned at the corners of her eyes—that this entire day, that her whole minutely planned extraordinary adventure, might turn out to be an extravagant failure. Why had she come at all? What was the *matter* with her—that she would even think of trying to run out on her own child, on her own life?

It was a great comfort to discover the museum's cafeteria. She needed to sit down, she needed a cup of coffee, she needed to eat something; part of her problem was simple hunger. (She'd been too excited that morning to swallow anything more than a cup of coffee.) She progressed through the cafeteria line with a sense of pace and deliberation, eventually settling on an egg-salad sand-wich, a piece of chocolate cake, and a cup of coffee.

Sally was beginning to feel she was getting everything back under control when, reaching the cashier, she came upon an unimaginable, a catastrophic discovery. She opened her wallet, where her twenty-dollar bill was securely stored, and—and *there was no twenty-dollar bill!* But how could this have happened, when, before leaving home this morning, she'd checked it three times, four times, five times? How could this have happened? It had been there!—yes, it had been there when she'd removed the other bills, yes, the two one-dollar bills, yes, in order to pay for her gasoline . . .

The truth struck Sally like a stinging slap to the face: When paying for the gas with the two one-dollar bills (when paying for the gas in her overexcited, agitated state), she'd somehow dropped the other bill, the twenty. Her twenty-dollar bill—all of her money—was gone!

This revelation came down like a judgment: *Twenty dollars—gone!*, and now it seemed she was only a minute or two away from a hot flood of tears. Sally started digging frenziedly through her purse, upsetting things, jumbling things, half the contents spilling out upon the floor (her comb, her compact, her handkerchief), as though the very components of her life were tumbling to her feet. In the bottom of her purse lay a nickel, and a dime, and a pair of pennies, but she was never going to make up enough to buy herself lunch . . . Her eyes were overflowing with tears, and of course she was aware that she was holding up the cafeteria line, delaying everybody while she went about spilling her life out on the floor of the Detroit Institute of Art—when a hand reached in front of her toward the cashier, bearing a ten-dollar bill in its fingers, and a man's voice said, "Please, if you'll allow me, I'd like to pay for that."

Beg your pardon?

Of course Sally could never normally have permitted a male stranger to do any such thing. But she swung round and discovered that the man with the ten-dollar bill was the most reassuring, the least compromising figure imaginable: a round-faced gentleman with thick glasses and a kindly crooked-toothed smile. His voice, too, was reassuring, for he had a slight stammer. What he had in fact announced to the cashier was: "P-p-please, if you'll al-la-low me, I'd like to pay for that." And behind the gentleman stood a woman (the deciding factor, in the end), an overweight middle-aged woman who said in a faintly southern accent, "Do, honey, do let him do it. It's all all right."

Sally let the kindly gentleman pay for her lunch. Shamefacedly, stammering herself, she thanked him and pumped his hand, and then she applied herself to the business of retrieving her belongings from the floor. And of course when he invited her to join them (they were a party of three; there was another man with them), Sally consented.

The woman turned out to be his sister, and the other man, his brother-in-law. Sister and brother-in-law were visitors to Detroit. They lived in Chattanooga.

The stranger who had paid for Sally's lunch turned out to be named Gordon Planter, of Grosse Pointe. Sally could be quite precise on these details because she was scrupulous about taking down both his name and address; she would of course pay back every cent she owed him.

In fact, in Sally's eagerness to clear her reputation and make plain that she had every intention of squaring her debt, she went over his name and address a number of times; it seemed she couldn't quite shut up. It turned out he was a doctor, and so what did she do next? She pointed out how disillusioned she'd lately become with the medical profession—none of the doctors she'd consulted had been any help at all with Luke's, her son's, asthma. Then she mentioned her divorce. *Then* she volunteered that she'd never been to Chattanooga; in fact, had never been to Tennessee; in fact, had never crossed the Mason-Dixon line—but a great-uncle had marched with Sherman through Georgia . . . Truly, truly she couldn't shut up. Well, the only sensible thing to do was to eat fast and beat a hasty retreat, but while hurrying through her chocolate cake she managed to spill a crumb—a gooey, dark, frosted crumb—on her white blouse. Honestly, she'd never made a bigger *botch* of things in her whole life.

Having planned to return to the Homer exhibition, Sally instead fled the museum. Without stopping even to try to clean up the chocolate stain, she climbed into her car and drove straight back to Stags Harbor. She wrote a note to her benefactor, Dr. Gordon Planter, as well as a check for $1.52, and that very evening—

needing above all else to put the last of this disastrous day behind her—she and her son marched to the mailbox and posted it.

And there the story might well have concluded. A source of squirming embarrassment would have become for Sally, in time, a slapstick misadventure, a droll anecdote she might have told on herself some years hence . . . Only, the letter she wrote that evening—May 12, 1968—made something of an impression on Gordon. It was somehow not the follow-up gesture he would have expected from that chatty, hopeless woman in the museum.

It was a gracefully amusing note, written on good paper, in a lucid hand. Close inspection revealed that it had been inscribed with a fountain pen:

> Dear Dr. Planter,
>
> Well I am back in Stags Harbor, having learned my lesson; I shall never leave the town borders again.
>
> How fortunate I was, when I made the mistake of thinking myself fit for outside society, to happen upon your indispensable assistance.
>
> The enclosed check cannot fully square our accounts, I fear, but I am hoping that it, plus the assurance of my deepest gratitude, will leave you not fully regretting our comical encounter.
>
> Yours sincerely,
> Sally Sultan

As it happened, Dr. Gordon Planter, for all his air of unflappability, was at that period in his life a vulnerable and a susceptible man—and that phrase *your indispensable assistance* reverberated within him. Forty-three years old, he too was recently divorced, his wife having left him under circumstances both painful and humiliating. (She'd gone off with one of his more successfully recuperated patients.) It cheered Gordon to think that in the eyes of this singular woman with the singular name, this Sally Sultan, he'd come across as someone who might be described as—as indispensable. And there was, too, his recollection that the woman, for all her air of abstraction and distraction (her belongings raining down on the floor, a smear of chocolate on her blouse), had been quite pretty.

The letter sat on what he still thought of as his wife's bedroom bureau. Gordon lived alone, in a big house in Grosse Pointe, two blocks from Lake St. Clair.

A few days went by and Gordon discovered, with some chagrin, that the encounter hadn't faded from his mind. Nor had her letter, even if it had disappeared physically after a cleaning woman's visit (eventually, after a thorough search, it turned up in the dining room). And on the Sunday following, two weeks after the meeting at the museum, Gordon woke up and resolved to do something highly atypical: He would drive up to Stags Harbor in search of Sally Sultan. Although he still couldn't put his hands on her letter, he did have her address. It was on the check, which somehow he'd failed to cash. The check for $1.52.

Now, Dr. Gordon Planter was a man of rare virtues—a man generous and gentle, scrupulous and conscientious—but no one would ever have labeled him daring or adventurous. He was keenly, almost morbidly susceptible to the fear of "stepping wrong": of proceeding where he wasn't wanted, or presuming on more welcome than he should. The decision to drive to Stags Harbor was unlike him, to say the least.

Another fact about Gordon (one that he generally succeeded in concealing from the world) was that he was reflexively, unshakably superstitious. As a matter of habit, Gordon scoured the world for auguries and omens—most of which (it turned out) cautioned him to hesitate, to deliberate, to back off. Hence, it unsettled him that on the way to Stags Harbor he twice got lost. Wasn't he being advised to head back home? Why had he set out in the first place? What was he after? He stopped in a coffee shop to clarify his thinking over a piece of Boston cream pie, during which it became evident that he didn't know why he'd embarked on this errand, or what he was after. In other words, there were powerful, persuasive reasons for beating a prudent retreat . . . Then Gordon got back into his car and, flouting every single one of the plausible warnings in his head, he proceeded toward Stags Harbor—toward his new life. All of which is how, on the evening of May 26, 1968, Sally Sultan, hearing a timid knock on her door, opened it to discover, to her astonishment, Dr. Gordon Planter.

Gordon had intended to arrive midafternoon, but his various detours and deliberations had delayed him. To his deep dismay, he'd shown up just as Sally was cooking dinner.

Sally was dismayed, too—to discover on her doorstep the doctor from Detroit in his gray suit and red necktie and gray felt hat. She was wearing a dusty brown housedress. She'd had a trying day. Luke had awakened her in the night complaining of stomachache, which in the morning turned into diarrhea, one trip after another to the bathroom. In the afternoon, to comfort him, she'd allowed him to draw with ink, which was always a mistake. He'd smudged not only his hands but, in a child's slapdash way, his cheeks and chin and lips as well.

In those first frozen moments when Sally opened the door to Dr. Gordon Planter, his explanation for his presence in Stags Harbor (something about being in the neighborhood, a consultation with a fellow doctor in nearby Bay City) made no sense to her. This was partly because Sally felt so flustered at the thought of the wreck of an apartment at her back (the place had no ventilation, and still smelled of Luke's diarrhea), and partly due to the onset of an attack of Gordon's stuttering. But after some hesitation, she invited him in. Gordon, having now found his voice, began to tell her about his sister and brother-in-law, both of whom liked Detroit so much, they were thinking of leaving Chattanooga. Gordon talked so enthusiastically, in fact, that Sally forgot about dinner—until a reproving black cloud billowed from the stove. She'd burned the grilled cheese sandwiches.

One stammering voice contended with another . . . Declaring himself responsible for the ruin of their meal—he'd shown a simple lack of manners in arriving at suppertime—Gordon announced that he would take the two of them out to dinner. Sally protested that Gordon would do nothing of the kind. Gordon insisted. Sally was more insistent yet—she made it clear that for her a matter of principle was at stake. Despite what she'd shown him so far, *she was no mooch*. Nor was she the sort of flibbertigibbet who tossed out her dinner when it wasn't cooked to perfection; no, Sally Admiraal wasn't the sort to let a bit of charred bread dismay her. The sandwiches were perfectly edible. They needed merely to be scraped. And she would be happy to make Gordon a sandwich, too—it was the least she could do. An unburned sandwich. (And Gordon? Though fearing he was once more "stepping wrong," he accepted—what else could he do?)

And so the doctor sat down at the kitchen table with the homely, unhealthy-looking, inky-faced little boy, Luke, who had been instructed not to start eating until the guest's food was ready. On the boy's plate were carrot sticks, applesauce, a burned and scraped cheese sandwich, and a hill of gray-green peas, rapidly cooling . . .

Sally confided that her son had had a stomachache in the night and Gordon delicately asked whether he might have a look at the boy. Sally consented. Gordon studied the whites of the boy's eyes, peered down his throat, felt the glands of his neck. Not exactly a robust specimen . . . Sally left the stove and came over to observe Gordon's various ministrations. He asked her a variety of medical questions—Did the boy drink milk? Did he have allergies? When had the asthma begun? Did the boy also have eczema? Had his blood been tested? Did he ever take vitamins?—and the two of them entered into a discussion that persisted until halted by an angry, acrid smell.

Oh my. Sally had burnt another sandwich.

This time, she grew *extremely* flustered. She announced that this sandwich was fit only for the garbage. A new one would take her just a moment.

And now it was Gordon's turn to demonstrate a little stubbornness. That was *his* sandwich, the black one in the pan, and he intended to eat it.

That's nonsense, you're my guest. I'm not going to serve you a burned sandwich, Sally told him.

And here lay the doctor's opportunity likewise to stand on principle: *He was going to eat what the rest of them ate.* He was the seventh of eight children, you see, and he wasn't about to ask for special treatment.

And seeing how adamant and righteous he was, Sally could only laugh with approval (showing Gordon, for the first time, what a pretty smile she had). Then she said, All right, let's all sit down to our feast together.

And so the family (or this threesome that would in time become a family) enjoyed their first meal together: They dined on Sally's burned and scraped grilled cheese sandwiches.

(Sally's story has come to a fitting and familiar stopping place. She reaches toward her purse, for a cigarette, then thinks better of it. Across the pond, the boy and girl have vanished. Its surface remains unbroken—nobody has been hurled into it, nobody either rescued from it or drowned. The pond is so still, there's little to distinguish scenery from reflection, the real world from the model world set at ninety degrees to it. I check my watch. It's three o'clock. Or nine in the morning, a Monday morning, in Manhattan. The mathematician in me relishes the notion that New York's a world also set at ninety degrees to this one—or so that six-hour time difference suggests. My former colleagues are beginning another workweek. And Sally concludes her tale.)

At the end of the evening, with every last crumb of the burned grilled cheese sandwiches conscientiously consumed, Gordon proposed that he return the following weekend. Would it be all right if he took them out to dinner next Sunday? And Sally, still feeling fresh from her divorce (though it was now a few years behind her), and extremely chary of all entanglements, and of course needing to be careful about appearances, explained apologetically that she didn't think that would be a good idea. Well, as a doctor, Gordon was also concerned about the boy's condition—could he come by next weekend to check on him?

And how was Sally to refuse the doctor that?

So Gordon dropped by on the following Sunday, in the middle of the afternoon. He sat in the living room, under the Winslow Homer reproduction, and drank seven cups of tea and, with only a little help from Luke, consumed an entire box of ginger snaps. But he did more than merely sit. This time he gave the boy a real once-over.

Clearly, Luke was in only middling health at best. So Dr. Gordon Planter proposed that the following Saturday he escort the two of them to Wake Hospital, in Saginaw, where Gordon had a friend, Dr. Paul Chapman, who was one of the finest pediatricians in the state.

And the following weekend he drove the two of them, in his elegant charcoal-gray Lincoln Continental, over to Saginaw, to see Dr. Paul Chapman. And the Sunday following that, Gordon arrived on Downward Lane in a state of exhilaration. He had spoken to Dr. Chapman, who had confirmed Gordon's suspicions. Luke was, among other things, anemic. Gordon, looking as jolly as any Santa Claus, brought forth from his sack some iron pills, as well as a new contraption, complete with a breathing tube, which he thought might alleviate the asthma.

It was a joyful moment. Gordon's ebullience was infectious and this time Sally readily assented to his proposal that the three of them celebrate with dinner out. They drove to Saginaw, to a restaurant Gordon had somehow heard of, which turned out to be alarmingly expensive. (Sally didn't wish to deepen her indebtedness any further.)

Even so, after a month of visits, she was discovering a certain relief in the doctor's presence. She had originally believed that Dr. Planter, with his stutter and ungainliness, was a man of few words, but it turned out that Gordon had quite a bit to say, chiefly about his divorce. He did most of the talking, she most of the listening— it was a gratifying relationship. Gordon, it became clear, was a haunted man. He hadn't recovered from the collapse of his marriage and his ex-wife crept into his every conversation. It was all Margie, Margie, Margie.

To Gordon's credit, he carried out such talk discreetly, elliptically—there was nothing in what he said that Luke shouldn't have heard. Not that the boy gave much indication of listening to Gordon anyway. Habitually timid with strangers, particularly male strangers, Luke seemed to spend the major portion of Gordon's visits in rapt concentration over his various drawings. (The boy was particularly fond of puzzles and mazes—never happier than when he'd situated himself within some elaborate winding labyrinth, from which he would eventually extricate himself.)

Sally sensed that in providing a listening ear she just might be doing Gordon some good. She wanted to help him. And the fact was, there was comfort for her as well in placing herself in his capable custody—in being chauffeured about in his luxurious Lincoln, in watching his fine doctor's hands undertake the humble task of replacing a faucet washer, in seeing him steer so assuredly through the nurses and the medical forms of that other sort of labyrinth, the winding corridors of a modern hospital.

But if there was comfort for Sally, there was also nervousness in the very essence of any such comfort. Gordon seemed intent on guiding her toward a world that wasn't her own. So that on the evening when the three of them drove to Saginaw for dinner, a number of things were troubling Sally.

She was unnerved by the expensiveness of the restaurant.

She was faintly annoyed at Gordon's air of self-congratulation in having come forward as Luke's medical savior, which she couldn't accept without a sense of self-reproach: Why in the world hadn't it occurred to *her* that the boy might be anemic?

And she was chafing a little at a remark Gordon had made as they'd climbed into his car. She'd used the expression *comme il faut*. And he'd looked at her in some puzzlement and pointed out that the phrase was French. Well, true enough, Gordon—no denying that. And he'd said, Where in the world did you ever come by a phrase like that? (Or had he in fact said, Where in the world did *you* ever come by a phrase like that? . . . The words continued to fester.)

In the restaurant, Gordon ordered the house specialty, a one-pound pork chop, with mashed potatoes and garlic bread; he clearly made no effort, unlike the ever-vigilant Wes, to watch his waistline. Sally, as a matter of principle, ordered the second-cheapest item on the menu, which fortunately turned out to be fried whitefish, a dish she was fond of. She tried to order a hamburger for the boy, but Gordon—high-handedly—overrode her. He ordered the boy the most expensive item on the menu, an immense T-bone steak—as "a source of iron."

Was there any more iron in the aristocratic cut of a T-bone steak than in the plebeian grind of a hamburger? Sally doubted it— and watched as the boy, manfully battling with fork and steak knife, tried to subdue a slab of meat nearly as big as his head.

Of course Luke couldn't begin to eat it all. Before long, he'd pushed his plate aside and turned over his place mat; he commenced another picture.

Gordon had a second martini and then ordered the cherry cobbler. Neither Luke nor Sally wanted dessert. Gordon insisted they try the apple pie.

While they waited for their desserts to arrive, Gordon happened to glance over at the boy's drawing. Identifying what seemed to be an elephant, he asked, "Are you drawing a zoo?"

(And at this point in her tale, Sally's glee and relish are so great, it would be a shame not to let her narrate it directly . . .)

"So then Gordon said to you, 'Are you drawing a zoo?'

"And you looked up, this little anemic seven-year-old boy who had again gotten ink on his face, and you said, 'I'm drawing Hannibal. And his brother Hasdrubal. Crossing the Alps.'

"And Gordon looked from you to me, from me to you, eyes bugging in his head. Things were not quite adding up. He didn't know *what* to say. But finally he asked me, 'Where in the world would the boy ever have learned such things?'

"And I told him you must have read it in the library—that you were a great one for taking mountains of books from the library.

"But Gordon *still* couldn't contain his amazement. The truth is, Luke, he hadn't paid you much mind, up until then—except for your medical state. I suppose he had too many problems of his own to work out. In any case, that's when he uttered the fateful words. And that's when I really let him have it. Poor Gordon, even now I can't believe what an ingrate I was. I'm so ashamed."

(But of course Sally looks far less ashamed than jubilant.)

"That's when Gordon said, 'Where would a boy of his *background* ever have learned such a thing?'

"Well. That did it. Of course it was that word *background*—that's what did it. It triggered what has always been my besetting sin, Luke—my ungovernable pride. Because all of a sudden it seemed clear as day. Just how Gordon saw us. *Background.* We were these, if you'll excuse the expression, these Tobacco Road folks he'd come in to rescue. We were these, excuse an even worse expression, white trash. He thought he was dealing with a couple of slum-dwellers who didn't know in which direction the sun rose in the morning.

"Well. I suppose it was one thing if Gordon saw me as some sort of charity case. I was in need of charity in actual fact, living as I was in the worst apartment in Stags Harbor. But it was another thing if he was regarding my little Luke as some sort of gutter waif.

"I was feeling guilty, of course, about not figuring out the anemia. And about housing an asthmatic child in such a terrible apartment. And about accepting so many favors. And now suddenly my weakness came to the fore, and so I sat right up and I said (oh it *mortifies* me even now to think of it!), I said, 'You may not realize it, Dr. Planter, but I'll have you know that tonight you are dining with the valedictorian of Restoration High School, class of 1956.'"

I interrupt Sally: "Good for you! And what did Gordon say?"

"Well he sat there stunned. As anyone might. No doubt asking himself, *Who is this lunatic of a woman sitting across the table from me?* I mean honestly, Luke, isn't that the *dumbest* boast you ever heard?

"But now I'd really gotten started. There was no stopping me.

There was absolutely no stopping me and I said, 'And another thing, Dr. Planter, you apparently do not realize who else you are dining with. You are dining with a boy with a highly unusual mathematical gift. You're dining with someone who is going to attend'—where in the world did I ever come up with such a notion?—'to attend Princeton University!'"

I interrupt again: "Well, I'm glad that at that very moment, when you were deciding my fate, you didn't pick Yale or Harvard. Princeton's a much pleasanter place."

"Truly, it was the devil himself inspiring me. For how else would I have come up with Princeton? It was as if I somehow *knew* that Gordon, as the seventh of eight children, as the poor kid from Newark who considered himself lucky to struggle through Rutgers, had always felt awed and intimidated by Princeton. Oh I couldn't have delivered a more telling reproof.

"But was I finished? *Oh* no. I said, 'Let me show you something, Dr. Planter.' And then I turned to you. I asked you (and I still recall the exact numbers, because I remember I combined your birthday with mine), I asked you, 'Luke, what is twenty-eight times nineteen?' And you, one split second later, you said—what would you have said?"

And it pleases me how rapidly I volley the answer right back at her—pleases me, even now, to be the boy with a calculator lodged in his head: "I would have said, *Five hundred and thirty-two.*"

"Five hundred and thirty-two. Precisely. That's what you said. And then a long pause. Gordon looking from you to me. From me to you. And then he gets out a pencil and paper and methodically works out the problem, and of course he comes up with five hundred and thirty-two. And then he looks us both over again, and I realized the three of us were on an entirely new footing. And you'd done it, my seven-year-old owl/boy. You'd put us there."

CHAPTER EIGHT

[handwritten: and the Commodore Hotel in Stags Harbor,]

RESTORATION—Wesley Cross Sultan, 63, *[handwritten: 62]* of 2135 N. Westhampton, died suddenly in Lyon Hospital in Stags Harbor, of heart failure. He worked for Great Bay Shipping for 42 years, chiefly in sales. He began his career in the Stags Harbor office, and after stints in Kalamazoo and Cincinnati, Ohio, he finished his career back at Stags Harbor. He retired two years ago in order to pursue full-time his civic pursuits. He was an active member of the Rotarians, the Restoration Chamber of Commerce, the Stags Harbor Betterment Society, and the Thumb of Michigan Prosperity Council. He was also active in the Restoration Episcopal Church, where for many years he sang in the choir.

He was born in Restoration and ~~was a graduate of~~ *[handwritten: attended but did not quite graduate from]* the old High School on Cherrystone Avenue. He was the son of the late Chester Sultan, the well-known businessman, and the grandson of Hubert Sultan, who served as the mayor of Restoration from 1908 to 1912. Old-time Restorationists will recall Sultan Furniture on Union Street, founded by Hubert and presided over by Chester until he closed its doors in 1935.

He was married ~~twice. His first wife was~~ Sally *[handwritten: three times. His first wife was Klara Kuzmak. He then married]* Planter (Admiraal), now of Grosse Pointe, formerly of Restoration. They were divorced in 1964. He leaves his wife, Tiffany, *[handwritten: from whom he was formally separated at the time of his death,]* and their two daughters, Jessica and Winnie; a son, Luke Planter, of New York; a brother, Conrad Sultan, of Miami, Florida; and a half-sister, Adelle De Vries, of Battle Creek. *[handwritten: with whom he had a son, Wesley Jr.]*

"You're *Luke*?"

No mistaking her tone. This is more than mere surprise—it's naked disappointment—and I suppose I should be used to this by now. Disappointment? It's what I reliably inspire on meeting for the first time someone who knew my biological father.

"I'm afraid so," I reply, which I hope will come off sounding winningly modest and wry but which turns out to be simply maladroit: I've made her conscious of how potentially insulting is the tone she has taken.

"Oh I didn't mean—" Tiffany begins. "It's just, it's just—well I'm so delighted of course to see you, wow to see you *finally*."

And I extend my hand in greeting just as she, on a kindred mission, hurries forward to embrace me. My fingers collapse up against her belly as, with a crisp snapping sound, she pins a kiss to my cheek.

I'm sure my face pinkens too—Tiffany's does. She swings round and cries, "Welcome to the humble abode . . ."

My appearance has surprised her, obviously; hers, on the other hand, closely approximates the mental portrait I've painted of her. She's a little shorter even than in my imaginings (she can't be more than five feet two), and broader across the hips, but even so, the dark-eyed face under the forest of brown curls seems familiar, as if I recognize her from photographs, although I don't think I've ever seen any photographs of Tiffany. She's pert and pretty and remarkably youthful. She might almost be a coed—a communications major at Restoration Community, say.

"I was just so *pleased* to get your letter, Luke. And I'm just tickled pink you could come by. Wait till you meet the twins. I hope it's okay, we're going to have barbecue."

"That's fine, just lovely, but honestly you don't need on my behalf—"

"Why it's no bother at all. Summer, most nights we eat barbecue. Maybe I've learned one thing anyway, being a mom these past six years? Kids'll eat most *anything* you burn a little on the grill first."

Tiffany laughs—or giggles—and winks at me. Frankly, I don't

know what to make of the nervous, overflowing warmth she's showing me (on the phone, she sounded a little aloof or wary). Or what to make of her deliberately quaint and cutesy vocabulary— "tickled pink," "humble abode." In truth the place is extremely humble—and as she breezes me through the house I catch a sense of superficial tidiness overtopping a deep disorder. An unwatched TV is running in the living room and in the kitchen I smell cheese, and maybe dill pickles, and then we're standing on the creaky wooden deck of her patio and she's calling, "Girls, girls, get over here. I wantcha meet somebody."

The backyard is narrow, but deep. At the far end of the yard, in the slanting, purply, late-afternoon light, twin sisters are playing in a sandbox. Doubtless the precious light is enhancing the effect, but it would have been an unforgettable tableau in any case: One of the girls, a beautiful thin child with short-cropped dark hair, wearing a lime-green T-shirt that glows unreally against the dull-green bushes behind her, raises and tilts her head, peering at us, the slant of her jaw highlighting all the more dramatically her face's exquisite bone structure. The resemblance is more than striking: it's eerie. Yes: she has my father's face.

The other girl (I'm afraid I hardly notice the other girl) glances up as well. But neither child gives any sign of a willingness to leave the sandbox. Our presence on the deck seemingly has little to do with them. They might be animals—a pair of fawns by the bank of a stream, for a moment halting their green browsing to stare, with less alarm than curiosity, at the fire-engine-red canoe gliding past them.

Then the small girl in whom my father is so painstakingly resurrected rises to her feet and her twin sister follows suit. They march toward the patio, each bearing in her arms a limp doll.

I feel some relief (and some regret—oh, I'm feeling all sorts of things!) when a little of the eeriness in the girl's appearance peels away as she approaches. She's just a girl, after all, and a grubby one at that—with orange popsicle stains around her mouth, and gray and brown smudges of yard dirt on her green T-shirt.

"Now this one's Jess," Tiffany announces. "And the other one's Winnie. Now I want you two girls to shake hands. This is Mr. Planter—this is Mr. Luke Planter."

Are they to be informed tonight that I too am Wes's child? And if so, is this a disclosure that ought naturally to fall to me? Jess's hand is sticky. The other girl, Winnie, does not extend a hand. Her right arm is already occupied with her dolly.

"Put it down, baby," Tiffany says—but the girl only hugs her dolly tighter.

"Put your dolly down. Do it now."

"Oh it's all right," I intercede.

"*Now*, baby. You do it, *now*." And this time there's a razor's edge in Tiffany's voice. Tough. This is the woman, after all, who chucked my father (my sixty-two-year-old unemployed father) out into the street.

But the child—Winnie—only presses the dolly to her chest. She has retreated a couple of steps and is canting forward, until the exposed plane of her downturned face, framed top and bottom by hair, is reduced to a few square inches: Her forehead has disappeared under her sandy bangs, and her chin and mouth are submerged in the dolly's frizzy locks.

Perhaps I'm predisposed to find in this girl's face a resemblance to Conrad . . . For wouldn't it be a wonderful poetic stroke if those two competitive Sultan boys were repackaged, a generation later, as the Sultan twins—a pair of strikingly handsome girls who looked no more alike than the boys had? So maybe I'm merely seeing what I want to see, but I believe I detect, in the confident breadth of the girl's face, and the sly obstinacy of those steady slightly hooded eyes of hers, a few touches of the old Master of the Mats.

Tiffany stares and stares with utter fixity at her daughter. If she were a magnifying glass, and Winnie a leaf, the girl would burst into flame. Finally, a tiny hand extends itself.

Eagerly I reach out my own hand and take a limp, sandy cluster of fingers into my palm.

"*There* you go," Tiffany says. "That's better. All right then, you kids can go back to your box."

And the liberated little girls, suddenly cheerful as can be, scamper off across the lawn and settle themselves once more in their shadowy sandbox. Tiffany drops into a white plastic lawn chair and motions me to sit down. I choose the farther of the two remaining chairs. She beams at me and says, "It's so fabulous seeing you here. Wes talked about you constantly."

Is this, I wonder, something of an exaggeration—or is it a polite, an outright lie? I say, "I didn't see him much." I add, "He never made any effort to keep in touch." And add further: "He left us when I was so young, it's almost as though he never was my father at all."

"Wes didn't mean things deliberately."

What I'm obviously tempted to reply is, *Are we to assume he all but abandoned his child accidentally?* Temper, temper. What I say instead is, "They're beautiful children. Your girls."

"*I* think so, but then *I'm* their mother."

And Tiffany laughs briskly, as though she'd gotten off a witty retort, winks heavily at me, as though she were flirting, and somberly—almost lugubriously—observes, "They're a big responsibility. Twins." Really, her tone, her demeanor, her body language . . . she's all over the map. She doesn't yet know how to respond to my presence, nor I to hers. Some degree of awkwardness must be expected, I suppose, when a man meets for the first time a stepmother who's younger than he is—and all the more so when the figure who unites the two of them is dead.

"Luke, can I get you something to drink? A wine cooler?"

"I'd love a beer if you've got one."

"They're homemade. The wine coolers. I made them myself."

"Well then a wine cooler sounds wonderful."

Tiffany bustles into the house—she has a bouncing, bounding walk—and returns a minute later bearing a tray that holds a large pitcher and some glasses. The drink she offers me is nothing I can name or identify. It's iced and pink and frothy on the top—sweet, with a slight burn underneath.

I'm glad for the drinks. Having the tumblers to play with eases our mutual awkwardness; we sit, and sip, and watch the children, and sip again. Tiffany asks after Sally and Conrad and I tell her a little about my recent visits with both.

In the distance, though rosy sunlight still hovers in the air, a cricket shakes its rattle. We're in the middle of an Indian summer weekend and the cricket is a reminder of what it's easy to ignore on such a day: September is waning.

"It sure is calm," I say.

"It hasn't been a calm *week*. I've been twice to the hospital."

"The hospital?"

"Winnie was stung by a bee and she's hyperallergic."

"I'm sorry."

Tiffany launches at once into an elaborate tale: the bee's arrival; its unprovoked assault; the roaring drive to the hospital; the shocking inattention of the doctors. Hers is a wandering story, but one whose theme is unmistakable: Winnie is one lucky girl to have so attentive a mother. Tiffany asks me about Manhattan ("I've always *fantasized* of going there"), and now I take over the conversation—hoping to demonstrate, I suppose, what a successful cosmopolitan go-getter Wesley Sultan fathered. We're staking out our territory, stepmother and stepson. Of course I mention nothing about having left Gribben Brothers.

Tiffany is the one who again steers the conversation over to my father: "You know, I miss Wes. Despite all the problems we had. I think about him every day."

And with this admission, Tiffany settles on me an expression so winsome, so poutingly doleful, so prettily proud, it takes me a moment to discern just how laughable her claim is . . . Do you mean to say that less than a year after the man who is the father of your children died, you still think about him daily? Oh, this Tiffany seems charming—and hopeless! How could my father have failed to find her attractive?—and how could he possibly have concluded that this was the woman he wanted as a partner into eternity?

My drive has left me feeling thirsty and I drink deeply from my peculiar pink drink. Tiffany drinks deeply from hers.

After a while she says, "Jess was Wes's favorite, I suppose because she looked so much like her daddy. My favorite's Winnie. With young kids, it's important you balance these things." And she fixes me with another self-congratulatory look. (Of course it's all too *perfect*—Tiffany's playing out her favoritism with the same transparency once displayed by Dora Sultan, that dour dutiful woman who sewed a name tag into Conrad's bow tie and left Wes's blank . . . And have I perhaps identified another variable in that straggling polynomial equation which in the end is Wes's life? Had he, at some level, married the image of his mother?)

Tiffany says, "But now when was the last time you saw Wes?"

"Quite some time ago."

Somehow I'm not going to admit to her—or admit to Wes in the grave—that I have the exact figure at my fingertips: nine years and a little over three months. "It was before you came on the scene." I add: "First my mother and Gordon moved part of the year to their condo in North Carolina. Then Wes moved to Cincinnati. Somehow he and I just didn't seem to cross paths."

"I think he was lone-ly," Tiffany sighs, and isn't there a hint of accusation in this?

My rejoinder, anyway, is somewhat defensive: "Particularly lonely in the last few months of his life, I suppose. I didn't realize the two of you had separated."

My words echo in the air.

"It simply was not *possible* for me to go on living in the same house with that man," Tiffany declares, and her words echo too.

For the second time this evening, I sense her formidable resolution. The flinty look in her eyes seems to ask: Have you come to accuse me? Have you come looking for a fight? (And you can't blame her for thinking this way, not while Adelle is telling anyone who will listen that Tiffany was instrumental in Wes's death. Deep in Adelle's heart, it seems clear, the pretty plump woman with the mop-top haircut sitting before me, whose frothy wine cooler I'm drinking, is a murderess.) Oh, Tiffany is ready for a fight.

I take what I hope is a concessive tone: "Tell me about your marriage. You know I'm divorced myself. Tell me anything and everything. I really know surprisingly little about the last years of Wes's life."

Up and down this quiet, windless suburban block, within one long rectangular backyard after another, dusk is falling. Restoration shares a time zone with Manhattan, though lying hundreds of miles farther west, and out here in Michigan it stays light far longer than on the East Coast. I'm not usually much of a drinker (and never was—even before, a few years ago, I was placed on medication that theoretically doesn't mix with alcohol), and Tiffany's homemade wine cooler has gone to my head just a little. The pink liquid harmonizes prettily with the day's final hues: the lavender light, the lit wire diamonds of the cyclone fences, and the stubborn fluorescence of Jess's lime-green shirt.

"Tell me about how you met," I say.

"Which version you want?"

"Are there many?"

"Wes's version? Or'd you rather have the truth?"

"Both, I suppose."

"Well, according to Wes, we met at the Grace Falls Episcopal Church in Cincinnati, Ohio. But I'd never been inside the place before when I met him."

"Then where *did* you meet?"

"A place called Gus's. It's not just a bar, it's like more a sandwich-type shop. It's a good crowd—lots of businessmen, not many worker-types. Wes always wanted me saying we met at Grace Falls, almost as if he thought Gus's was a stripper joint. But it was nothing like that. Everything was all in his mind."

"He could be a bit—"

"He didn't want to be the sort of man would meet his wife along when she's waitressing, you see, while me, I've never been ashamed of what I am. It's just like college. When we moved up here from Ohio, Wes wanted me telling people I graduated Ohio State, me who did two semesters at Holdwell Community, me whose father deserted the family and whose mother was a school cook, how likely was Ohio State, I ask you? It was again the same thing exactly. He didn't want to be married to the kind of woman that doesn't have her B.A."

"Well you know he himself never—"

"Of course not. Right. Exactly. He himself never. But it's as if if *he* could never complete anything, *I* had to have a B.A. from State. Give me a break."

"I understand how you feel."

"Exactly. That's the point."

We exchange confirming nods and sip our drinks. Over Tiffany's shoulder, the very first star of the evening breaks through the blue—the winner in a marathon race whose course extends over light-years. Somewhere I read once a memorable statistic. The most distant object visible by day—the sun—lies some eight minutes away at the speed of light. The most distant visible by night— the Great Andromeda Galaxy—lies some two million light-years away. In terms of visible boundaries, then, night is some 100 billion times bigger than day.

"You've got to understand, it was impossible to live with him."

"That doesn't surprise me," I tell her, and feel myself nodding sagely—feel myself exhibiting a vast, multidimensional, astronomical calm. Yes, the drink has gone to my head.

"What it was, eventually? I *outgrew* Wes. You have to understand, I was only a kid when I met him."

"Right," I say. "Correct."

"Exactly. I was twenty-two, and he was positively this *gentleman* figure, wearing this glowy silver suit and being all so friendly and kind. But without ever coming on to me was the thing. He'd done that, it's all over, I wouldn'ta give him the time of day."

"I understand," I say. "I appreciate."

"I'm no innocent, I'm not suggesting. At twenty-two I was already married and divorced, did you know that?"

"No, I don't think I did. Kids?"

"Nope, but a miscarriage. I was water-skiing. It was stupid."

"These things happen." I hunt for a synonym. "They eventuate."

"You know one thing Wes used to do? We'd go into a restaurant or something, he'd say to the waitress, 'Now what do you recommend for a couple of newlyweds?' He thought it got you better service that way, and maybe sometimes we did get a free drink or a piece of cake, but he was doing it *years* after we'd been married, and it was mortifying."

It was mortifying: Yes, it was the very way Sally had described how Wes, back when he was courting *her,* employed the identical stratagem. For he stayed true to the old ruse—but how different the circumstances! How different his world had become, some thirty-plus years further on. *It was mortifying* for Sally because Wes's question suggested to a stranger the existence of racy intimacies that she, his proper betrothed, wouldn't consider granting him. And *it was mortifying* for Tiffany because it reminded her, who continued to look like a schoolgirl, that she had stepped up to the altar with this beaming, leering, snowy-haired man . . .

"My divorce was one more thing Wes didn't want me spreading round. But the point is, Wes was so *persuasive,* I really did mostly nearly believe everything he told me. He was some big shot, he was indispensable to Great Bay, he was practically running their Cincinnati office, and when they transferred him back to Stags Harbor, it was going to be wow a great promotion. But not even Wes was able to turn it into a promotion when they fired him."

"Fired him? Isn't that a little harsh? He was due to retire."

"That's one way of looking at it. That's *Wes's* way, but I tell you I learned eventually if you were looking at something Wes's way, you'd better be preparing yourself for a nice shock. No, they pushed him out, didn't want to pay his health insurance, and he was fighting back tears the day he like oh so casually announced the big news to me. Right there where you're sitting . . ."

And while this may sound hard-hearted, it cheers me to hear about those fought-back tears of my father's. Or my response to them cheers me: I feel a hot, welcome discharge of sympathy coursing through my chest—sympathy, if not exactly for the wily, oily old salesman who sat in this very chair with tears in his eyes,

then at least for the kid in the snapshot taken at his brother's graduation, tilting his wrist to expose his fancy watch to the camera. I
feel sorry for that small-town *gallant* with the elaborate pompadour
and his upcoming life of whittled dreams.

I drain my drink and say, "It seems he had less and less to hold
on to. His job. His previous children. His marriage to you."

"Wes was impossible to live with. It was *so embarrassing,* him
always coming on to other women—always hitting on my friends."

"He kept that up? Even the last few years?"

"*Even* the last few years? *Especially* the last years."

"I'm sorry . . ."

"Evening, folks, and my, my, don't the two of you look comfy."

I don't know if this is a man's voice or a woman's. It's a throaty
greeting in any case, followed by a harsh bark of laughter. I swing
around and see, stepping out of the dining room onto the deck, a
tall, bony woman in a pair of khaki shorts and an olive T-shirt. Who
is this? Whoever it is, she entered the house without knocking.

"Hel-*lo,* hel-*lo,*" Tiffany calls—sings—and adds, "Talk about
your pleasant surprises—d'you have time to join us? We're having
wine coolers." Tiffany leans toward me and explains, "Patty's just
coming off some wicked laryngitis."

"Tiffany's famous wine coolers," Patty in turn says to me, and
supplies a confidence of her own, in a whisper that breaks harshly:
"She puts buckets of *vodka* in them." And another hacking laugh.

Something about this woman instantly rubs me the wrong way.
I suppose I feel I've been making progress with Tiffany—learning
things—and any interruption would be regrettable. But in Patty's
particular case, something in her long and narrow face, with its
loose-jawed, almost vulpine smile, instinctively makes me edgy.

Patty takes the chair beside mine and crosses her lean legs,
which are very tan, and lights a cigarette.

"I have someone I want you to meet," Tiffany says. "Patty, this is Luke Planter. Wes's son. Luke, this is my friend Patty Boudreau. Patty lives down the street."

"Wes's *son*?" Patty echoes, as though incredulous.

"Not with *me*," Tiffany pretends to explain, and giggles. "By an *earlier* marriage."

From her voluminous pitcher, Tiffany pours Patty a drink and, without asking whether I'd like another, refills my glass, as well as her own.

Until now I haven't noticed the third glass waiting on the tray. Oh. Tiffany has been expecting her friend. And Patty will be here for a while.

"I can't believe you're Wes's *son*." Patty blows a doubtful cloud of smoke my way.

"I'm afraid we don't look much alike."

"Oh it's not that . . ."

She gives me a cool, openly measuring stare, then turns and nods at Tiffany, who nods in corroboration and giggles—a comprehensive female exchange of information I can't begin to decipher. But what *is* evident is that with Patty's arrival the ambience of our little patio conversation has shifted.

It seems I've become some sort of exhibit. This should make me nervous, and yet the atmosphere gradually warms. The two women talk about each other. Patty explains to me what a splendid mother Tiffany is; Tiffany tells me how indispensable Patty is to the main office of the Haggerty Construction Company. An odd protracted crepuscular glow has come down from the heavens, as though our boozy leisureliness had succeeded in retarding the flow of time. The children, in their shadowy sandbox, continue to play with fawnlike quietness. Tiffany has mentioned a barbecue, but when will she get started? A covered grill waits on the edge of the deck. So far as I can tell, Tiffany hasn't made a stab at a start at a beginning of a dinner . . .

At first I assumed it was a joke, but it seems Patty was telling God's own truth in reporting that Tiffany spikes her wine coolers. My drink burns, pleasantly, in my throat. The stars are clarifying in the sky just as my vision begins to blur.

"Patty is an absolutely *fabulous runner,*" Tiffany tells me. "She's been doing it for *years.*"

This might seem an unlikely assertion, given that since her arrival Patty has nursed her laryngitis with half a dozen cigarettes. Still, she has those stringy runner's muscles in her calves and thighs. Patty exudes a strange, conflicted air of malady and vigor, vice and virtue.

I ask her, "How much do you run?," and Patty croaks back, "Usually 'bout forty miles a week," and I say, "That's quite a lot," and "There's no *stopping* her," Tiffany inserts.

"There's no stopping me. It's an affliction."

"Fortunately, it isn't contagious," Tiffany says. "*I* haven't exercised since seventh grade."

"Since your first period," Patty points out, and coughs out another laugh, as Tiffany giggles brightly.

They're a study in contrasts, the two friends: Tiffany, short and plumpish, with beautiful fair young skin; Patty, long and stringy, tanned, a little haggard.

Tiffany goes into the house, presumably to fetch some food at last. Patty swings toward me and says, "Wes was always talking about you."

"Wes? Did you know him well?"

"Course I did, Tiff's my best friend. We even have the same birthday. Same year and everything."

Same year? I would have figured Patty for five years older, anyway. Or ten.

"He was always on about how smart and well-educated and everything you were." This comes from Tiffany, who returns not with food but with a lit pair of scented candles, which she sets on the white plastic table between us.

"I don't know about that . . ."

"First in your class—weren't you first in your class at college?"

"Heavens no. Nothing like."

Absurd as it might sound, potent feelings of shame well up inside me. I see the two women once again glancing at each other, and their faces in the candlelight share a look of knowing cynicism. It seems they both feel taken in: Once again, once again they've caught Wes Sultan in a bald-faced lie.

So it isn't an urge to defend my own academic prowess, Lord knows, but to refurbish my father's deservedly shaky reputation for accuracy, that inspires me to boast, pathetically, "But I did graduate Phi Beta Kappa. As a math major. And I did graduate first in my high school class." I add, "That must have been what Wes was thinking."

"Wes was always going on, too, about how successful you are," Tiffany says. "In business. In Manhattan."

The look Tiffany gives me is open, discriminating, fervent. *Are you a fraud, too?* it wonders. *Like your father?* Her big eyes flicker in the candlelight and I'm struck in this moment of earnestly exchanged glances by just how extraordinarily pretty she is. More than that. Is she too short?—too plump to fit society's prevailing standards of beauty? Maybe, but all such reservations melt away in the darkness and for a moment I feel sure I see Tiffany as my father once saw her. Those blue eyes of his peered out from under the ivory crown of his pompadour and glimpsed a creature who incarnated all the youth and vivacity and delicacy, all the sweet, ingenuous credulity, that are the world's true, best bounties. He unpacked his finest wares for her—his dusty patter, his hoary jokes, his incongruously boyish gestures, his fluttering eyelashes—and he felt them "take" in the young woman before him. She was proof positive, wasn't she, that he hadn't lost a thing? And that any recent failures with women were no more his fault than his career disappointments? Surely it wasn't his fault . . . No, weren't such failures the fault of a world (an increasingly sloppy, slovenly, ill-mannered, ill-dressed, profane world) that had abandoned its allegiance to the obsolete virtues he embodied?

And I'm reminded of a weird evening, early in my tenure at Gribben Brothers, when I went out to dinner with quite an international crew. We were discussing a Delaware-based petrochemical company. There were a couple of Japanese bankers, and a Korean, and a German, and a Swiss, as well as my boss at the time, Jason Gillespie. Over dessert and coffee Jason launched—out of the blue—into a little discourse about cockroaches. Jason could be an overpowering presence—suave and genteel and handsome and ruthless—but his face looked bloated and bloodshot with drink and I had the feeling he was about to overstep the bounds. I was wrong. He explained that cockroaches can continue to mate even after they've been decapitated. "The little fuckers are too damned stupid even to know they're dead." This observation, which stunned the table, was succeeded by a strained and befuddled silence, during which many napkins were contemplated. And then Jason made his point: "What we're looking at here, gentlemen, is a fucking corporation too damned stupid to know it's dead."

Well, it turned out that no businessman anywhere—in New York, in Europe, in Asia—had ever uttered a comparison quite so trenchant and witty as this one of Jason's. Ringing, resounding laughter followed, and a joyous refilling of wineglasses . . . But the words later came back to haunt me when I realized that much the same thing could be said about Great Bay Shipping. Yes, the institution to which my father gave his life turned out to be a brainless, headless organization, managed by people without the least notion of contingency planning. To anyone who knew anything about business, the history of Great Bay Shipping was a reeling from catastrophe to catastrophe, the busy extraction of each new resource until, one unforeseen day, the last of them went dry.

And those words of Jason Gillespie's came back to haunt me further when I realized they might likewise be applied to my father himself—a man slow to recognize that the horse he'd bet on, the company he'd chosen to carry his life, was hobbled in one foot. And having finally noticed his error—or having been thrown from his hobbling horse—what did Wes do but lurch away on his own and plunge into one ill-planned, underfunded get-rich scheme after another, throwing his savings away? Had the company held him back over the years? Oh no. No, it seems the company had *protected* him from his own foolishness and incompetence—and what a humbling lesson *that* must have been for Wesley Sultan to digest as he entered his seventh and final decade . . .

Of course it would be the easiest thing in the world, sitting in a pricey French restaurant in Manhattan over profiteroles and crèmes brûlées, to dismiss Wes and his entrepreneurial visions—and easier still to dismiss Wes's final wife: a short, fleshy Midwestern college drop-out and divorcée and single mom who prided herself on her "homemade" wine coolers. But the light shifts, or perhaps a single candle flickers on a backyard patio, and suddenly this very woman is the embodiment of all the world's preciousness, and the man who loved her is a seeker after a heartbreaking excellence—and how must Wes have felt when Tiffany told him she had "outgrown" him?

So I want to think that I, in some circuitous but not laughable fashion, am defending my father when I puff myself up a bit: "Well, Tiffany, that's a funny world, doing the sort of business I do in New York." The sentiments feel legitimate; in this moment, I

might still be on the Gribben Brothers payroll. Might still be someone who was once put in charge of restructuring $450 million of
Jeppco debt. And got the paper placed in record time.

"There are always people more successful than you are," I go
on. "And always people who used to be more successful who are
now out on the pavement, looking for a job. Looking for *your* job.
There's a lot of luck involved . . ."

"Wes said you used to fly all the time to London."

"That's right. I once flew there three times in eight days."

"I love to fly," Patty declares and I think she intends her declaration to soar. But not having spoken in a couple of minutes, her
voice emerges as a croak—less the sound of a bird, about to take
wing, than a frog, up to its hunkers in silt.

Tiffany at last summons the children from their dark-
swallowed sandbox. They march toward us silently out of the
depths of the night. To my surprise, to my profound delight, one
of them rubs up against my arm, clambers into my lap.

"Would you look at that!" Tiffany calls. And both women
laugh with pleasure.

"Hello, Wendy," I say. It's the other one—the one who doesn't
look like Wes. Meanwhile, Jess climbs up into Patty's lap. Only the
twins' mother sits without a child.

"It's Winnie," Tiffany corrects me.

"Of course it is," I murmur into the girl's sandy hair. Of course
it is. The wine, or vodka, has bedeviled my brain. "I'm afraid I'm
inexcusably bad with names."

"Wes was just the opposite," Patty points out.

Of *course* he was. For he'd worked at it until it became a simple
reflex . . . And all at once I can picture him at the age of about
eighteen, sitting in a drugstore in Restoration, Michigan. It's 1953,
and Wes is poring over a magazine article titled "Making Your Way
to the Top." (Meanwhile—as my boozed-up imagination takes

wing—I can even picture the writer of the magazine article. The author of "Making Your Way to the Top"? A desperate bottle-hitter, many times fired, with a mortgage payment due on his house in the Bronx, and a daughter whose teeth need straightening, and a mother-in-law with a bad knee, tap-tapping out his article while throwing down shots of cheap gin.) The article advises young Wes to pay special attention to names, not just the important people but the underlings too. This is practical wisdom which the eighteen-year-old boy-man takes fully to heart. Oh, can't you just see him, in conversation a few days later, stroking a grateful aged secretary with her name—someone whose boss doesn't appreciate her, and whose boss's clients don't appreciate her, and whose long-deceased husband didn't appreciate her? Wes appreciates her . . .

Wendy, Winnie—actually it's all the same to the warm, light-weight bundle in my lap, who doesn't care what she's called and who within moments has fallen sound asleep. What about her dinner? Something in me would naturally prefer to have her sister in my lap, little Jess. Though perhaps it would feel disorienting to have Wes's face, metamorphosed into a beautiful girl-child's, so close to my own.

Tiffany at last puts some hamburgers on the grill, which, it turns out, was readied before my arrival. The sleepy bed of coals has remained hot. Patty blows the smoke from a fresh cigarette over the head of the little girl in her lap. I down my drink and it seems the last of the day's light is swallowed up. Night has fallen and a chorus of crickets begins to sing that song titled "There Used to Be No Houses Here, This Used to Be a Forest." I've had *way* too much to drink.

Tiffany offers to lead the children up to bed, but both Patty and I protest. They'll wake up when the hamburgers are ready; in the meantime, we're happy to have the girls in our laps.

In fact, neither of the children fully awakens when offered

their dinner. A few bites of hamburger, a couple of carrot sticks, and they curl back up into slumber . . .

I notice (and am proud of myself for so observantly noticing) that my own burger is charred on the outside and raw within. I don't mind. I accept another glass of Tiffany's silly but lethal wine cooler. Drinking it is like getting hit over the head with a *very* large stuffed animal. Resuming our conversation where we'd dropped it hours or days before, when Patty arrived, Tiffany says, "Wes made it impossible to live with him."

"Impossible," Patty echoes.

"Absolutely unforgivable."

"Totally—totally *unforgivable.*"

"Hitting on all my friends. I mean honestly."

I find my tongue. "Well, it's all behind us now," I declare, eager to curtail all such talk. For these are hardly words appropriate in the presence of children—or, for that matter, the presence of a non–family member like Patty.

But it's Patty herself who renders most of my scruples sadly irrelevant: "Did he honestly think I would do that to Tiff? My best friend in the world?"

"Did he—" I begin, and then halt. I already know the answer.

"A *number* of times," Patty supplies eagerly. "Including right here. In this house."

"In my bedroom," Tiffany adds.

"A *number* of times in Tiffany's bedroom," Patty echoes.

Okay: and maybe I should no longer be forgiven my naïveté . . . I don't know. But if I'm to relate truthfully the evening's events, I can't conceal just how bewildered I'm left feeling at this particular moment. And how dizzy. No doubt things would be different if I hadn't—immediately, instinctively—found Patty so unappealing. Perhaps if I'd caught her on a day when she didn't have laryngitis, or wasn't chain-smoking despite having laryngitis, I might have seen her in another light. I don't know. Yet something about Patty Boudreau gives me the *creeps,* and that a sixty-plus-year-old Wes (a Wes who had seemingly reached a point where he could hardly fail to descry at the horizon the prospect of a grim and solitary old age) would risk his marriage so flagrantly and spectacularly for a woman like *this,* and his wife's best friend besides . . . Earlier in the evening, studying Tiffany's face by candlelight, I'd momentarily felt a keen spiritual affiliation with my father: a vision of how his young wife might have come to symbolize everything that was bright, generous, clement and vibrant in the universe. But if I want to get nearer still to Wes, I'll have to dig deeper. I'll have to understand why, at his age, he would jeopardize everything that was bright, generous, clement and vibrant in the universe for this leaking chimney of a woman in the plastic lawn chair beside me . . .

"I wouldna have minded so much," Patty goes on, "if he hadn't been such a Jesus freak. Talk about hypocrisy."

"A Jesus freak?" I say.

"Absolutely. The least you can do is keep your trousers on while you're talking about Jesus. I mean, *Jesus.*" Patty looks to Tiffany for verification.

Tiffany nods sympathetically.

I speak sharply: "I don't think anyone's ever described Wesley Sultan as a Jesus freak." And I too look for Tiffany's approval.

"Well a church freak," Tiffany offers, by way of compromise. "You know he insisted on going every week."

"He was in the choir," I point out.

"It didn't matter." Tiffany shakes her head mournfully. "He woulda gone anyway. He even went when he was on the road."

"When nobody would know," Patty points out.

"That's really sort of like showing off, isn't it?" Tiffany says.

"And he was getting more and more that way," Patty notes.

"You're saying people like Wes shouldn't go to church?"

I don't know whom my question is addressed to; in any case, nobody answers it. The evening's first real hint of uncontrolled anger—mine—dissolves in the air. The two women are being more levelheaded than I am, I realize gratefully. We sip our drinks. "Luke's just gotten divorced," Tiffany announces to her friend.

"Some time ago, actually," I append.

"Patty's divorced, too, isn't it funny? Here the three of us sit, all in our thirties, and we're three divorcées. And a widow. It does give you some doubts about marriage or romance, doesn't it?"

"I think of the word *divorcée* as applying only to women," I point out. "Though there's no reason why it should," I add fair-mindedly.

"Either way, it's something you have in common. The two of you," Tiffany confirms, and she gives me the little push of what I guess would be called a meaningful glance, and only then, belatedly, do I ascertain why Patty is here tonight.

Patty is here because the two women have speculated that I just might make a suitable partner for her.

It's a realization that breaks like a wave over my head, lifting my unsteady legs out from under me. Patty and me . . . The two of us . . . I'm struck first by a frantic sense of my own shortcomings. After all, I've so sorely disappointed them. (Tiffany's initial greeting—"You're *Luke*?"—is still ringing in my ears.) And I'm struck second by an urge to beat a hasty retreat. (It seems everything about this evening is misconceived.)

And in my own uneasiness I don't immediately recognize just what an extraordinary tribute Patty's presence here tonight is, finally, to my father in his grave. I will grasp this only tomorrow, in an ascending airplane, while staring out a round window, through a hangover headache, at the flat countryside surrounding the Detroit airport . . . However badly Wes behaved as a husband, Patty nonetheless drove over here tonight hoping to meet a younger version of Wes, a newer model. If he was *impossible* and *unforgivable,* she was willing even so to give him another try.

When, maybe half an hour later, I get up to go, I'm still feeling apologetic—or apologetic anew. I have to wake up the little girl in my lap, Winnie, and it turns out she has cut off the circulation in my legs and I wobble like a drunken man—like the drunken man I am—to the front door. The city of my brain, located at the confluence of a river of wine and a river of vodka, has flooded over; its streets are mostly impassable.

The twins wear faces of sleep-smeared befuddlement. After the darkness of the patio, the lights within Tiffany's house—my father's former house—jab at my eyes. The unwatched television still talks to itself. When Tiffany, holding Winnie by the hand, chants, "Say good night to your Uncle Luke, sweetie," it takes me an analytical moment to identify what's wrong with this picture. For I'm not the girl's *uncle.* No, *brother* is more like it. I kiss Winnie on the top of her sandy head.

Then my father, down in his newest incarnation, looks up at me from under a crown of cropped raven curls and says, "Night, Uncle Luke."

"Good night, angel," I whisper, and deposit another kiss on a child's head, taking deep into my lungs the scent of her curls, her black living hair . . .

And now I have only the two adults to deal with.

In the dark foyer of the house, I swing toward Patty, to give her a farewell kiss, and my lips land upon her nose.

Patty snorts with amusement and says, "That how you do it in New York?" and she takes charge of the situation . . . My proven ineptitude gives her a kind of carte blanche. "Hold still," she tells me, and I do. We size each other up. And then Patty, with a husky can-do chuckle, steps toward me, directly toward me, and plants her mouth securely on mine. Our kiss isn't long, perhaps, but it isn't short, either. Oh, it's lengthy enough that I hear my step-mother, Tiffany, while my lips are pressed against Patty's, while my eyes close and open and close once more, first release a little squeal-ing giggle and then bring her hands together in a clap of approving gaiety.

And now is the moment to face down my stepmother. What is expected of me could hardly be clearer—or more baffling. Big-eyed Tiffany looks *very* amused. I step forward, lean down, and (How in the world has such a duty befallen me? What in the world is the world coming to?) wade inebriatedly into my task. We kiss. And do I imagine it—the quick swipe as our lips meet? The slick mischievous flicker of her tongue against my teeth?

CHAPTER NINE

and the Commodore Hotel in Stags Harbor,

RESTORATION—Wesley Cross Sultan, ~~63,~~ 62 of 2135 N. Westhampton, died suddenly in Lyon Hospital in Stags Harbor, of heart failure. He worked for Great Bay Shipping for 42 years, chiefly in sales. He began his career in the Stags Harbor office, and after stints in Kalamazoo and Cincinnati, Ohio, he finished his career back at Stags Harbor. He ~~retired two years ago~~ *was effectively fired two years ago but claimed to be retiring* in order to pursue full-time his civic pursuits. He was an active member of the Rotarians, the Restoration Chamber of Commerce, the Stags Harbor Betterment Society, and the Thumb of Michigan Prosperity Council. He was also active in the Restoration Episcopal Church, where for many years he sang in the choir.

He was born in Restoration and ~~was a graduate of~~ *attended but did not quite graduate from* the old High School on Cherrystone Avenue. He was the son of the late Chester Sultan, the well-known businessman, and the grandson of Hubert Sultan, who served as the mayor of Restoration from 1908 to 1912. Old-time Restorationists will recall Sultan Furniture on Union Street, founded by Hubert and presided over by Chester until he closed its doors in 1935.

He was married ~~twice. His first wife was~~ *three times. His first wife was* Sally Planter (Admiraal), now of Grosse Pointe, formerly of Restoration. They were divorced in 1964. *Klara Kuzmak, He then married* He leaves his wife, Tiffany, and their two daughters, Jessica and Winnie; a son, Luke Planter, of New York; a brother, Conrad Sultan, of Miami, Florida; and a half-sister, Adelle De Vries, of Battle Creek.

from whom he was formally separated at the time of his death,

with whom he had a son, Wesley Jr.

"You don't look well," Conrad tells me. We're marching across a parking lot under a punishing Miami sun that lashes you from two directions—down from a hazy sky and up from the blazing asphalt. His remark seems like a preemptive strike. *I* don't look well? When

I've met him recently, it's been evening and we've sat across from each other in some soft-lit restaurant. To glimpse him outdoors, in the unmerciful noonlight of this sweltering September day, is to behold quite another figure: He's a cumbersome pale near-elderly giant tortoise of a man sweating profusely into the shell of his too-tight bottle-green polo shirt. Conrad looks querulous, and over-burdened, and faintly befuddled.

"I feel fine," I tell him. "Maybe Miami agrees with me."

"Or maybe it's your new line of work."

"New line of work?"

"So I gather. My sources tell me you're no longer at Gribben Brothers."

His sources? It can only be Sally . . .

The glass door of the hardware store leaps open when Conrad's mammoth body lumbers onto the entrance mat. If it hadn't, presumably he would have marched right through it; the old wrestler isn't to be messed with this afternoon.

Immediately, a wave of refrigerated air hits us, and with it a new line of discussion. Conrad doesn't seem to recall leaving any conversation dangling, and he starts in anew, energetically: "Tell you something? They're all crooks in this place. Do me a favor, Luke? Do a little shoplifting. I'll make some distraction, you shove an air conditioner into your pants. Serve them right, last time I'm here the cashier tries telling me I gave him a ten. I say it was a twenty, and *I* say he was a thieving bastard."

"Maybe it was an honest mistake."

"Maybe I'm a giant tea biscuit? Contact paper, where the hell's the *contact paper?*" This concluding question is barked at a young man in a Jerry Garcia T-shirt who clearly doesn't work here and furthermore, even if he did, surely couldn't help us; he has the puffy-eyed, indrawn look of someone so high he can't tell up from down.

And so it goes . . . Conrad's performance in the hardware store might be comical, I guess, if presented as some sort of film sketch. But as experienced firsthand, up close—*as his companion*—it's pretty horrifying. When the kid in the Jerry Garcia T-shirt tardily shrugs his shoulders, Conrad purses his lips and releases a flabby, flatulent splutter and swings around so grandly that he jostles an elderly gentleman who—holding up three long black screws to the light—is engaged in a painstaking series of comparisons. Conrad doesn't excuse himself, nor does he excuse himself when he bumps into a young father cautiously wheeling a baby stroller. And when, after a good deal of circular wandering, he locates the contact paper and a clerk willing to assist him, he says, "Christ, is this all the choice there is?" so witheringly that the clerk beats a retreat. Unassisted, Conrad eventually settles on the store's least annoying contact paper and shuffles empty-handed over to the cash register, where he's informed that he should have brought the roll up with him; it will be measured and cut there. "Excuse me, I assume most of your customers are telepathic?" Conrad asks. "That why you don't have a sign to tell them that?"

As he drives me back to his apartment, I get some inkling of what's eating at Conrad today. While he was away last week, his Cuban cleaning woman installed contact paper in the kitchen cupboard. As a "surprise." Conrad doesn't like contact paper; I suppose it's fair to say he doesn't like surprises, either. "I particularly don't like contact paper when it's got *deer* prancing on it." He tried removing it, but the paper hung on stubbornly: it seems he'll never strip the shelves down to bare wood again. "For *life*—I'm stuck with contact paper for life now!" Defending herself, the cleaning woman explained that the paper would be easier to wipe down—it would keep the roaches under control. "Now I ask you, what would you rather look at when you reach in for a potato chip—a little scaredy-ass cockroach or a big-eyed Bambi?"

Back in his apartment, Conrad brightens a little. The building is called Ocean Prospect, which allows him an opportunity, once more, to rail against its builders' greed and mendacity. "What I've got is a view of a building looking out on a building maybe looking out on a building looking out on the sea." He's on the fifth floor. Miami's a city I scarcely know, but I gather it's a place—dense like a rain forest—where everything's stretched to unnatural heights through competition for sunlight. You might say that Conrad's apartment lies closer to the forest floor than to the canopy's crown; it's surprisingly dark in here.

. . . And more modest than I would have expected. Although Conrad retired early a couple of years ago, when his cancer was diagnosed, he had a long and presumably reasonably successful career as an accountant. He's never had dependents and ought by now to be sitting on a considerable nest egg. But his money certainly hasn't gone into home decoration. With its bare walls and spare, utilitarian furnishings, this place looks more rented than owned.

Yet this impression, too, is misleading. Conrad's apartment, I'll eventually discover, is a storehouse of hidden luxuries. Although he's not much of a cook, his kitchenware will turn out to be first-class (Noritake china; beautiful Calphalon pans; German steak knives). His unostentatious little stereo speakers will prove to be fountains of booming lucidity, even though Conrad has no deep interest in music. (His catholic CD collection is chiefly devoted to "greatest hits"—Beethoven, Bob Dylan, Tchaikovsky, the Drifters, Streisand, Sousa, Sinatra, Gregorian chant.) His Leica camera equipment is of semiprofessional quality, although it seems he rarely meets a moment worth recording on film . . .

There's one exception to the rule that Conrad's extravagances are neat, recessed, and unflashy, and his name is Rusty. Rusty stands in a golden cage beside the window, his crooked gray scaly hands clasping a dowel rod. Green, red, yellow, he's a spectacular parrot—a creature brighter not only than everything else in the apartment but brighter than everything else in the jungle he was born to inhabit. Occasionally he lets rip a raw, gargantuan *squawk* that rattles the door hinges, but most of the time he gets by, like his master, on rumbling grumbles; clearly, Rusty's a creature who nurses a good many grievances.

Without asking what if anything I might like to drink, Conrad sets two open bottles of Molson's Golden ale on the glass living room coffee table. And two bowls brimming with macadamia nuts. This, too, I will learn about Conrad (for in the next few months I'll learn a lot about him: this odd, crotchety, embittered, aggressive, insightful, ailing man and I will forge a real friendship), that he rarely asks you what you want. Refreshments materialize wordlessly—thrust at you, like some sort of challenge.

Conrad sits with his back to the window. I sit facing him. If Ocean Prospect had an ocean prospect, I suppose I'd be gazing out across the bounding main. As it is, I contemplate the apartment building across the street.

"All right, let's hear it—what the hell's going on?" Conrad wraps his question in a tone of mock anger.

"Beg pardon?" I say.

"You've quit working. Yet you're down here all the time. What's the new line?"

"Why do you assume I have a *line*?"

"Taken up cocaine running, have we? I mean, what the *hell's* going on?"

He has, belatedly, picked up the conversation we dropped on entering the hardware store, and I see suddenly that there's nothing *mock* in Conrad's anger. I've mystified him. He's feeling—in a way he cannot quite place—manipulated. And he doesn't like it.

I say: "It was Sally who told you. Wasn't it."

"So it's true, then. You turned in the golden meal ticket? You're unemployed?"

"Yes, I suppose it's true, but no, I'm not exactly unemployed. It was Sally, wasn't it."

"What do you mean—'not exactly unemployed'? You telling me it's some sort of *job*—poking around interviewing various sad-sack Sultans about their family history? Like we're the Kennedys or the Rockefellers? Like somebody's *paying* you to talk to Adelle? Tell me it's true and I'll tell you I'm a little green Martian. Some-one's *paying* you to interview fat old Conrad?"

He tosses down a substantial handful of nuts and, jowly face vibrant with self-satisfaction, chugs his bottle of beer.

"That's not what I meant. I meant I still have a fair amount of money, my own savings, and it needs managing. So I'm still in the investment game, only on a vastly reduced scale. Meanwhile, this other business, this looking into what you call family history, is something else. Call it a personal quest."

"You know what? You're looking really god*awful*. If you got time for 'personal quests,' you might take up the task of restoring some color to your face. You look worse than I do and I at least have the excuse of being a sick man. You're supposed to look *healthy*, for Christ's sake. You're just a kid."

"I'm nearer forty than thirty."

"And I'm nearer a hundred than zero. Incidentally, my sources tell me you had some kind of breakdown when that girl left you."

"That girl had a name. Angelina. And she wasn't just a girl. She was my wife. And I didn't have any breakdown. Except for court dates involving the divorce, and things like that, I don't think I missed more than a week's work over it."

It's the first time I've ever really snapped at Conrad and my open anger certainly does nothing to chasten him. Rather, he looks overjoyed at having gotten a "rise" out of me.

He says, "You know what I think? I think you've taken up the so-called mystery of poor screwy brainless Wes because you can't solve the bigger mystery of why your marriage exploded."

"You know what I think? I think you don't know what you're talking about."

"I gather the girl gave you quite a shock."

"Okay. It was quite a shock."

"I hear she made a chump out of you. A really spectacular chump."

"For a while. Maybe. Look, I was hardly the perfect partner—"

"Love's vicious. You didn't know that? You shoulda asked me *years* ago. Cupid? Little bastard kid's a sociopath. Love? It's the one thing in the world a man should never be romantic about."

"You've become quite the aphorist."

"The whoozit?"

"Forget it."

"And now you're saying I don't know what *aphorist* means?"

"Oh Christ, then why in hell did you ask?"

"Forget it."

And I'm not sure how, but it seems I've been outmaneuvered.

I begin again: "You were hard to reach last week. You were away."

"On vacation."

"My sources tell me you were in the hospital."

"Okay. Okay, it was an unusual vacation. And you tell your 'sources' I hope she chokes on her next wedge of Brie cheese."

But these words are uttered without bitterness. Along with the shadows of a premature dusk, a peaceable wash of melancholy has eddied into the room, gently lapping us both, and allowing me to confess, "Maybe there's some truth in what you're saying. About me and my quest. I don't know, oh hell, maybe I needed something else to brood about. But I do believe, I really do, there's also a real logic in what I'm doing. Is it so unreasonable to suppose that the more I figure out my father's life, the more I'll understand my own?"

"Oh, it's reasonable. Somebody might even call it *astute*. It just happens to be dead-ass wrong." Conrad reaches behind his head and tugs thoughtfully on his silver ponytail. "Look, Wes can't tell you anything because Wes didn't know anything—he never acted on a single real *idea* in his life. Wes never had a philosophical moment. And you know what? I didn't either, never had a single idea, until twenty-seven months ago. You want to know what turned me into a philosopher? My dick hardly works."

It's not a remark that invites any obvious follow-up. I look at him blankly, I suppose.

"That's not supposed to happen when they zap out your prostate with a pair of fancy scissors, using quote nerve-saving techniques close quote. But the damn thing hardly works anymore. They diddle you with all sorts of machines, for God's sake, and rub you with witch's milk, for all I know, but at the end of the day they just want you to skedaddle on home when you tell them, *My dick still hardly works.*"

Conrad pauses. He's assessing the situation—seemingly weighing me up as a suitable confidant. I say nothing. Across the room, with what sounds like self-punishing thumps, gorgeous Rusty whets his beak against the bars of his cage. And Conrad chooses to continue: "It's an experience'll make a philosopher out of any man. Suddenly you have to say, What else have I got in my life?"

"And?"

"And?" Conrad says.

"And what answer did you come up with?"

"Precisely. That's just it. Go ahead. You tell *me* what's still left in my life that ought to mean more to me than this bowl of macadamia nuts. Ja know I put on twenty-five pounds since January?"

"You do seem to be—"

"Would you shut up? Or at least quit euphemizing, if there is such a word? Christ, what am I supposed to do, take up an interest in the opera? Spare me, I'd rather watch paint dry. Start visiting art museums? I have a sweet little story on that score, actually, involving your mother, as so many sweet little stories do. This was some years ago, she comes down here I don't know why, she never had any use for Miami."

"Maybe she wanted to see you?"

Conrad shrugs this one off: "Anyway, Sally's here and she suggests we head off to some lunatic art gallery. Always out for self-betterment, you know our admirable Miss Admiraal. Anyway, we get there and there's a special exhibition of shoelaces."

"Come again?"

"Once is plenty, thanks."

"Shoelaces?"

"You think I'm kidding, I only wish I was kidding. But here's a so-called artist who works, if that's the right word, with shoelaces. Plain white shoelaces. Two-packs-for-a-buck shoelaces. Drag-'em-in-the-gutter shoelaces."

"And?"

"And in one of his creations he's nailed a shoelace to a piece of plywood. In the next one he's stapled it to a cardboard box. The next one, he's glued it to a gunnysack. The show's called 'Only Connect,' wouldn't you know, and the artist has a big I suppose you could call it manifesto up on the wall, explaining how in some of his works the shoelaces are tight and in others they just sort of dangle down, and how sometimes he uses glue and other times brads or staples or tacks, and in the very last one, I suppose it's some sort of *culmination,* he has used a *shoelace* to attach the shoelace."

Sometimes when Conrad tells a story he'll pause momentarily, and his hooded eyelids will half-close, and his eyes will fly up in his skull. Oh, it's a spooky thing: For just a second, you find yourself conversing with a dead man . . .

But Conrad's gaze returns, he hasn't gone anywhere, his eyes engage my eyes, he's as lively as ever: "And Sally wanders past three or four of these creations with that dear irresistible *deferential* look on her face—but after a while even she has to give up. And meanwhile I'm gaping slack-jawed at all this stuff, trying my damnedest to keep my lunch in my belly, and what does Sally say as we're leaving the place? She says, 'I'm sure you have a better sense of what the artist's doing than I do.' Do you understand what I'm saying? Do you see how perfectly *adorable* this is?"

"I'm not sure I—"

"No?" Pause. "Well, in her dear sweet totally illogical way"—pause—"Sally assumes, though she'd never put it this way"—pause—"she assumes the exhibition's some sort of fag thing. She doesn't understand it? Well that's only to be expected, because it's a fag thing, isn't it?"

He has made another confession of sorts. I say, "Are you sure she—"

"And don't you love it? Don't you love *her*? The logic's just so delicious I'll be grateful to her forever. *I'm* supposed to be interested in looking at shoelaces glued to plywood? Come again? Could you run that one by me again?" Conrad holds up a cupped hand to his ear, like an elderly man pleading deafness. "Just because I like boys, it naturally follows I'm hot for shoelaces? Is that it? And now that I don't go after boys, am I supposed to turn to art galleries for my entertainment? Maybe go see if the artist with the shoelaces has turned over a new leaf—or maybe I should say put the shoe on the other foot? Hell, has he moved on to toothbrushes, maybe? Tweezers? Q-Tips?"

Conrad's big jowly face is all wrenched awry—with amusement, rancor, exasperation, affection, vitriol. His burning restless gaze settles, predictably, on the bowl of nuts before him. He tosses down another tranquilizing handful and says, "Are art galleries supposed to be my substitute? Or maybe philosophy? I tell you, I've done more thinking in the last two years than in the whole rest of my life and you know what's the one conclusion I've reached? *Thinking stinks.* You can put that one on my tombstone: *Here lies fat Conrad, who said, Thinking stinks.* It's a vastly overrated activity. As far as pleasures go, I can think of all sorts of activities that beat thinking all to hell."

And another look slips into his eyes: a hard, naughty, and maybe wistful look. Conrad says, "You do know, don't you, she was always keeping me away from you?"

"Beg pardon?"

"Even after she and Wes broke up, you know she and I stayed friends over the years, in our fashion, but *you* didn't see much of me, did you? In that regard, our meek and mild Sally was the lioness and you the cub, and I think it would have insulted me if it hadn't been so goddamn funny. Who in the world did she think I *was*? What depravities did she think I was capable of? What I wanted to say to her, in addition to other objections that were even more obvious, was this: Sally, your dear little wunderkind's not my type. Hell, you never *were* a boy, Luke, you always were a little man, at ten you were more the accountant than I ever was. You were all sorts of things, kiddo, but at fifteen I can't imagine you were *any-body's* heartthrob. Nobody's—not even the leery old queer at the edge of the school track, watching the boys jump the hurdles. Not even a heartthrob for the sweet hopeless girl who's far too chunky to make the cheerleading squad. Look, I don't mean to be cruel."

"And I certainly don't take it cruelly, Uncle Conrad."

"If you 'Uncle Conrad' me again, I'll pack a handful of these macadamias up your sinuses." Yet he looks pleased with my little parry. He picks up another handful of nuts and—for all I can see—jams them up *his* nose: His big hand comes up and covers his lower face, a moment later descending empty. He says, "Look, I know your type. Admit it, even as a boy, you never had any real healthy interest in porn, now did you?"

"In—"

"Pornography. Dirty pix? Gaping yearningly at somebody's privates? No, hell no, not you, Luke. Heavens no."

It's a measure of the weird, burgeoning complexities of my dealings with my uncle that I feel a little shamefaced: It embarrasses me to have to confess, "A big interest in porn? No."

"In your next reincarnation, maybe you won't skip the best phase in life."

"Mm?"

"Youth."

"Tell me about their breakup, Wes and Sally."

"What's to tell?" Conrad shrugs his enormous shoulders. Rusty from his corner of the room mutters a bitter stretch of parrot philosophy.

Conrad says, "She simply caught him too many times with lipstick on his undershirt—or undershorts—and when she finally chucked him out on his ear, that was that. You do understand, don't you, that our meek Sally Admiraal is the toughest little lady ever to come out of Restoration? That it's no accident, it's completely inevitable, that she winds up sitting so pretty in France. I understand she's moving there . . ."

"Hardly *moving* there. She's just decided to stay on till Christmas. She'll come home for a while first, straighten things out, then head down toward Nice or Montpellier. Where there's more sun. She's arranging to take French classes. Maybe in the end she's more full of surprises even than Wes."

"Sur*prises*? *Sally?*" And Conrad is off again, launched by the fuel that best propels him: indignation. "But obviously the one most remarkable thing about Miss Sally Admiraal is that everything she's ever done is one hundred percent predictable and if I'd given it ten minutes thought I could have told you she'd be staying on till Christmas. Of *course* the little *A* student's gone back to school. And of *course* she's doing it in France. Because she's free now—she's free at last, now Wes is dead."

"Wes—so what are you saying? How exactly would that have freed her?"

"And my advice on this so-called quest of yours? Give it up. Fire yourself and find a new line of work. Because you obviously don't understand anything."

And now I guess I've finally had enough; I *am* hurt. I repeat my question: "How would that have freed her?" And I push him a little: "I mean, Wes had his own wife, his own kids, his various organizations he belonged to. Surely *he* wasn't stopping Sally from moving to France for a few months."

"Organizations?"

"Well . . ." I can tell from Conrad's face that I'm about to be flatly contradicted. "The Rotarians, the Restoration Chamber of Commerce, the Thumb of Michigan—"

"You're thinking Wes was actually going to meetings? Of organizations like that?"

"What are you saying? He never joined?"

"Of course he *joined*. And probably attended a few times, looking to make connections—what I suppose he called 'contacts.'

But how long would it take before someone let him know he was
no Hubert Sultan—that he was a financial lightweight? How long
before somebody hurt his pride?"

"You're saying he felt inferior to them?"

"And superior too. Oh, if life was only as simple as you make
out, Luke, hell we might all climb into a rocket ship and blast off to
Mars. Life here on earth would already be solved. Christ, Wes *knew*
those guys. He'd known them ever since high school, those Rotar-
ian types with their wide-ass suits. They bored him back then, and
they bored him now. And they infuriated him. Because they'd got
their hands on all the money somehow. That was the stinger:
Somehow they'd got their hands on all the money."

"Okay, all right, go ahead, then: Make my life more complicated. Tell me about Wes's years in Kalamazoo. Tell me about the
Zidlers."

"What in hell do you know about *them?*"

"Not much. I first heard the name from you, actually. Last time
I came to visit. And I asked Sally about them."

"And?"

"And she told me she didn't know much about Wes's Kalamazoo years."

"Oh, is that right? Ignorant, was she?"

"She must know something. But I'm sure you know more than
she does . . ."

And it seems I've hit upon just the right phrase. You can see in
his face how Conrad warms to my words. For he is once again the
man with the monopoly—the one with the goods.

Well, he will have me wait a moment longer . . . First he goes
to the kitchen and fetches two more bottles of beer, then over to
the bathroom, where, behind the half-closed door, I can hear what
I don't want to hear: painful spaced grunts as the urine finds the
bowl. (And another anecdote: a funny—ha-ha—story from my

days at Gribben Brothers. It seems there was a company president who decided to fire an incompetent executive. But on the big day, he happens to hear the man in the bathroom, groaning in the effort to pass his water, and somehow can't fire him after that. The upshot of the story? Well, if this were a Christian morality tale, the executive would turn a corner and become a credit to the company. Were it a simple illustration of corporate ruthlessness, the executive would rise to the top and ax his former boss. But in fact, their entire division was downsized a month later and they both lost their jobs. The lesson of the story? Pity is irrelevant, ha-ha . . .) And yet for all his grunting, when Conrad returns to his couch, his face wears a gleeful expression.

"Come on," he says, "it's time for a drink"—as if we haven't been drinking—"we'll go to my local."

So we troop back out into the heat and climb into Conrad's car and drive again to the little Mexican dive, La Rosa Rosa. This time around, caught in Miami's stop-and-go traffic, I realize what I missed the last time we drove out here after many drinks: Conrad's "local" is miles and miles from his apartment. Not that I mind the drive. It's clear that if I'm patient, I'll eventually be treated to a tale Conrad has been saving: Wes's adventures in Kalamazoo with the Zidlers. Whoever they are.

So I sit tranquilly in the passenger seat while Conrad punches the accelerator and swears at various "idiot drivers" along the way. What *does* concern me is how even a short walk in the heat leaves him panting for breath. When we reach the inadequately air-conditioned La Rosa Rosa, he settles with a grunt of exhausted relief into one of the booths. The various posters—Mazatlán, the jaguar, the pop singer in the pink party dress—continue to buckle from the walls. "Your local isn't very local," I say.

"It's my local," Conrad says.

"How often do you come here?"

"Most every day."

"However did you choose this place?"

"I just chose it."

"But why *this* place?"

"I just chose it," Conrad declares with a finality that cuts off further questions. What draws him to La Rosa Rosa? His attachment to this little dive is unmistakable. I've been with him in many public places—restaurants, a hardware store, a grocery store, a post office—but this is the only one where his voice grows gentle. Clearly, there's a story attached to this place, and it looks equally clear (an accurate surmise, it turns out) that he's never going to tell it to me.

"How are you, Graciela?" he inquires, almost tenderly, as the limping old proprietress wanders over with a basket of taco chips. "How's the leg?"

"It's the leg," she says. "It hurts."

"I'm sorry," Conrad replies, and adds in a tone that surprises me, for it sounds almost proud, "This is my nephew. Luke. From New York City."

"I've been there."

"You liked it, Graciela?"

"Not like here."

"Two rum-and-Cokes," Conrad says, placing my order for me.

And only after the drinks arrive and he has sipped deeply does Conrad commence the story he has promised me:

"Wes moved to Kalamazoo in 1970," he begins. (*Actually, 1971,* a voice in my head declares, but I keep my mouth shut. It seems Conrad the accountant has never gotten a date right in his life. Even so, the story he narrates has a ring of authenticity . . .)

It seems that shortly after moving to Kalamazoo, Wes took up with the wife of one of the chief executives at Great Bay Shipping. Pamela Zidler. A risky thing to do, but evidently a passion neither could rein in. According to Conrad, "They were humping every hour on the hour."

Wes was in his mid-thirties at the time. Pamela was a decade or so older, and her husband, Harry, a decade older still. The Zidlers had no children. Needless to say, the affair had its explosive potential—a hustling young salesman, new to a little midwestern city, flagrantly taking up with one of the bosses' wives—but somehow it didn't explode. Wes and Pam kept up their daily humping, at a white heat, one month after the next . . .

And when the situation finally broke, it did so in an unforeseen way: One morning, Pamela found Harry on the bathroom floor. He'd had a stroke, which left him partially paralyzed on his right side. Well, the boss was finished being a boss: There was nothing for Harry to do but elect early retirement.

And what everybody in town wanted to know was, had Harry suspected Pam and Wes all along? And had his suspicions contributed to his stroke? Most people figured Harry must have guessed the truth, but if so, what he chose to do next was inexplicable: He took Wes under his wing. The young salesman became the stroke victim's favorite companion.

Night after night, the two of them used to sit up watching television, or playing gin rummy (which Wes played badly), or simply drinking a beer on the back porch if the weather was fine. And when Harry had a second stroke, this one far more debilitating, Wes moved in with the Zidlers.

There was plenty of room, plenty of beds. Wes and Pam had a real palace to play in. Twenty years before, in order to please his pretty young wife, Harry Zidler, who had family money behind him, had constructed in this levelheaded midwestern city a fantastic castle/villa, with a watchtower and genuine marble floors from Italy. Oh, this place was far finer than the old mansion on Crestview Boulevard that Wes had lived in as a boy, before the collapse of Sultan Furniture; it was finer than anything Wesley Sultan had ever known.

And once installed within it, Wes became all but indispensable to the Zidlers, since Harry turned out to be more comfortable with Wes than with any of the men or women actually paid to assist him. Harry relied on Wes to wheel him around, to help get him in and out of his chair.

"Oh, Wes became a perfect little *son* to Harry," Conrad tells me. "Strolling him to the park, helping him get dressed, cleaning up after he'd soiled himself—and meanwhile racing to hold down his job at Great Bay. Oh, Wes was a very busy boy . . . And Harry? Harry for his part couldn't have *been* more grateful. Tears would overflow his eyes when he'd thank Wes for everything he'd done for him. He used to call Wes the son he'd never had. And he used to plead with Wes, tears spilling down those elderly cheeks, to look after Pam when he was gone. Isn't this a heartwarming story?"

"And why do I think it won't have a heartwarming conclusion?"

Conrad's merry hooded-eyed grin really is something to see. If it's possible to look impish when you weigh over two hundred and fifty pounds, he manages it. He says: "In particular, Harry used to beg Wes to prevail on Pam not to sell the house after he was dead and gone. Because Harry *loved* that house—one of the finest homes in the western part of the state—and he wanted Pam to hold on to it forever. He worried that *she* worried she couldn't afford to keep the place up. And so Harry went very conscientiously through all the financial papers with Wes—the stock holdings, the bank accounts, the will, everything—to demonstrate without any doubt that Pam would have *more* than enough funds to live on as a widow. Because, you see, everything would go to

Pam after his death . . . which really meant everything would go to Wes, because whatever else you wanted to say about Wes, he did have Pam Zidler wrapped round his . . . his little finger.

"So everything was in place to put old Harry to bed for good, and yet the doddering old bastard wouldn't go. Somehow kept right on living, getting worse and worse, maybe he had another stroke, he was a total mess, yet at the end of each day still breathing. Years went by. Yes, for six long years Wes paid his dues, carrying Harry here, carrying him there, feeding him and dressing him.

"You know what they always tell you about some guy who's soiling his pants and can't wipe his runny nose? How they always say, 'At least his mind isn't affected,' or 'He's still sharp as a tack'? Well, that's exactly what they said about Harry, but the truth is, Harry seemed totally gaga, this lopsided old geezer in a wheelchair drooling onto his birthday cake . . .

"Six long years of this, and finally Harry does go off to meet his Maker, and maybe he honestly hasn't been quite so gaga all along, because do you know what? Do you know what?"

"I think I'm catching the drift."

"Are you? And isn't it too delicious for words? . . . Oh kiddo, isn't life the best thing going? It's so good, it's addictive, isn't it? It's so good sometimes, I can hardly bear it.

"So: that last will and testament that Harry'd shown Wes? The one leaving everything to Pam? Well, well. Turns out it wasn't quite Harry's *last* will and testament, was it? No, it had been superseded, hadn't it? Long ago. And the follow-up will, the valid and completely airtight will, it was a little different, wasn't it? The first one left everything to Pam and the next one left her—nothing. Zilcho. But you know what? You know what?" Oh, I think Conrad's having more fun than I've ever seen him have. Jollity is radiating from his face's every pore: it has reddened his cheeks and wet his eyes. "Well: Harry's will may have neglected Pam, but it didn't neglect Wes. And do you know what Harry left Wes? In repayment for those six years of carrying him out of a chair and into a chair, and mopping up the piss that hadn't found its way into the bowl? Harry left Wes a—you guessed it!—a set of luggage. Now what did Harry mean by that? What *could* the man have meant by that?"

Conrad dabs with a napkin at the laughter-laden tears in his eyes. For one moment, he wears a look of entreaty—I'm being asked to join him in his mirth—and then, quite abruptly, he swings around, showing me his face in profile. He's peering over at the poster of the pop singer in the pink party dress. Seen from the side, Conrad's head, with its solid brow and tight drumstick of a ponytail, possesses a hefty dignity.

"The story pleases you," I say to him.

"It doesn't please you?" He's still regarding the poster. All the humor has left his voice.

"You feel Wes got what he deserved," I say.

"You don't?"

"You don't think he was genuinely fond of Harry?"

"You do?"

"And what happened to Pam Zidler?"

Conrad again swings around, giving me so blank an expression you might suppose I'd asked after one of the story's peripheral characters, rather than one of its principals. He's slow to answer: "Well, Wes *left* her, of course. Skipped town as soon as he could. Took up his old beat in Stags Harbor."

"You think Wes didn't love her? He only cared about the money?"

"Oh God why do I bother? Why do I bother telling you *anything*?" And Conrad—truly—smites himself on the forehead, a great theatrical resounding slap. "Don't you—*won't* you see the point? Isn't it clear? Wes had to leave because he'd been *beaten*. He'd been made a fool of, and that was the one thing he could never tolerate. The beautiful, *beautiful* thing about that story? It's that the man in the *diaper* made a fool of Wes . . ."

We drink our drinks in silence. Conrad swallows another handful of taco chips. "Home?" he says.

"Home," I reply.

We drive back through the heat and the Miami traffic. Again by tacit agreement we let our conversation drop until we reach our destination. Only when we've settled once more in Conrad's shadowy living room, with new bottles of beer and a replenished bowl of macadamia nuts before us, do I say, "But you were telling me about Sally. You were telling me she was tough with Wes . . ."

And once more, although these little errands have left him panting for breath, Conrad is off and running: "When she threw him over, it was *over.* It was *basta,* bastard. It was *nada más.* And poor Wes couldn't understand the concept. *'Forever?'* Blink, blink, blink, those gorgeous eyelashes of his. *'Forever?'* Up and down goes the sculpted Adam's apple. *'Forever? What's that?'* Is it any wonder, after Gordon died and Wes showed up at Sally's place, thinking he might resume things just as before, kapow, she blackened his eye?"

"She gave him a black eye?" But this *couldn't* be true.

"*Course* she did."

"I don't believe it."

"You go and ask her . . ."

"Simply not possible."

"*Ask* her."

"I will. I will ask her."

"That's *her* story—you make her tell it. And don't let her wiggle out. I just wish I could be a fly on the wall—to watch Sally explain to her son how she gave the kid's father a big black eye."

"I still don't believe it."

"Suit yourself, but it's like I told you. In the end Sally's a lioness. And what was Wes in the end? A hyena."

The comparison pleases Conrad, eliciting from him his own hyena's happy bay of laughter, to which Rusty contributes a raucous bark of amusement. A jocular moment in the jungle . . .

I say, "But tell me more about Wes. What did he do when he first discovered the truth about you?" There, I've crossed another threshold.

"The truth about me? I'm not sure there *is* a truth about me."

"About being more interested in boys than girls."

"Oh *that?* We never discussed it."

"Never? You never discussed it? Really?"

But why in the world not? Hard to believe that Conrad—iconoclastic Conrad—would let mere inhibitions silence him . . .

"But you want my guess?" Conrad says. "My guess is, it mostly pleased him."

"Pleased him? How?"

"Don't be a cluck. By now I'm sure Rusty's got this better figured out than you do."

"Meaning?"

"Meaning I wasn't going to chase Wes's *girl,* wasn't going to show him up the way I did in a gym or on a track. For a guy like Wes, that was very reassuring. You know how you meet sometimes, or you read sometimes, somebody saying *everybody's* queer, at least to some degree? Well, maybe I'd believe it if it hadn't been for Wes. But he was somebody whose world was a place where men didn't *count,* men weren't completely real.

"They were obstacles, they were competitors, and they were the bosses, the people running Great Bay, so you could hardly ignore them, no actually you had to spend a great deal of time and effort learning how to *manipulate* them, which was, as my little story about the Zidlers ought to make clear, something Wes never quite mastered. But men? Boulders in the road. Treat 'em with care, watch out for 'em, go round 'em, maybe even dynamite the bastards, but in the end they're just these great big hulking dry *rocks.*

"If only Wes had been God and could have designed the world? What would it look like? Well, he'd've got rid of most of the men, I can tell you, except for himself. Lord knows, he would never, *never* have had a son."

And Conrad regards me cruelly. Clearly he's aware that at some psychological level he himself has just killed me off . . . Yet this time I outmaneuver him. Has he sentenced me to death? In response, I offer him (I offer the dual cancer and cardiac patient) ongoing life. I say, "Wes wouldn't have got rid of *all* the men. He would have kept a brother—somebody to contend with. To define himself against. Somebody without whom his life would have lost so much of its meaning."

It's in moments like these that I've already begun to feel quite fond of Conrad. For the way he looks at you when you score a point off him. The little acknowledging pause when something registers. His gaze is more than respectful at such times. It shines with the trained athlete's dispassionate admiration for the deft stroke, the well-executed stratagem. He peers hard at me and chugs the rest of his beer.

I get up to go to the john, passing on my way what has to be Conrad's bedroom. The door's closed but ajar. I don't hesitate, although feelings of guilt lead me to employ the side of my shoe rather than my hand. (Am I reluctant to leave fingerprints?) I nudge the door open, peer inside. And what I view strikes me with the honed force of an epiphany. There's an enormous bed, with a black funereal bedspread. And across from it, where you'd expect a television, an aquarium. The thing is absolutely huge—of a size appropriate to some showy seafood restaurant or swanky office lounge. Aquariums are something I know a little about, having kept over the years both a twenty- and a thirty-gallon tank. Conrad's aquarium must hold two hundred gallons of water.

It's an oceanic, a saltwater, environment. There are intricate coral grottoes, spiny urchins, wan voluptuous-fingered anemones. Carnival-colored fish flicker through the flooded garden of Conrad's tank. He has put hours and hours into it—and hundreds and hundreds of dollars. But I've never heard a word about it.

The pump releases a benign hum, soothing as a cat's purr.

I stand there frozen, my mind carried off—I'm in a state of childish enchantment.

I'm feeling, I suppose, like a police detective who has stumbled upon some clue that, though not yet fully analyzed, seems certain to crack the case. For somehow it all makes *sense*: that in his living room Conrad would keep a beautiful but cacophonous and cantankerous parrot, and in his bedroom a hushed, gorgeous, palatial garden. (Just as it makes *sense*—though it will take me a few days to forge this particular connection—that a man whose father drowned in a chilly northern lake would wind up sleeping beside a balmy, jeweled marine kingdom.)

When I return to the living room I say, "I went to see Tiffany."

"Jesus, you've been a busy boy."

"And she said something similar to what you're saying."

And of course Conrad is immediately goaded: "Similar? Good Lord, say it ain't so, Luke. Because if I've begun sounding like *Tiffany*, you can cancel everything I've just said. Similar? Am I devolving into some suburban bimbo, sopping up the spirits every night on my backyard patio? Have two years of philosophizing left me sounding like Tiffany?"

"She said Wes didn't care about anything except being loved. By women exclusively, I think she meant."

Needless to say, I expect to be contradicted. I've begun to formulate an all-but-infallible rule: In Conrad's world, *anyone's* judgments about Wes, except his own, are completely off the mark . . . And Conrad doesn't let me down: "Wes didn't care about driving a splashy car? Wes didn't care about wearing an expensive watch? It's poppycock she's talking. Let me tell you a story about Wes. Now listen to this one . . .

"Okay, when he was, let's see, fourteen, Wes became absolutely *obsessed* with our father's suits. These were still hanging in the closet, though the man had been moldering for years, and Wes wanted to have them altered for himself. Now what kind of a fourteen-year-old boy, you might well ask, would become obsessed with wearing his dead father's business suits? The answer is: Wesley Sultan. Momma refused at first, but Wes kept it up and kept it up and kept it up, and for his sixteenth birthday she relented and I can still remember, it was a *very* hot day [A hot day? Wes's birthday fell in November.] and Wes was parading around the house in this suffocating gray wool pinstripe suit, and I don't think I've ever seen him looking more pleased with himself. People might say I was in the closet for a long while, but Wes was in there in a much more unusual and obsessive way; he was in our dad's closet, dreaming of wearing the dead man's suits. That's who Wes was."

This is a new story to me—and a rich and wonderful one. What a singular young peacock this fellow is, whose finery is a charcoal-gray old fogey's business suit!

And for just a moment it seems I have him: The quarry has been flushed from his covert. Here's a genuine sighting: He stands before me. In the little row house on Scully Street, beside the Michicabanabee River, Wes Sultan, age sixteen, gazes wholeheartedly into the mirror on the wardrobe in his mother's bedroom and I stare out at him.

The year is 1950. Wesley is wearing an old-fashioned gray

wool suit which, though recently altered, is still a little large for him. The tailor has left him room to grow.

And growing is just what Wes intends to do. The mirror—that fathomless treasure trove—encases all the gliding, dancing lusters of the coming years. Slowly, he pivots left, pivots right, jubilating in what he sees. Isn't life the best thing going? And Wesley smiles at the world—which is to say, he smiles at himself. He fires a glance deep into the mirror's vertical catacombs of silver and glass, far into the future, where our gazes fuse at last. He all but recognizes me.

CHAPTER TEN

and the Commodore
Hotel in Stags Harbor,

RESTORATION—Wesley Cross Sultan, ~~63,~~ of 2135 *62*
N. Westhampton, died suddenly in Lyon Hospital in
Stags Harbor, of heart failure. He worked for Great
Bay Shipping for 42 years, chiefly in sales. He began
his career in the Stags Harbor office, and after stints
in Kalamazoo and Cincinnati, Ohio, he finished his
career back at Stags Harbor. He ~~retired two years~~ *was effectively*
~~ago in~~ order to pursue full-time his civic pursuits. *fired two years* *ago but claimed*
a nominal He was ~~an active~~ member of the Rotarians, the *to be retiring*
Restoration Chamber of Commerce, the Stags Har-
bor Betterment Society, and the Thumb of Michigan
Prosperity Council. He was also active in the Restoration Episcopal Church, where for many years he sang
in the choir.

He was born in Restoration and ~~was a graduate~~ *attended but*
~~of~~ the old High School on Cherrystone Avenue. He *did not quite* *graduate from*
was the son of the late Chester Sultan, the well-
known businessman, and the grandson of Hubert
Sultan, who served as the mayor of Restoration from
1908 to 1912. Old-time Restorationists will recall
Sultan Furniture on Union Street, founded by Hubert
and presided over by Chester until he closed its
doors in 1935.

from whom he He was married ~~twice. His first wife was~~ Sally *three times. His*
was formally Planter (Admiraal), now of Grosse Pointe, formerly *first wife was*
separated at of Restoration. They were divorced in 1964. He *Klara Kuzmak,*
the time of leaves his wife, Tiffany, and their two daughters, Jes- *He then married*
his death, sica and Winnie; a son, Luke Planter, of New York; a
brother, Conrad Sultan, of Miami, Florida; and a sis- *with whom*
ter, Adelle De Vries, of Battle Creek. *he had a son,*
half- *Wesley Jr.*

Half the people my age I meet in New York are fantasizing about
opening a restaurant—the other half are writing a thriller. My generation's dreams of escape seem to center on either food or crime.

There's little doubt into which camp Carolyn Dahlberg, who lived across the hall from me my freshman year in college, falls. Food fantasies aren't in her line somehow. She's one of many old classmates who are Princeton-style "refugees from the law"—people whose professions took all sorts of curious twists when their legal careers soured or collapsed. After being turned down for a partnership at Paul, Weiss, she opened a detective agency.

In the dorm, the joke about Carolyn was that most of her conversations began *You won't believe what just happened to me.* She was a tireless talker—someone who took more pleasure in her spectacular mishaps (*You won't believe . . .*) than most people do in their triumphs. I run into her on Third Avenue and we catch up over a cup of coffee. It's been nearly ten years since I last saw her, but she's hardly changed: still fair and slight (she can't weigh much more than a hundred pounds), with a little kid's chipped front tooth. She looks like an unlikely adventuress, and yet she's the only person I know who has scuba-dived in the Japanese naval wrecks in Truk Harbor, or once broke a hip jumping out of an airplane.

I think Carolyn has always seen me—perhaps understandably— as someone whose life is just a little dull, and she perks right up on hearing I've left Gribben, with no tangible future. Suddenly she has far more questions than I have answers. This lady detective leaning forward in the booth across from me keeps repeating, insistently, *Luke, your story doesn't really add up,* until I recall what I suppose I've mostly forgotten: I always liked Carolyn Dahlberg better as a concept than as a companion. She makes a person nervous.

As we're leaving the restaurant, I think to ask her about the possibility of looking up a stranger whose trail has grown cold— about finding someone who has moved away, drifted off.

"Easiest thing in the world," Carolyn tells me. "Usually. Not a lot different from property law—which incidentally I always loathed.

Mostly dreary stuff—dusty afternoons in the registry of deeds, old phone books, telephoning old employers . . ."

I tell her there's somebody I'm curious about, a relative I've never seen. Carolyn says, "When I went into this business, I figured I'd go broke, but there'd be tons of excitement. And I was half right. Jeez, you might as well be shepardizing cases all day. You honestly want me to find a missing relative? My experience is, they're like sleeping dogs . . ."

"How much would it cost me?"

"Let's call it a freebie, if you'll figure out what my next gig ought to be. I need a real job, Luke."

Carolyn gives me a mournful look, but I'm aware that this conversation, too, is happy grist for the conversational mill: *Things got so bad, I pulled Luke Planter off the street and asked him to find me a job* . . . "Carolyn, I'm the last place to look for career advice."

"Then let's call it eight hundred dollars."

I tell Carolyn I'll think about it and a few days later I call back and give her the go-ahead. (And maybe I'm more like Carolyn than I want to think. For the notion of being able to say, *You won't believe this, but I once hired a private detective* holds inordinate appeal for me.) And in less than a week, I receive by fax a name, a Pittsburgh address, and a phone number. Carolyn has thrown in for good measure an education summary (Catholic high school diploma, one year of community college) and an employment record (auto-parts store, supermarket assistant manager, health club manager). As well as a bill for six hundred dollars. I fire off a letter that very afternoon:

Dear Wesley Giardina,

Although you and I have never met, we have a great many things in common. My name is Luke Planter. But I was born Luke Sultan, on May 19, 1961, in Restoration,

Michigan. My father was the late Wesley Sultan and my
mother is Sally Planter, the former Sally Sultan, born Sally
Admiraal. My parents were divorced when I was three and I
was later formally adopted by my mother's second husband,
Dr. Gordon Planter, who passed away four years ago.

It seems one of the things we share, therefore, is a
biological father.

I am an investment banker (with Gribben Brothers, here
in Manhattan), who in his spare time is compiling some
family history. For obvious reasons, I've been eager to track
you down. At the moment, I am doing a little research into
the life of Wesley Sultan, which as you can imagine is quite
a tangled affair. I would be especially interested to learn
whether you yourself have memories of Wesley that you
wouldn't mind sharing with me, either by letter or,
preferably, in person. My job occasionally takes me to
Pittsburgh and I would be quite pleased to meet with you
there at your convenience. I would also be quite interested
in any "family lore" you might know—any anecdotes about
Wesley you may have heard from your late mother or from
other relatives. Also, I would be very keen to see any
photographs you might have.

Although it is my interest in family history—particularly
Wesley—that has prompted this letter, I would very much
like to meet you independent of my project. We may have
more in common even than we know.

Yours sincerely,
Luke Planter

Not a nibble for three weeks—no note or call—and then the following handwritten letter, its penmanship a chaotic jumble of
capitals and lowercase letters, cursive and printing:

Dear Mr. Planter,

Sorry I can't help you but I'm afraid you are under some mistaken Impression. You say you were eager to track me down but I'm afraid you have found the wrong man and so you'll just have to keep right on tracking. (or trucking) My father was Johnny Giardina, born and raised here in Pittsburgh, and the old boy may have got up to some weird business in his life but I'm pretty sure going around under an alias like WESLEY SULTAN wasn't one of them. I've never been to Restoration Michigan, or to Detroit either; maybe I'll go there some time. Sounds like quite a hopping Place.

Good luck

Wesley Giardina

He's never heard of Wesley Sultan? The letter throws me for a loop. On the one hand, I haven't a doubt in the world I've found my half brother. On the other, I realize (more and more clearly with each reading) just how closely I've skirted catastrophe. My dashed-off letter? It might easily have detonated a land mine. Good Lord, why hadn't I foreseen this? Foreseen that Klara Kuzmak/ Sultan/Giardina would cover her tracks thoroughly? No, my half brother, Wesley Giardina, has never heard mention of his true father and namesake, and when my letter arrived out of the blue he must have taken me for a lunatic—which under the circumstances was a mercy and a kindness. The alternative? It was so ugly it made me squirm.

The alternative? I arrive in Wesley Giardina's life like some sort of postal mugger—stepping out of the shadows in order to shatter the foundations of his existence. Who could say what zealously protective, whitewashed version of events Klara Kuzmak created for her son before she died? As Lou Gehrig's disease took away first the use of her fingers, and then her hands, wasn't there all the more reason for clinging to an artificial past? For me to destroy her rendition of things would be an absolute desecration of her grave . . . What *had* I been thinking?

The second time around, showing a good deal more reflection and circumspection, I write as follows:

Dear Mr. Giardina:

Many thanks for your letter, which indeed corrected a mistake of mine.

I will continue my research into my family history with greater accuracy, thanks to you. Actually, since I last wrote you I did succeed in locating the person I was looking for (the one I mistook for you). I apologize for the mistake.

I don't suppose I can strongly recommend Restoration, Michigan, or even Detroit, to someone who has never been there. I'm sure what those places have to offer can already be had in Pittsburgh.

Yours cordially,
Luke Planter

I post the letter from Kennedy Airport. I'm again on my way to France.

She's a sunny soul by nature, but even so Sally seems cheerier now than at any time since her widowhood began, four years ago. She is chatty and exclamatory, wide-eyed and indefatigable. She says, "I simply cannot stop marveling." She says, "I gape out my window in the morning and declare, 'Truly, this isn't where I'm living.' And yet this is precisely where I'm living." She says, "Who could have foreseen it? It's all so marvelously improbable that *I* would wind up here."

"Happily so?"

"Happily? Blissfully. I think this must be the prettiest place I've ever lived."

I've just rolled up on her doorstep. I'm feeling jet-lagged and disassembled and dazed and a little blissed-out myself. After a long, bumpy, stormy flight from New York to Paris, and a shorter but equally bumpy and stormy flight to Nice, I was set down in what felt like a rare global oasis of tranquillity. The winds had slipped into a doze, the clouds had evaporated, and the sun on the hills and valleys of this matchless countryside came down broadly, sweetly, evenhandedly.

In a little rented sky-blue Renault I drove up and down meandering mountain roads for an hour or so, giddily overjoyed with my surroundings even while fretting that I might be more tired than I supposed; I had Hollywood visions of winding up halfway down a hill, buried in a tangle of flowering vines, car upended and wheels still spinning. Disaster had been tracking me ever since I left New York. Could it be that I'd shaken it off my trail at last?

Here in the south of France, in the town of Mare aux Cerfs, somehow Sally has found a beautiful little apartment for herself in what I'd call a row house if this were Manhattan. But this is a medieval French village and she's found an old, sloping slice of a house on an old, sloping street—a neighborhood that has the tilted reality, the skew lines, of a fairy tale. There's a little sitting room and a dining room and a good-sized kitchen downstairs, two bedrooms and a study upstairs, and a thriving, appealingly untidy garden out back. She urges a nap on me, but I'm not yet ready to sleep. She makes me a cup of tea and again urges a nap, but I insist instead on a walk through town.

There are no sidewalks on Sally's narrow street and we stride on cobblestones, past a butcher shop (dead chickens plucked only to the neck, their undecapitated heads still feathered) and a patisserie (whorled little pastries ornate as orchids). The scrolled orange tiles that make up the roofs of this town gleam in the afternoon sun.

In my jet-lagged, head-slightly-rotated way, I'm coming up once more against a sensation of all but boundless ignorance. For here is one more world I don't know anything about; nothing is familiar here, everything is new. That I'm ignorant about the architecture is only the least of my lacks. I know next to zero about the town of Mare aux Cerfs or its workings, the history of the region, the flow of its commerce, and, most telling of all, the language in which such dealings are carried out, a language I last studied twenty years ago, for two years in high school, and a language in which, moreover, my mother is now—slowly, to be sure, with many stops and starts, and yet steadily—negotiating her way around. It grows apparent that Sally Planter, née Admiraal, has refashioned a European tie that is far realer to her than it will likely ever be for me. She whose grandparents emigrated from Utrecht, and whose childhood reverberated with mumbled Dutch admonishments, is getting around in yet another Continental tongue. She steps into a boulangerie and asks for a baguette, *pas trop cuite,* and into a pharmacy, where she determines, after consultation, which of two seemingly identical sunblocks is actually more effective, and into a papeterie, where she buys *cartouches* for her *plume,* and into a *crêmerie,* where she settles on a cindery disk of chèvre and asks the fromager if it is *prêt à manger ce soir* and he laughs and tells her it's *prêt à manger maintenant* and *ce soir aussi; ce fromage* is *formidable!* And what's more impressive still is to see that Sally is, already, not only recognized but welcomed in all these charming little establishments. In just a few weeks, that characteristic brio of hers (or perhaps the phrase is *joie de vivre*) has impressed itself upon the neighborhood shopkeepers, overcoming her various fumblings and incomprehensions. Sally's joy in life is a participatory joy, openly inviting others to share in it—which they do, assembling around her a community within the community.

She leads me to what she describes as her "favorite brasserie," and over *cafés noisettes* she says to me, "We talked a lot about religion last time, in Domat, and I told you all about how the POOF Band, the Christian rock band, had chased God right out of that old Dutch church in Restoration, but I now learn that the Grosse Pointe Unitarians aren't doing any better." After years of drifting from church to church, Episcopal to Methodist to Presbyterian, Sally in her late forties had found a seemingly permanent home with the Unitarians. "Maybe you remember the minister—now ex-minister? Peter Prescott."

"S."

"Mm?" Sally says.

"Not an *M*. An *S*. Peter *S*. Prescott. He clung to the middle initial."

"Truly your memory's amazing . . . Anyway, I'm afraid he's gotten himself into an unspeakable scandal."

"Unspeakable?"

"Sexual."

"Of what sort?"

"You don't want to know."

"He ran off with one of the ladies in the choir."

"Worse."

"He ran off with one of the little boys in the choir."

"Worse. He makes someone who ran off with a choirboy look like a choirboy."

"Geez, I really *don't* want to know."

"Suffice it to say that the entire congregation doesn't know whether to laugh or cry. But the grisly details really don't matter, my point is that, as I sit here in France, contemplating my life, I do feel that everything back there across the Atlantic, back where I really live, is coming undone. Is there a church left in the country that looks both sane and dignified? That doesn't leave you feeling you're watching a soap opera written by a drug addict? How was Conrad, incidentally? Speaking of coming undone."

"Well he looked exactly like what he was—somebody who'd recently been in the hospital."

"And did he talk to you about what put him there?"

"Not a word of that. I don't know anything except what you've told me."

"And I don't know much. He had the prostatectomy two years ago, but evidently his PSA count is up, which suggests they didn't get all of it. But where has it gone to? A CAT scan and a bone scan didn't turn anything up." With her love of virtually any sort of specialized nomenclature, Sally naturally absorbed, during her years as a doctor's wife, some medical fluency. "And it seems at least two of his coronary arteries are ninety percent clogged, and needless to say his blood pressure is through the roof. Oh, I do sometimes think Wes was lucky to go so quickly. It would have shattered him, oh it would've broken his proud manly heart, to go the way his brother's going."

"Unfortunately, the hospital stay did nothing to curb his appetite. A meal these days with Conrad is a sort of dinner/theater spectacle."

"Maybe it's his way of hurrying the whole business along? Or maybe it's the opposite—trying to convince himself the cancer's under control. If end-stage cancer usually wastes you away, then isn't it a *good sign* to be growing fatter and fatter? Either way, it's a grim fix to find yourself in, isn't it? To be wondering whether it's cancer or heart disease that will get you first?"

"I'd bet on his heart. He told me he's put on twenty-five pounds since January."

"I'm not sure I *want* to see him at the moment. I think the

technical term is *cachexia,* by the way. The medical term for wasting away." And now the mother bird's doing something she has
been doing for thirty-six years: feeding vocabulary to her fledgling.

I say: "Food seems to be a substitute for a social life."

"Count on Conrad to find a substitute more dangerous for him
than the alternative."

"The alternative?"

"Than promiscuous gay sex . . ."

It's a surprising remark from Sally. Despite all her travels, her
encyclopedic reading, and her running familiarity, as a doctor's
wife, with the medical hazards of intimate behavior, still the reticences of an upbringing in the shadow of the Christian Reformed
Church run deep. To this day, she's somebody who will flinch
involuntarily at an unexpected profanity. In addition, she's a great
one for family discretion; the Admiraals "don't go telling tales"
about one another. Finally, she remains prone to a vestigial impulse
(faintly ludicrous, given my age, and yet touching all the same) to
shield her child from the wilder forms of adult behavior. She had
made it quite apparent, over the years, that Conrad's romantic
forays are nothing the two of us ought to discuss.

So I feel I've been provided with a momentary opening, and I
leap into it: "Tell me about all that—about your dealings with
Conrad. When did you first guess the truth about him? Was it Wes
who told you?"

"No, it wasn't Wes. Was he in denial about his brother? Or
didn't know yet? I'm not sure, but it was Conrad who finally spoke
up. I'd had my suspicions, but he didn't actually come clean until
long after I'd divorced Wes and married Gordon, and I don't suppose that's any accident."

"Meaning . . ."

"Meaning, Conrad and I didn't really become friends, become
easy with each other, until after I divorced Wes."

"Because . . ."

"Because he couldn't really like me until I'd thrown Wes out? I don't know, Luke. I can't tell you how often, dealing with those brothers, I had to throw up my hands and say, *The waters are too deep for me.* You recently asked to see all my old Sultan photographs, and surely you've sensed it yourself: the extraordinary intensity of those two boys. They were simply more vividly *there* than other people. I don't mean to say a single thing against your father"—and there's a faint lurch in the conversation, a jarring recognition that in this particular conversation *your father* is an ambiguous phrase—"against Gordon, but that was something that took a little getting used to. Gordon didn't wear his intensity on his sleeve. In many people's eyes, I suppose he might have looked a little pallid beside those Sultan boys.

"And one of my first thoughts after I'd heard that Wes had passed away was, *Now Conrad can go too.* He'd won this particular race. Outlasted his brother. And the odd fact is, and I hope I'm wrong, but the odd fact is, I'll probably turn out to be right: I can't imagine Conrad will outlast Wes by all that long. I wouldn't be at all surprised if they both died at exactly the same age: sixty-two."

"Which gives Conrad only a year to go."

Sally's gaze holds steady, though she blinks rapidly. "I suppose it does."

I wind the conversation back one notch. "But eventually Conrad did level with you? About his social life?"

"Oh I don't know if he ever *leveled,*" Sally says. She glances round the brasserie. She wants another coffee. "If intensity was the primary trait of those Sultan brothers, deviousness wasn't far behind. Conrad likes to play games, and as the years went by, and he lost that aloofness of his youth, he volunteered all sorts of admissions. He became a great one for shocking non sequiturs. But I gather there was a time when he was very promiscuous. He certainly never had the knack of settling down with one person, I'm not sure why."

"Maybe because he's absolutely and utterly impossible?"

"That might have something to do with it. In any case, it's regrettable now, when he so much needs looking after, there's nobody to take care of him."

"But he talks to you about his illness? He always shuts the door in my face . . ."

"Well he *does* talk to me about it, albeit in his typically mordant and combative way. I suppose he likes to complain to me. This has something to do, I gather, with his notion that I—alone on the planet—lead some sort of charmed life. I can just see and hear him." Sally narrows her eyes, in impersonation of Conrad's hooded grin, and in a gruff, lowered voice declares, 'Has cancer struck *her* yet? Oh no, not *her,* not our Sally, despite all those cigarettes . . .'

Oh, but she has Conrad down! In this brasserie in the south of France, she has placed him before me in all his vast, exasperated merriment. I say to her, "I think he scares people off."

"He's had a hard time. He'd probably deny it now, but he had a very rough coming out. I don't mean to play amateur sleuth, it's presumptuous of me to talk about it, who am I to sit here sipping a fancy coffee in Mare aux Cerfs and making pronouncements about my ailing ex-brother-in-law in Miami?—but I've often thought that's the reason Conrad has no interest in anything you might call cultural life. Long ago, back in our Restoration days, when he didn't know anything, when *none* of us knew anything, and he was in a state of absolute denial, I think he came to the conclusion that cultural life was the province of women and homosexuals. Poetry, painting, classical music—it all belonged to the homosexuals. As such, it had nothing to do with Conrad Sultan, who cared only about running track and wrestling and throwing a football. And when it came time to find a profession, he wasn't going to be any hairdresser or dancer or interior decorator—God knows, he was going to be an accountant. And the rather sad and amazing truth is, I don't think he's ever conquered those initial prejudices. Am I making sense to you?"

"Quite a bit, I think. Though I gather there was one painting he coveted."

"Mm?"

"A Chicago street scene."

"Oh the famous *Michigan Avenue in the Rain*! You can't believe the battle waged over that one. The two brothers went to war."

"And Wes won."

"I suppose Wes won."

"By getting Adelle to say she'd only *lent* it to Conrad."

"Oh but you must understand: Adelle wasn't lying. No, I'm sure of it. No, by the time Wes got through with her, she was totally convinced that lending it is precisely what she'd done. He was very persuasive."

"So why the big battle? I gather the painting's ugly."

"Oh it's ugly all right. It looks like what it probably was: something you'd buy in a hotel lobby. Yet Dora loved it. Why? I think in her eyes it stood for everything that's cultured and refined. Chicago was a dream for her—as much as France has been a dream for me. That's why Conrad wanted it."

"And that's why Wes didn't want Conrad to have it?"

"Oh I suppose."

"It became a question of which boy was in fact the rightful owner of Mother's dreams."

"I like how you've put that."

"Thank you."

"But I was telling you about Conrad's innate conservatism, his I'm-an-ordinary-accountant's uneasiness with certain forms of out-landishness. You know, I was in a swanky restaurant in Miami with him when the maître d' seated a man and woman at the table beside us. Well, it became clear in one minute that this was a gentleman of very florid, feminine gestures. And clear in another minute that the woman *was* no woman. And what was so interesting was Conrad's response: *It drove him up the wall.* We had to leave; we couldn't even stay for the drinks we'd ordered. And this wasn't twenty years ago; it was in the last year or two. Given his love of shocking remarks you might think nothing would have pleased him better than to take me to such a place—but oh no, he was miserable.

"And in some obscure way it's all connected to his hatred of California. Miami was meant to be lively but also grounded and *unweird*. He wanted to be near the beach, he wanted to see the young men, I suppose, and it may be hard to envision but Conrad on a beach was himself once something to see: He exuded physical *strength,* as well as an athlete's grace, and I remember one occasion when a storm was blowing in, and the sea was all a shiny silver gray, and the sky was silver gray—Winslow Homer colors—and out of the breaking waves looking just like some sort of Greek god strides bronze Conrad. The man was truly beautiful.

"So it made sense he loved the beach, unlike Wes. And yet he didn't want to be out on the West Coast with what he called 'all the weirdos.' Sometimes Conrad could sound more like your average accountant than your average accountant."

"Tell me about Wes and the beach."

"Wes? I suppose he felt bested by Conrad. He was like you—his skin never would take a tan—and he fretted that his shoulders were too narrow."

"He felt like a weakling?"

"Oh it was all so ridiculous. Wes was so handsome, with or without his clothes! You know what was maybe the most amazing thing about him? It was the way he stayed so handsome, whatever

level you inspected him on . . . I mean that man had truly beautiful *ears!* Most people's ears are nothing to write home about—
mine have kept me from wearing my hair up for years—but I
remember one day looking at Wes's ears and realizing they were
picturesque. Like fabulous glowing seashells. And when he went for
a physical, I don't doubt for a minute the doctor with his tongue
depressor used to marvel at what gorgeous tonsils Wesley Sultan
had."

"I met Tiffany recently. And the twins."

"Tiffany?" Sally sips deeply from her empty coffee cup. "And?"

"And she was pretty much what I'd envisioned. But the reason
I mention it is because I was amazed, really, how much little Jess
resembles Wes. You talk about gorgeous Wes with the flashing blue
eyes—well I've recently seen the six-year-old version."

"That girl's going to have men jumping out of office buildings
for her."

Yet for all of Sally's cheer and levity, melancholy weighs the
corners of her eyes. And why not? How could she fail to experience some heartache at the notion that the purest radiance she'd
ever known—Wes's charm, Wes's charisma—has been reborn in a
world removed from hers?

"We should go back," she tells me. "You need to lie down,
you need to sleep. Then I want to hear all about your visit with
Tiffany . . ."

So we amble back through the sunlight to Sally's new apartment. She brings out for display her French textbook, her class
notes, her homework assignments. She is enrolled at the Académie
Varoise de la Langue Française, an institution whose sole building
is, she tells me, far less imposing than its name. Her instructor is the
iron-haired Mme. Guendouzi, the most immaculate human being
in God's creation, who has branded two of Sally's homework
assignments *"un peu sale."* None of the students, not one, has

escaped the stigma of being *sale,* not even Mme. Jeong, a young Korean woman who during class incessantly scrubs her hands with Handi Wipes. Meanwhile I find something hugely heartening in Sally's amusement with her classmates, and in her flexible ability to transplant herself and flourish in a new routine and a new home— and also I find here something reproachful, as my thoughts drift to the fly-by-night little apartment on East Seventy-ninth Street where I've lived the past two years. (And this is perhaps the place to acknowledge publicly what these pages doubtless have already reflected: With each paragraph assembled here, I'm feeling a stronger impulse to step forward and plant myself center stage. It's a temptation I mean to resist, largely restricting myself to those parentheses and brackets so congenial to the mathematical mind, or at least to the ex–math major—though I do intend, as a reward for good behavior, to grant myself the last word . . .)

I go upstairs and lie down for half an hour, until I realize that, although my brain's loopy with fatigue, I'm not yet ready to sleep, and we climb into the Renault and I drive down to the beach.

In the summer, this narrow stretch of sand (on one side encroached upon by a string of hotels and brasseries and bike-rental shops, on the other by an incoming tide that pushes its prone bathers back upon themselves) must be a dense tapestry of flesh. But on this warm, sunny Saturday in October, it's relatively empty. There are people playing badminton, and a scatter of children are chasing a yapping little terrier. I strip down to the bathing suit under my trousers and walk steadily into the cold sea, which deepens rapidly.

I'm a poor swimmer, and a distrustful one—a fitting grandson to the Chester Sultan who drowned in Lake Huron in 1942. When I let go of the land, dropping my legs behind me, I shiver with a midwesterner's instinctive uneasiness at the sea's sweeping power. When was the last time I swam among waves? I can't recall—can't recall anything, for it seems one result of my surrendering to the sea is the washing away of the very underpinnings of my memory. Pushed mindlessly this way and that, I couldn't put a sentence together if I tried. It's all I can do to count one by one as I breaststroke into the bobbing swells—ten strokes, twenty strokes, thirty, forty, fifty. A wave splashes into my mouth and the Mediterranean's ancient salt flavor on my tongue (a flavor that, way down deep in the brain, ought to taste like home) is a shocking, burning thing. I give up the fight, circling round and capitulating into a sidestroke which, with the sea's help, brings me within moments back to shore.

People talk about the moon's "borrowed light." My mother sits in borrowed shadow, that of somebody's else's vast umbrella. Its owners must have set their towels and picnic basket beneath it hours ago. The sun has since moved on, and the umbrella's shadow along with it, inching into an empty stretch of sand now claimed by Sally. Even in the shade she wears a long-sleeved cotton turtleneck, a floppy straw hat, and sunglasses. Her skin, unlike mine, can hold a tan, but neither of us has ever had much use for the sun.

Still, it's hugely cheering to have before us a shifting, shouting parade of nearly nude souls—people whose skins lap up the sun the way a cat laps cream. Spirits are high. Under the dark shade of our umbrella, shuttered behind our sunglasses, we might almost be moviegoers sitting in a darkened theater. The film we are watching is called *An October Day on a French Beach*. With a cast of dozens, if not hundreds. People drift by; conversations chase one another down the sand. It's all a shaggy-dog story, in which a shaggy dog actually materializes—far down the beach, its body prone on a towel, confronting the incoming waves with noble, leonine placidity.

Torsos are narrower than they would be at home.

A few of the women are topless.

Sally says, "To think I grew up in a house where dancing wasn't permitted. Along with cardplaying and theatergoing, it was one of the 'notorious trio.' You think I'm kidding, but the phrase is genuine, I believe it came down as an official Synod pronouncement. Such activities were invitations to the devil. And somehow I wind up on a topless beach. Honestly, if my parents could see me, their every worst fear would be confirmed."

Some twenty feet away, a young German woman (more girl than woman—she can't be older than eighteen) is playing an odd form of badminton. The racket is shorter than a conventional racket and the birdie is broader and solider. She is wearing no top and the bottom half of her bathing suit is a crisp V about the size of a pocket handkerchief. Her legs are lean and muscular and her breasts are high and full and am I the only person on the beach who feels that under the circumstances there's something wonderfully improbable in the concentration she invests in her game? For she's quite skillful, and her boyfriend/opponent (a hollow-chested ponytailed kid also wearing a V of a suit, who might play better if he didn't insist on keeping a cigarette poked in his mouth) is no match for her. Farther off, a group of frantic small boys is repairing a sand castle undermined by the incoming tide. And farther still, little polycolored sailboats glide, the V's of their sails inverting the V's of the skimpy trunks on the narrow hips of the men and women bathers.

"I'm going to have my second smoke of the day," Sally says, and I watch—taking pleasure in her pleasure—as she ritualistically prepares for that first, finest puff on a brand-new cigarette.

As she exhales, she announces, "I'm feeling bad about something," and in fact this seems a perfectly opportune moment for an admission beginning *I'm feeling bad . . .* For Sally is radiating contentment, and on such a day, in such a place, nothing she might confess could possibly upset either one of us very much. She says: "Wes died owing me a substantial amount of money."

"But surely you're okay. Financially secure. If you're not, perhaps I could—"

"Sweet of you to miss the point, Luke. But I'm not upset on my own behalf." She inhales another cloud, exhales. "I'm upset on yours."

"On mine?"

"Let's face it. I'm never going to get that money back, am I? And if I hadn't given it to Wes, I could have set it aside for you. You've read my will, Luke. You know you're the principal legatee."

"So you loaned money to Wes?"

"After Gordon died. Different times. And I'm still feeling guilty about it. I tried to tell you before. That day in Domat, sitting in the abbey chapel. I meant to tell you then. But I suppose the place intimidated me; the fear of God got into me . . ."

"How much money?"

"Seventy-seven thousand seven hundred and fifty dollars."

"Hey, you weren't kidding."

"*Plus* interest, if anyone was counting, which of course no one is. In retrospect, that's one of the humorous aspects to it: Wes's absolutely *insisting* that the money be repaid with interest."

"Good Lord, it's a fair amount of money. Actually, I'm surprised, frankly. I thought Wes did okay, financially. They must have paid him decently at Great Bay."

"Not enough. And evidently less and less as the years went by. You know how the company nearly went under. He was working largely on commission, and the company was offering him less and less that anyone could sell. But it wasn't living expenses most of the money went to. It was investments."

"Investments?" And didn't I have a right to sound skeptical? Wasn't this my field, after all?

"You know how Wes was always scheming."

"That's something most people outgrow, after a loss or two: the schemin' and dreamin'. They learn to keep it down to a couple dozen lotto tickets."

"Oh I'm sure Wes bought those too—Wes bought the whole kit and caboodle, I'm afraid. At first it was some sort of diesel-engine company. And then I think a reforestation process. The truth is I didn't have the heart to refuse him. Wes was so desperate to break free and show everyone at Great Bay what he could do. That's the phrase he kept using, 'to break free.' How was I going to refuse him?"

"Now wait a minute. Let's just hold on one minute. Given that I'd made a career, a if I may so successful career, in investment banking, wouldn't you think he might have wanted to consult with me?"

"Wouldn't you think that that's why he wouldn't?"

Sally's logic is better than mine.

I say to her: "And you really thought you might get your money back?"

"That's it exactly: I really thought I *might*. Stranger things had happened in my dealings with Wes Sultan."

"And it's all gone?"

"I assume so, and I feel more guilty than I can say. I honestly cannot *tell* you how guilt-stricken it's left me feeling. I keep think-ing about Gordon, who was always so frugal about his savings, so conscientious about ensuring I'd be provided for after his death . . ."

The poor Catholic kid from Newark: That's how Gordon liked to picture himself. He, too, had wanted to break free and show them what he could do, and in his unflashy way he'd man-aged precisely that, with a solid medical practice and a lifelong habit (unimaginative but in the end irreproachable) of buying a few good blue chips and never budging from them. At his death, he'd left Sally an estate of just under $900,000, not including the house in Grosse Pointe and the condominium in North Carolina.

"So you're out eighty grand. Your finances are still in good shape."

"The fact is, until recently, when you left Gribben, I thought the money wouldn't much matter to you. That was my rationalization, you see."

"And it won't matter. For heaven's sake, listen, it's your money, not mine."

"Well, you may be sitting on a comfortable nest egg at the moment. But you don't have a job, dear, and I assume your funds are finite, just like the rest of ours. How long can you carry on like this? This is your third flight to France in a few months."

"I told you, the flights are free. When I left Gribben, I had over four hundred thousand miles banked in frequent-flyer accounts."

"But you don't have four hundred thousand now. Do you see what I'm saying? Things run out."

Things run out . . . The contingency Sally is pursuing is dark, and spooky—and almost as remote as, let's say, the cloud formations arranged over the town of Stags Harbor on my fourth birthday—my first birthday after my parents' divorce. My memories of earliest childhood are distressingly few. I do much better after Gordon came on the scene, when I was seven, but with his arrival, money worries ceased to be a primary concern. Only if I went far far back, where all my memories blurred into family folktales, could I find accounts of genuine necessity and exaction: that foul, fabled, ferocious land called Want, in which young Sally Sultan, having been disowned by her parents for divorcing Wes, sometimes was forced to swallow all pride and go hat in hand to borrow twenty dollars from a neighbor. A single mother, young Sally had watched her nickels and dimes with care, and still she sometimes would discover, at the end of the month, that she couldn't meet the electric bill, the phone bill, the car payment. What had those days been like for her? Of course Sally has always been a worrier—and back then she must have woken up fearful, and gone to her lonely bed fearful, she must have tallied the sums in her head, over and over and day after day, only to ascertain, as the vicious knot in her stomach pulled itself tight, that again she'd come up short . . . Everything in the passage of my own remembered life, which essentially began in Grosse Pointe and proceeded from there to Princeton and from there to Manhattan, was terribly remote from that dark land of Want. For me it was all something of a lark: I liked these tales about the basement apartment on Downward Lane.

Does it upset me to learn that Wes squandered some eighty thousand dollars of "my" money? Hell, I want Wes to have it—want to resurrect him and present him with the check myself. No, what pains me in Sally's tale is something else: the image of Wes as the classic doomed "small investor," plumping down his dream-stake on a roulette wheel spun by a hand he couldn't see, with all the gambling proceeds to be gobbled up by a "house" he couldn't identify. (There are times when—I have to think—virtually *every-one* in the investment game, even the most ruthless, greed-mad, gung ho capitalist, must feel something far more profound than deep reservations: occasional shuddering moments of true horror at a glimpse into a system that consumes the weak as thoughtlessly as a cruising shark tears the leg off a swimmer.)

"Luke, I know I should have drawn the line at ten thousand. Or let's say twenty. But I never could stand up to Wes. If I hadn't felt by rights it was *your* money, I suppose I would have given him everything I had."

"Never able to stand up to him? I hear otherwise, incidentally. Conrad tells me you once gave Wes a black eye."

Sally swings round and inspects me—her gaze asks, *Is this a story you're ready for?*—before taking a deep drag on her cigarette.

Then she says, "Do you want the short version or the long version?"

"The no-stone-unturned version. This sounds exactly like my sort of story. I want to hear how Sally Admiraal, well known for brushing away mosquitoes rather than swatting them, came to give my father a black eye."

"Well now"—she sighs—"this was shortly after Gordon died. Not more than a month or two. And one night there's a knock on the door and in comes your father."

"Come to pay his respects to the widow."

"I didn't know what he'd come for actually. Anyway, I led him into the kitchen. I'd just been to the grocery store.

"Was I in a shaken state? Yes, I was, Luke, because, expected though Gordon's death had been, the actual dying had torn me up. I don't mean merely that it made me *very* sad—though it did. And *very* lonely—though it did. It also made me irrational, and one sudden fear was that poverty would descend on me overnight. (Actually, maybe I would have been better off if this fear had continued to haunt me—it might have prevented me from subsidizing Wes to the tune of eighty thousand dollars!) In any case, I'd gone to the grocery and bought just the sorts of things I used to buy after Wes left us, when we hardly had two dimes to rub together: I bought Spam and deviled ham and tin cans marked down because they were dented.

"So now you have the background, Luke. And there we were, Wes and I, in the kitchen, and wouldn't you have thought, under the circumstances, with Gordon something like a month in his grave, and both of us in our fifties, Wes actually almost sixty, and a new father of twins besides, truly it never occurred to me that—that he would make a pass at me." Sally manages to look and sound outraged—or nearly manages it, for isn't there just a hint of merriment lurking at the corners of her eyes, and out along the vibrating edges of her voice? "But that's exactly what the man did! And he didn't seem to have a doubt in the world about the suitability of what he was doing! I told him to stop and he didn't stop. And I told him to stop and he didn't stop. And for just one moment I got very *angry.* It was one thing if Wes was always going to be having these affairs, but another if he was going to have one with me. I'd been his *wife,* and surely there's something unseemly about having an affair with your *wife.* In any case, I reached behind me and I—can you tell what popped into my hand?"

"A can of Spam."

And merriment comes out plain—it's dancing in her eyes—and Sally says something that, under the circumstances, could hardly please me more: "You've got the instincts of a real storyteller, Luke. A can of Spam is exactly what it was."

"Kapow."

"I'm sure *kapow* is a bit of an overstatement," Sally corrects me. "I didn't hit him *hard,"* she points out. "It felt more like a push than a hit."

"But you gave him a black eye."

"Well, he bruised easily. Like you."

My jubilant laughter appears to reassure her somewhat, even if she doesn't join in. She goes on, pensively: "And I do have to say, in many ways it was the most effective let's call it gesture I ever made toward Wes. I think I so flabbergasted him he never even *considered* making advances again. From that point on, we were on a completely different footing—one that lasted for the rest of his life."

"And that's a 'footing' I still don't fully understand. It would never have occurred to me, for example, that you were regularly lending him money . . ."

"You know what I think? I think it's time I had a glass of wine. Why don't we have a glass of wine?"

I throw on shoes and a polo shirt and we make our way up to the awninged terrace of one of the little cafés abutting the beach. Sally orders a kir royale and I do too, although at this point I hardly need a drink—sleeplessness has set my head aspin.

Sally and I have long had a tacit understanding that either one is free to cut off an uncomfortable conversation—we don't press each other too close—and I'm wondering whether by calling for wine she's shutting the door on a painful line of inquiry. But soon after our drinks arrive, she lights another cigarette and resumes the conversation where we'd left it:

"Surely you've discovered that Conrad can give you all sorts of information I just don't have. But I don't think even *he* knew how things stood with Wes and me these last few years. Wes kept turning up. The truth is, I didn't let on to anybody just how often Wes turned up. He was forever driving down from Restoration to Grosse Pointe, some hundred and eighty miles round-trip, often for nothing more than a cup of coffee. He always had a new problem, or a new scheme. I suppose I was a sort of adviser. I suppose I was his confidante."

"This was after Gordon died?"

"Mostly. No—not completely . . ." And it surprises me, it delights me: Who would have supposed this admission would bring a blush to Sally's cheeks?

"Of course there was never anything improper," she murmurs, but what do mere technicalities signify, in a case like this? When your conscience stands in the dock? When you already consider yourself guilty, as she manifestly does?

And it seems I understand a good many things all at once . . .

Even before Gordon died, Wes succeeded in beguiling Sally back into his world. Nothing untoward, no improprieties—no, no, and yet on the plane of the spirit he had conscripted her. There were contacts between them that had to be concealed from Gordon, and later, even after Gordon's death, contacts needing to be concealed from Tiffany . . . And I saw how Wes had largely triumphed, notwithstanding the famous Night When Sally Blackened His Eye with a Can of Spam: He contrived to lure her into that clandestine world—concealed meetings, small lies, ongoing chains of deception—where he was most comfortable.

Sally says: "It's very simple, really. Wes was a proud man. He didn't want everyone knowing it each time he hit a little snag. That's understandable." But her statement might as well be a question: *That's understandable?* There's an imploring note to her voice.

She goes on: "Wes sometimes felt people were hostile to him and the truth is people were probably even more hostile than he realized. People don't like womanizers. Maybe I ought to narrow my generalization and say, People in Restoration, Michigan, didn't like womanizers. Maybe they're commendable figures here on this French beach. But back there, and back then, it seemed *men* didn't like womanizers because I suppose they were jealous; and *women,* particularly married women, felt misused by them, at least afterward. The fact is, among my women friends, one or two of whom it later turned out had actually gone to bed with him, everyone wanted me to *hate* Wes.

"But honey, I could never hate Wes—at least not for long. I merely found him impossible to live with, which is another matter.

"You know what? I sometimes felt, watching the way people responded to Wes, and later thinking about the utterly heartfelt indignation that women who'd bedded my husband were willing to express on my behalf—I sometimes felt, and I know I shouldn't be saying this to you, do understand I don't mean this the way it may sound—I sometimes felt, about the whole range of romantic, of sexual, activity in the world around us, I felt that the one safe generalization is: *Almost nobody's happy.* Honestly, why else would they *care* so much who Wes was pursuing? There's simply so much unbelievable *resentment* in the way most people gossip about others' romantic lives. Why are small towns so poisonous? What were we all so afraid of in Restoration, Michigan? And in the Christian Reformed Church? If you listen not to the *what* they're saying but to the *tone* in which it's said, you understand that for many people the bitterest, most painful news they can ever possibly hear is: Two neighbors right down the street have been making love just like a pair of rabbits."

She brings out this last image as though it were daring, and new. Oh, there's something touching to the look of faintly addled triumph on Sally's face: For all her circumlocutions, she has struck a belated blow against those pharisees who were her husband's relentless attackers.

And would the people on this beach look more forgivingly on Wes? From underneath the café awning, the strip of sand seems a wholly indulgent place. The land of Cockaigne . . . The topless girl has set down her badminton racket to lie prone on an enormous Babar beach towel, while her boyfriend rubs suntan lotion into the tops of the backs of her thighs and into the slight pale overspill of her buttocks. A pair of pretty girls in bikinis—*young* ones, tiptoeing on the edge of puberty—stroll along, arms folded self-consciously across their chests; they are followed by a pack of five equally young boys, who call muttered assessments, ridicule, praise, pleas. Their words don't carry up to the café—and I wouldn't understand them if they did—but whatever they're saying stirs the girls to not quite suppressed smiles. And a man I'd idly grouped under what Sally calls Conrad's "orientation"—a handsome, bronze, slight-boned man who has paraded daintily up and down the beach in a pair of whisper-scanty turquoise bathing trunks—at last meets the figure he has been awaiting. It's a woman, as bronze as he is, and in greeting her he nuzzles his hips up against her hips, giving her a sort of crotch-kiss.

Sally signals to the waiter for a new round of drinks.

"Give me an example," I say. "Of some of the bitterness or hostility Wes faced."

"Well what about Bernie?"

"Bernie? Adelle's Bernie? Bernie hostile to *anybody*?"

"Yes, oh absolutely yes—Wes's own brother-in-law, sweet sleepy never-an-unkind-word-for-anybody Bernie. I remember returning to Restoration for a Christmas party—this was long after I'd married Gordon and we'd moved to Grosse Pointe—where Bernie had too much to drink, something he did maybe once a year. And he starts very earnestly explaining to me that deep down Wes is just like Conrad, I'm speaking sexually now, only Wes won't admit it. Do you see? According to Bernie, this accounts for the womanizing.

"And I said to him, 'Bernie, you're talking about somebody who used to be my husband.' I said, 'Wes may have all sorts of psychological quirks, and maybe he has trouble dealing head-on with the truth at times, but I can assure you that his attraction to women is genuine.'

"I got a little stern with Bernie, which was very gratifying. I felt like one of those Victorian spinsters in a *Masterpiece Theatre* production—you know, the mousy ones who can be counted on in the penultimate episode to reveal that they're going to stand on principle. And of course whenever anybody gets stern with Bernie, he collapses like a soufflé.

"But twenty minutes later he's back, more in his cups than ever, and he's developed a new theory. It's, heaven help us, sexual inadequacy. *That's* what's at the root of Wes's womanizing. He isn't able to perform, or he doesn't really enjoy it, and this is the shortcoming driving him so impulsively into the arms of new women.

"And once again I take him to task. I explain to Bernie that he's talking about somebody I've been married to, and I assure him that he couldn't be more wrong about this inadequacy business. Or about the other, either."

"The other?"

"The not enjoying it. I suppose I'm being vague and euphemistic with you, just as I was with Bernie, though afterward (many times over the years, in fact) I wished I'd spelled it out precisely, because I think frequently of something Wes used to say. It was a joke. It wasn't macho bragging, no, it was mock-macho bragging. It was a sweet boyish boast, that's all, but it was true nonetheless. He'd say, I love fucking—saying it with a sort of sweet boyish surprise, as if it was a revelation he'd never quite gotten over. And maybe *that's* what I should have told Bernie: *Wes loved fucking.*"

Well, it was the first time I'd ever heard the word on Sally's lips. Thousands of miles away, in the Restoration Christian Reformed Church on Grand Elm Street, no doubt the pulpit has just exploded like a giant kernel of popcorn. Still further off, in Heaven, stunned choirs of angels have broken off their eternal chanting. Yet things go on just the same on the beach at Mare aux Cerfs—where private parts are going public, and oil is being kneaded into flesh, and the entire frieze of warm near-naked bodies has given Sally license to confide matters she has never confided in me before. I'm struck by a sensation, as we sip our drinks on the café terrace, that all our recent conversations in France have been drifting toward this juncture: the one where seemingly no conversational terrain is off-limits and I can ask whatever I choose.

But how far do I—how far would anyone—want to pursue these things? Do I inquire now whether she recalls the evening of my conception? And what the two of them discussed that night? And precisely where the act was consummated, and in what position, and whether the resulting pregnancy was intentional? (Or were they hoping no child would result who might, thirty-six years later, pose such vexing questions?)

And why does her little anecdote elate me so?

Why? No doubt my pleasure is rooted in simple male vanity. (Obviously I'm keen to hear, coming off a failed marriage and an aborted career, that my often hapless, much-divorced, prematurely unemployed biological father was more than a caddish seducer—he was a memorable lover. Male vanity runs so deep that even among those Cistercians of the abbey of Coppée, doubtless there was some devout medieval monk who, kneeling at morning prayers in his unheated stone cell, savored the occasional thought that his father was a damned rogue . . .) But I'd like to think I was heartened too on Wes's behalf. For with each passing month in my quest I'd grown more solicitous of him: of the skinny high school kid with the big grin and the big ambitions, and of the old salesman with his white pompadour, befuddled to have arrived at a future where inhospitality awaited him at every doorbell . . . And while I'm pondering such questions, Sally takes up the narrative thread again. Oh, I know what *she's* doing. She is fulfilling a compact with a dead man. She is surmounting her natural reticence and modesty in order to do right by Wes—to do right to the father by way of the son:

"I'm happy to say I make no claim to wide experience in these matters. But I'm a woman who has been married twice, and I know what I know. And one of the things I know, and one of the things I should have made crystal-clear to Bernie, is that, A), Wes certainly wasn't motivated by any lack of pleasure, and, B), for him it wasn't merely a matter of his own enjoyment. Wes wanted to please. In most everything, Wes wanted to please.

"Needless to say, he was utterly flummoxed by the women's movement, calling into question, as it did, his old-fashioned gallantry. What was Wes going to do with hairy-legged women who resented his trying to open doors for them? In various ways he'd become quaint, and naturally he hated that. Anyone would. The sixties and seventies were hard for him. He didn't like rock music, he distrusted all those slovenly hippies who distrusted well-groomed salesmen. He had no interest in drugs. But one of the funny aspects to it all (you're probably too young to remember this, Luke) was that right about then the human race discovered something you might suppose they would have discovered aeons ago: that women were one half of the equation when a married couple went to bed. That's the way it felt for us in Restoration, anyway, where suddenly all those magazines that used to carry articles about how to slip-cover your sofa or how to keep your Thanksgiving turkey from drying out now began advising us on how to make our men more responsive in bed. In retrospect, it was all so wonderfully ludicrous! All my married friends, grown women with three or four or five children, had suddenly discovered the existence of sex. Suddenly the air buzzed with talk about women 'sensitizing' their men and I finally realized how ahead of the game Wes always had been. He may have become quaint and antiquated, and yet apparently he knew what all sorts of sophisticated, *au courant* men were just now beginning to learn. I shouldn't be talking this way, obviously I shouldn't be talking this way to you, I can't believe I'm speaking like this to you, Luke, but I used to get so God-damn excuse me *tired* of everybody slamming Wes. He wanted to bring *pleasure,* and you can say all you want about his being a narcissist, you can read a few magazine articles the way Bernie did and conclude that it was merely selfish egotism motivating Wes, but damn it surely selfishness that takes the form of generosity has something to be said for it."

"And what about Gordon?"

"Gordon?" And Sally looks at me blankly. I'd swear that she fails, for just an instant, to recognize the name of her second husband. And in all my interviews—with Sally, or Adelle, or Tiffany, or even Conrad—this seems to be the common motif: the moment when, as they're recalling Wes, an amnesiac glow slips over their features. Thinking of him, they forget everything else they ever knew. And it wouldn't surprise me to learn, despite all the wrongs done to her, that on her paralyzed deathbed Klara Kuzmak, too, shone for a moment at the thought of Wesley Sultan.

I say: "Gordon was the same way? As Wes?"

Just moments before, Sally had said, "I can't believe I'm speaking like this," and I too am marveling at the knowledge that never in our lives have we had a conversation as open as this one. And yet it seems that boundaries exist even in this new territory. What am I asking her, in effect, but *Hey, how was my adoptive father in the sack?* And this is none of my business. For if Sally has a duty to do right by Wes, she has a kindred duty to do right by Gordon. A curtain comes down—it seems my stint as a voyeur is over.

Sally says, "My whole life was different—everything was different—with Gordon. In many ways, I honestly feel he saved my life. He rescued me, he rescued the two of us. I think I'll have my third cigarette." But she has lost count. This is her fourth.

Sally says, "You know in his unflashy way I honestly think Gordon was a genuine hero. He had a gift that is far, far rarer than it ought to be, or than it's supposed to be: He truly forgave the insults and the slights inflicted on him. That takes a great soul. I've told you before how my parents initially disapproved of him. That was partly his Catholicism, but partly what they held against him was that he would consider marrying *me*—a divorcée with a little boy, living on Downward Lane."

"It's a Marx brothers joke: Nobody is suitable to marry our daughter who would agree to marry—"

"And of course that's it! That's just what it was. But then it turned out, as the years went by, there were benefits in having an ultracompetent doctor for a son-in-law. And when first Poppa and later Momma got sick, who was there to ensure that they got the very best medical attention available? And who was loyally at their bedsides every God-damned day—excuse me, somebody better shut me up, why is it I can't manage to get a sentence out today without cursing like a sailor?"

Sailors? Out beyond the last swimmers, a few dwindled poly-colored boats are drawing designs upon a sea like a pale chalk-board. Their little triangular sails are the symbols of a special kind of math—the geometry of the sensualist—and the curves they trace are a record of a pure pursuit of pleasure. Meanwhile, over-head, the sky's another sort of chalkboard. Employing another sort of chalk, a silver jet trails a feathery white line. Good Lord, it's a beautiful day . . .

I say: "I've been mulling over a remark of Conrad's, about you, which didn't make much sense to me at the time. He said you couldn't really do what you're doing now, couldn't move to France for months at a stretch, until Wes died. That you felt you had to be there for him."

"You know how Conrad overstates things . . ." Sally pauses, though, pulls reflectively on her cigarette, and changes her tack: "But I suppose I did feel somewhat solicitous. Toward Wes. Partic-ularly as his marriage came undone."

"So just how close were you and Wes at that point? How often did you talk to him after Gordon died?"

"It varied, honey, it depended on Wes. *He* always contacted me—or he'd just show up, in the middle of a Saturday afternoon, and was I going to throw the man out without a cup of coffee? I worried of course about Tiffany, about the suitability of my hav-ing tête-à-têtes with another woman's husband. That may sound ludicrously narcissistic, given that I'm not far from being a senior citizen and Tiffany is still a very attractive *girl*. But I certainly don't want to sound like Nancy Reagan at Charles and Diana's wedding, explaining that she chose her outfit so as not to upstage the bride!"

"You've got a ways to go before you sound like Nancy Reagan."

"The truth is Wes needed to talk. I used to pray—I'd pray nightly—that that marriage would hold together . . . And then things got still more complicated when Tiffany started telephoning me."

"Really? Often?"

"Often enough. Poor girl, I think she felt I might have useful insights into Wes's character—I might be able to help." Sally reaches too late for the ashtray. Her cigarette drops an exploding load of gray powder on the tabletop. "The fact is, I wanted nothing more in the world than to help her—to help them both. She was so young, she couldn't understand Wes's *vulnerability.* Of course I had to wonder how much good I'd done either one when they separated—"

"I gather she threw him out."

Sally winces, pulls again on her cigarette, then faces the truth straight on: "All right, when she threw him out."

"She says she had good cause. She . . ."

But this time I'm the one who hesitates. Does Sally know that Wes, even at the end, was propositioning his wife's friends? Perhaps she does. In any case, she cuts me off: "I'm sure she had good cause."

I break the ensuing silence. "Eighty thousand dollars."

"Honey, I can't tell you how ashamed I feel."

"You shouldn't. You were trying to help him."

"But I couldn't say no."

"Exactly. You couldn't say no."

Sally corrects me: "No, I mean I *couldn't* say no. I lacked the willpower. Do you see what I'm saying? I loved Wes."

"Of course you did."

"No, I mean I loved him. I mean I went on loving him. I mean, oh honey"—and the urgent raw exploratory look in her blue eyes tests me, and pleads with me—"I mean I was in love with him. I mean I was in love with that man until the day he died."

And now it seems the two of us have arrived at the last admission, the one situated even beyond her employment of a long-forbidden word: For we're speaking now of that variety of *love* which lies on the other side of *fucking.*

Until the day he died . . . My eyes drift over the pale chalk-board of the sea. Two things—it seems I recognize two things simultaneously. (But in actual fact one probably follows the other in rapid succession.)

I realize first that this woman, whom I consider the wisest person I've ever known, with all of her bookish wit and her endless measured qualifications and her great calm ironic but unbitter amusement at life, has always been a fool for love—a fool for the man with the picturesque ears and the marvelously good-looking tonsils.

And I realize that it's been precisely in her recognition of her essential nature, and her accommodation to it, that much of her wisdom resides.

Still staring out over the sea, I say to my mother: "So Conrad was mostly right. You wouldn't have felt free to move here while Wes was alive."

"All right: Yes, there's a good deal of truth in it. I couldn't let Wes stray *too* far away. I had to be nearby. Yet there's another impulse at work here. You must understand—this has been something of a lifelong dream of mine: someday I'd move to France and study French. You know the story of my studying French in high school."

"Your father wouldn't allow it."

"He disliked the French, who were a frivolous people. But we had a neighbor who was French, Delphine Queffelec, a war bride, who was willing to teach me. So I sneaked around; I learned it all catch-as-catch-can. And from the start, I dreamed of going back to the source, of learning things right."

She signals to the waiter. We're each going to have a third kir.

"The reason I go into it all again, Luke, is to show you that I've *always* had a sense of obstacles in my pursuit of French. Yes, right up until Wes's death there was always some reason why this aspiration of mine, this vision of myself sitting right here, in a little café on the beach near *the town where I live*—why it wasn't practicable.

"And I can't tell you how odd it is suddenly to be able to say to myself, *I can move to France if I want to.* Honey, I can't tell you how odd it is to have the obstacles at last removed.

"And why are they removed? It's because Poppa's dead, twenty years now, and Gordon is dead, whose practice kept him too busy for extended vacations in France, and Wes is dead, who may not actually have needed me around but who convinced me he needed me around, and whom I learned to keep at a distance but whom I couldn't bear to be *too* distant from, and my son is long grown and living on the East Coast, and it looks as though Conrad is dying. Let me tell you something: If you find the landscape of your life is open and clear, it's because it's unpeopled."

And how am I to reply to Sally, who looks so crestfallen and forlorn? I say, "Unpeopled? You have more friends than anyone I know . . ."

"You know who I miss? It occurred to me the other day: I miss God. I miss the fierce, fulminating, frightening Lord Almighty of my childhood. Not that I've joined the 'scoffers and naysayers,' as Momma used to call them, and yet at that Unitarian church I selected because it seemed so enlightened and so appealingly life-embracing I can't seem to locate a God who frets one way or another about what I or anyone else does. This is a God whose motto seems to be *I'm okay, you're okay.* And one more stern presence is subtracted from my life . . . No, the only deeply disapproving, censorious force left in my cosmos is Conrad, bless his prickly heart, and when he dies that will be one more obstacle, one more curb on my behavior subtracted. He'll no longer be there to chide me for my extravagance, or for daring to outlive my husbands, or for any of twenty other offenses. Heavens, I'll miss him. When he dies, I'll be one step closer to freedom—only think of the cost involved. The truth is, I'd give anything to have Wes materialize once more on my doorstep with one of his absurd get-rich schemes. It was all so gorgeous and seductive—those golden, dreamy plans for his new life. Honey, I'd love to let him let me toss another eighty grand down the drain . . ."

When I get back to the States, a strange envelope awaits me. After a moment I recognize the haphazard blend of capitals and lowercase, cursive and printing:

Dear Mister Luke Planter,

That first letter of yours got me to thinking and before long it got me doing some of what you call research of my own. Nothing much came of it until I went to an Aunt of mine here. She may be getting on in years, as they say, but she knows a lot more about a lot more than she lets on.

It seems there's been a good deal of lies being spread around here on all sides over the years but nobody did more of the Lying and the Spreading than old Wesley Sultan.

Though to judge from your last letter maybe you're just as big a liar as good ol' Wes ever was.

By the way if you're looking for your halfbrothers and halfsisters I hope you understand, the list doesn't stop with me.

I already wished you luck with your <u>research</u>. When you're all finished with it I hope you'll print it up in a great big deluxe HEAVY book. Then I hope you'll tie it all up with a gold ribbon, and tie the other end to the end of your dick, and go toss it over the side of the nearest bridge.

Wesley Giardina

CHAPTER ELEVEN

and the Commodore Hotel in Stags Harbor,

RESTORATION—Wesley Cross Sultan, ~~63,~~ *62* of 2135
N. Westhampton, died suddenly in Lyon Hospital in
Stags Harbor, of heart failure. He worked for Great
Bay Shipping for 42 years, chiefly in sales. He began
his career in the Stags Harbor office, and after stints
in Kalamazoo and Cincinnati, Ohio, he finished his
career back at Stags Harbor. He ~~retired two years~~ *was effectively*
~~ago~~ in order to pursue full-time his civic pursuits. *fired two years*
He was ~~an active~~ *a nominal* member of the Rotarians, the *ago but claimed*
Restoration Chamber of Commerce, the Stags Har- *to be retiring*
bor Betterment Society, and the Thumb of Michigan
Prosperity Council. He was also active in the Restoration Episcopal Church, where for many years he sang
in the choir.

He was born in Restoration and ~~was a graduate~~ *attended but*
~~of~~ the old High School on Cherrystone Avenue. He *did not quite*
was the son of the late Chester Sultan, the well- *graduate from*
known businessman, and the grandson of Hubert
Sultan, who served as the mayor of Restoration from
1908 to 1912. Old-time Restorationists will recall
Sultan Furniture on Union Street, founded by Hubert
and presided over by Chester until he closed its
doors in 1935.

He was married ~~twice. His first wife was~~ Sally *three times. His*
from whom he Planter (Admiraal), now of Grosse Pointe, formerly *first wife was*
was formally of Restoration. They were divorced in 1964. He *Klara Kuzmak,*
separated at leaves his wife, Tiffany, and their two daughters, Jes- *He then married*
the time of sica and Winnie; a son, Luke Planter, of New York; a
his death, brother, Conrad Sultan, of Miami, Florida; and a sister, Adelle De Vries, of Battle Creek. *with whom*
he had a son,
half- Wesley Jr.'

He may have left other
children as well.

Just outside Restoration there's a popular diner, O'Donnell's,
located beside the Michicabanabee River. The restaurant's builders
had two constructions to think about—the restaurant itself and its
parking lot—and you might suppose, mathematically, that they had

a 50 percent chance of getting it right: of setting the restaurant beside the scenic river. But, predictably, they did it the other way round, placed the parking lot next to the Michicabanabee and the restaurant beside the parking lot, so that diners have a view not of the river wending down through pine and birch and hemlock, but of large, hungry people unpacking themselves from their minivans and pickups, marching purposefully toward great platters of chicken-fried steak and beer-batter onion rings and Hawaiian macadamia hot-fudge sundaes . . .

I breakfast at O'Donnell's and head west across the state to Battle Creek. It's a discouraging, billboard-plastered drive. Given a fifty-fifty chance of getting things right, here were my fellow Michiganders consistently getting them wrong. *Oh my home state!* I'm thinking as I cross into Pheasant Ridge, surely one of the ugliest housing developments on God's green earth. *Things don't have to be this dismal!* is the thought uppermost in my mind as I pull into Adelle and Bernie's driveway. This is weather to accentuate the unsightliness in anything and everything. It's a dark leafless November day and the lusterless sky looks like a painted backdrop of coat after coat of leaden gray. Sunlight, moonlight, starlight— no hint of a glint could ever pierce such a color. Having passed literally hundreds of TV satellite dishes on my drive, I find it only fitting that I wind up parking underneath one, and discover Bernie watching a football game.

Bernie is so often the butt of family jokes (not only from Conrad, who is dependably ferocious, but even sometimes from Sally) that it isn't easy to regard him fully as a person in his own right . . . He seems placed on the Sultan family stage purely as a provider of comic relief. Bernie's a big slope-shouldered man in his fifties, with a baggy sagging face and a haircut that belongs on a little boy: a full head of downy sandy-brown hair forever springing up in unruly cowlicks. It creates a constant impression—often accurate—that he has just risen from bed.

We shake hands in the living room, I talk a little about the drive. Bernie asks me about New York, about my mother's stay in France, about Conrad's health . . . but all the while his gaze keeps stealing to the TV screen. Adelle repeats an offer, already extended a number of times over the phone, that I stay on here in Pheasant Ridge for Thanksgiving dinner, now only two days away. "Our guest room is just crying out for visitors"—she squeezes my arm—"and we'd adore having you, wouldn't we? Bernie?" And Bernie, perhaps sensing that freedom's to be won through a conscientious attention to hostly responsibilities, tears his gaze from the television and declares, "We would be just *thrilled,* Luke. Truly, indeed we would."

I follow Adelle out to the kitchen, leaving Bernie to his game. I sit at the kitchen table, taking the same chair I occupied a few months ago, beneath the framed sampler proclaiming HOME IS WHERE THE HEARTBURN IS. This time, instead of breakfast cereal / marshmallow / chocolate chip / butterscotch chip squares, Adelle offers me pumpkin cookies, maple pecan cookies, and another pile of charred gingerbread men.

"You need to rest a moment," she tells me. "Then we'll be off."

She and Bernie have promised me a "tour of the town."

She points out the two postcards on the refrigerator from my mother and nods in a dazed, respectful manner as I explain about Sally's French classes. Adelle is visibly in awe of this woman who divides her time between Detroit and North Carolina, who jets around the world by herself, and who (perhaps most to the point) may be the only woman in the world whom Wes could never put fully behind him.

Adelle sees my glance drift over to the needlepoint sampler and says, "I suppose you think it's *kitsch,* don't you?" and the truth is *kitsch* isn't a word, or a concept, I would have expected Adelle to come up with. "But I like *kitsch,*" she goes on, and the point is obvious, isn't it? That even here, in the De Vries household in Pheasant Ridge, a suburb of Battle Creek, life is being lived in an atmosphere of self-conscious irony. Even the woman who lives beside the needlepoint sampler that says HOME IS WHERE THE HEARTBURN IS sees herself as gently lampooning the sort of woman who lives beside a needlepoint sampler that says HOME IS WHERE THE HEARTBURN IS.

"Actually, if it's all right with you—" Adelle begins, and the expression on her face is so dire, it's as if she's about to confess to something calamitous. But it turns out her news is simply that Bernie won't be coming with us. He hardly slept a wink last night. And she's pretty sure he's coming down with a cold.

So Adelle and I climb into my rented car. It has begun to drizzle. She guides me through the wet streets. She also tells me about her neighbors the Crumleys, Herb and Bev, whom I would be meeting if only I were able to accept the Thanksgiving invitation. And about the raccoons that made a home in the neighboring elementary school. And about the son of the local police chief, recently arrested in Chicago for shoplifting more than three hundred dollars' worth of merchandise from a place called Delilah's Closet. Women's lingerie—do you believe it? And about the flooding in the basement. And about her neighbors the Donaldsons' poodle, Buckles, hit by a firetruck (although Adelle herself believes it wasn't really an accident but a kind of suicide, the Donaldsons treated Buckles so shabbily). I make no effort to steer the conversation. Though I scarcely know this woman—my aunt from a marriage that ended a few years after my birth—I know her well enough to understand that any conversation must circle round to Wes before long.

It turns out that I'm visiting the "best-known city of its size in the world" (a determination probably arrived at by the local chamber of commerce). Of course it owes its renown to the Kellogg brothers, John and Will Keith, who a hundred years ago made Battle Creek a health center to the nation. The word *sanitarium* was coined by John, Adelle tells me. It's a shame—she goes on—that tours are no longer given at the Kellogg's factory. In its place is Kellogg's Cereal City USA, our destination.

Cereal City turns out to be a closely guarded, security-conscious land, wary of kidnappers and hostage-takers. Specifically, it frets about its three favorite sons, those little rascals Snap! Crackle! and Pop!, who never go anywhere without the constant bodyguard of a trademark symbol. In the museum's prose, this makes for an odd mixture of whimsy and legalese: "At the top of every hour, Snap!™ Crackle!™ and Pop!™ race around the silo with Tony the Tiger™ announcing the winner." Adelle and I watch a film in which Sunny the Sun and the Sweetheart of the Corn introduce us to the Kellogg brothers. We wander through the museum, peering at old photographs, old cereal boxes, and old black-and-white televisions that have reached that previously only theoretical limit of program-free programming: They show nothing but commercials.

Dr. John Kellogg was, it turns out, an evangelist, touring the country on behalf of his meat-free, smoke-free, sugar-free, caffeine-free, alcohol-free vision of "biologic living." He wanted nothing less than to reform the nation's diet. Doubtless it's no one's fault—it's simply the way of the world—that the doctor's original mission was lost. The town that once tried to market lima bean flakes, as a boon to national health, now traffics in Cocoa Frosted Flakes and Sugar Pops.

We don't stay long in Cereal City USA™. We drive to downtown Battle Creek, such as it is, and slip into a cavernous bar/microbrewery, where we both order amber beer.

"You were talking about Thanksgiving," Adelle says, but of course it's she who has been talking of Thanksgiving, she who has been doing nearly all the talking today.

"Right." The beer turns out to be delicious.

"Well, I found something that might interest you."

And what she unearths from her purse indeed interests me very much. It's a color snapshot of Wes. I suppose he must be at least sixteen, although he doesn't look it. His double-breasted suit is presumably one of those inherited from his father—one which his mother allowed him to alter when he turned sixteen. He is stand-ing before a colossal Thanksgiving turkey, wielding outsize carving utensils. He is very much the man of the house—or such is his aspiration. The photograph suggests a daunted clumsiness. This bird's splendid carcass is too much for Wes. Doubtless the task would be better taken in hand by Conrad (by the skinny little kid with the crew cut, staring so intently, so acquisitively at the plump golden bird), whose athlete's general confidence of movement has already, in his early teens, declared itself.

"Oh, I *like* this," I tell her. "It's a very appealing picture. Isn't it amazing how much the young Wes resembles little Jessie? You know I went to see Tiffany since I saw you last."

"*Tiffany?* If I was you, I wouldn't have anything to do with *her,* Luke. *I'd steer clear.*"

The vehemence, the raw hostility of Adelle's response is not at all what I expect. Last time we got together, she seemed so proud about having "no problem" with Tiffany. I say, "Oh I don't have anything to *do* with her. It was the first time I'd met her, actually."

"Steer clear, is what I say." And so baneful a look clouds Adelle's face, she might be warning me against cobras, or opium, or elephantiasis. Her glass of beer, most of which she has already downed, has left a foam mustache on her upper lip. "Steer clear of the little *bitch.* That's what I say. Oh she'll manipulate you. Just like she manipulated Wes. You have to understand, she's one of those women who gets anything they want. She wants a child, here's a child—here's *twins,* for God's sake. That's what Wes gave her. She wants a house instead of an apartment? Okay, here's a house."

It's an unlikely scenario, Lord knows: Wes the sugar daddy. Does Adelle understand that Sally, deep in the background, played the role of secret banker? Does Adelle have any idea that Wes died eighty thousand dollars in his ex-wife's debt?

Adelle races on: "You know I went back too, back to Restoration since I saw you last. And I found something out—yes I did. I didn't actually see Tiffany, but I did talk to a friend of mine who happens to have been a neighbor of theirs, of Wes's and Tiffany's, and you know what she told me? Something very interesting. You know what she told me? She said that Tiffany found another man. And *that's* why she threw Wes out, do you believe it? She found another man."

"Yes," I say, "I think I'd heard something like that."

"You'd *heard* it?"

And Adelle's sharp little eyes stab at me . . . Oh, she's all riled up: What in the world was *I* doing knowing secrets about Wes that *she* didn't know?

I say: "I guess I heard it from Conrad. Or maybe Sally."

"Well that makes it worse. Much worse, doesn't it?" Adelle's voice has lifted. It's become a cry of injustice: "It's even worse that Tiffany would be so *open* about it, isn't it? That *everyone* would know about it. It's all just so whore-y, do you believe it? She'd go after *any*body."

*Any*body? I feel a dumb warm blush climb my face at the thought of Tiffany's open wet kiss of farewell . . .

And Adelle hurtles ahead. It's as if having drunk a beer, or simply being in a bar with a beer before her, has given her license to become someone else entirely. The woman who bakes cereal squares in her suburban ranch house has been transformed into a foam-mustached, tough-talking middle-aged barfly. "Well I'll tell you something else, something maybe you didn't already know, did you know Wes had found somebody new by the end? When he was staying at the Commodore?"

"No," I say, "I didn't know that."

"That's just the *point,* isn't it? Your not knowing. Because Wes believed in discretion. I think I was the only one he told." And she regards me triumphantly.

"And who was the someone?"

"Well, not to gossip. Wes had discretion? I do too."

"I don't mean to pry."

"So this mustn't go beyond this table. I'm not sure even—"

"Honestly, if it's confidential—"

"Her name was Nancy Croker."

"And what does she do?"

"She was just someone Wes *met.* It's not what she does. I guess she works at the Department of Motor Vehicles. I guess they met when he was renewing his driver's license."

"And she's—how old is she?"

"Late forties? And not *nearly* pretty enough for Wesley, if you want the truth, but at least she was a genuine, caring person. She had a real cross to bear, but she wasn't a whiner how Tiffany was. She has a boy locked up in Jackson. Selling horse."

Horse? I nearly laugh aloud . . . Surely Adelle has been watching too much TV.

"Is that right?"

"Heroin."

"Yes. And Wes? He was seeing a lot of her?"

"Oh I suppose so. He moved a lot of his things out there. She lives in Gastaw. But it wasn't anything, really. I think he was lonely at the Commodore, anybody would be."

"But he kept his room at the hotel?"

"Absolutely. He wasn't going to commit to Nancy if his heart wasn't in it. They both understood that. It was just a physical arrangement. There were no illusions, no deceptions, no false hopes."

Hearing the blithe tone of "just a physical arrangement," you might suppose this was a world Adelle was on intimate terms with. But one glance at her face assures you otherwise. The uncomfortable truth about Adelle is that it's hard to believe any male ever looked upon her with potent desire—even thirty years ago—and impossible to believe, if there was such a person, that he happens to be the man reclining before the TV set in the living room back in Pheasant Ridge. Still, this hasn't slowed her down, or soured her. She's a good soul. And the most fiercely protective mourner anyone could ask for. The spirit of goodness assumes all sorts of forms, but perhaps it's never so touching as when it emerges in someone you might expect to feel shortchanged by life.

Adelle says: "It was one way to heal himself."

"No one told me . . ."

"Well it wasn't something anybody advertised. And Nancy wanted things kept quiet, for obvious reasons. She was in the middle of a divorce herself."

And what is going on inside my head as I sip my beer and this latest revelation unfolds? Not much surprise, obviously: How long could Wes be expected to live a celibate's life in the Commodore Hotel? No, I suppose what I'm mostly feeling is a mixture of weariness and chagrin. Am I always going to come upon another twist in the road? And what am I supposed to do now—track down Nancy Croker?

I say, "Did Tiffany know about her?"

"It wouldn't surprise me. She's a terrible gossip obviously. But Wes did want to keep it from her. Despite everything, he was still hoping to reconcile. If only for the children's sake."

"But he really loved Tiffany, didn't he? And he was heart-broken when she threw him out?"

Adelle hesitates—even though I'm merely echoing everything she told me during my last visit. If I'm reading her expression correctly, a pair of opposed forces is contending inside her. On the one hand, she clings resolutely to this image of Wes as a victim of unjust heartbreak, retreating to his sister for solace and counsel. On the other, it grieves her to grant Tiffany so much lasting authority, such unmerited powers of attraction.

But the outcome is in little doubt—for in the end Adelle's priorities are fixed. Her allegiance belongs to her dead brother. She says, "Well of course. Of course he did. That's how Wes was—so sensitive. He always was. There'd been other women, over the years, who broke his heart."

"Tell me about them," I say.

"It just happened. Over the years. That was the thing about Wes almost nobody understood about him. He was the last thing from a playboy. He took it all so seriously. And poor kid, he never learned just how hard the world could be: Time and again, he'd wind up heartbroke, that was Wes." Abruptly, Adelle's conversation takes a sharp, veering turn: "Are you seeing anyone special, Luke?" And the beak of her nose is aimed at me.

"Special? Me?"

"Anyone in particular?"

"No—nobody in particular. Not at the moment. I mean, it's not as if I'm not open to—"

"I heard you had a nervous breakdown when she ran left. Angelina. When she ran off with—"

"You mustn't believe everything Conrad tells you. It *was* Conrad, wasn't it?"

My aunt deals me a sly and self-congratulatory look, one that announces, *I don't reveal my sources.* Then she drives her point home: "When I heard you had a breakdown, I said to myself, That's Wes's boy all over."

Under the circumstances, it's not a link I'm eager to ratify. I say to her, "Oh I hope to find somebody else soon. It's just—I guess I'd like to finish all this first."

"All this what?" my Aunt Adelle asks me. "I don't follow."

"Finish this project, I guess. As you know, I've gotten very interested in my father—in the whole Sultan family, you and Conrad, too, the full story. I've been trying to figure out Wes's life. That's my project."

"It's quite a big job," Adelle notes.

"Bigger than I ever thought."

"That's what I discovered. Because I had to do much the same thing."

"The same?" Needless to say, *I'm* hardly following *her* . . .

"Figuring things out. Just like you. And I had a deadline to deal with."

I say, "I'm not quite sure I see—"

"Why, when I wrote the obituary."

It's as though I've been winged in the head by a rock. I simply don't know what to say . . . "The one in the *Restoration Oracle*?"

"That was me."

And the look upon my aunt's face? I read there uncertainty, and an appetite for praise, and the burnished, abiding pride of published authorship.

"I just assumed someone at the paper wrote it."

She accepts this as a handsome compliment. We've ordered new mugs of beer and her deep, plunging swallow links her to factory workers all over the planet; it's the deservedly satisfied swallow of someone whose eight-hour shift is over, a reward for work well done. "Well-l-l," she sighs. "They didn't have one prepared. Can you believe it? Grandson of the former mayor, and they don't have one prepared! And they were short-staffed, on account of the flu epidemic. Obviously, Sally was the one to have written it. She's the journalist. She would have done it so much more beautifully than I could, *you* know her gift for language. But she didn't want to."

"Maybe she thought it wasn't her place—since she and Wes were divorced."

"Maybe." Sally's elevated motivations evidently are not meant to be questioned—only accepted. "So I did it. I wrote it, and I submitted it. Of course they edited it. They said it didn't 'fit the usual format.' Whatever that means. I told them, 'Wes didn't fit the usual format either.' That's what I said: Wesley Sultan didn't fit any usual format. And I started with ten typed pages, which they said was much too long. They said they wouldn't give Michael Jackson that long a one, if *he* died, and I told them in fact Wes was a much better singer than Michael Jackson, who I'm told won't go anywhere without all those hocus-pocus special effects."

"I gather he had quite a nice voice. Wes."

"He had one of the God-damned finest voices I've ever heard," Adelle recklessly cries, and dips into her beer, surfacing with a freshened creamy mustache. "Nothing fancy—there was nothing fancy about Wes's singing. It was just pure beauty. That's all: pure beauty. You had to appreciate pure beauty, to appreciate Wes's voice."

We finish our beer and drive back home through the drilling rain. The gray day's steadily darkening. By the time we're seated in Adelle's kitchen once more, the sky's a black presence against the windowpanes. Bernie is snoring in the living room. The television is running.

I say, "I suppose ten pages was a little long for a local newspaper."

"What do you write about someone you've known your

whole life? What do you say about your own brother? Obviously, you put down the facts, you get all the little details right—"

"Obviously."

"But that isn't the whole story, is it?"

"Not by a long shot."

"And when do you quit? When do you know you're finished?"

Oh, she has hit the very question—the thorn that daily jabs at me. When and where *do* I quit? Is my next stop to be the Department of Motor Vehicles? Or one step further—the jail that holds Nancy Croker's horse-peddling son?

I say to her, "Well in my case, I think I'm nearly through."

"And what do you do with it? What do you do with everything you've assembled, everything you've learned?"

And an unexpected fierceness colors Adelle's voice, and colors her creased and devoted, homely face. On either side of that vast nose of hers, the little eyes have flared up with grease-fire quickness. Her artist's portrait was finished—ten whole pages—and no one would ever ask her for another. *But what was she supposed to do with it?*—and with the collection of Wesley Sultan anecdotes which hadn't fit into it and which she, with a diligence and an ardor and a single-mindedness that utterly eclipsed my efforts, had collected over a lifetime? Don't the two of us share—who share so little—a common passion and avocation? And isn't she saying to me, *What do I do with my life?*

Sometimes it all seems preordained: a homely middle-aged woman sits in the homely kitchen of her homely home, a plate of burned and broken gingerbread men stacked like so many accident victims before her, while in the living room a sportscaster drones over the slumped, slumbering torso of her husband, and what does she finally say but *What do I do with my life?*

And what is her nephew to reply?

What can I possibly give her? Her face hardens, her eyelids flutter (her pain is suddenly palpable), and I very much want to give her something. It's impossible not to like Adelle: the loyalist, the archivist, the keeper of the flame.

I say, "That's why I'm so glad to talk to you. You remember so much."

But it seems I haven't quite hit on the right words, or the right gift. She replies, "Bernie says my memory's my curse, it keeps me living in the past." And she goes on looking miserable.

I say, "I'm sure Wes would be touched, to be remembered so lovingly," which does soften the creases in her face, though she points out, "Bernie says I only look at one side. He says I have a blind spot for Wes's weaknesses."

I say, "I suppose men in particular can be hard on Wes," and she says, "Bernie certainly can be. He thinks there was something wrong with Wes, that's why he chased after women so much," and suddenly I think I see my way clear . . .

I recall Sally's description, on the beach at Mare aux Cerfs, of her run-in with Bernie at the Christmas party where, emboldened with drink, he'd presented his theories about Wes's "inadequacies." Oh, Sally was right about Bernie: From the misleading softness of his La-Z-Boy recliner, he has been waging a limited war for years—sniping at Wes, working to undermine Wes. And maybe you can't blame Bernie in the end. Years ago, he married a woman who embraced wholeheartedly a male ideal he himself could never emulate. What marital recourse was left him but to work, from the depths of his La-Z-Boy, toward the bankruptcy of her dreams, toward her inner life's impoverishment?

What was there for him to do but to tell her, over and over, that her idol was tarnished?

And what is there for me to do but snipe at the sniper? I long to say to her, Bernie has it all wrong. Long to set before Adelle's eyes the young cock of the walk, the kid-husband who would jubilantly announce to his kid-wife, *I love fucking.* My destination is clear . . .

"So he started up with another woman after Tiffany," I begin. "Stayed active right until the end, did he?"

"Oh Nancy wasn't really anything. She doesn't count."

"Other men often must have been jealous of Wes—of his appeal to women."

"His whole life, that's what it was: hounded by jealousy."

"You know you read so much nonsense. Just recently I was reading an article somewhere, all about how anybody involved with lots of women must have psychological problems. But what about gays, what about Conrad? Does he have a psychological problem if he takes a lot of men for partners?"

"You're absolutely right he's got a problem. Conrad seems *troubled* to me; doesn't he seem *troubled* to you?"

"No but my point was actually the very opposite one, that mere promiscuity per se hardly means—"

"He's always been hard to talk to on the phone. All that sarcasm, and it doesn't matter if you called him, if you're paying maybe a dollar a minute, you *still* have to listen to him say the opposite of what he thinks."

"Well as you know, he's not well. Physically I mean. His health really does seem to be collapsing. Anyway, the point—"

"But now it's this bitterness, and silence, and they're new, aren't they? He's gotten so *fat,* and not just physically."

"My point is that maybe Wes took up with lots of women simply because—"

"It's simply impossible to carry on daily life with Conrad anymore. Try giving him a simple 'Happy birthday' call. You'll see what I mean."

I'm like a man at the wheel of a car whose brakes have gone

out on a winding, rain-slick hill, but I keep on trying to steer the conversation: "I suppose everybody's life is very complicated, when you get down to it, but that doesn't mean there aren't a few simple aspects. Maybe Wes liked women."

"You're saying Conrad is a whaddayacall—a misfeminist?"

"A . . ."

"Someone who doesn't like women?"

"No, I was simply making a point about Wes."

"He certainly can be rude to me. Conrad."

"I was saying that sometimes what you see on the surface may be perfectly accurate. Maybe Wes just liked women."

"He liked them more than a man ought to. They kept breaking his heart."

"I keep reading these stupid articles," I say, steering into the skid, "and it seems anyone who ever gets involved with lots of women is immature or troubled. Do you ever hear things like that?"

"All the time." Adelle shakes her head in absentminded agreement. But still she fails to make the connection I'm so heavy-handedly placing before her.

And then you can almost hear it: the click in her brain. Her eyes light, her open mouth snaps eagerly shut. She says, "D'you know what Bernie was always saying? He said Wes was no different from Conrad really. That neither one had any genuine interest in women, only Conrad at least had the gumption to admit it. Or he said that Wes was—inadequate, physically inadequate in some way, and that's why his love affairs kept collapsing, that's why he kept always having to go after somebody new."

"That's not what Sally tells me."

"Sally?"

And a look of respectful surprise dawns on Adelle's features at this reference to the woman who dispatches such bright, eloquently phrased postcards from unimaginable places with unpronounceable names like Guadeloupe and Bruges and Aix-en-Provence.

And Adelle says: "You talked to *Sally* about all of this?"

"Well I gather that she'd sometimes heard the sorts of innuendos you're referring to. The sorts of things Bernie might imply. And she wanted to defend Wes. Or perhaps I should put that another way. She wanted to pay a sort of tribute to my father. She wanted me to know that although the marriage collapsed, in various ways the two of them had been extremely happy." Is there something unseemly in what I'm doing? Probably. I push on . . . "And that things on the you know physical level, long ago, things between them had been extremely satisfying."

And is there in all the world any other revelation that would have brought such radiance to my Aunt Adelle's features? More than anything else, wasn't this what she yearned to hear—that the wandering hero who'd beached up at the Commodore Hotel, shoulder-to-shoulder with transients and alcoholics and all sorts of unspeakable riffraff (when he wasn't covertly shacking up with a not-yet-divorced-woman-from-the-Department-of-Motor-Vehicles-whose-son-was-a-druggie-and-a-jailbird), had indeed once embodied all the romance of the handsome prince of a fairy tale? That Bernie had it all wrong? And that a queenly woman, today residing in the castled land of France, had, back in her princess days, once found in Wesley Sultan everything her heart desired?

CHAPTER TWELVE

and the Commodore Hotel in Stags Harbor, ~ *and 27 Arrow Road, Gastaw,*

RESTORATION—Wesley Cross Sultan, ~~63~~, 62, of 2135 N. Westhampton, died suddenly in Lyon Hospital in Stags Harbor, of heart failure. He worked for Great Bay Shipping for 42 years, chiefly in sales. He began his career in the Stags Harbor office, and after stints in Kalamazoo and Cincinnati, Ohio, he finished his career back at Stags Harbor. He ~~retired two years ago~~ *was effectively fired two years ago but claimed to be retiring* in order to pursue full-time his civic pursuits. He was ~~an active~~ *a nominal* member of the Rotarians, the Restoration Chamber of Commerce, the Stags Harbor Betterment Society, and the Thumb of Michigan Prosperity Council. He was also active in the Restoration Episcopal Church, where for many years he sang in the choir.

He was born in Restoration and ~~was a graduate~~ *attended but did not quite graduate from* the old High School on Cherrystone Avenue. He was the son of the late Chester Sultan, the well-known businessman, and the grandson of Hubert Sultan, who served as the mayor of Restoration from 1908 to 1912. Old-time Restorationists will recall Sultan Furniture on Union Street, founded by Hubert and presided over by Chester until he closed its doors in 1935.

He was married ~~twice. His first wife was Sally~~ *three times. His first wife was Klara Kuzmak, He then married* Planter (Admiraal), now of Grosse Pointe, formerly of Restoration. They were divorced in 1964. He leaves his wife, Tiffany, *from whom he was formally separated at the time of his death,* and their two daughters, Jessica and Winnie; a son, Luke Planter, of New York; a brother, Conrad Sultan, of Miami, Florida; and a sister, Adelle De Vries, of Battle Creek. *with whom he had a son, Wesley Jr.,*

He may have left other half-children as well.

Conrad greets me like this:

"You tell me I'm looking well, I'll toss you out on your silly-looking nose. What's the matter with your nose, anyway? Y'ever break your nose?"

"In fact I did. I got hit by a crew oar. Which took some doing, since I never rowed crew."

"Next time, don't have it set by the guy from the local auto-body shop."

"You're looking well, Uncle Conrad," I reply.

His eyes glint, his full lips pucker into a near-grin. Silver-haired Conrad remains fully at home in a world of adolescent banter, of boyish put-downs—exchanges that call him back, presumably, to an era when he and my father went after each other day after day, year after year.

He says, "That's *well* spelled with an *h* at the front."

In truth, he isn't looking well; in truth, he's looking like hell; and my first glimpse of him turns my stomach soft and fluttery. His color's all wrong . . . Once when I was a little kid I sliced open an apple and some thirty years later the shock of what I found there remains fresh in my mind. An intruder had got into the fruit before me: not a worm, or no ordinary, moist little worm—but a creature that had hollowed out for itself a dry, dusty, cobwebby chamber. Conrad? For all his size, he looks like a man hollowed out, somebody harboring any number of dry dusty gray chambers within him.

"You just can't keep away from Miami, can you, Luke?"

"I suppose not."

"You must have all sorts of relatives here."

"I have an uncle. Name of Conrad."

"I mean in-laws."

"My in-laws are in Connecticut."

It's partly one of Conrad's jokes, I suppose, and partly a suspicion that I've been stretching the truth: He doesn't seem fully to believe that Angelina and her family didn't float ashore in Miami on a leaky raft. In fact, Oscar, my father-in-law, or ex-father-in-law, has a thriving dental practice in Westchester County. Gloria, my ex-mother-in-law, plays the viola in a semiprofessional string quartet.

"You came down for the warm weather . . ."

"I came down to see you, Conrad."

The warm weather? What lies outside Conrad's living room window is hardly *weather* as we usually think of it. The sky is a sickly, sallow, sunless, unearthly no-color—more off-putting even than that lusterless November sky draped over Adelle's Battle Creek. Granted, *it isn't cold,* and maybe that's all most Miamians ask of their weather: *Just so long as it isn't cold . . .* But what is the likelihood, walking under a heaven of this sort, that you'd ever stumble upon some novel thought, some bold realization? What sane person wouldn't prefer to be in New York, where (if last night's weatherman called it right) even as I lounge here in Conrad's living room snowflakes are descending?

"I understand Sally's back."

"Will be. In two days. Home for Christmas."

"And happily settled in the Grosse Pointe mansion? Or will it be the North Carolina condo? Or is she off again to a château in the south of France?"

"It's back to Michigan. At least for a while. You know I saw Adelle."

"And refused to stay on for Thanksgiving. You were her second choice, by the way. She invited me first." He laughs, or snorts in place of a laugh, and Rusty in his cage by the window throws off a comradely rasp of merriment.

Conrad's in a feisty mood today, but that's all right. I have all the time in the world. I can outwait him.

He eyes the paper bag under my arm. "You brought me a present."

"It's an incendiary device. You and I, we're going to bomb City Hall."

I open the bag and pull out a bottle of cognac. It's quite fancy stuff: Hine Antique, at nearly ninety bucks a bottle. Such distinctions are mainly lost on me, but it's what Conrad once, when I took him out for a meal ostensibly paid for by Gribben Brothers, ordered after dinner. I set the bottle down on the coffee table, beside his open bottle of beer.

He says, "Pricey stuff."

"You told me you didn't feel like going out, I thought I'd bring the best of what's out there in here."

"You have luxurious tastes. Just like your mother." Conrad poses this as a reprimand, but even so, I can see he's pleased with the gift.

"There are glasses in the kitchen," he tells me. "Get the good ones, with the blue stems, they're up above the sink. And taco chips on the counter. And guacamole and sour cream in the fridge."

Out in the kitchen I'm again reminded of Conrad's willingness—for all his railing at my expensive tastes—to indulge himself in a few fine things: the Calphalon pans, the German knives. But always in restricted numbers. The glasses, the blue-stemmed "good ones" in the cupboard over the sink? There are only two of them. It seems Conrad long ago concluded he wasn't the party-throwing type.

So I set out on the coffee table an unlikely little snack: barbecue-flavored Doritos, guacamole and sour cream, and two glasses of very pricey cognac. Conrad has drained his beer in the meantime.

The cognac (Conrad swallows an inch of the stuff at one go, then pours himself a second inch, which he sips) appears to cheer him. He talks for a while about Hillary Clinton, whom he calls "Hellishly Clinton"; he is of course a Republican.

"So what did you dig out of Adelle?" he asks suddenly.

"Beg pardon?"

"What's the most recent tidbit in this ghoulish little grave-robbing project you've undertaken?"

We scrutinize each other over our glasses. I say: "I gather there was another woman. After Tiffany."

"Of course there was . . ."

"Know anything about her?"

"I can guess. An even more pitiful case than Tiffany? Probably. Kites checks, shoplifts, peddles heroin."

"That's her son you're talking about."

"Say what?"

"Evidently she's got a son who's a druggie. Doing time in Jackson State."

"Perfect. And the lady herself? What's her *scoop*?"

And whom does this last question remind me of? It reminds me of *me*. Conrad is parroting—parodying—my role of eager intern-journalist. "She works for the Department of Motor Vehicles."

"Love it. Wes takes a woman from the DMV for a ride. That's just perfect."

Pleasure at his little witticism inspires Conrad to knock back the rest of his cognac. He pours himself another inch (he seems to relish this business of apportioning himself carefully measured doses) and sips modestly.

"He left quite a complicated trail, didn't he?" I say.

"Nothing complicated. Just messy. There was nothing at all complicated about Wes."

"I can't say that's my impression."

"He's very simple. That's what makes this whole detective's quest of yours so laughable. I saw somewhere that some archaeologist turned up some graffiti in the old Roman catacombs. Two thousand years old, and do you know what it said?"

"I don't think so."

"It said: *I, Joe Roman*—or Tiberius Tiberio, or whatever his name was . . . It said: *I, Joe Roman, screwed a lot of women here.* That's Wes."

"Better run that by me once more. The Wes part."

"That's Wes, goddamn it. That Roman was his great-great-etcetera-grandfather."

"Yours too, then."

"I'm speaking *spiritually,*" Conrad corrects me, reprovingly, and swallows the rest of his cognac and pours himself another inch. He really is looking godawful today. So godawful—gray and dented and bloated—it seems my pricey gift may just finish him off before the afternoon's out.

"I'm still not sure I see—"

"*That's* Wes. Isn't it obvious? Here's this Roman guy, dead two thousand years, who left as legacy one statement: *I screwed a lot of women here.* Nothing else. But probably that's the one sentence, if he could leave only one, he'da chose to leave. And what of Wes remains, when all's said and done? What would he choose to hear us saying about him, if he could look down from heaven at the two of us sitting here? *There sure were a lot of women . . .* You already told me, didn't you, you never had much use for porn?"

"I'm afraid that's right."

"Me either, anymore, but I once spent a great deal of time, hours and hours, poring over my precious little ink-smeared smut collection. This was back when you might say I hadn't fully reconciled myself to certain aspects of my nature. This was straight porn, men and women, no gays or lesbos, I suppose I thought it might straighten me out, though I don't suppose there's such a thing as straight porn to a nonstraight mind, you find yourself bending a few details slightly, you see?"

"Sure."

"No you don't but anyway this was hard-core stuff—real contraband in those days. Black-and-white pix, half the shots out of focus, and busloads of homely models, lots of appendectomy scars and scabby elbows. But maybe because it *was* straight porn, it didn't take me long to see just how small and limited and *narrow* it all was." And his eyes *narrow* at the word—peering hard at me through two tight slits. "If you look at it with any kind of dispassion, you see there aren't many things a man and woman, or for that matter a man and a man, can do to each other."

"Yes."

"But that's just it. That's where Mother Nature steps in. Making sure most of us never *can* look at it with dispassion. Wes never did. Wes was somebody who had one and only one ambition in his whole life: He wanted to write on the wall of the Commodore Hotel *I, Wes Sultan, screwed a lot of women here,* and he wanted people to unearth his message two thousand years from now."

Of course I can't let this go by. I say, "Surely there was more to it than that? What about all his efforts to make an impression? How about how hard he worked to charm even some woman he hadn't the slightest—"

"Oh Wes's *charm*! You know the only real ambition Wes ever had?" And to look at Conrad's bright and expectant expression, you'd swear he hadn't just, moments before, both asked and answered this very question. But this time around he takes a new angle. "He wanted to hear a little voice inside his head announcing, *It's working, I'm charming her.* Anybody—even the withered crone behind the counter at the neighborhood candy store! I remember I must have been about four, Wes was about six, and old Mrs. Grinspan behind the counter was maybe a hundred and six, and what was Wes doing? He was *flirting.* Probably didn't even know the word back then, but it's what he was doing. Batting his famous eyelashes, giving her a little rap—and inevitably he'd walk outa that place with a pocketful of candy. You know what was the most delicious sensation in the world for Wes? It was to hear a little voice inside his head announcing, *A woman just gave me a pocketful of candy.*

"Do you see what I'm saying? *Wes was simple. We're all simple. Men are simple.* What do *women* want? Who the hell knows. What do *men* want? Simple things. The dumbest thing about men? Not seeing how dumb they are. You telling me you're not simple, Luke?"

"I'm not telling you much of anything . . ."

"You're not simple? Then you're not a real man. Simple as that. Think about *Playboy* magazine." And it seems the cognac, on top of the beer he has apparently been downing all day, is doing its work, warming and reviving Conrad's slumping frame. He's canted forward, head upheld and eyes flashing in his oversize skull. Blimp that he is, he is again successfully airborne. "Not *Playboy* now, but the way it used to be—maybe before your time?—when the whole damn editorial staff hadn't yet managed to find a woman's crotch. It took them ten or fifteen years of hard, steady searching, but in the end they did indeed succeed in finding the crotch.

"But I'm thinking back to the old days, the way the magazine was when all those old Restoration duffers, those men who were friends of my father's, would open it up and—surprise!—there was a pair of tits. And they'd open it up the next month and—surprise!—another pair. And the next month—surprise!—another set, and the next month—surprise! . . . But the *real* surprise, if you think about it, is that month after month the surprise could still *be* a surprise. And yet it was, kiddo. It was. Each month these accountants and sales reps and insurance salesmen and real-estate appraisers, men all over America, would open it up and find this big bouncing shocking *surprise* . . .

"It's all so *simple,* that's my point. I told you what the richest experience in the entire world was for Wes, you want to hear what it was for me? It was to meet some kid, twenty let's say, who looked like the straightest boy in the world, and then to discover he wasn't straight. That's what did it for me. I wanted the one who couldn't *possibly* be queer, and who turned out to be queer. I wanted the one who looked like he'd grown up on Mom's Sunday pancakes, the one who looked like he'd never been troubled by a kinky thought in his life—he couldn't *be* too healthy and too corny-looking for me, provided it wasn't some put-up tarty corniness. The sexiest state in America? Where else but Utah, with all these blond Mormons in ties and jackets, no drinks, no drugs, no *coffee* for God's sake, and eager as hell to get shameful Conrad into a corner and tell him the good news about God and the wisdom of the Elders!

"I guarantee you one thing about Wes. No matter how many times he heard it, each new time that little voice inside him announced, *It's working, I'm charming her,* it was just like a miracle had been achieved. It's a pretty meager-looking miracle if you step back and look at it, but Wes never did step back. It's 1970 and here's Wes the salesman driving some back road in rural Michigan, listening to country music and checking his hair in the rearview and asking himself what kind of reception he's going to get from the secretary at some windshield wiper factor. It's 1980 and here's Wes the salesman driving some other back road in rural Michigan and checking his hair and wondering how he'll fare with the waitress at the diner. Hell, he was endlessly content with his miracle. To him, it was the greatest miracle the world had to offer.

"And it was just the same for me. In *my* little miracle, a voice in my head declared, *But he's queer after all!* This goddamned Mormon, or this Boy Scout or police cadet, or this football captain who's going steady with the head of the cheerleaders, is *queer after all*. Again it's not much of a miracle if you think about it, but who ever stops to think about it? The only thing the man on the prowl is interested in? His daily miracle. We're all like little kids, standing openmouthed in front of some magician at a fair, saying, *Show me that trick again*. Mind you, not until the last couple of years did I even bother to think it through. I had better things to do than think: I was a man pursuing his daily miracle. Piss time."

Conrad heaves and grunts his way to his feet and shuffles from the room. Outside, nothing's changed, the sky remains exactly the same unhealthy shade of no-color—earthly weather is a thing of the past.

There are no books in this living room, no paintings on the wall. A few framed photographs stand on the table beside the couch (including the snapshot in which a clowning Wes has donned Conrad's graduation cap), but these have a transient air. What you feel here isn't so much a passion for spareness as a sense of disengagement, as if these must be the quarters of someone who couldn't locate anything worth placing in his bookcase or upon his wall. I hear a toilet flush, and Conrad takes control of the conversation while still shuffling down the hallway toward me:

"Oh I've gotten into all sorts of tangled-up business, at midnight a man makes any number of compromises, but you know I never had much interest really in the beach-boy types with their oiled muscles and itsy-bitsy slingshot trunks. From the start you knew who they were and what they're up to and there's no miracle in them—although I needed big muscles myself, because the one thing I can tell you if you're going after the straight-looking guys who can't *possibly* be queer is that most of them aren't and they may take a swing at you. The road to heaven? Lined with perils."

He collapses into his chair and downs the rest of his cognac. He pours another inch into his glass—his sixth? his seventh?—and stares at me soulfully and says, "Kiddo, I'm worried about your drinking."

"About *my* drinking." My initial splash of cognac hasn't yet been drained.

"Absolutely. Don't you notice whenever we two get together we wind up shit-faced?"

"It's hardly the case that I—"

"Wouldn't our conversation be more interesting if you promised never again to open a sentence with *It's hardly the case . . . ?*"

"Hey—"

"Or, *My own opinion is . . .*"

"Look—"

"Look, you're on medication, isn't that right? Have been ever since that girl left and you had that little nervous breakdown, right? And here you are, drinking the hard stuff in the afternoon . . ." And my Uncle Conrad shakes his head ponderously, lugubriously at me.

I meet his glance, drain my cognac, and say to him, "Point one: I've been on medication since before Angelina and I separated. Point two: I never had a nervous breakdown and you've *got* to stop talking like I did, you've even got Adelle thinking I'm some sort of psychic invalid."

"What medication?"

"Various."

"What medication?"

"For different things."

"What medication?"

"Sixty milligrams of Inderal—that's a beta-blocker—and Nardil, fifteen and thirty milligrams, on alternate mornings. That's an old-fashioned antidepressant, and fifteen and thirty means, incidentally, I'm on lower doses than more than half the people I know."

"You're *spooked,* face it, Luke. Eyes like a hare and look at the way your hand shakes. I notice it each time you pick up your glass."

"It's the Lithium. Four hundred and fifty milligrams at bedtime. Shaking's a common side effect. And Zoloft, fifty milligrams, also at bedtime."

"You're pale, you're shaky, your hair's coming out in handfuls, your eyes are bloodshot."

"Oh and ten milligrams of Ambien. That's for insomnia. I'm cutting back on all the dosages now that I've left Gribben . . ."

"You look like a patient in a shell-shock ward."

"I feel *swell.*"

"I don't know what it is about your generation," Conrad continues dolefully, downing his drink and dipping a Dorito first in the guacamole and then in the sour cream—leaving a green ribbon in the latter. "None of you can cope with reality, can you? You're all on drugs, aren't you? All the little pleasures of this world just aren't enough for you, are they?"

It's a comic send-up, surely—this version of a Conrad Sultan ready to extol the elementary joys of rose-gardening, or a glass of cold water, or a brisk constitutional at dawn. But then he says, "With your dad dead, I suppose it ought to be my job to tell you to watch it now and then," and all at once I can't say to what degree the mournful look on Conrad's face, or the abruptly maudlin tremble in his voice, is in fact genuine. "Kiddo, you've got a lot of time left to fuck things up. Young people always think they need to fuck things up—but they don't. Life will do it for them. What's your hurry, Luke? Look, I don't want to see you die the way your father did."

"Mm?"

"In a bar."

"But he died in a hospital."

Conrad shakes his heavy head. "Wes was dead. By then. By the time they got him to the hospital. Dead by the time the ambulance arrived."

"A bar?" I say, after a moment. "Where?"

"Stags Harbor."

"And what was its name?"

"The Silk and Satin Saloon."

"Of course it was," I say. "What else would it possibly be named?"

"It's no way for you to end up," Conrad tells me.

"Piss time," I counter, and rise to my feet. I feel a little wobbly, though I've had very little to drink. But Conrad's words are dizzying—his entire presence is dizzying . . .

On the way to the bathroom I pass his bedroom and all at once I feel a powerful longing for another look at that aquarium. I want to verify my memory—to see whether Conrad's aquarium is as pure and imposing and magically ornate as what I recollect. But the door's closed. For a moment I lean my head against the door, catching—maybe—the rich, cleansing hum of the filtration system. Or maybe it's my own—medicated—blood in my ears.

On the way back from the bathroom I turn the knob and nudge the bedroom door with the side of my shoe. It opens slowly. The aquarium is still in place, as outsize and ornate and as magical as ever, but this time I notice something new about the room—a far less spectacular feature. On the wall between the bed and the aquarium hangs a painting. It's a nondescript gray canvas in a garish red-and-white frame. A painting? This can only be the artwork that triggered one of the fiercest battles the two Sultan brothers ever fought. Yes: agoraphobic Dora Sultan's treasured vision of downtown Chicago. *Michigan Avenue in the Rain.*

When I return to the living room, Conrad has found a new tone and subject:

"Tell me about Hibernation."

"Bernie? He spent most of my visit watching a football game."

"And Adelle?"

"*Very* down on Tiffany this time around."

"And that surprises you? You had to fly out to Michigan to figure that one out?"

"She'd changed her tune. Last time I'd seen her, she went on and on about how Tiffany broke Wes's heart. As if nobody else ever had. This time around, she made it sound like Tiffany was just one in a string of broken—"

And once again I've said something to stir Conrad into high dudgeon: "Wes's heart *broken*? Jeezo Christo, it's the most absurd thing I ever heard. Honestly, *don't* you understand anything? That that was merely the last step in the Great Wes Sultan Act? His little trademark finale? The one that proved how *sensitive* he was? Actually, actually it was the one real inarguable stroke of genius in the guy. You hadda hand it to Wes. Your average Don Juan, he makes a conquest and walks away without a second thought. Maybe even takes *pride* in never giving the woman a second thought. Well, Wes prided himself in being a Don Juan with a Difference, a Don Juan for Our Times.

"If for Wes the richest phrase in the universe was *It's working— I'm charming her,* what was the second-richest? It was *Poor sensitive Wes really got his heart broke this time around.* Don't you see? Don't you understand how much he *enjoyed* going to Adelle with another tale of heartbreak? Wes was never *happier* than when his heart got broke . . . God help him, he saw himself as some sort of country-and-western singer. Don't you get it? How *sweet* it was, when a relationship was coming undone and he was dumping another woman, to say to her as he was buttoning up his shirt, *You know, honey, I really fell for you?* From Wes's point of view, nothing was more noble than declaring after a night in the sack with some woman he hoped he'd never see again, some woman who was missing a front tooth or weighed two hundred pounds, to declare, *I know I don't mean anything special to you but gee, darlin', you really turned my head there for a while.* And this went on for forty years! He took his darlin' act on the road, Wes went out on tour, and he played the same act night after night for forty years! Look, I guaran*tee* you, America today is positively chockablock with sixty-plus-year-old women, most of them probably fat as fat Conrad, who occasionally say to themselves, *Once, once I broke the heart of a beautiful boy.*" The image is finally so disturbing to Conrad that nothing is to be done but to dip an entire fistful of Doritos all at once into the sour cream and to bite down upon it in a great shattering clatter. Still chewing, he revs right up again: "Wes's heart *broken?* The first thing you have to realize about Wes is that *whatever* he ever said about love or sex or passion was absolute nonsense." The sweeping grandeur of this denunciation brings a lick of joy to Conrad's crafty eyes. "He never in his life made an honest remark on the subject.

"Wes's heart *broken?* If it ever was, it was Sally who did it. Because it turned out she had backbone, and Wes never figured on that. Turned out when she said *enough,* she meant just that. Wes could never get his head around it. Couldn't believe he could train those blue eyes on Sally, do the big soulful swallowing with that gorgeous Adam's apple of his, sigh and promise her, *Everything will be different, I'll take you to the moon,* and she could reply, *Sorry, I've got other plans.* Of course it scared him that her IQ was about double his. (Let's see, seventy times two is one forty. . . . Yep, that's about right.) He worried she'd finally seen through him. It was the beginning of the end for Wes, who would later discover other women, too, who would say *Enough,* and all sorts of folks at Great

Bay Shipping whose hearts didn't go pit-a-pat when he batted his eyelashes. So he had his fall, just the way Mother had her fall—she fell all the way from Crestview Boulevard to the duplex on Scully Street."

"I went over and looked at that place. The last time I was in Restoration."

"You know what the weird thing was about Scully Street? The really painful irony? The thing that Wes could never see and Mother could never see? It's this: that Scully Street was actually a helluva nice place to grow up. Had the Sultan family fallen? Hell, Luke, we'd fallen into clover. You had the park right there. And the Michicabanabee River. And if the guy next door sat on his porch in his T-shirt all day and didn't cut his lawn, well you didn't have to worry anymore about what the neighbors thought . . . Summers in particular, those were lovely down there. Summer nights," Conrad says, or sighs, and the look on his face is as far as I'm concerned a new face, the tone in his voice a new tone. For this is the expression, and the pitch, of a man looking deep into his past and locating there, gratefully, beauty and liberality and ease. This is the closest I've ever seen Conrad come to a nostalgic interlude. "Summers, down by the Michicabanabee, we used to see fireflies, hundreds and hundreds of them, and Wes and Adelle and I would go out hunting them with mason jars. And the better you did, the more your jar glowed; those jars glowed just like lanterns. You know what I'd heard somewhere? Some kid told me, I don't know if it's true. But I always wanted to see if it was true . . . I heard that sometimes when frogs swallow a firefly their throats will glow for a second, they'll glow with the light they've swallowed inside them."

There's a glow in any case—delicate, but enduring intact over half a century—on Conrad's face. He takes another shot of cognac and says, abruptly, "You know, something tragic has happened to me."

I give him a sympathetic nod. I'm naturally supposing that he's alluding to his health problems—to those little dry dusty gray rooms being hollowed out inside him. But I ought to know better. Even an ailing Conrad, and a tipsy nostalgic Conrad, isn't about to go soliciting my sympathy in so open a fashion. "It's just horrible," he murmurs. "I've become a philosopher."

"About your own life?"

"About my own life, and Wes's, and yours, and Sally's—about everyone's. I told you last time, you can put it on my tombstone: *Thinking stinks.* I'd trade every interesting thought I've had in the past two years for one more of my little miracles."

He pats at his crotch and says, "I said as much to Sally maybe a year ago. I explained that I'd figured out the central mystery of my life, but I didn't find it all that fascinating really, and she said to me, 'But what about culture, Conrad?' Now tell me something, Luke. Is there anything in it—culture? What's the real point of culture?"

Oh, now there's a look of pleased arch ingenuousness on his face—but also, if I'm reading him right, some gravity too.

"I'm working on that one, Conrad."

"Now this is the woman, remember, who once guided me to an art exhibition of shoelaces glued to plywood. Am I going to look at one of those artworks and say, *My life's mystery is restored?* And is the Metropolitan Opera or the Louvre Museum in Paris really much more than plywood and shoelaces? Luke, I don't like art. [No, Conrad, though you fought like the devil for *Michigan Avenue in the Rain.*] Or music. Or the movies. I used to like TV, even though everybody says it's an insult to your intelligence—but Jesus, I've always liked insults. And then, what the hell, it finally got too stupid even for me. So what am I supposed to do all day but eat all day, and drink all day? You get the monkey off your back and what have you got? Nothing. You're not free, you're just broke.

That's when you say, Wait a minute, at least I used to have a *monkey.* Instead, I'm stuck philosophizing . . .

"You know I read somewhere that scientists, physicists I guess, were trying to come up with their big TOE, do you know what I'm saying?"

"Not *precisely*, Conrad." I pour myself a second drink.

"A Theory of Everything—a theory to explain everything."

"Oh well yes, actually I—"

"So one day, what the hell, what did I do? I came up with a theory that, if it doesn't explain everything in the world, comes pretty close. You want to hear my theory? You want to have the whole goddamned world explained to you once and for all?"

"Very much."

"All right, it goes like this: *Every time an idiot's born, I'm a little better off.*" And the expression upon the man's face truly is something to behold: a look of absolutely incandescent triumph. No doubt about it, my Uncle Conrad is expecting applause, congratulations, awe.

"Maybe a little amplification . . . ," I suggest.

"All right, all right. Look, take hotels. What sort of idiot pays three dollars for a bag of chips from the minibar when he knows he can get a bag four times the size at half the price one block down the street? The answer is: an *idiot* idiot. But I'm an accountant, so let's look at it from the accountant's point of view. The sort of person who pays the minibar price, the person who says, *Go ahead and rob me blind,* he's the one keeps the hotel profits up. He's the one allows them to keep room rates down, you get what I'm saying? *The idiots are subsidizing me.* Okay, take airplanes. What sort of idiot is it who buys a newspaper for two hundred bucks—which is basically all the value you're buying—*Here's your complimentary newspaper, sir*—when you fly first-class? The answer is: an *idiot*

idiot. But they're just the sort of idiots who keep my own ticket price down. Once again: *They're subsidizing me.* You could extend this out well beyond the field of economics, incidentally. It pretty much explains how the world works: *Every time an idiot's born, I'm better off.* It's also why you've got to be grateful anytime anybody builds an Idiot Attractor—it gets them out of our hair for a while. Man, they can't *build* enough riverboat casinos to suit me.

"Do you get it? *Every time an idiot's born, I'm better off.* It's what I tell myself whenever I go shopping or to the post office and I have the bad luck to run into an idiot. In my mind I say to him, *Thank you, my friend, you're making my world a better place, you goddamned idiot.* It's what helps me keep my temper."

"But you have the worst temper of anyone I know, Conrad."

"But think how much worse it would be if the world weren't full of idiots! Christ, man, they're the only thing holding me together . . ." And with the last stroke, his big ruddy round face glows once more like a mason jar full of fireflies. He has out-bantered me, hasn't he?—out-bantered the Princeton boy, the megamoney Manhattan finance man? Amusement, jubilation, self-righteousness dance in his eyes. And something in addition: a boyish look that declares, *I've won! I've won!*

But abruptly Conrad's gaze goes cold, his features harden. He drains his glass and says, "Okay, fun's fun. But isn't it time you told me what you're doing?"

"Beg pardon?"

"I mean, cut the shit."

"Beg pardon."

"And quit *pardoning* me, or *pardoning* yourself, Mr. Prissy Etiquette: what's the matter with *What?* for God's sake?"

It's all come on so fast . . . No, this is no joke, and the sincerity and the amplitude of Conrad's rage are puzzling. I've never seen so many facets of the man as I've been seeing this afternoon, and yet this particular side to him isn't one I'm eager to meet. No, for the first time in my life, as the old wrestler thrusts his shoulders toward me, and trains on me that hooded reptilian glance with which, forty years before, he must have psyched out one opponent after another, I feel genuinely fearful of my uncle.

"I'm afraid I don't understand you, Conrad . . ."

"But I've just *explained* it, weren't you *listening*? There's no big mystery so far as Wes is concerned. Period. Okay then: How long can you go on pretending to play Sherlock Holmes when there isn't any mystery?"

"I'm still not sure I—"

And Conrad erupts, cries with a great howling wail of a voice: "Goddamn it, it's Sally, isn't it?"

I haven't a clue what he means, not a clue . . . I only know his dark apartment shudders with anguished feeling, that every last bit of raging intensity in his gaze is authentic. I say: "Please, I don't understand. What do you mean?"

Conrad says: "Of *course* it's Sally, it's always *always* bright little Sally, pulling the strings behind the scene. I can just hear her now, in that goddamned sweet charitable voice of hers, *Go visit your Uncle Conrad, Luke, he's lonely and miserable.* And, *He's very ill, Luke, go get to know your uncle before he dies.*"

For a few seconds I sit there dumbstruck. Then I say, softly, "But Sally has nothing to do with it, Conrad. Completely nothing at all to do with my being here."

And Conrad storms on: "What are you expecting me to believe, *huh*? That the New York high-finance hotshot comes down here because he just can't get enough stories about a small-town loser like Wes Sultan? You weren't in any such hurry to see Wes when he was alive."

"Maybe I'm making up for things . . ."

"Or maybe you're making things up! You telling me you quit

your megabucks job just to track down the doings of a pathetic little flimflam like Wes Sultan? You may have had your famous nervous breakdown, buddy boy, but you're not as batty as that. No no. You? You're a cagey little shit."

More softly still, I say, "Point one: Yes, I gave up my job in order to do things like sit here with you. Point two: Yes, I quit my job in order to pursue the 'doings' of a small-town loser like Wesley Sultan. I'm afraid you're going to *have* to believe it, Conrad. Because it's all true."

"That so? Okay, then tell me one thing: Where does it lead you? Tell me just one thing: What's the what-for? What's behind all your careful little grave-digging?"

The brutal pressure of his gaze squeezes out of me what I haven't yet confessed to anyone: "I'm going to write a book . . ."

"*A book!*" Though Conrad takes such outsize satisfaction in inhabiting a world in which he can predict virtually everything, he manages to sound utterly flabbergasted. "A book about what, for Christ's sake?"

"A book about my father . . ."

"But Wes never read a book!" Conrad snaps back.

"Not *for* him. *About* him."

"A book about *Wes*? A *book* about Wes?" And now it appears Conrad isn't so much incredulous as indignant. He leans forward and his rage—if that is what it is—threatens to break over my head.

"Yes, I am going to write a novel," I answer him. And to loose these words into the open air—to set them fluttering around our heads like an uncaged bird, as though Rusty had gotten free and were whipping and flapping around our ears—is somehow to clarify for myself just how unreally, preposterously colossal is this, my innermost ambition. I'm going to write a *novel*? You mean, *I'm* going to write a novel? Based on characters like Wes, and Adelle, and *Conrad*? Why not declare instead, *I'm going to construct an inter-*

planetary space probe in my apartment or *I'm going to locate King Solo-mon's mines . . . ?* It's an all-but-insurmountable undertaking, isn't it? Because (so I've come to see) in order really to write a novel, I would have to do something only people in novels ever seem to do: remake my life. Not merely change my job, uproot my every routine, replot my ambitions—but dig down into the very soil of my life and reconfigure the fixed roots of my thinking.

Conrad calls me back to reality: "A novel about *Wes!*"

And I hear the hurt in old Conrad's voice—and all at once it's apparent that what's irking him *isn't* a sense of family privacies breached, of confidences betrayed. No. No, what vexes him is in fact a sensation of being shortchanged. Yes, it strikes Conrad as *unfair . . .*

A novel about Wes? What in the world had *Wes* accomplished to merit being the Sultan brother selected as the subject for a book? Had *Wes* been captain of the wrestling team? Had *Wes* set the school hundred-yard-dash record?

A new idea dawns upon him: "A novel about *Wes,*" Conrad marvels. "But then—but then *I* would be one of the characters."

"Well it's not as though I'd be taking every literal detail and—"

"It's impossible to write a novel about Wes without making me one of the characters. That's impossible," Conrad unbudgeably declares.

"I'll change your name of *course,*" I grandly, glibly announce, sweeping my hands through the air just as though I were waving a wand.

"Change my name?"

"I'll make you—I'll make all the characters a composite."

"Change my name!" And—yes—Conrad has turned indignant once more, more so than ever. "If you change my name, Luke, I'll come at you with a crew oar and break your silly-looking nose. Change my *name!* Why, the very idea is absurd. It's ridiculous, it

ought to be illegal. It probably *is* illegal. I'm sure it's libel, not to use the legal name of who you're talking about.

"Jesus, don't you see anything? Luke, you've got to get me down *exactly*! Otherwise, what's the point? What good's a Conrad who's only half a Conrad, who's merely obnoxious instead of insufferable? If you're going to do it, *do* it, baby. Just say the hell with them all and do it. And I want you to get down the little speech I just made, about men looking for nothing but a daily miracle, and I also want you to insert into your novel my big TOE, which I consider one of the most profound contributions to philosophy in the twentieth century. Remember it: *Every time an idiot's born, I'm a little better off.* And you must get down exactly how *fat* I am—" And Conrad lifts his shirt, lifts it high to expose a tremendous slumping mountain of white belly—and only now do I realize just how drunk he must be.

"And I want you to make sure you don't skimp over what an absolute *slob* I was, especially when I was eating . . ." And Conrad with a sweeping athletic flourish of one of his big hands scoops a dollop of guacamole onto his index finger and smears it across the bridge of his nose.

"Get in goddamned *all* of it. You've got to go the whole hog, Luke—you've got to do the whole big fat barbecued *pig.* It's all life's cruel-humored ingenuity you've got to get in, its love of really sick jokes—I'll never forgive you if you don't do my situation justice."

Conrad grandly empties his cognac and returns the glass to the table with a bang. A green dab of guacamole hangs on its rim, where it has edged up against the bridge of his nose.

He eyes me squarely and says, "Goddamn it, you know what the bitch of it is, Luke? The goddamn bitch of it is this: I probably won't still be around by the time you actually get around to publishing your book . . ."

(Was it painful to utter those words? It's painful to transcribe them. Oh, it's all too painfully ironic for words, isn't it, Conrad? That you—you who were forever throwing off confident, wrong-headed predictions—should somehow manage to get things right on the one most vital question confronting both of us . . . Old friend, dear silver-ponytailed friend, I wish I could ask you now, *Have I done right by you?* Have I done your situation justice? Clearly I haven't, if I neglect to mention how in the end you outfoxed me one last time. You had prepared a final surprise, hadn't you? And I failed utterly to foresee the closing twist, lurking in your last will and testament, the one stipulation lying just beyond your Restoration gravesite, with its view in the distance of the winding Michicabanabee . . . All your money, your apartment, your belongings, even Rusty and your aquarium and *Michigan Avenue in the Rain*— whom else would you choose to leave your entire estate to but to . . . to the *rich widow* whose extravagances you deplored, the one who inevitably would, or so you always with such bitter satisfaction speculated, *wind up with all the chips?* Doesn't it, as you used to say, *make perfect sense?* What more gratifying final stroke was there than this vindication of all your own gloomy, merry prognostications? Whom else must all your possessions go to, in the end, but to your brother's wronged wife?)

"Justice!" cries the impossible, irreplaceable man with a war-paint stripe of guacamole on his nose. "Luke, I demand you do me justice!"

CHAPTER THIRTEEN

and the Commodore Hotel in Stags Harbor, *and 27 Arrow Road, Gastaw,*

RESTORATION—Wesley Cross Sultan, ~~63~~ 62, of 2135 N. Westhampton, died suddenly in ~~Lyon Hospital in~~ *the Silk and Satin Saloon* Stags Harbor, of heart failure. He worked for Great Bay Shipping for 42 years, chiefly in sales. He began his career in the Stags Harbor office, and after stints in Kalamazoo and Cincinnati, Ohio, he finished his career back at Stags Harbor. He ~~retired two years~~ *was effectively* ~~ago~~ in order to pursue full-time his civic pursuits. *fired two years ago but claimed* He was ~~an active~~ *a nominal* member of the Rotarians, the *to be retiring* Restoration Chamber of Commerce, the Stags Harbor Betterment Society, and the Thumb of Michigan Prosperity Council. He was also active in the Restoration Episcopal Church, where for many years he sang in the choir.

He was born in Restoration and ~~was a graduate~~ *attended but* ~~of~~ the old High School on Cherrystone Avenue. He *did not quite* was the son of the late Chester Sultan, the well- *graduate from* known businessman, and the grandson of Hubert Sultan, who served as the mayor of Restoration from 1908 to 1912. Old-time Restorationists will recall Sultan Furniture on Union Street, founded by Hubert and presided over by Chester until he closed its doors in 1935.

He was married ~~twice. His first wife was~~ Sally *three times. His* Planter (Admiraal), now of Grosse Pointe, formerly *first wife was* of Restoration. They were divorced in 1964. He *Klara Kuzmak,* leaves his wife, Tiffany, and their two daughters, Jes- *He then married* sica and Winnie; a son, Luke Planter, of New York; a brother, Conrad Sultan, of Miami, Florida; and a sis- *with whom* ter, Adelle De Vries, of Battle Creek. *he had a son, Wesley Jr.*

from whom he was formally separated at the time of his death,

He may have left other children as well. *half-*

"It was some sort of weird homing impulse. I don't know how otherwise to describe it. A little voice in my head saying I had to be back with my family for Christmas."

"I'd've been happy to go out there."

"Oh I knew you would, and wouldn't that have been enchanting—Christmas in Mare aux Cerfs? No, my feeling wasn't *logical*. It was simply an irresistible impulse, ordering me back to my family for Christmas, and never mind that you're my family and you were willing to fly out there to meet me. And that's how it happens that I've come back to *this*."

This *this* of Sally's is a heavy wet blanket of winter slop, irregularly heaped on the lawns and sidewalks and streets of Grosse Pointe. Additional slop is coming down. The flakes are wet and adhesive, clumping into gummy gray-white wedges on each wiper blade. I'm driving my mother's big boat of a Buick. We're on the way to what must be, she promises me, *the world's largest video store*.

It's late afternoon on a winter day in the Detroit suburbs and it seems I've journeyed a great distance from those lucent afternoons in Mare aux Cerfs when the light felt more magical than any light in years—afternoons when your eyes long for arms that could embrace the world whole. Since then, it's as if skies keep getting darker, *thicker*. This one's a wall of cement. You'd need a jackhammer to break through it—to break through into that other, otherworldly light which, even today, may have gently deposited itself upon the slopes of Mare aux Cerfs.

Christmas has come and gone. Christmas was yesterday, and doubtless today ought to be a day for remaining indoors, grateful for shelter and family. But not even freezing rain and snow can keep Detroiters house-bound today. The roads are clogged with cars, all fleeing the hearth, the dining room, the embrace of the family circle. The turnoff to the Hopewell Mall is backed up for what must be a quarter mile.

The Buick's heater purrs, the wipers cut their languid arcs, traffic starts and stops. Ahead of me stretches a thronging sea of red lights (brake lights, taillights), reflected off the dripping sides of cars, off the snowy puddled pavements. It's not much past noon, but already night appears to be falling. "You'll be back in the sun in three days," I remind her. Sally is flying to Miami to see Conrad.

"I had such a peculiar conversation with him a few nights ago."

"Tell me."

"He must have been more in his cups than usual. It's the only thing I can conclude. It was a different Conrad from the one I'm used to."

"Tell me."

"For one thing, he was apologetic."

"That doesn't sound like Conrad. Apologetic about what?"

"About practically everything. About our entire history of dealings. I do mean our *entire* dealings—he literally went back to the first time Wes escorted me to the old Sultan home on Scully Street and I met a skinny sandy-haired college boy named Conrad. Also he was very self-pitying."

"*That* doesn't sound like Conrad."

"I mentioned the New Year and do you know what he said to me? He said, 'It's weird to know . . .'" Sally pauses and I understand I'm once again being appraised: She's wondering whether to shield me from some demonstration of life's harshness or cruelty— from some "unpleasantness." Of course I know as well as she does that Conrad's dying, and if over the last few years she has lost a husband and an ex-husband, I've lost an adoptive father and a biological father. No matter. In a sector of Sally's mind forever impervious to logic or experience, a vestigial parental superstition continues to operate, telling her, *What is not spoken before your child will not touch him* . . . "Well, he said to me, 'It's weird to know you're seeing the last New Year of your life rung in.'"

"Really?"

It's not the sort of line I'd expect from Conrad. If anything, it's a pronouncement Sally herself might deliver (in her characteristic tone of proud meditativeness, of rational wistfulness—careful words overlying a reservoir of hurt and fear). And all at once it seems the prospect the two of us are obliquely confronting, as we drive to the world's biggest video store on the day after Christmas, is that of her own passing . . .

It's many years away, surely, yet even so there's no question that before she goes Sally would like to see my own life more settled. As long as she's on the planet, it's her duty to see me *placed* some-where—and aren't my joblessness and my childlessness and the collapse of my marriage persuasive evidence of some flaw or shortcoming in my upbringing? Oh, none of this is *logical,* but who could be logical on a gray day after Christmas in the Detroit suburbs, with sleety snow falling, and talk of another death in an already-dwindled family?

Sally's upset about Conrad, she isn't altogether happy to be home, she's getting inklings that the upcoming year will be a hard one, and I'm sorry to be adding to her worries. Things were differ-ent for her when I was jetting over for visits in France. Now we've both returned to the town where I grew up, and how exactly is she to explain to her neighbors and friends this divorced and unem-ployed son of hers? As we drive along, both of us are grimly sens-ing that reality has returned (reality at bottom often consisting, for a Michigander, of a handful of sleet tossed at you out of a darken-ing sky).

Reality returns, too, in the guise of a blazing video store the size of a small French village. I say, "Hey you weren't kidding—it *must* be the biggest in the world."

We stroll through aisles and aisles and aisles of entertainment, and you might think it would be easy to locate something we want to watch tonight. But it isn't. Somewhere along the line, as year by year Hollywood's movies turned bloodier and bloodier, Sally made a resolution to quit sitting through anything "too gruesome or queasiness-inducing"—which seems to rule out half the new movies. And neither of us wants to sit through anything "too soupy"—which pretty much eliminates the other half. It's a depressingly familiar story: What do you prefer tonight—the murderous, or the maudlin?

We wander round the store. Dozens and dozens of televisions are clamped to the ceiling, so that wherever you stand you're in sight of a screen—on each of which, when I look up at one point, Arnold Schwarzenegger is threatening to beat up a robot.

As it happens, at that moment I find myself halted right beside an eight-foot-tall cardboard stand-up likeness of Arnold. If he's larger-than-life in real life, in this celluloid supermarket he's bigger yet, he's larger-than-larger-than-life: he's a godlike figure in this environment where little folks—dwindled folks, like Sally and me—shuffle about in an uneasy search for some un-unappealing diversion.

We finally settle on a BBC Sherlock Holmes episode, "The Return of Holmes," one in which (according to the back of the box) Conan Doyle, having killed off his most famous creation in a previous story, resurrects him in response to popular demand. When we're seated in the car once more, watching the windshield wipers go about their steady business of *clarifying, clarifying* (the sleet is still coming down), Sally says, "The oddest thing happened after your last trip to France. The day after you flew home, I was visited, I guess you might say, by some sort of overwhelming spell of gloom. Or depression? Maybe self-doubt . . ."

"Well I'm *sorry.*"

"It was the oddest thing ever: I could hardly move. I could hardly bring myself to get up from that chair in the study and make myself a cup of tea."

"I certainly hope I wasn't in any way the cause."

Sally's reply surprises me: "But I think you *were.* Indirectly,

Luke. And I mention it now only because no lasting injury was done, after twenty-four hours the spell essentially lifted. I say 'you *were*,' because I'd spent so much time during your visit raking over the past—Wes and Conrad and crazy Dora and beautiful glowing-haired Klara and Momma and Poppa and Gordon. That sort of retrospection may occasionally be a good thing for the soul, even a necessary thing, but obviously it stirs everything up, and who among us can look back on the whole of their lives without real *pangs*?

"Anyway, you'll recall that that's when I finally 'fessed up to you about lending Wes all the money. (And it seems I'll never quite square that with my conscience. There's a good argument to be made that I betrayed not only you but also Gordon and I suppose Tiffany—I was interfering in their marriage, wasn't I?) And I got to thinking, in a very methodical way, a cataloguing sort of way, about all the people I'd betrayed or deceived over the years. And maybe sometimes my behavior was justified (like not telling Poppa I'd signed up for a French class in college) and maybe sometimes it wasn't (like not telling Gordon I'd lent Wes money), but the point was just what a maze I'd created. 'Oh what a tangled web we weave . . . ,' as the poem says. Deceiving Gordon about how often Wes and I were in contact. And then deceiving Tiffany likewise. And later deceiving Wes after Tiffany started calling me for advice. And deceiving *you* on a number of fronts, trying to protect Wes I suppose. And I began to wonder: Were Wes and I really all that different? Am I much less fundamentally deceptive than he was? And had his habits simply rubbed off on me? Or did it all run a little deeper: Was a taste for deception one of those shared traits initially drawing us together?"

"Oh come *on*, you've got to be kidding."

"And yet I'm *not*, or at least that's truly how I was feeling, but I don't think I've quite made my point, which is: Even if the rest of us don't practice deception on the grand level that Wes occasionally did, don't we all wind up, even the so-called truthful people, living inside a *very* tangled web?"

Oh, I see it exactly, the observation Sally in her modesty hesitates to voice explicitly. She can't quite permit herself to say, *I think I'm a basically honest person*—a boast that, touching as it does on the condition of the soul itself, would strike her as even more unseemly than *I'm intelligent* or *I'm charming* or *I'm good-looking*. Honest of course she is, and the point she's making hinges on her core honesty. You begin with a few discreet silences, you add a couple of deliberate ambivalences, you toss in a scatter of white lies—and before long even the person of firm integrity has created a labyrinth of deceptions.

Later, when we're settled at the dining room table over cups of milky tea and lemon cookies, I take up the conversation again: "You said Conrad was apologetic . . ."

"About his whole life. He said he was sorry he'd been so barbed with me."

"With you? With everybody. He *must* have been soused."

"You know what he said? He said he'd never forgiven me for remaining loyal to Wes. Now isn't that odd? Don't you think that's odd? He said that given the way Wes treated me, I should have remained furious forever. (And isn't it funny just how moralistic *Conrad* can be on the subject of Wes's philandering?) But anyway, he said he couldn't forgive me for forgiving Wes, for remaining his loyal wife. And you know what I said? I said, 'But I've remained loyal to you, too, Conrad.' And you know what he did?"

The reddening of her own eyes announces in advance the—stupendous—thing that Conrad did next. And if Sally's feeling taxed and embarrassed, there's triumph too in her voice as she declares, "Well: Conrad started to cry."

"Good God, that's something I can't picture."

"But Luke, I'm struck by a sense—I don't know how to put this without sounding grandiose, and possibly lugubrious—a sense of a vanishing world. Honey, Wes's death—I'm only now realizing—hit me far, far harder even than I would have imagined. Maybe that's not so surprising (after all, he was my first great love), but I do feel what I'm talking about is larger than Wes: as though an entire world's vanishing." She helps herself to another lemon cookie—her fourth—and says: "And you can remind me that that busy little world centered in Restoration, Michigan, was impoverished and uncultured. Or you can *show* me just how impoverished and uncultured it was, you can set me down in Arles, whose Roman ruins and every historic cobblestone are a weighty indictment of my upbringing. But in the end I can only reply to you, It doesn't *feel* like an impoverished world. Oh, no: It felt as complete as any-where on the globe and perhaps that's what being young really is: the gift of taking with you, wherever you go, a sense that the pos-sibilities of the place you're in are infinite. I keep thinking of Toledo Heights Park, in Restoration, which as you recall is on a sort of hill, so the whole town—such as it is—lies outspread below you, and I used to meet Wes there when we were courting. (And you can see what an old woman I've become that I employ a word like *courting,* but that's what it was, I assure you.)

"Anyway I keep thinking of the two of us in Toledo Heights Park, and one evening, as I've mentioned to you, he actually asked if I was a virgin. What in the world did he think? I was Sally-the-nose-in-her-book, I was Sally Admiraal the good daughter of the Christian Reformed Church, I'd been kissed by at most half a dozen boys, all of them notably fumbling and shy, and here was Wes doing something more intimate, in a way, than proposing marriage to me.

"And I've just been feeling, especially these past few months, it began really to hit me around Thanksgiving, Luke (which is inter-esting because of course there's no such holiday in France), that an entire world is ending, and it's absolutely going to *break my heart* when Conrad passes away.

"Here's somebody who has spent the last forty years sniping at me. Here's somebody with whom I've spent the last forty years pretending that sniping wasn't sniping—but do you want to hear me say something I shouldn't say? I think Conrad's in a sense in love with me. Not passionately, not sexually—I'm not yet quite such a dotty old lady as that. But spirit to spirit, Luke. It doesn't make sense? Well, who said love ought to make sense? He always wanted not just my approval but something more—maybe he's always wanted me to reaffirm what crazy erratic Dora used to make plain on her more lucid days: that he was the more lovable, or more worthy, of the two Sultan brothers. Is that a terrible thing to say? I think he needs me . . .

"Or perhaps I should point out that in some way (I'm sure you won't misconstrue this) I've been in love with *him,* in love with the good-looking but, from a woman's point of view, always safely unreachable of those wild Sultan boys. And he was so handsome! Do you see what I'm expressing so inadequately? That it's hard not to love the one without loving the other—the two of them were so close, in their funny, fiercely competitive way. And now Conrad's my last remaining link, he's my tie to a vanishing world, and when he goes, that girl in Toledo Heights Park, stuttering with shock to be asked whether she's a virgin, will be further away than ever." She reaches across for another cookie, catches my eye, and mumbles, a little sheepishly, "All that weight I lost in France? I can feel it coming right back on."

"It's the holidays. We all overeat."

"And I didn't finish Proust," she confesses. "I got bogged down."

"You've been reading other things. Closer to home. Calvinism and the history of the Dutch immigrants in Michigan . . ."

"With Monsieur Proust, I got three volumes in and decided I wasn't doing him justice. So I started over. That was the mistake," she adds mournfully.

"I do understand what you're saying, though, about a vanishing world. Conrad, he's the last link." And then I recall another: "Of course there's Adelle . . ."

And between us, in another quick exchange of looks over the dining room table, there's a shared quivering acknowledgment of shame. We've done it too: We've overlooked Adelle. Oh, the world itself has conspired to overlook Adelle, and even the theoretically impartial eye of the camera lens does it all the time—how else to explain why, in photograph after photograph, Adelle emerges as a smudged, shadowy presence?

Poor Adelle . . . For no good reason that anyone can possibly see, when she was born Life declared, *This will be an utterly lusterless child.* And when it was time for her to wed, Life declared, *Her mate will be a man whose afternoons are spent dozing before a screen on which tiny muddy uniformed men pile on top of each other in pursuit of a muddy ball.* So mine is a protest against Life itself when I insist, "But it's not as though Wes will have completely vanished. After all, he left various children. Including a son sitting right here. And including a daughter who looks uncannily like him."

"I've had a couple of letters from her . . ."

"From Jessie?"

"Jessie? From Tiffany."

"Good Lord, what did she say?"

"They're in the den."

"Can I see?"

"Well—of course. But there's something you might want to look at first . . ."

I follow Sally into the den. When she tries the lamp beside the big oak secretary, the bulb blows. There's an explosive blue-white flash, and a little *ping,* and then shadows once more. I turn on the dim lamp beside the TV, by whose pale glow Sally, after a minute's searching, locates an envelope.

It's a letter from someone I haven't thought about in years, Agnes Callahan, a friend of my mother's from Restoration days. Why is Sally showing me this? My Sherlock Holmesian surmise— an accurate one, it turns out—is that she is seeking to palliate various revelations still to come . . .

The letter from Mrs. Callahan strikes a tone that, my guess is, typifies the correspondence of widows with widows. The implicit message behind its bright, chatting updates is, *We are carrying on.* She first apologizes for not writing Sally sooner. She is living now in Mexican Way, Arizona, outside Phoenix. She talks at some length about the weather, the golfing opportunities "way out here," the various professional successes of her children and her sons-in-law and daughters-in-law.

It's not until page three that I reach what I suppose is the letter's core and inspiration. Agnes Callahan is offering, in gingerly fashion, condolences on Wesley's passing—not an easy burden, given that Wes was someone whose reputation in Restoration wasn't the best and was someone, besides, whom Sally divorced some thirty years ago.

Mrs. Callahan reports that she last saw Wes three years before he died, at her daughter Lucy's wedding. (Wes had been among the guests because Lucy had somehow befriended Tiffany.) As the night wore on, Wes danced with the bride, and then with the bride's mother (Mrs. Callahan herself), and finally he approached the bride's grandmother.

"Well, you remember, Sally, how badly Mother was ailing in her last years. The rheumatoid arthritis was really something awful (she finally had to have her hip replaced) and she suffered also from angina and emphysema. So when Wes approached her, I was very quick to refuse on Mother's behalf. He was a little insistent, and I naturally went on refusing, until it became apparent that Mother actually very much wished to dance with Wesley. I'll never forget it! She said to him, 'Young man, I haven't danced in more than twenty years.' And Wes replied, 'Well I'm honored that you've waited so long for me.' And I'll be darned, Sally, the next thing anybody knows, Wes had Mother up on the dance floor, spinning her slowly round and round. And I can't *tell* you how many times Mother referred to that dance in the year before she died."

"It's a lovely anecdote," I say, looking up from the letter.

"Isn't it?" Sally's eyes are shining.

"Always the gentleman."

"Of course he was, but don't you also think Wes's reply, about being so honored, was quite clever?" Sally is clearly eager to ensure that Wes, who was rarely praised for his wit, receive his fair due in this regard as well.

"It was perfect," I reply. A silence ensues. "You were going to show me Tiffany's letters," I say at last.

There's a slight, reluctant hitch in Sally's movements as she hands them over—which I begin to understand the moment I catch sight of the childish penmanship's big balloonlike loops.

The first of the letters, dated November 3, reads as follows:

Dear Sally!

I hope this finds you happy and everything in FRANCE! We are all fine. Halloween has come and gone and you'll never guess what Jessie went as, Wes. That's right, she decided to trick or treat as her own father! I wish you could have seen her. I gave her some sideburns with an eyebrow pencil and I put some gray in her hair with talcum powder and in a suit and tie borrowed from a boy down the block. I'll send photos as soon that they're developed.

Sally, while I was going through Wes's papers recently I found some evidence of something that surprised me very much. Maybe I'm wrong, but it seemed like it was the case you loaned Wes various sums over the years, which he didn't tell me. (you know Wes) Otherwise I would have thanked you before, long ago. Obviously.

Now this was a total surprise to me, and the money wasn't any small sum from my point of view. Even if Wes didn't invest the money too wisely, let me say I'm grateful to you. I think people that know me will all say I'm a grateful person. I just hope it isn't too late to say THANK YOU.

Now with Wes gone and everything you may be feeling quite different now, but actually I'd be completely grateful if you thought it might still be appropriate to send another loan to Wes's family. I'm just asking you to think about this. Even if he's gone of course his kids are still here. You know I've always admired you more maybe than you know, and I wouldn't be asking except that Dr. Cole (the dentist) predicted that Jessie's teeth will come in crooked and I don't see any way when I look into the future I can handle everything.

This past summer I met Luke (at last!), and I can see why Wes was always so proud of him and said he got your brain power. You must be proud too.

The kids put you every night in their prayers, and Wes too. Jess the other night said to me, Is Daddy's hair combed the same way in Heaven.

Yours sincerely,

Tiffany

And the second, dated November 15:

Dear Sally,

I'm sure that France is the most elegant place on earth and I know that you are so happy there. I never studied French, but I did study Spanish back in high school: Buenas dias!

I wrote you a letter, I don't know if you got it. Maybe you did, if you did you don't have to worry about me now. I wanted to tell you what happened to me. You're almost the first person to know it. I'm going to be married! (Again)

His name is Russell Bradway and both kids just love him! The first time she met him Jess said she planned to marry him, little did she know I would get there first! He's an automobile salesman but very steady. (seven years at the same dealership) In my other letter I was worried about our financial situation but please ignore all that. (forget it) Everything will be fine again and wish me all the happiness in the world. I do for you.

Love,

Tiffany

Of course laughter's an inadequate response at such a time, but what else is a person to do? I feel it leaking out of me—pure jets of mirth—in little snorts and giggles. More than anything I've encountered so far, Tiffany's pair of letters lend a bouncy absurdity to this family quest I formally embarked on when I cleaned out my office desk at Gribben, six months ago, on a sweltering day in June. Days have gotten colder, and darker, since.

Is this where my father ended up? Did the man who in his twenties married Sally Admiraal wind up here? Is the voice in these letters that of the woman whose loss emotionally bankrupted

Wesley Sultan? I think of Conrad proclaiming, *Wes was simple,* and for a moment Conrad's right and everything's clear as glass.

You do have to wonder: Did a white-haired Wes Sultan, one hard-pressed afternoon, lift his strained gaze to some vast Midwestern cumulus-cloud configuration that was new to him, that was new to the very heavens, and did he ask himself, frantically, *How am I going to hold on to the woman?*

Was Wes's "tragedy" as ridiculous as that? Perhaps it was. *Oh yes, life is like that . . .* a contemplative voice inside me concurs, meaning, *Life's a bitch,* meaning, *Life's a series of pitiful erosions,* meaning, *Life could be defined as that force in the universe that undertakes the systematic humiliation of all its Wesley Sultans.*

In the sickly half-light of the den's dim lamp, it seems only fitting to match embarrassing revelation with embarrassing revelation. So, passing the airmail envelopes back to Sally, I say to her, "I've got something to tell you I should probably have told you before. I chased down my half brother. Klara's son. Wesley Giardina."

"Oh Good Lord . . ." And Sally regards me warily, eagerly. "What is he doing?"

"Managing a health club."

"And what did he say?"

"Very little, actually. He wrote me an obscene response. I gather there's a certain amount of hostility to Wes even now . . ."

"He's living—"

"In Pittsburgh."

"And you got his address from Conrad?"

"Conrad? No, although probably I could have, he seems to have his hands in every pie. No, I guess I wanted to take a more complicated line. You know when I started all this—this whole business of looking into Wes and the truth behind his life—I had this notion that I was going to discover my father. Well maybe I have, to some degree, but what I really feel I've done is discovered an uncle and an aunt, Conrad and Adelle. And you, too. I mean I hope it's all right for me to say this, but I feel that your life, too, has come clearer to me." I add: "I go out in search of the dead and I find the living . . ."

My words are meant to be heartwarming, frankly, and I have every confidence that that's how Sally will take them. Why, then, does she nod so blankly—or uneasily?

Then she says, "And there's something I haven't told *you*. Something I perhaps should have told you long ago. Only, I wasn't sure how much you wanted to know. It's only lately I've come to understand how really determined you are, Luke. This is a hard thing to discuss—it's something that has tormented me over the years. Oh heavens, this is very, *very* difficult. Hold on."

Sally goes out into the kitchen—she's on a cigarette run. I take a seat on the couch. Is there another room in the world that has as much resonance for me as this den? This is the room Gordon loved best of all rooms in the world and these are the last walls he ever saw. It was here, too, a few months before his death, he uttered perhaps the most moving lines I've ever heard anybody utter. I was sitting beside him when he got a phone call from a friend at the hospital. His latest test results. He hung up, glanced over at me, his adopted son, and said, "Bad news, I'm afraid." We looked at each other for a moment. Two generations, and not a drop of shared blood between us, but the naked exchange of glances was secure: it would hold over time. When Gordon spoke next, he stumbled over an inessential word but—as was clear from the proud, forthright look in his eyes—he showed himself steadfast in the clinch. He said: "It seems I'm ga-ga-ga-going to die."

Sally returns and sets a pack of Salems and a lighter on the coffee table. She's nervous. I'm nervous—and fearful. And *excited,* for what statement in the universe could be more exhilarating, when delivered by one of your parents, than *There's something I haven't told you . . .* ? As if all life's essential mysteries might, even yet, be deciphered.

Sally has spoken sorrowfully of gaining weight, but in the flare of the lighter her face looks drawn and haggard and for a moment I'm conscious of the unfleshed skull beneath her skin. She inhales deeply, exhales a spectral cloud, and says: "Oh my. Well. Well, as you know, Conrad always kept a sort of eye on Wes over the years. And in many ways he was the only real source of information I had. You could say Conrad snooped around, and maybe there's some truth to that, but he was also quite useful to Wes, who sometimes needed a counselor or an intermediary. You've heard all this, how Conrad was the one who smoothed things over with Klara Kuzmak, for example. But many, many years later, after I'd divorced Wes and married Gordon, I was given a pretty strong indication, Conrad was characteristically oblique but I think the import of what he was saying was hardly in doubt, I was given the impression—Oh dear Lord . . ."

Even by Sally's standards, her delivery is growing roundabout. She pulls again, hard, upon her cigarette. "Well: I was given a pretty strong indication that the secret marriage between Wes and Klara was not quite officially terminated—or at least not quite officially terminated at the time when, I'm afraid, when Wes and I were married in the Restoration Christian Reformed Church. He somehow—well—honey, it seems Wes maybe somehow failed to actually follow it through. You see? You know how Wes had trouble following things through . . . Well, in this case your father maybe failed to follow it through . . . through to an official divorce."

And for just a moment, studying Sally's anxious, shadow-cratered face, I undergo a feeling of total bafflement, before, in the obscurity of this familiar room, everything clarifies. A bright light breaks over the entire planet, and I say to her, "But that means—

Jesus, that means your marriage, your whole marriage to Wesley, would have been invalid." And everything grows brighter still: "That means, without knowing it, you were sitting day after day on a sort of bomb. Think about it: You were waiting to discover that your entire existence, at least in the eyes of your neighbors and your parents and the church, was one tremendous shocking scandal . . ."

And Sally, exhaling a triumphant plume of smoke, cries, "But isn't that *like* you, Luke! Bless you, child, isn't that *kind* of you to think first of me! Don't you see it has all sorts of other repercussions? Repercussions for you?"

"Of course it does," I reply, and the sentence that follows— words as straightforward as hers have been elliptical—constitute the richest, most satisfying utterance that has issued from my throat in years: "It means I'm a bastard."

"It means, possibly, you were born, technically, out of wedlock, Luke."

Perhaps I shouldn't feel quite so jubilant. Poor earnest Sally's all atremble, hunching over herself as though to conceal herself behind a cloud of smoke . . . Poor Sally's just a little girl suddenly, quivering before something vaster even than Poppa and Momma: before God Himself, Whose glittering sword of justice sweeps like a comet through the icy black cosmos.

"Okay, sure, I see the point, okay"—I chatter on—"let's call it out of wedlock. So what—hm? What possible difference could it make to anybody now?"

"Luke, I wasn't brought up in the sort of household that countenanced illegitimate children . . ."

"Hell, *you* can't be blamed for what you didn't know. It's Wes who's responsible. *He's* the one will have to argue it out with his Maker."

"I somehow didn't expect you to take it like this."

"So how should I take it? Should I be horrified? Embarrassed? No, I think I *like* this latest bit of news. I do. It's just what I wanted to hear. I've been searching for the crowning touch in Wes's career—maybe now I've actually found it."

"Over the years, I kept asking myself over and over, How in the world did all of this happen to *me?* I try to make sense out of it all." And Sally is coming round. With the burden of her secret at last removed from her shoulders, feeling almost giddy with relief, she's now doing what she does best: looking back over her days with a born storyteller's eye and linking one event to another. She is weaving her life into a satisfying narrative whole, a rich tapestried sequence—a tapestry whose central character is modest little Sally Admiraal of Restoration, Michigan, improbably placed in the role of global wanderer. "All I wanted, all I expected, was to raise a family in my own hometown, Luke. Do you ever get the feeling the world's a sort of movie with wonderful screenwriters but a terrible casting director? Why was *I* chosen to play this part? I never harbored a bohemian ambition in my life."

"But who better than you, Sally? To play the footloose divorcée in the south of France whose divorced and unemployed son discovers he's illegitimate?"

"That's *not* the way I see myself, young man, and it's certainly not the way I see you."

"But I *like* to think I have unconventional origins. And I like to think that when I die, I'll leave a tangle for the obituarist."

"Well *I* like to think that certain information stays in the family. Including what you've learned here this afternoon. You must promise me, you must solemnly swear, not to breathe a word of this to anybody . . ."

And I offer my oath: "I solemnly swear," I tell her. (And you'll have to forgive me, Sally, but by now there's no point in my denying that there isn't a single ancestral grave I wouldn't rifle, in my headlong pursuit of a few corrections. Does this sound ruthless? I suppose so, but let's not forget that my quarry is elusive as the yeti, or Bigfoot, or the Loch Ness Monster. For I'm out hunting nothing less than the truth about a liar, and who in my shoes wouldn't trade the family Bible for a packet of squalid letters, a few compromising photographs? Sorry, Mom.)

The day's last light is spent and the windowpanes give nothing back but a flat blackness. We've come to the end of the line. The New Year is so close, I can almost reach out and touch it. The future beckons. It's right there, just behind the closed door of the den. In the next room lies another season—the return of spring, just a few months off, when daffodils, cut from Sally's own backyard, will stand in the vase on the desk in the very den where Gordon died.

. . . Or perhaps behind the closed den door lies a different spring. The past beckons. It's April Fools' Day, 1952, and the sun is filling the wineglasses of the big elms on the streets of Stags Harbor on this day when Wesley Cross Sultan will outmaneuver Miss Henrietta Scoobles and land a job at Great Bay Shipping.

A silence has descended upon the room. Sally and I are at the turn of the year, where past, present, and future commingle and blur. And Wes is closer than you know—

But when Wes enters the room, it's not from any expected door. Sally cries, "Oh but you didn't see the photograph! Look in the envelope!"

"Mm?"

In the second of the two airmail envelopes I find it. A snapshot. It's Wes—or the closest approximation remaining on the planet today. It's six-year-old Jessie, in her Halloween costume. Kids always love dressing up as ghosts, but what an exceptional, dear, lively, queer, incomparable little ghoul the girl-child makes! She's wearing a man's miniature gray suit, and a red tie, and Tiffany has done a marvelous job with the girl's hair—transforming a pixie cut into a big gray glorious crowning pompadour. Here's the man who got old Mrs. Callahan up on the dance floor, artificial hip and all, that arthritic grandmother who had waited for him on the sidelines, watching the dancers turn, for twenty years. And Jessie has instinctively reproduced not just the quizzical tilt of the head but also my father's beseeching and hopeful gaze . . .

It's night and the room is ankle-deep in shadows. Oh, the den is awash with ghosts: the ghost of Gordon, who built this house and lived his life in it and died here in this room, and of white-haired Wes of course, and of glowing-haired Klara Kuzmak, whom I never met, and, further in the shadows, of Henry and Kathy Admiraal, who watched their only daughter drive off with a devilishly handsome salesman in a red convertible, and of Dora Sultan, who today endures only in a few curled and cracking photographs but who may once have housed in her belly the first unthinkable stirrings of a daughter conceived in adultery. If they have been importunate (as ghosts will be), they have also been (as ghosts must be) patient. Their time has come: the turn of the year: We've reached one of those borderless moments when the departed are given the run of the house . . .

A ghostly mother says, "I could heat up some more tea," and her ghostly son replies, "I'm okay."

"Can I get you anything else?" one ghost says.

And the other ghost answers, "I think I've got everything I need."

CHAPTER FOURTEEN

Wesley Cross Sultan, 62, of 2135 N. Westhampton, Restoration, and the Commodore Hotel in Stags Harbor, and 27 Arrow Road, Gastaw, died of cardiac failure in the Silk and Satin Saloon in Stags Harbor. His entire professional career was spent at Great Bay Shipping. He worked there for 42 years—not long enough, apparently, to inspire any reciprocal feelings of loyalty or obligation among Company management, who effectively fired Wes two years before his death.

He worked chiefly in sales, mostly out of the Company's Stags Harbor office. For a six-year period in the seventies, he worked in Kalamazoo, and for a five-year period in the eighties, in Cincinnati.

Despite his long and stable career, Wesley might reasonably have been described as a man without a compass. Or perhaps as a restless soul who never went much of anywhere. Although he retained his good looks to the end of his life, evidently he felt too old, on leaving the Company at the age of fifty-nine, to seek out salaried employment elsewhere. He set off on his own, embarking on a number of speculative, poorly researched investments. These predictably came to nothing. Wes was probably handicapped by knowing no other employer than Great Bay Shipping, a notoriously ill-run organization. (Personnel records would indicate, erroneously, that he joined the Company at the minimum age of eighteen; in truth, Wes at the age of seventeen altered his birth certificate in order to render himself prematurely employable.)

Distraught and disoriented at the loss of his job, and eager to conceal from friends and family his feelings of humiliation and betrayal and heartbreak, Wes grandly announced that he was retiring in order to devote himself to various community and commercial organizations: the Rotarians, the Restoration Chamber of Commerce, the Stags Harbor Betterment Society, and the Thumb of Michigan Prosperity Council. It seems fair to say, however, that his ties to these organizations were lukewarm at best.

The deceased's affiliation with the Restoration Episcopal Church was perhaps a different matter. Cynics might be quick to declare it no accident that he joined the community's wealthiest congregation; a good argument could be made that this decision, too, was business-inspired. Yet there can be no question that Wesley Sultan, with his fine voice—a thin but clear tenor—loved singing in the choir. And the church's sumptuosity may have held natural appeal for a man who was unfailingly dapper, even a bit of a dandy.

So where did Wesley stand with God? If that's a line of inquiry ultimately beyond the charge of any obituarist, nevertheless a strong case could be made that the deceased was a person of cryptic but intense private yearnings. In the last years of his life he became an increasingly regular churchgoer, attending services even when his job took him on the road. It's certainly possible that Wesley's religious fire was stoked by internal intimations of mortality; he may well have silently recorded various early warning signals of the heart disease that killed him.

He was born in Restoration and attended Restoration Central High School, although he failed to obtain his diploma. He dropped out a few months before graduation to begin working at Great Bay Shipping. His formal education ended, then, at the age of seventeen. Informally, there was little additional schooling; Wes's reading was largely confined to the *Restoration Oracle* and the *Detroit Free Press*.

The deceased was heir to a distinguished local family. His paternal grandfather, Hubert Sultan, was the mayor of Restoration for two terms, from 1908 until 1912, when his bid for reelection foundered amid accusations of financial irregularities, including graft and embezzlement. (Although Mayor Sultan was never proven guilty of anything more venal than a lack of discernment in his appointees, it must be noted that financial irregularities are a persistent Sultan family theme.) Wes's father, Chester Sultan, ran Sultan Furniture, Restoration's leading home-furnishings supplier, until the business collapsed in 1935. He drowned in Lake Huron in 1942, in an accident involving alcohol. (Problems with alcohol, too, are a Sultan motif.) His death may conceivably have been, but probably was not, an act of suicide. Wes and his younger siblings, Conrad and Adelle, were reared mostly by their mother, Dora Sultan, whose mental health was apparently undermined by the sudden collapse of the family fortune. She turned agoraphobic in her old age, and for most of her life may well have been an undiagnosed manic-depressive.

And Wes's self-image? He appears to have regarded himself as the balked scion of an illustrious midwestern family—a family whose glory days, it seems fair to say, he failed to reinvigorate. When viewed at some distance from the small town of his origins, the "tragedy" of Wesley Sultan naturally assumes a diminished and provincial flavor, although it could well be argued that the contours of his life speak volumes about a country hurtling forward so rapidly that its values and mores, its jokes and idioms, its graces and ambitions expire even before the generation that begot them. Wesley Cross Sultan's tale might be viewed as that of a man who slowly perceived that his charm had grown quaint, that he was someone whom the world had outrun. (Or so it might be interpreted by a 36-year-old man of the next generation, who is to be envisioned revising Wes's obituary in a little bar in Miami, La Rosa Rosa, alone, working with his head down, taking comfort in the rumble of Spanish voices around him. He's a 36-year-old man prepared to swear that—in the light of life's overriding darkness—the loss of anybody who once, in his own local corner of the cosmos, threw off something of a glow is no small-time tragedy. Prepared, further, to swear, with the runaway lyricism of someone sipping his third rum-and-Coke, that some mystical equivalence obtains between all extinguishings of the light—be it the flare and fade of a supernova or, on some stump by a Michigan riverbed, a swallowed firefly, glimmering for an instant in a frog's translucent gullet . . .)

Wes's marital history was extremely complicated and may never be wholly untangled. He was married first to Klara Kuzmak, born in Cracow, Poland. Wes had one child with Klara, a son named Wesley, currently residing in Pittsburgh under the name Wesley Giardina. Klara died of amyotrophic lateral sclerosis in 1977.

If, as the scanty evidence suggests, Wes's marriage to Klara was never formally terminated, then his subsequent "marriage" to Sally Admiraal, also born in Restoration, was on his part an act of bigamy. They were divorced, or "divorced," in 1964. Wes later married Tiffany Fitchett, of Cincinnati, Ohio, from whom he was estranged at the time of his death and by whom he fathered twin daughters, Winnie and Jessica. There is some evidence that he may have fathered other, unacknowledged children.

At the time of his death, Wes was survived as well by a brother, Conrad, of Miami, Florida, and a half-sister, Adelle De Vries, of Pheasant Ridge, Michigan. And also by a son, Luke Planter; formerly of the New York investment firm of Gribben Brothers; now a novelist.

A NOTE ABOUT THE AUTHOR

Brad Leithauser was born in Detroit and graduated from Harvard College and Harvard Law School. He is the author of four previous novels—*Equal Distance, Hence, Seaward,* and *The Friends of Freeland*—four volumes of poetry, and a book of essays. He also edited *The Norton Book of Ghost Stories*. He is the recipient of many awards for his writing, including a Guggenheim Fellowship, an Ingram Merrill grant, and a MacArthur Fellowship. He recently served for a year as *Time* magazine's theater critic. An Emily Dickinson Lecturer in the Humanities at Mount Holyoke College, he lives with his wife and their two daughters, Emily and Hilary, in Amherst, Massachusetts.

A NOTE ON THE TYPE

The text of this book was set in Bembo, a facsimile of a typeface cut by Francesco Griffo for Aldus Manutius, the celebrated Venetian printer, in 1495. The face was named for Pietro Cardinal Bembo, the author of the small treatise titled *De Aetna* in which it first appeared. Through the research of Stanley Morison, it is now generally acknowledged that all old-style type designs up to the time of William Caslon can be traced to the Bembo cut.

The present-day version of Bembo was introduced by the Monotype Corporation of London in 1929. Sturdy, well-balanced, and finely proportioned, Bembo is a face of rare beauty and great legibility in all of its sizes.

Composed by NK Graphics, Keene, New Hampshire
Printed and bound by R.R. Donnelley & Sons,
Harrisonburg, Virginia
Typography and binding design by
Dorothy Schmiderer Baker